GRACEFIRE

BOOK ONE

Vera Bell

# OF FLAW AND SCORN

Gracefire Series, Book 1



Published by
TIMEBOUND PUBLISHING LLC
Georgia, USA

Cover Design by Vera Bell

Printing History
First Edition: Timebound Publishing / 2026
10 9 8 7 6 5 4 3 2 1

The Library of Congress has catalogued this edition as follows:
Names: Bell, Vera, author.
Title: Of Flaw and Scorn / Vera Bell.
Series: Gracefire.

ISBN: 979-8-9946805-1-3

Author Website/Contact: VeraBellAuthor.com

# Dear Reader

Imagine it's summer of 795 A.D. Without warning, longships with dragon heads slip from the northern mists and strike the Irish coast with unimaginable terror.

The Viking raid on Rathlin Island—the first recorded in Irish history—marked the dawn of a new era. Driven by ambition, scarcity, and the promise of plunder, Norse warriors stormed the monastery and burned it to ash. The monks, isolated and unprepared, spent centuries gathering sacred treasures, only to watch them looted and destroyed. Yet the greatest loss wasn't gold or silver, but people—torn from everything they knew and carried into an uncertain fate.

That first strike and the fear it ignited form the historical backdrop for this novel. Though later centuries brought more complex interactions between Norse and Irish peoples, such as trading and settling, this story is rooted in that initial encounter, marked by violence, captivity, and spiritual upheaval. But beyond war or conquest, this is a tale of what follows. What happens when love grows where it shouldn't? When light breaks into the darkest places? When the unlikeliest of hearts longs for something greater than itself?

As in history, in this story, two vastly different worlds collide. One is Christian. The other, pagan. One follows the Gospel—the Good News of redemption and salvation. The other is ruled by strength, honor, and fate.

To reflect the spiritual divide between my characters, I've included epigraphs and verses drawn from sacred and mythic texts. Each of the first forty-three chapters opens with a stanza from *Skírnismál—The Ballad of Skírnir*—the fifth poem from the *Poetic Edda* and a cornerstone of Old Norse mythology. Because the classic translation by Henry Adams Bellows can be difficult to follow, I've chosen quotes from a more accessible, poetic rendering by Marius Harridsleff at vikingr.org, used here with his kind permission. His work beautifully captures the Norse worldview—harsh, mythic, and elemental—while remaining clear and resonant for modern readers.

In the poem, while Odin is away, god Freyr climbs his high throne and gazes across the worlds. In the land of the giants, he sees Gerd, a radiant maiden whose arms shine with light. Struck with longing, Freyr grows heartsick. Though love between gods and giants is forbidden, he confesses his desire and sends his servant Skírnir to win her—bearing gifts, threats, and a magic sword. When treasure fails to sway her, Skírnir turns to threats and dark curses. Only then does Gerd agree to meet Freyr in nine nights. Although he finds the wait unbearable, they are finally wed. Gerd's reluctant acceptance and their delayed union echo the novel's deeper tensions between desire, sacrifice, and surrender.

In contrast, the final two chapters' epigraphs draw from Scripture to reflect the story's enduring message—love that bears all things, mercy that restores, and a God who does not abandon His people but pursues them with purpose and hope. Throughout the novel, several well-known Bible verses appear as markers of faith. But while that faith offers comfort, it also calls for justice over vengeance, mercy over wrath, and forgiveness through grace. In the end, the closing verses speak not only to redemption, but to the unshakable promise that even in sorrow, love endures, and a greater plan is unfolding.

While Freyr and Gerd's tale of longing, bargaining, and forbidden love mirrors Brigit and Reidar's journey—and even a third character's—it does so to a point. At its heart, this novel is about second chances. How love can bloom in a world ruled by violence. How even the fiercest warrior may hunger for something more. And how, even in darkness, light is never beyond our reach.

Though fictional, the main male character, Reidar Valorborn, is loosely inspired by Håkon the Good, a tenth-century Norse king remembered for his strength, wisdom, and unexpected openness to the Christian faith. You can read more about him in the Historical Note at the end of the book.

Lastly, both *Skírnismál* and Scripture are rich with the supernatural. In one, magic and manipulation blur the line between longing and power.

In the other, grace confronts darkness with unyielding light. The contrasts are sharp—fate versus free will, coercion versus consent, vengeance versus redemption—yet the parallels are striking. Each text wrestles with good and evil, with what it means to pursue something beyond oneself, and with the cost of that pursuit.

As a side note, though I wrote the novel with *Skírnismál* in mind, the decision to place each stanza as an epigraph came after the final draft was complete. And yet, remarkably, each one aligned with the deeper message of its chapter. Sometimes, stories really do write themselves.

I am thrilled to share this journey with you,
*Vera Bell*

P.S. For bonus scenes, sneak peeks, and exclusive content, sign up for my newsletter at VeraBellAuthor.com. And if you enjoy this book, I would be honored if you left a review at Amazon or your favorite retailer site. Your support means the world to me!

**For the flawed, the scorned,
and the wondrously
redeemed.**

# Map

Viking Raids in Ireland

Late 8th – Mid 9th Century A.D.

Viking Raids in Ireland
Late 8th – Mid 9th Century A.D.
Shetland Islands
NORWAY
Hebrides
Orkney Islands
SCOTLAND
Rathlin Island
ATLANTIC OCEAN
Derry
Dalaradia
Inishmurray
Maghera
Bangor
Armagh
Movilla
Downpatrick
Inishofin
IRELAND
Louth
Monasterboice
IRISH SEA
Slane
Holmpatrick
Dublin
Roscam
Kildare
Clonmacnoise
Glendalough
Inis Cathaig
Clontert
Seir
Birr
Lismore
ENGLAND
NORTH SEA
Scelig Mhicil
Cloyne
WALES
N
W
E
S

# Cast of Characters

## Ireland and Norway

|  |  |
|---|---|
| **Astrid Eldarsdottir** *(OW-streeth)* | Shield-maiden, Reidar's former betrothed |
| **Brigit O'Clery** *(BRIH-jit)* | Irish woman from Rathlin Island, taken as a thrall |
| **Caoimhe** *(KEE-va)* | Brigit's woman servant |
| **Cearbhall mac Bressal** *(CAR-ull mak BRESS-al)* | Brigit's first husband, Irish chieftain |
| **Gudbrand** *(GOOD-brahnd)* | Angel |
| **Gyda** *(GEE-tha)* | Reidar's *fostra* (foster-mother) |
| **Harald Fairblade** *(HAH-rahld)* | Former jarl of Ljosstrond; Reidar's father |
| **Eldar** *(ELD-ar)* | Astrid's father |
| **Mairead** *(mah-RAID)* | Brigit's good-sister, Cearbhall mac Bressal's sister |
| **Orm the Oaf** *(ORM)* | Reidar's *hirdman* |
| **Padraig** *(PAW-rig)* | Christian monk from Rathlin Island |
| **Rathnait** *(RAH-nit)* | Brigit's mistress in Dalaradia |
| **Reidar Valorborn** *(RAY-dar)* | Harald Fairblade's son and rightful heir to the Ljosstrond jarldom |
| **Saoirse** *(SEER-sha)* | Brigit's maidservant |
| **Sigrid** *(SIG-rithr)* | Astrid's cousin |
| **Sveinulf the Querulous** *(SVAYN-ulf)* | Reidar's *hirdman* |
| **Thorsten** *(THOR-sten)* | Reidar's younger brother and *hirdman* |
| **Ulf** *(OOLV)* | Reidar's *hirdman* |
| **Vargr Bloodgale** *(VAR-gr)* | Reidar's uncle, usurper, and jarl of Ljosstrond |

# Glossary of Irish and Norse Terms

Irish words and pronunciations provided with assistance from Ciara Hall, a Northern Irish translator. Norse words, names, and pronunciations referenced from *Lexicon Poeticum* (lexiconpoeticum.org) and the *Dictionary of Norse Mythology* (vikingr.org).

|  |  |
|---|---|
| **A chroí** *(ah-KHREE)* | My heart (Irish endearment). |
| **Æsir** *(EYE-seer)* | The principal gods of the Norse pantheon. |
| **Althing** *(ALL-thing)* | An assembly or governing council in Norse society where laws were made, disputes settled, and decisions voted on. |
| **Asgard** *(AHS-gahrd)* | The Norse realm of the gods, home to the Æsir and a place of power, glory, and divine rule. |
| **Baldr** *(BALL-dur)* | The Norse god of light and purity, whose death at Loki's hand marked the first shadow of Ragnarök. |
| **Blodhefnd** *(BLOTH-hevnd)* | Blood vengeance; the duty to avenge a slain kinsman in Old Norse society. |
| **Bodhrán** *(BOH-rawn)* | A traditional Irish frame drum. |
| **Brynhild** *(BRIN-hild)* | A fierce Valkyrie and shield-maiden, famed for a legend of love and betrayal. |
| **Karl** *(KAHRL)* | A free man in Norse society, typically a landowning farmer or warrior of the middle class. |
| **Eir** *(AYR)* | The Norse goddess of healing and mercy. |
| **Fenrir** *(FEHN-reer)* | The monstrous wolf of Norse myth, fated to break free at Ragnarök and devour Odin. |
| **Fomorian** *(foh-MOHR-ee-uhn)* | A race of giant monstrous beings in Irish mythology, associated with chaos, darkness, and the sea. |
| **Fostra** *(FOHS-trah)* | Foster-mother or nurse in Old Norse society. |
| **Freyr** *(FRAYR)* | The Norse god of fertility, prosperity, and peace, who weds the giantess Gerd after a mythic courtship. |
| **Freya** *(FRAY-yah)* | The Norse goddess of love, beauty, and magic. |
| **Frigg** *(FRIG)* | Odin's wife and goddess of marriage and prophecy. |
| **Galdr** *(GAHL-dr)* | Old Norse magical chants or incantations used in sorcery. |

| | |
|---|---|
| **Gerd** *(GAIRTH-ur)* | A giantess in Norse mythology associated with the earth and fertility, who becomes the wife of the god Freyr after a mythic courtship. |
| **Hel / Helheim** *(HEL / HEL-hime)* | The Norse realm of the dead |
| **Heil** *(HAYL)* | Hello in Norse (addressed to a woman). |
| **Heill** *(HAYL)* | Hello in Norse (addressed to a man). |
| **Hersir** *(HAIR-seer)* | A local chieftain or nobleman in Old Norse society. |
| **Hirdman** *(HEERD-man)* | A personal armed retainer of a Norse lord (plural: hirdmen). |
| **Huskarl** *(HOOS-karl)* | Household warrior sworn to a jarl or king (plural: huskarlar). |
| **Jarl** *(YARL)* | A nobleman or high-ranking leader in Norse society, equivalent to a earl. |
| **Kirtle** | Medieval Irish woman's gown. |
| **Lawspeaker** | A legal authority in Old Norse society who presided over the assembly and recited the law from memory. |
| **Léine** *(LAY-nya)* | A long linen tunic or traditional Irish shirt. |
| **Ljosstrond** *(LYOHS-strond)* | "Light Shore" in Norse. A fictional coastal settlement whose name joins *ljós* ("light") and *strǫ nd* ("shore"). |
| **Loki** *(LOH-kee)* | The cunning trickster god of Norse mythology, known for deception and chaos. |
| **Midgard** *(MID-gahrd)* | The world of humans in Norse cosmology, positioned between Asgard (realm of the gods) and Hel (the underworld). |
| **Mjolnir** *(MYOHL-neer)* | Thor's hammer; symbol of protection and consecration. |
| **Nithing** | A coward or villain; the worst kind of man in Norse |

| | |
|---|---|
| *(NEETH-ing-er)* | society. |
| **Nithingsverk** *(NEETH-ings-verk)* | A coward's deed; a vile, dishonorable act. |
| **Odin** *(OH-thin)* | The Norse Allfather god of wisdom, war, and magic; ruler of the Æsir. |
| **Ragnarök** *(RAHG-nah-rohk)* | The prophesied end of the world in Norse mythology. |
| **Runes** | The characters of the ancient Norse alphabet, believed to hold magical power. |
| **Scian** *(SHKEE-an)* | Irish double-edged personal dagger used in daily life. |
| **Skírnismál** *(SKEER-nis-mahl)* | An Eddic poem in which the god Freyr sends his servant Skírnir to woo the giantess Gerd. |
| **Skol** *(SKOHL)* | A drinking toast; "cheers" in Norse culture. |
| **Skoggang** *(SKOHG-gahng-er)* | A Norse outlaw; a person banished to the forest and stripped of protection by law. |
| **Thor** *(THOHR)* | The Norse thunder god, protector of gods and humans, wielding his mighty hammer Mjolnir. |
| **Thrall** | A slave in Norse society, typically captured in raids or born into servitude. |
| **Valhalla** *(VAL-hall)* | The hall of the slain where Odin receives fallen warriors. |
| **Valkyrie** *(VAL-kir-ee)* | A supernatural maiden who chooses those who die in battle and carries them to Valhalla. |
| **Volva** *(VUL-vah)* | A seeress or prophetess skilled in Norse magic and divination. |
| **Yggdrasil** *(IGG-drah-sil)* | The great tree of Norse myth, whose roots and branches connect the nine worlds. |

# Scorn

My Great Scorn is an unseen chain wrapped around my waist, so heavy it steals my breath. It bound me the day the savage Norsemen descended upon my land and took everything from me. My family. My home. My freedom. Seven long, cruel winters have passed, and still, they take. I have forged link upon link for every vile thing done to me, and their number is now beyond counting. Yet the first remains unchanged, for it belongs to the heathen boy Reidar, whom I hold accountable for all my sorrows.

**— Brigit O'Clery, 20, Rathlin Island, Éire, 803 A.D.**

# Flaw

Seven winters past, I met my Great Flaw and named her Ingrid—a name fit for a goddess. It was a folly worthy of a green boy on his first Viking voyage, but not of Reidar Valorborn. For all her beauty, her bronze tresses coiled like snakes about her shoulders, and her emerald eyes burned with such searing scorn they could turn a man to ash. If Odin wills that I find her, it would be only to prove she is no goddess and to rip her from my heart once and for all. For a jarl can afford no flaws, and I will be jarl—no matter the cost.

**— Reidar Haraldsson Valorborn, 22, Ljosstrond, Norway, 803 A.D.**

# PART ONE

## Eleven Apples, All Made of Gold

*Rathlin Island — Dalaradia, Éire*
*795–803 A.D.*

# Chapter One

## Shadowbane
***Reidar***

*Go now, Skirnir! and ask my son*
*What is troubling him so;*
*And get an answer, for he is*
*Deeply in love.*
— Skírnismál, stanza 1

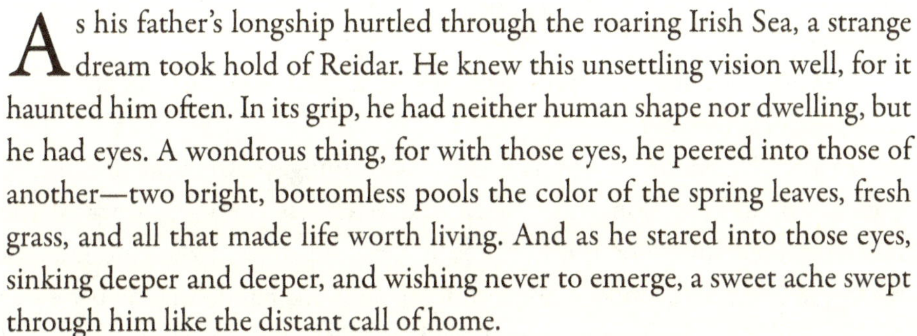

As his father's longship hurtled through the roaring Irish Sea, a strange dream took hold of Reidar. He knew this unsettling vision well, for it haunted him often. In its grip, he had neither human shape nor dwelling, but he had eyes. A wondrous thing, for with those eyes, he peered into those of another—two bright, bottomless pools the color of the spring leaves, fresh grass, and all that made life worth living. And as he stared into those eyes, sinking deeper and deeper, and wishing never to emerge, a sweet ache swept through him like the distant call of home.

To his annoyance, Reidar woke as he always did—before he could glimpse the owner of those mesmerizing eyes. He pushed himself upright, blinking away the remnants of slumber. The tides had calmed. Some rowers sat at their thwarts, watchful and silent, dipping their oars in measured strokes. Others lifted their shields from the gunwale hooks and set them at their feet, helms in their grip.

"By Thor"—he scrubbed a hand over his face—"how could I have slept so long?"

Above, his father's splendid sail of red and gold stripes billowed full, the favorable wind carrying the longship forward.

Reidar stood and stepped to the prow, fixing his gaze on the land rising ahead. Even through the haze of the falling evening, it burst with the bright hues of the gems his father brought from the Eastlands raids last summer. He called them emeralds, those large, shining green stones Reidar could study all day, imagining the faraway lands where such treasures lay free for the taking. The treasures and the thralls—strong men and comely women who yielded great profit in the Westlands markets and made his father, Jarl Harald Fairblade, a wealthy and powerful man.

For the past three summers, Reidar had begged Harald to take him along on a voyage. He'd been ready after his twelfth winter—tall, broad, and skilled with his battleaxe and sword. Soon as he turned thirteen, he'd attended his first Althing, where he received his arm ring, lay with a woman, and defeated each of his peers in the much-celebrated weapons practice. At fourteen, he bested most of his father's men and hunted and felled a bear without aid. But Harald Fairblade never broke his rules, not even for his firstborn. So Reidar Haraldsson would go a-viking after he'd seen fifteen winters and not a day sooner.

"Steady now." Harald's hushed command drifted over the deck and faded into the thickening mist.

Reidar's heart fluttered in pace with the thrilling splash of the oars slicing the waves as the longship made its relentless passage toward the mist-shrouded hills. For the hundredth time, he stroked the fine inlay of his sword's pommel, smooth and comfortable in his hand. Shadowbane was his father's gift—its double-edged blade inlaid with silver and gold and tempered to perfection. It was the best one in Ljosstrond, worth sixteen head of cattle and fit for Odin's Hall.

All his twelfth winter, Reidar had pondered the name. It came to him as he watched the blade catch the light, straight and powerful as it was. By the gods' favor, Shadowbane was a weapon to cast light into the heathen darkness, to add to his father's wealth, and to bring honor to their bloodline.

He clenched his jaw, pushing away the memory of his *fostra's* shiny eyes and trembling chin as she bid him farewell, painting his face with coal while muttering incantations against fear. The old woman needed not fret. Reidar Haraldsson may not have yet drawn his first blood, but he would soon earn the name he'd coveted since he was small—Reidar Valorborn.

The rain fell as the lush hillside grew near. The cool rivulets slid down Reidar's neck and seeped beneath the wolfskin wrapped around his shoulders, but he scarcely felt them. His body hummed like the thunderclouds before a storm. His soul longed to run, fight, and conquer. His heart yearned to show his father how ready he was.

"Green Éire—we meet at long last." His uncle, Vargr Bloodgale, came to stand beside him, stroking his well-worn axe haft with a large, calloused hand. "Your first raid, hmm?" His clap to Reidar's shoulder nearly sent him reeling. "A boy is not a man until he proves to the gods he is a warrior fit for Valhalla. Are you ready to make your first kill, Reidar the Sapling?"

Reidar lifted his head and fixed his menace of an uncle with a cold stare. "See that you do not get in my way when I am in battle rage." Reidar's voice emerged in a low rumble despite his effort to steady it like his father did when faced with a thinly veiled insult.

Vargr erupted in a nasty laughter that stopped as abruptly as it started. With a cold smile, he bent his thick neck to Reidar's ear, and the sharp mixture of sweat, mead, and urine filled his nostrils. "See that you do not get in mine."

Harald Fairblade approached before Reidar could reply, so he swallowed his fighting words as he did too often with his father's dung of a brother.

"Odin is watching over us." Harald squinted into the falling dusk. "He gives us cover." He glanced over his shoulder at the four longships following closely behind. "They will not see us beach."

"Unless they have already spotted us." Vargr laughed. "Then your son will have his first blood before sunup, and Loki willing, I will have the pleasure of a woman. Did your father tell you, Reidar—?" Vargr licked his lip; he didn't dare call him names in Harald Fairblade's hearing. "These women are not like the ones back home. They are ignorant heathens, and from them you take what you wish."

"Vargr." Harald's voice deepened with warning. "The women, if comely or skilled with housework, will yield good profit, as the men will, if they are strong." He touched Reidar's shoulder. "We come for the spoils, not to spoil our plunder like ravening beasts with neither sense nor reason."

Reidar nodded and said nothing. He wished his uncle had remained in Norway as had been planned all along. But the cursed man changed his mind after his wife died in a strange accident that left her with a broken neck. Surprising all, Vargr joined the voyage after her send-off, claiming distance might dull his aching heart.

The mist lifted a bit as they drew near, revealing the outlines of a strange longhouse. It sat atop a bluff rising sharply from the rocky shore—too squared, too ordered, nothing like the solid, sloped roofs of home. Dark and silent, it seemed built to keep men in, not welcome strangers.

Vargr gave a low whistle. "Odin is indeed with us today, brother—a monastery!"

"Monks." Harald scoffed. "I had hoped the boy would face some challenge on his first raid."

Reidar squinted, studying the gloomy structure. Monks were men who gave up all their earthly pursuits to worship a God unlike any he knew—one who allowed Himself to be beaten and nailed to a cross. Reidar couldn't make sense of such a God. He seemed pathetic, meeker than a lamb, weaker than a child. How could they worship such a one? His favorite Thor, the ruler of thunder and lightning with his *Mjolnir*—a divine hammer—was worthy of worship. The Allfather Odin, the fearless ruler of Asgard and the eternal seeker of wisdom, was deserving of adoration. So was Freyr with his flawless art of fertility and good harvest, and even Loki the Trickster, with his unceasing cleverness, if not the occasional lack of honor. But that unseen Christ of theirs, who went to His death without so much as a protest, defied all reason. Yet according to his father, all Westlanders worshipped him. Such folly didn't sit right with Reidar, and he wouldn't be Harald Fairblade's son if he did not weigh it against steel and sense.

The rain slowed to a drizzle, and the air grew eerily silent, save for the low hum that drifted from the hills ahead. Chanting. An odd emptiness enveloped the longship. A stillness on the wind that slithered down Reidar's spine—an invitation and a warning in one.

"Gold and silver weigh well on a scale—" Vargr spat—"but no self-respecting Eastlander would give coin for these feeble monks, if they even survive the crossing."

A half-known outline caught Reidar's eye while his father and uncle studied the dour walls of the monastery. A splattering of mist-shrouded huts stood a distance away, small skiffs docked on the beach.

"Father, look—" He touched Harald's arm. "It is not only the monastery."

"A poor fishing village." His father shrugged. "Fishwives are homely and ill-tempered. The men might yield some profit if we can find Eastlands fish traders to deal with." He smiled. "Still, it is a choice granted by Odin. Is it the monastery or the village for you?"

A strange sensation crept into Reidar's veins—a thrill mixed with something that made the fine hair on his arms rise.

"The village." He gripped his pommel, struggling to still the excitement in his voice. "The feeble monks are no match for my Shadowbane, Father."

"Good choice, Son." Harald patted Reidar's fair, drenched locks. "We'll enter the village side by side at the monks' first call to prayer."

A thin silver crescent peeked through the rain clouds, casting a glimmer of light onto Shadowbane.

Reidar hid a smile, thanking Thor for the favor. "Will we hear it, Father?"

"Oh, we will." Harald chuckled. "It is a sound unlike any other."

And for the second time that evening, an odd shiver prickled over Reidar's skin.

# Chapter Two

## Fear

***Brigit***

*I know I will face harsh words,*
*If I go to speak with him,*
*And get an answer, for he is*
*Deeply in love.*
— Skírnismál, stanza 2

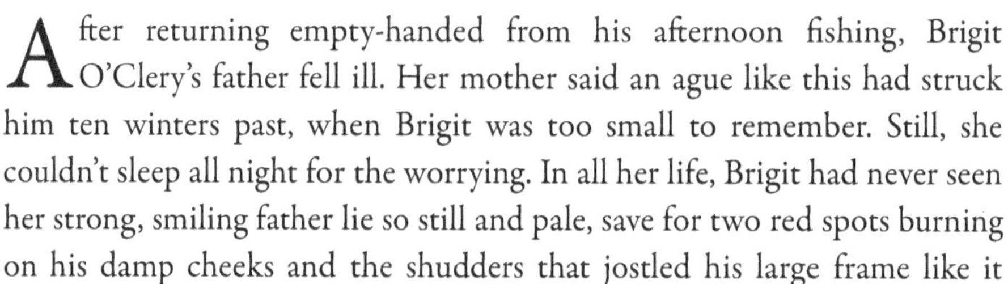

After returning empty-handed from his afternoon fishing, Brigit O'Clery's father fell ill. Her mother said an ague like this had struck him ten winters past, when Brigit was too small to remember. Still, she couldn't sleep all night for the worrying. In all her life, Brigit had never seen her strong, smiling father lie so still and pale, save for two red spots burning on his damp cheeks and the shudders that jostled his large frame like it weighed nothing at all.

When at last Brigit fell into uneasy slumber, her mother woke her up, her eyes lined with shadows and a deep groove etched between her brows.

"It's nearly sunup." She smoothed Brigit's hair away from her face. "Run into the wood, child, and bring back yarrow root, elderflower blooms, and wild strawberries. I'll make a tincture for your father. It shall soothe the fire in his blood."

Brigit blinked the sleep from her eyes. Her father lay abed as before, his flesh afire with fever that held fast. She rose, rinsed her face with cool water from the basin, grabbed her small wicker basket and a patched woolen shawl, and stepped outside.

The world lay hushed in near-darkness as Brigit made her way toward the forest, shivering with the morning chill and weariness. The thick mist hung over the village like a blanket, but most of it would burn away with the rising sun. It mattered not—she knew the wood as well as her own shadow.

The yarrow with its clusters of wee white blooms was easy to spot, and Brigit used her sharp *scian* to dig up the plant's healing root. Glad to be done with this chore, she shook off the bits of soil, dropped the earthy knotted tangles into her basket, and stood. The elderflower was everywhere this time of year, but she would pick the blooms on her way back and place them atop wild strawberries lest they bruise.

Despite the somberness of the morning and her father's illness, Brigit's mood lifted at the thought of her next task. She liked gathering wild strawberries in her lovely, quiet wood, and she especially liked their tangy sweetness, so unlike any other. Maybe after making the tincture, Mother would let her mix a bit of honey into the berries to eat with her porridge.

The sun rose steadily over the wood, chasing away the mist and revealing the bright, red clusters scattered throughout. Brigit closed her eyes and drew in a long breath, reveling in the head-spinning aroma of rich soil, crisp morning dew, sweet birch and willow leaves, and ripened wild strawberries.

The first trill of the thrushes announced the monks' impending rising to toll their bell. Her friend, the young monk Padraig, explained it was to announce the end of the night and the beginning of the new day, which they heralded with the morning prayer called Lauds. The monastery was a good neighbor to the village and paid the fishermen well for their daily supply of mackerel, haddock, and pollock. All the fine grain, ripe cheese, and fresh honey the O'Clerys enjoyed came from the monks, as did their holy sacraments and benedictions.

Brigit ventured deeper into the forest, humming a praise hymn to Saint Padraig. She'd listened, enthralled, when the monks sang it at the last gathering. Though captured and enslaved, he found comfort in his faith and even went on to banish darkness from Éire.

*Christ with me,*

*Christ before me,*
*Christ behind me,*
*Christ in me,*
*Christ beneath me,*
*Christ above me...*

Before long, Brigit's basket was half-full, but she continued to a clearing ahead, where she would pick the choicest berries. Then, she would hurry home and pluck the elderflowers along the way.

She froze at the thrum of men's voices. Their rowdy laughter and strange, rolling cadence were unlike anything she'd heard in her thirteen winters.

One shouted, his voice like the crack of a whip.

Her hand flew up to the small wooden cross she wore on a cord around her neck. Heart pounding like a *bodhrán*, she pressed her basket close. How could there be strangers in her wood?

A few yards away, a man said something in an uneven, guttural tongue. Another gave a bark of laughter. The first man muttered in reply. Through the branches, a shock of pale-yellow hair caught the sunlight.

*Run!*

A flock of sparrows exploded from a large oak above. A creak of twigs. Approaching footsteps.

If she ran now, she'd surely be noticed.

Suffocating on her breathing, Brigit pressed her back into the trunk of the oak and willed herself to fuse with it.

*Our Father in...in heaven...*

The Lord's Prayer caught in her throat, drowned by the grim tales a Northumbrian merchant told when he last brought linen and iron to Rathlin. He called them Norse savages, for they came out of cold, heathen lands that lay to the north of Christendom, to plunder, arson, murder, and enslave all that had the misfortune of crossing their path. Shuddering and making the sign of the cross, he'd whispered they were a race of barbaric, marauding giants with cold eyes and yellow hair, sent by the devil himself straight from the pit of hell, for they had no souls.

That was two winters past, when Brigit was eleven. For a long time after, she feared to shut her eyes at night and lurched at the slightest noise and the faintest shadow. But the Norsemen never came to her island and never would. Padraig said Éire lay too far for them to bother when they had all the riches of Hebrides and the Orkney Islands within their reach. After a while, Brigit's fears had abated, then gave way to the pressing matters of helping her mother with unending tasks of cooking, weaving, mending, and cleaning—

A stranger stepped from the trees, his face half-shadowed but eyes glinting like ice.

Brigit's heart slammed against her ribs, depriving her of breath and rooting her to the spot.

The man stared at her. He drew closer.

Gasping, Brigit pressed a fist to her mouth to stifle a shriek, yet it still escaped from her into the wood. His hair, lighter than the palest stalk of wheat at the peak of summer, was shorn close on the sides but hung long and tangled at the top. Across his chest lay a round shield with strange, swirling carvings. At his right side rested a sword sheathed in a scabbard; and at his left—an axe with a blade as cold and sharp as the look in his eyes.

The ground tilted beneath Brigit's feet as the man headed straight to her oak.

He stopped feet away.

Blood freezing, she squeezed her eyes shut and gripped the basket with fingers so numb, they didn't seem to belong to her. And neither did her mind, for while it screamed for her to run, her legs refused to obey as if bound by some enchantment.

A verse her mother taught her when she woke in a cold sweat after the Northumbria merchant's visit rose to the top of her mind:

*Save me and guard me...*

*With You, I walk in light, never to fear....*

"*Heil.*" The man was upon her, his voice deep and terrifyingly foreign.

Heart hammering, Brigit opened her eyes. She blinked. While uncommonly tall and wide of shoulder, the savage was not a man but a boy of no more than fifteen winters. His eyes were the color of the brightest sky, and the expression in them was more curious than cold. Brigit let out a slow breath. They were strange eyes—large but elongated and sitting above high, broad cheekbones. Yet he was only a boy, for his face was smooth and free of a beard save for a pale sprouting above his lip.

Brigit's gaze fell on the large, sharp axe at his leather belt—an instrument of death if ever she saw one. She squeezed her eyes shut again.

*Our Father...*

She needed to leave, to run back as fast as her legs would carry her, so she could bring the basket with the medicines to her mother and warn the monks and the village.

"Reidar." The boy's hand brushed against her arm, his touch shockingly light and warm.

Brigit's eyes flew open. He was pointing to himself. Brow quirked, he gestured toward her and turned his palm over in question.

"Brigit," she squeezed out.

He scratched his forehead. "Brih-gid." Odd, how he said her name, as if trying to warm to it but failing. He shook his head. "Ingrid."

Brigit glanced past him as the rough voices of his people grew louder. Very slowly, she took a wee step away from the oak.

The boy looked at her basket, then said something in a strange, heathen tongue.

Did he want her wild strawberries? Brigit lifted the basket with cold, stiff arms. "Take it," she forced out. "It's yours."

He grabbed a handful and stuffed them in his mouth. "Mmm..." He nodded as if he knew the taste and liked it.

Breath held, Brigit took another step toward the path home.

Swift as lightning, the savage boy blocked her way, his expression friendly but firm, like her father's when he taught their hound to obey.

But Brigit was no hound. Stomach hardening, she bit her lip and held up the basket to the savage boy once more. "Take this. I'm going home."

He didn't stir.

Brigit swallowed, her words emerging shaky and thin. "I must go home."

"Home?" The way he echoed the word in his strange, savage way made it sound like something wicked and not at all what it meant.

"Home." She clenched her jaw. "I—go home."

The boy Reidar shrugged—the word meant nothing to him. With an incomprehensible half-smile, he reached into her basket again and took out a single berry. Haltingly, almost uncertainly, he extended his hand and brought it to her mouth.

Speechless, Brigit drew back. How did these savages, who didn't even know girls could feed themselves, have sailed all the way to Éire? Thoughts racing, she dropped her gaze. Maybe he was only after sharing a meal and would let her go once it was done. Brigit pulled away from his fingers and reached for the strawberry.

The savage boy shook his head and nudged the berry to her lips.

Brigit stared into his pale blue eyes. Would he let her go if she ate it? She allowed him to feed it to her. But she hadn't even chewed it properly when he bent to her mouth. His breath smelled of wild strawberries, and his lips were a stark mixture of warmth and iron against hers.

Brigit's heart thumped so loud, it hurt her ribs. Yet his kiss was so light and fleeting, it seemed he'd changed his mind.

"Ingrid." He lifted his head and gave her a blinding white smile, which made his broad cheeks ride even higher and turned his eyes into bright blue slits.

Brigit blinked against a gut-wrenching realization. Though chaste, this was her first kiss—stolen by a stranger.

The voices of his people reached them in a harsh, barking laughter. Brigit lurched back and slammed her shoulder into the tree trunk. She hardly noticed the sting.

"Please—" She gestured behind her with a rigid hand, then to herself, then toward the wood. "I must return *home*."

The boy straightened with decision and took her by the wrist. "Home."

"Let me go!" Brigit's heartbeat rushed into her ears as she struggled to wrench her arm from his unyielding grip. The savage ignored her, pulling her after him toward the voices in long, easy strides.

The world tilted as she followed him into the familiar clearing. Nothing about it was familiar—not the sharp tang of sweat and iron in place of the sweet scent of damp earth and fresh grass, not the terrible, unnatural silence that descended upon their entry. Brigit's vision flickered at the edges as a throng of fur-laden, symbol-marked giants stared at her with cold, foreign eyes. A legion beyond counting. Her pulse pounded in her head, drowning out the silence. The world blurred into a haze as one giant laughed and headed straight toward her.

Her knees buckled, and the boy circled his arm around her shoulders and murmured something he likely thought soothing in his barbarian tongue. A wicked, soulless heathen. He'd dragged her here when he could have let her go!

The man stopped paces away, and an icy chill rolled down Brigit's spine. Although he couldn't be more than twenty winters, he was built like a rain barrel—a Fomorian of the old tales. For a long moment, he studied Brigit with his small, deep-set eyes. Her stomach twisted. They glinted with something terrible, as though he would devour her whole if not for the others there.

The boy Reidar bit out words that had the tone of frustration, and the Fomorian tore his bone-chilling gaze away from her, turned to the gathering, and declared something in a low, groveling voice. A few men laughed, some shook their heads and rolled their eyes.

Brigit's chest clenched against her ribs. Another moment, and they would tear her to shreds like the ravening beasts they were.

She jerked her head up as the boy's grip tightened on her shoulder to the point of pain. Brow lifted as if in amusement, but eyes glinting with mute, cold loathing, he gave the Fomorian a curt, controlled reply—a challenge and an order in one. The Fomorian scoffed, reached into the belt that circled his thick middle and produced a sizable gold bracelet that dripped with shiny red and green stones.

Brigit's blood ran cold. She was being bought and sold like yesterday's catch.

Suddenly, the boy Reidar seemed taller and harder around the edges. The Fomorian trained his ugly eyes on him, then rummaged in his belt again, and added a heavy gold torque to his offering.

All color drained from Reidar's face, and Brigit thought he would deal the bigger man a blow. Instead, he said something low and soft, then released Brigit. It was so abrupt, she lost her footing and tumbled onto the dew-soaked grass with a loud gasp. Her basket fell from her hand, and the wild strawberries scattered all over like drops of blood.

*Run! Now!*

Quickly, she scrambled back to her feet, but before she could bolt into the wood, the boy grabbed her wrist again. With his free hand, he snatched both treasures from the Fomorian and hurled them onto the ground with something that sounded like a terrible curse.

The Fomorian scowled and stepped closer, towering over the boy.

Near them rose the trunk of a great yew, and Brigit leaned against it, unable to quell the tremors running through her body. Her thoughts scrambled, recoiling at the notion of being seized by this beast.

Another man approached—as tall as the Fomorian, but fairer of face and with the bearing of a chieftain.

Unblinking, Brigit stared at the heathen marks covering his head, where it was shorn on the sides, and his long, wheat-colored plaits streaming down his back.

The man trained a stony gaze on the Fomorian and barked something that sounded like an order.

The Fomorian spat, picked up the bracelet and the torque, and stalked off.

With hardly a breath, Brigit drew away from the yew and toward the wood, trying to ease her arm from the boy's grip. His large hand tightened on her wrist in response, hard fingers digging into her skin.

She parted her lips to tell him once again she needed to go home but stopped short. His face no longer held any trace of warmth or curiosity as he fixed his piercing gaze upon her.

Her heartbeat climbed to her throat, her need to get home turning hot and frantic.

With his free hand, the boy pointed at her, then at himself, struck his chest with an open palm, and spoke in a voice that brooked no argument: "Thrall."

The chieftain shook his head and muttered to the boy. Then he flicked Brigit a cold, indifferent glance. "You—slave," he said in rough, broken Scots, walking away. "You—his."

Brigit's heart raced like a caged bird. She wanted to scream, to pull free, to run. But her captor was twice her size and had the strength of two men, so she squeezed her eyes shut and begged God for help.

# Chapter Three

## Home
***Reidar***

*Please tell me, Freyr,*
*Foremost of the gods,*
*What is troubling you so?*
*Why are you sitting here alone*
*For so many days?*
— Skírnismál, stanza 3

Reidar shoved down a nagging twist in his gut at the sight of Ingrid's panic-stricken face. Surely, such misgivings had no place here. He, Reidar Haraldsson, on his glorious raid of Éire, had been the first of Harald's men to claim a thrall. And what a thrall she was! He needed no obscene offerings from his uncle to know her price, for he'd never seen such beauty. Her eyes, rimmed with long, dark lashes were the precise hue of the shiny emeralds he loved so well. Her silky hair, the color of burnished bronze streamed down to her waist like a filly's mane. The shape of her lovely face struck him as sweet, soft, and entirely blameless. She was like a kitten—small and delicate—yet with a hint of claws tucked beneath all that loveliness. An irresistible enticement.

He longed to gather her into his arms and see if she would fit against him. The wanting unsettled him, and it was all he could do to plant a gentle kiss on her berry-stained lips. For the girl was young, the first beguiling marks of womanhood scarcely upon her. But in two or three winters, he would take her as his lover. His and none other's. He'd even named her to his liking.

Around them, men stuffed the last of their morning fare into leather bags and tested their blades.

"Do not fret, Ingrid, you are mine," he mouthed, uncertain why he bothered to speak at all, for the heathen girl didn't have his tongue.

Her green eyes widened in response as she stared ahead, unseeing and unblinking.

Reidar flinched as if struck, his strange dream taking hold of him in daylight. The girl's eyes were like the trees around them, like the rivers in the bright sunlight, like life itself. Like the eyes from his vision.

Scoffing, Reidar shook his head. *By Thor, enough of this.*

His gaze fell on her wrist—his tight grip must have hurt. Reidar loosened his fingers, but she didn't seem to notice. He rubbed his forehead with his free hand, uncertain how to proceed. Harald Fairblade had split his men in half. In short order, Reidar would be setting off to the village with his father to claim thralls and valuable supplies. The other group, led by the blasted Vargr Bloodgale, would make for the monastery for its gold, silver, and strong young monks. Then, they would load the longships with their loot and sail back home. And he, Reidar Valorborn, would return a Viking and with his own lovely concubine.

The cold knot in Reidar's gut returned as Ingrid's arm trembled beneath his hand. He couldn't very well bring her along on the raid. He glanced around—he would tether her to a tree, then come back for her. None of her countrymen would lay eyes on this wood henceforth. But what of the wild beasts?

The girl stifled a gasp and blinked. Two large, shiny tears rolled down her lovely cheeks.

The knots in Reidar's stomach tightened. "I will not hurt you, Ingrid," he ventured in the most soothing voice he could muster, hoping his tone proved words enough. "I will keep you safe."

The girl wiped at her face, then fixed him with her glittering gaze and breathed something in her strange, lilting tongue. Once again, he caught that unknown word, *home*. If only he knew what it meant. But if it was a thing she'd left behind, he could provide it for her. Once they were back in Norway, he would give her anything she wished, for his father lacked for nothing.

He studied her, struck by a sudden idea. Maybe it was something simple he could give her even now.

"Home," he echoed, releasing her wrist so he could turn up his palms in question. "Home?"

Her eyes filled with such hope and longing, he'd give anything to see calm and content in their place. Reidar pushed such folly away. This girl was his first resplendent plunder, and she belonged to him with or without her *home*. His accursed uncle was right in some ways—she wasn't like the Norse girls back home. He had no need to conciliate or win her over.

Ingrid's eyes bore into him as he battled these unbefitting feelings. Then she pointed to the wood and made the unmistakable sign of the roof over her head. "Home," she said very clearly.

"Ah." Reidar tipped back his head and gave a low whistle. That was one thing he would not give her. "No." He trained his gaze on her and slowly shook his head.

They both lurched at the blare of his father's horn.

Reidar squared his shoulders, heart pulsing and muscles tensing as the world hardened into stark relief of a thrill mixed with something that had to be bloodlust. The men were smearing their faces with war paint, grabbing their axes and shields, lining up in two formations. At last! The time for wavering was over. The mounting urgency honed his thoughts to a keen edge. His course lay clear as sun on snow. He would take his concubine to the edge of the wood, conceal her there, then return for her after the raid and bring her to the longship, along with all the other thralls they claimed.

Breath quickening, Reidar pulled a length of rope from his belt and grasped both her wrists in his. He didn't allow his heart to squeeze at the way all color drained from her lovely face and at the sight of her small, helpless hands shaking in his. And at the unmistakable ice in her gaze that cut through it all.

"Do not fear me, Ingrid." His racing heart robbed his voice of intended gentleness as he bound her wrists and tightened the knot. "By Thor, I will never hurt you."

Chest heaving, she spat out a reply, her voice filled with such scorn he flinched.

The clanging on the shields and the men's battle cries drowned out her words.

"Walk fast and do not fight me, Ingrid." Reidar pulled hard on her rope and headed to his father, hoping she understood his unwavering intent, if not his words.

She did not fight him. She followed like a filly on a lead—first to Harald, then through the wood. Too small to keep up with his pace, she nearly ran behind him, her face pale as freshly fallen snow.

With all his might, Reidar pushed the thoughts of her from his mind. She would do, for nothing would stand in the way of his first raid. For he would fight, conquer, and plunder no worse than any of Harald Fairblade's men. Better and mightier. He would make his father proud. He would prove his uncle wrong. He would earn his coveted name of Reidar Valorborn.

The rope in his hand jerked. A man behind spat out an oath. Without breaking pace, Reidar glanced over his shoulder. The girl had stumbled and nearly took a tumble. She had lost her lovely wide-eyed look during this short march. Her eyes were rimmed with red, face tear-streaked, hair ruffled. Reidar's breath hitched, but he crushed such unseemly stirrings. A pity. Yes, a pity and nothing more. When this was over, his thrall would do well to clean up and put on a glad countenance for him.

The first rays of sun peeked through the canopies and brushed her cheek, and with them, a strange ache pierced his chest. Despite himself, Reidar imagined their roles switched, and him captured, bound, and led by the rope amidst a throng of terrifying foreigners.

The delay cost him, for several men quickly closed the gap between him and his father. Harald peered behind him, eyes glinting against charcoal. "There will be others, Son. Leave her. She is slowing you down."

A long, sonorous din filled the wood along with the soft morning light. It reverberated through every leaf and branch, then rose to the sky and faded into the billowy clouds above. The sound sent a shiver down Reidar's spine.

"The bell! The monks are gathering to pray." His father lifted a brow, picking up his pace. "All in one place and oblivious to anything aside from their Christ. Odin is truly with us today!"

A myriad of rays burst into the wood, bathing everything in their bright, warm light. They streamed over the girl, painting her in white—a stark contrast against the coal-smeared faces of Reidar's people. But shining as she was, her gaze on him lay heavy as lead.

Heat, fast and rough, surged through him like a hard blow. She detested him. Yet it was only as it should have been. He nearly stumbled himself with a sobering realization. What gain was there in claiming her as his thrall? Of bringing her to Norway? He may have thought her alluring, but she did not find him so. Not after such indignities. She would never come to him of her own free will, nor be his lover when she came into her bloom. She would only despise him for the rest of her life, maybe even try to kill him.

The thought of her loathing him filled Reidar with such gloom he shuddered. But it also brought a burst of welcome clarity. He did not allow himself to question it, yet his gut still twisted as he caught up with his father, for his pride recoiled at having to make such a request. Harald Fairblade would surely see it as a crack in his courage and not the measured, sensible choice it was.

With a plea to Thor, Reidar blew out his breath and turned to his father. "I would not leave her, nor bring her to Norway," he said, struggling to sound as sure and commanding as Harald himself. "I would take her back to her home."

"Home?" Harald Fairblade stared at Reidar like he was seeing him for the first time. "Time to awaken from your enchantment, Son. Her home will be ash and rubble before the day is done."

Reidar swallowed. He hadn't considered that. "Why destroy the village?" He shrugged, striving for nonchalance. "Is it not enough to burn the monastery?"

His father shot him a frown and said nothing.

Reidar understood the weight and the merit of setting fire to the Christians' holy places. His people were a force to reckon with. At the very sight of them, those meek, kneeling fools should cower, eagerly offer up their treasures, and be grateful for being taken slaves and not drowned or worse. Yet Ingrid wasn't a monk, and the notion of her cowering or left without a home grated worse than an axe blade against a whetstone.

Reidar drew closer to his father. "Do not burn the village, Father. She will be without a home then." He set his jaw. "Look how helpless and frightened she is. Let her keep her home."

They were at the edge of the wood, the low huts and the monastery steeple rising in the thinning mist.

"These heathens are not like us, and you have much to learn, Son." Harald shook his head. "The men must have their many rewards for coming along on a voyage. But I will indulge you, for leaving her behind is wise." He spared a glance at Ingrid. "She may not live to see our shores—a poor use of the afterhold's worth. Find a grown woman, skilled and strong, and take her instead."

The rope strained in Reidar's hand, and the girl gave a sharp cry of pain. He came to a halt, freezing at the sight of her small body lying face down on the ground.

He dropped the rope. "Ingrid!"

The girl lifted her head, unseeing, then shook herself and scrambled to her feet. Her face twisted with agony as she jerked her right foot up and stared at Reidar with wide, accusing eyes.

Harald Fairblade's men skirted around them, some with curious glances, others with overt looks of disapproval.

"Leave her, Reidar." His father's voice called from a widening distance—a command, curt and cross, and to be obeyed.

# Chapter Four

## Flaw
***Reidar***

*How can I tell you,*
*Young hero,*
*Of my great sorrow?*
*Though the sun rises every day,*
*It never brings relief to my longing.*
— Skírnismál, stanza 4

"I am coming, Father," Reidar bit out and went to the girl.

Ignoring the chuckles and the lewd comments, he squatted before her and thrust out his hand. "Let me have a look."

She made to draw back, but he grabbed her ankle and felt around it with his fingertips. It was small and fragile, and judging by her yelps of pain, badly sprained.

"Thor and Odin, why do you do this to me?" Reidar gritted his teeth as the last of Harald's men passed them by.

Ingrid sank down on the forest floor. Her skirt hiked up as she did so, and Reidar let out a loud oath. Her knee glistened with bright red blood, mixed with fragments of her torn gown and specks of dirt. The wound needed cleaning and tending lest it fester.

Reidar peered longingly after the men as they vanished from sight. His body hummed with an urgent need to kick something very hard. Instead, he stood and looked around. They had passed a small creek, he remembered.

Fists clenched, he exhaled a long, steadying breath and pointed toward the wood. "I will look for water," he ground out, unable to keep the anger from his voice.

The girl shrank back.

He made an impatient drinking gesture, then pointed to her knee. "To clean this."

Reidar didn't wait for her reply. He barreled back into the wood, cursing his ill luck every step of the way. He found the creek soon but had neither horn nor cup to carry the water. He shut his eyes, breathing hard. He should abandon this foolish task, this useless girl, this cursed wood and join his father on his first splendid raid. But the thought of leaving Ingrid there, scared and injured due to his recklessness, made his stomach turn.

"By Thor's Hammer! What is this madness!" He tore a strip from his woolen tunic and dipped it into the cool stream until it was drenched. There was a bright patch of moss clinging to the root of a nearby tree. He grabbed a fistful and marched back.

The girl remained where he had left her.

A distant scream pierced the calm. Heart pounding, he peered toward the shoreline. Through the trees, a ribbon of smoke curled into the sky. Harald's party had entered the village. And instead of basking with them in the raid's glory, he was here, tending to this heathen girl like some foolish healer woman!

Reidar shut his eyes and tipped his head back. He needed to rein in his fury, or he'd only hurt her more. He pulled in a long, shuddering breath, then let it out.

"Stay still," he barked, losing the fight with himself.

Ignoring Ingrid's panicked protests, he squeezed the water from his strip of wool onto her knee. Her face turned deathly white. She gave a loud gasp and clenched her fists.

The heat left Reidar in a swift, cleansing wave, and along with it came the obvious solution.

"Shh." He smoothed an errant strand from her cheek. "Shh, I will make it better."

He stilled himself against her yelps as he patted the dirt from the wound and covered it with moss.

"All better now, Ingrid." He forced a smile and stood. "I must join my father." He gestured toward the village, then at her. "I will come back for you."

All color drained from her face. She raised her hands to him.

Reidar grew cold all over. How far out of his mind had he gone to leave her in the wood with her wrists still tied? Mute, he pulled on the knot, and the rope slid off, eliciting a new gasp of pain. Deep purple grooves etched her thin wrists where he'd bound them. Angry red welts marked her smooth, lovely skin.

He picked up the rope and tucked it into his belt. His limbs felt too heavy, so he plopped down onto the ground and stared at his big, daft hands, the raid fever gone like it had never been. Mere moments before the monks rang their bells, he swore by Thor to never hurt her. Now she was badly injured in four different places—all due to him. It had to be Loki, his uncle's favored god, who had played this ill trick on him, keeping him from drawing his first blood.

Reidar shivered—he had spilled his first blood, but from the last person he wanted to bleed. Something stung at the back of his nose, and he clenched his fist, wishing to deal himself a hard blow. But that wouldn't help the girl, so he tore off another strip from his tunic and bound her tiny ankle with as much care as he could muster.

They were alone in the wood—none to hurry him along, cast disapproving glances, or offer lewd suggestions. He took her hands into his and brushed his thumbs over the welts on her wrists. "I am sorry for hurting you," he choked out. "And I release you from bondage, Ingrid. I will take you *home*." He pointed his chin at the huts in the distance.

"Home?" The girl searched his eyes at the sound of the familiar word.

He nodded and dried her cheeks with the back of his hand. The girl stared, then rewarded him with a faint smile, sweet and lovely like the rest of her.

The raid hovered as distant as Norway itself. Reidar could not fathom fighting and plundering now. He lifted his face to the sky with a silent query to all the gods of Asgard. Were they angry with him for taking pity on his spoils? For how else to explain his shameful exchange of the thrill and honor of the raid for an Irish girl's shy smile? How else to account for the indisputable truth that this smile was worth more than any loot from the raid?

"Home," she repeated, then added something that could only be words of gratitude.

Reidar said nothing. His uncle's mocking stare and the humiliating *Reidar the Sapling* burned through his mind like a brand. His voyage back loomed shameful and empty-handed, laden with well-deserved taunts and sneers. He'd have to think of something—some way to justify this unforgivable folly, unworthy of a warrior. But he needed not hurry now, so he relaxed in the wood's stillness and studied Ingrid's heart-breaking face, committing it to memory.

Brows raised, she studied him back, and for the first time, her gaze wasn't filled with fear and scorn. In their place shone surprise and something that made Reidar unaccountably happy—approval.

His father said there would be others, and Reidar knew he was right. But in that moment, he also knew in his marrow he'd never meet anyone like this small, heathen girl. He didn't care for the way the knowledge squeezed at his heart, so he stretched out his arms, then raised them to show his intent to carry her.

Eyes downcast, she nodded her consent.

With a gentleness he didn't know himself capable of, he reached beneath her thighs and lifted her in his arms. She felt soft as clay and was light as a feather. Slowly, he walked toward the edge of the wood, peering into the distance. If the raid was still afoot, he would wait until it was done, then bring her to her hut. And if it was finished, so much the better.

Reidar set off, reveling in the warm, comfortable feel of her against his chest and in her sweet scent of fresh honey and morning dew. He glanced down as she went slack in his arms. Her hand clutched something at her breast as she closed her eyes and mouthed silent heathen incantations. He hadn't noticed it before—a small wooden cross, simple and stark compared to the inlaid, jeweled ones plundered from Northumbria and Iona.

He shivered as the weight of knowing sank in, clear as the lifting mist—the girl had charmed him. She must have been a skilled sorceress too, for he felt neither fear nor alarm as she opened her mesmerizing eyes and gazed into his soul. The peace and calm in them took Reidar by surprise. What sort of God wielded such power?

The outlines of the huts grew clearer, then rose before him, grim and silent. He was glad Ingrid settled her silky head against his chest and closed her eyes again, for he'd spared no thought for what his people had wrought upon her *home*. Keeping his pace steady, he stepped through the village. The silence pressed against him like a presence, glum and mournful, the salt-laden breeze thick with the tang of blood, fear, and death. The skin at his nape crawled—Harald's men had done quick work of the little village.

Doors hung wide open, their wooden frames swinging on broken hinges. Shattered pots and half-spilled grain littered the ground marked by his people's heavy footprints. A woman's torn gown lay at his feet, and a distance away, near to the shore, lay the woman herself, her disrobed body twisted in an unnatural way. He tore his gaze from the corpse. Along the beach, skiffs stood overturned; tangled nets sprawled like spider webs. Reidar came to a halt as the tide receded, revealing more corpses caught in its ebb and flow. Still, Harald had not set the huts ablaze.

Reidar snapped his head at the monastery as a sharp stench of woodsmoke bit at his nostrils. The flames licked its walls, mounting and swelling, thick columns of black smoke rising into the bright blue sky.

He drew away and toward the sea. A clash of familiar voices and deep laughter filled the silence, mixing and mingling with the clang of iron and the snap of wood against the hulls as his people loaded their spoils onto the longships. A long line of thralls stood roped together beside trunks and bags of loot. Harald Fairblade had done well, and Reidar needed to unburden himself and join his father.

He exhaled sharply through his nose as a woman's low wail cut through the harsh, barking voice that could only belong to Vargr Bloodgale. A sharp crack of a whip was followed by a thin, terrified scream.

"Ingrid."

The girl's eyes flew open. She lifted her head, took one look around, and shrieked, flailing in his arms. Whether from the horror of what she saw or from the pain of her injuries, he didn't know. But whatever the cause, he could take no more.

"Where is your *home?*" He jerked his chin at the huts. "Where?"

She stopped screaming and pointed at one. Its door was, thankfully, shut, and no telling what horrors awaited her within.

Reidar went to the dwelling and deposited her onto the ground before it. He grabbed an oar lying nearby and handed it to her.

She stood, leaning on it, careful not to bear weight on her hurt ankle.

He swallowed against his thundering heart. This was good, wasn't it? He'd spared her village from fire and delivered her home. Beyond that, he could do no more—save bring her to Norway against all common sense and Harald Fairblade's explicit command.

"You can come with me and be my thrall." Despite himself, he pointed toward the beach. "Or you can take your chances here—" he gestured around—"and be free."

She appeared to understand, for she gave an emphatic shake of her head toward the shore, then stared at her *home* with such wretched eyes he had to look away. Her yearning to go in, warring with the terror of what awaited there, mirrored his own so sharply it twisted his insides.

He forced it down, but it remained. An eternity seemed to have passed since he met her gathering her daft wild strawberries, and in that time they both aged a decade. With everything in him, Reidar longed to cast himself into the sea—to wash himself clean of this day and the dark shadows in her gaze. Hollow on the inside, he tipped her face toward him with his forefinger and searched her emerald eyes.

She met his gaze.

They stood motionless, as if they both had turned to stone.

He swallowed, glimpsing something in her hair—a small twig tangled there. He pulled it free and studied it, delaying his departure. It was shaped like the rune Algiz—a stick figure with arms reaching toward the sky. A rune of life and death and of the protection and guidance from the gods.

He took her hand and pressed the twig into it. It would take all the gods to help her now.

She frowned at the twig but closed her fingers around it.

Reidar shot a glance at the longships. Half the chests had been loaded, and the thralls were being driven aboard. It was time to go.

"Reidar—" He pressed a stiff hand to his chest and pointed to her lips, seized by the aching need for her to remember his name.

The girl blinked and shook her head.

"Rei-dar," he repeated.

Her shoulders dropped for a breath. "Reidar," she echoed in her strange, lilting way, her gentle, girlish voice ripping him apart.

Head heavy and dull, he nodded and straightened. Then he marched to the beach without a backward glance, tearing at his daft, leaking eyes with a viciousness he should have saved for the raid.

He shook himself hard. He'd not shed another shameful tear for this heathen girl, for she came perilously close to breaking him. In the short time he'd known her, she'd managed to deal his honor irreparable harm. And he'd done well to leave her behind, for Reidar Valorborn, Harald Fairblade's firstborn, would never show weakness. Not before his father, not before Vargr, not before any of the men.

He squared his shoulders and lifted his chin high. While the girl wasn't ripe enough for any of them, save his depraved uncle, she was woman enough for him. He'd tell them he indulged himself with his spoils before laying her to waste.

The damage he'd done to his face stung as he wiped his eyes. How to account for that? His stomach roiled at the notion, but he knew he'd laugh all the same when he told them she'd marked him as he took from her the little she'd had to give.

# Chapter Five

## Trouble
***Brigit***

*I don't think your longing is*
*Too great to tell me,*
*Since we were young together,*
*We can trust each other.*
— Skírnismál, stanza 5

In a cold, benumbing daze, Brigit watched the boy Reidar march toward the beach. Something appeared to be wrong with his face, for he kept both arms raised to it. But when Brigit glimpsed his destination, his face no longer concerned her. Behind him, five long, lean ships rocked on the waves, each wooden prow carved into the face of a terrible fanged creature.

As a small child, Brigit once dreamed of a beast sailing from the mist, its jaws gaping, eyes glowing like fire. She'd stood rooted on a shore of ash, unable to flee, the wind tangling her hair as the beast's maw gaped wider than a cave. Not a soul lingered with her. No voice broke the silence. It was as if the world itself had turned its back on her. And when she woke, she'd wept the tears of one utterly forsaken.

Now she remained still as a post, breath coming in swift puffs against the suffocating smoke that surged her way. Prows rising against the sky, the dark shapes of the Norse ships that loomed beyond the heathen boy resembled great beasts at rest. Beside them, savages were heaping their plunder into chests and hurling them overboard like so many buzzards.

Brigit's heart drummed a frantic beat in her ears. Several Norsemen shoved forward the monks and the villagers, bound like cattle. She searched their faces, but the distance blurred their features into shadows. Still, she saw some stumble while a few brave souls fought against their bindings, only to be struck down with the butts of axes. Amid the waves crashing against the shore, the air rang with Irish cries, Norse shouts and laughter, and the thuds of chests hitting the decks.

Brigit's breath caught as she glimpsed a slight, gangly figure in a long robe. A guileless smile, a warm loaf, a sweet honeycomb—the images rushed through her, hazy and distant as a dream. Her hand flew to the cord around her neck, clutching the wooden cross the young monk, Padraig, had given her on her name day. He was too kind, too gentle. He'd never survive such depredations.

In her horror, she forgot her ankle, but she ought to have minded it for she nearly fainted as her foot touched the ground. The sharp pain jolted her back to herself. In her free hand, she was still holding the twig the boy Reidar had pressed into her palm. Heart thumping, she tucked it into her belt and stumbled toward her hut's entrance.

"Mama—" She pushed the door open, halting at the threshold.

The table lay upended against the cold hearth. Shattered pots littered the floor. In the corner, her father still lay upon the bed, unmoving.

A dark, deathly stillness clung to the wreckage like a shroud. The air hung thick with something foul and choking that twisted her gut. She quelled it. Father must have taken a turn for the worse. Soon as she found her mother, she'd tell her of her misadventures, then hobble back to the wood and gather the medicines.

"Mama, come out. They've gone." Brigit darted a wild glance around. Surely her mother had hidden from the savages. She would have heard them coming and pressed herself beneath the bed, or squeezed inside a chest, or climbed up in the rafters—

"Mama—?" Brigit's voice came thin and strangled as she peered into every dark corner of the thatched roof.

She fought to suppress the sobs that threatened to burst forth like thunder on a stormy day.

A dreadful hush settled over the hut, cold and unnatural, disturbed only by her noisy, uneven breathing. She dug her fingers into the oar, then loosened them. She needed not fret. Her mother was a clever woman, and she'd surely slipped into the cellar where they kept grain, vegetables, and salted fish—

A distant cry split the silence, so piercing it spread into Brigit's fingertips. A woman's wail of agony. Stomach roiling, she staggered back to the entrance and peered at the beach, wincing against a shot of pain in her ankle. The ships rocked on the edge of the shore; the savages strained to push them from the sand.

Brigit returned to the ruin that had been her life. She stood motionless, staring at the planks her parents used to cover the cellar. They lay tossed aside, the entrance ripped asunder.

She stumbled forward.

Empty.

She stepped to their only chest and threw it open.

Empty.

She raised her head toward the bed, breath heaving like a tide. "Da..."

No answer came from the dim corner.

Slowly, one limping step at a time, she approached her father. The foul smell thickened.

A pitiful wail burst from her lips as she slipped on something slimy like fish guts, lost hold of her oar, and tumbled onto the floor, spreading her hands out to halt the fall. Her fingers slid against the sticky muck, and she knew what it was by its sharp, metallic stench and by the eerie stillness of her father.

Suffocating on her breathing, Brigit struggled up and came face to face with a deep gash in his throat that no longer dripped with blood.

She screamed.

She hobbled out of the hut.

The world spun as she caught sight of her hands, smeared with crimson. Her screams turned to hoarse gasps that tore at her chest, depriving her of air. A yard away, a disrobed woman lay bowed in an unnatural position, her sightless eyes staring off into the wood. A bit farther, the old man Declan and his wife Cara lay side by side, both drenched in blood. Beside them, the small girl Eilis from two huts down and her little sister Aoife lay feet apart. The ancient man, Tadhg, lay farther still, his face frozen in a grotesque mask of horror. Had they been here all along, even as she stood with the boy Reidar, echoing his name?

Stomach heaving, she scanned the beach. The Norse ships had gone, swallowed by smoke and mist.

It took all of Brigit's remaining strength to remain upright as a terrible truth settled over her like a crushing stone. She was completely alone on what only that morning had been her happy island. Her home.

She collapsed to her knees on the cold, sodden earth, her body convulsing with violent heaves. The boy Reidar knew what his people had done—what awaited her—and still, he left her to her fate. He could have taken her. He should have taken her even if she fought him.

She retched until nothing was left, then dropped her head into her hands, trembling with her whole body as his piercing blue gaze flashed through her mind. He'd given her a choice. Her! A wounded girl of thirteen winters! He'd wished her to remember his name. Savage! Did he fancy she'd live long enough in this graveyard for it to matter?

*The Lord will provide.* Her mother's words floated in Brigit's mind, then faded. On this day, the Lord abandoned Rathlin Island and everyone who called it home, leaving them to rot in the wake of heathen wrath.

As if from elsewhere, Brigit took stock of herself: hurt ankle, bloodied knee, mangled wrists. She curled up where she knelt and wept herself into oblivion.

She woke in the dark of the night to the lashing wind and the indifferent whisper of the waves lapping at the shore. Shivering, she wrapped her arms around her. The dead had not been given proper Christian burial and no doubt wandered near—maybe even where she lay. She stopped breathing as a distant wail cut through the darkness. A banshee, mourning the poor souls' unrest!

"Lord, p-please have mercy on their souls... Please save, give..." The prayer wasn't coming, so as quietly as possible, Brigit crawled toward her hut. Gagging, she came to a halt at the entrance—the smell had gotten worse.

Then a horrid notion made her freeze in place. Her father's spirit surely wandered here now. What if he took it into his head to haunt her?

Heart hammering, she crawled to a nearby tree and remained there until daybreak, praying as best she could and not daring to close her eyes.

Her mind cleared with the rising sun. She would retrieve her oar, find an empty hut—there had to be one—then scavenge for any remnants of ale and food. And then, as Padraig said, sufficient for the day was its own trouble.

But nothing was sufficient any longer. For two days, Brigit hobbled from hut to hut, finding each turned upside down and filled with sights no young girl should witness. The savages had taken everything—not a sip of ale, nor a crumb of bread, nor a sliver of fish remained. They must also have taken her mother, for she was not among the dead. Yet the thought that she lived offered Brigit no solace.

Throat parched and ankle throbbing, she scraped charred bits of fish stew from the bottoms of blackened cauldrons, licked soured milk from the shards of broken crocks, and upended empty flagons for the last bitter drops of ale.

At dawn of the third day, she ventured to the farthest hut. No corpses or signs of violence marked the place, and neither food nor drink remained inside. For as long as she remembered, the villagers murmured of a strange man who lived here alone, keeping to himself even when the others gathered to mend their nets or share the day's catch. He fished like the rest of them but never lingered at the shore, always slipping back into his hut instead. Children whispered that he spoke to the sea, that he wasn't quite right in the head.

By the hut lay an upturned skiff, its hull stripped but nearly mended. The man must have been making repairs when the Norsemen took him.

Brigit's ankle had healed so she walked without leaning on the oar, though she still stepped with care lest a bolt of pain halt her in her tracks. She glanced at the wood. Perhaps she'd grown hale enough to venture there now and forage for some berries.

She winced with a flicker of memory—a single wild strawberry pressed to her lips, cool with morning dew and bursting on her tongue like honeyed wine. And with it flashed the image of the boy Reidar and his stolen kiss. To her dismay, he was never too far from her mind with his sky-blue eyes and wheat-colored hair. And the thoughts of him curdled, turning more bitter with each torturous day and each bone-chilling night. He'd saved her from his people, but it'd have been better if they'd taken her along with her mother. It'd have been kinder if they'd killed her. It'd have been more merciful if she hadn't been born at all.

As if come to life, the skiff moved, and a hand appeared from underneath.

Brigit shrieked, heartbeat roaring in her ears. But just as she spun to hobble away as fast as her ankle would allow, the hand lifted up the boat, and from beneath crawled out a man. Brigit's shrieks turned frantic. She backed away. He was likely no man at all, but a brazen unrested soul, come to haunt her in broad daylight!

The specter stared at her for a confused moment, then darted a wild glance around and stood, shaking himself like a dog. "Begone!" He crossed himself with large, fretful hands. "Be at rest and leave the living be!"

It must have been the hideous mix of gnawing thirst, sapping hunger, and dark sorrow that slowed Brigit's thinking, for it took her a long, stunned silence to gather his meaning.

"I'm Brigit O'Clery," she choked out at last, "and I am still living, more's the pity."

The man stared at her, then approached, hands fidgeting as if with an invisible net. He was in his midlife, not yet old but not young either. Still, save for the strange manner of his hands, he seemed hale and not at all dying of thirst like she was.

He studied her with fixed, wide eyes, then raised his hand and poked her shoulder with his forefinger. "You're but a girl!" He scanned the shore, muttering something under his breath. "They're coming back! Soon, too!" His sharp cry turned her blood to ice. "Haste, haste—I must mend my boat! Shh—they'll hear!"

Brigit drew back from the flash of madness in his eyes.

"The fiends' coming is nigh, girl—you hear? With the turning tide the hell-spawn comes again!" His voice emerged thin and shrill as he turned to his skiff.

Suddenly, he froze. "There's ale and salted fish in the cellar—beneath the bed." He shot Brigit a chagrined glance over his shoulder. "Eat and rest. We sail for the mainland at noontide."

# Chapter Six

## Scorn

***Brigit***

**Seven Winters Later**

*From Gymir's house,*
*I saw a maiden,*
*She was dear to me,*
*Her arms shone like the sea and sky.*
— Skírnismál, stanza 6

Brigit woke at dawn to a cold bed and the hounds' vexing barking outside. Three nights now, and still her husband had not crossed the threshold of her chamber. Lord Cearbhall mac Bressal was quite besotted with his newest fancy. His new concubine was a cunning girl who laughed at his every dull jest and gazed into his eyes like he was Niall of the Nine Hostages in the flesh.

Brigit flounced to the window with a look of disgust. With luck, he'd never come here again, and she would be free of his sordid attentions at last.

She pressed her small wooden cross to her chest and closed her eyes. Many winters past, a kind young monk named Padraig gave it to her. Her father carved a wee fish upon it, and her mother threaded it onto a thin leather cord. She scarcely remembered their faces now—they had turned to a blur. Brigit grasped the cross, letting it dig into her palm until she felt its edges. It was all she had left of her parents and her girlhood cut short. It was also the only remaining link to her fading faith, and she clung to it time and again to ward off the Great Scorn that lived inside her, hard and unrelenting. But it burned so wild and wide, she could scarce name what she despised most.

On some days, it was her detestable, philandering husband, whose touch she abhorred. On other days, it was her shameful barrenness, though she suspected the fault lay with him—he'd never fathered a child on any woman. Still other times, it was the dark, draining certainty that her fate was to live out her sad, lonely life in this bleak house, among her husband's abominable kin, who loathed her no less fiercely than she did them. There were days, too, when she couldn't deny her scorn turned inward, for she was a woman wed and ought to have loved her husband. For even if he left much to be desired, he had wed her—a peasant girl with nothing to her name—and cared for her as a husband should. He clothed her in fine garments, gave her a well-appointed chamber with her own maidservant, and provided meals she'd never dreamed of.

But on most days, with rage as bright as the flames that devoured Rathlin Monastery seven winters past, she loathed the Norsemen who took everything from her. For they alone were to blame for her accursed, wretched life. They alone had ensured she'd have no hope and no future. And at the top of the hill that was the Norsemen, stood the boy Reidar, whom she scorned above all for leaving her to such a fate instead of taking her away from it.

Aye, that was why she deplored him—for that reason and none other. For after the mad but kind man, whose name she never learned, brought her here, to Dalaradia, to a distant relation of his, her life became a living purgatory.

His cousin Rathnait, stout and red-faced, had refused her outright, saying she had six mouths to feed. But after Brigit tearfully vowed she would cause no trouble but cook, clean, weave, mend, churn butter, and tend to the children and the livestock from dawn to dusk, the woman grudgingly relented. Huffing and spitting, Rathnait tossed a filthy straw pallet by the door and warned Brigit she'd be thrown out at the first sign of idleness. Her compensation would be the roof over her head and a single meal each day she worked—and no food if she feigned an illness and shirked her work.

It was then Brigit had acquired her Great Scorn—for Rathnait, for her leering husband who pinched her when his wife wasn't looking, for their cruel children, and for the Norsemen who'd sentenced her to a life of servitude at thirteen winters. Yet she worked hard and made do, dastardly as it was. Then one day, it was her ill luck to be milking the cow when the Dalaradia chieftain, Cearbhall mac Bressal, took a fancy to ride across his lands. She was eighteen winters then, a woman grown, and once he saw her, he wanted her for himself.

Her mistress had surprised her with her fortitude. Standing firm, with her meaty hands at her waist, Rathnait declared to her overlord that Brigit was a God-fearing girl and a valuable servant, and he could have her only if he wed her proper and paid the full bride price, besides. After some haggling, Brigit was sold for five head of cattle and a small plot of land.

Cearbhall mac Bressal was twice her age and hard on the eyes, yet she'd foolishly thought him the answer to her prayers. Her wedding night had disabused her of the notion, for it was the most detestable of her life, followed by countless others. The misery lasted until her husband took a concubine. Brigit was nineteen then and fancied it a turn in her fortunes. But the chieftain soon tired of the girl and returned to Brigit. The pattern repeated itself often, and her Great Scorn grew greater every time.

Still, she loathed the Norsemen more. For if not for them, she'd have remained with her loving parents until she came of age, then wed the kind boy from her village who always smiled and brought her lovely rocks and shells. He, too, was taken by the savages, for she saw no trace of him when she hobbled from hut to hut with the oar the boy Reidar gave her before leaving her there to die.

Brigit wiped at her eyes and reached beneath her pillow for the swath of cloth that held his twig. Apart from her cross, it was the only thing that filled her with light. Oddly, it was nearly shaped like a cross, save the angled lines rose up like arms reaching toward the sky. Scowling, she closed her fingers around the wee bundle. Brigit could never unravel the knots in her heart, for they pulled and throbbed with the memory of the boy Reidar. For seven long winters, the thoughts of him brought on an incomprehensible mixture of searing loathing, unbecoming tenderness, and unbearable bewilderment. Why should she hate him so when he saved her from his own people in the only way he knew? Worse, now a woman of twenty winters, she longed for him in every shadowed corner of her heart and in her every bone and sinew. Surely, she was cursed to have fallen for her foe—and one gone, never to return. And perhaps this wicked curse was at the very root of her Great Scorn.

But worst of all, Brigit no longer felt certain that Christ loved her. In the dead of the night, when her abominable husband snored beside her as she sobbed with shame and self-pity, she wondered if her God had forsaken her. Then, after getting her fill of tears, she repented. Eyes squeezed tight and fingers gripping her cross, she begged forgiveness for doubting Him and for her unrelenting longing for the heathen boy, whose memory, fed by her imaginings in her ghastly marriage bed was the only thing that kept her from opening her own veins.

Outside, the hounds broke into another fit of barking, this time followed by snarling.

Brigit stuffed the cloth with the twig beneath her pillow and stood. She shivered in her husband's mandated shift of thin, fine *léine*, which afforded little warmth against the morning chill.

The din came to an abrupt halt as she reached for her fine woolen shawl and wrapped it about her shoulders. Every hair on her nape prickled as countless muted footfalls swept through the courtyard. Before she could move, a loud crash shook up the house. It rang with sounds that turned Brigit's blood to ice and stomach to lead.

A cacophony of voices and laughter.

Rough and guttural. At once foreign and terrifyingly familiar.

Her heartbeat pounded in her ears with the finality of a night terror come to life.

Crashes of iron against wood. A woman shrieking, wailing. A man pleading. Bold words that sounded like curses. Laughter that turned vicious.

*Father, help me, help me...*

Frantic, she scanned her small chamber. Nowhere to run. Nowhere to hide.

Her gaze fell upon her chest of drawers—too small. Behind the bed—she'd never fit. The crawling space beneath it—too tight.

The voices grew nearer. Footsteps followed. They came to a halt outside her chamber.

Heart leaping from her chest against ugly, hoarse sobs, she dashed to the corner farthest from the door and crouched there.

Someone kicked the door open. She squeezed her eyes shut and mouthed the Lord's Prayer with cold, trembling lips. The footsteps approached—heavy and determined. She covered her head with her arms as the person stopped a foot away. A mixture of sea, wet fur, and man filled her head.

Ceaseless, deafening stillness stretched.

She sensed him squatting before her.

"You." A deep, Norse voice spat the Irish word with a scoff.

She pressed her back into the corner, shaking like a leaf.

"Look." The voice held a new note—consternation mixed with vexation.

Brigit peeked from beneath her forearm and came face to face with an enormous axe hanging from the man's belt, and a long scabbard with a Norse sword pommel at the top. She shut her eyes again.

*Our Father in heaven...* She couldn't tell whether her prayer broke from her as a sob or if her tears fell in silence. The words remained locked in her mind.

The man said something curt in Norse, and she knew he commanded her to look at him. She didn't stir.

A large, rough hand grabbed her arm at the wrist and wrenched it away from her face. Her stomach heaved and roiled. Her heart turned into a frantic bird inside her chest. Another instant, and it would burst.

The man murmured something that sounded like an oath. He released her arm.

She peered up through the blur in her eyes and wished she hadn't. Before her loomed a giant, the likes of which had ravaged her island, his head concealed beneath an iron helmet with a nose guard that cleaved his face in two.

The chamber tilted like a fishing skiff in a tempest. This time, the boy Reidar wasn't here, and this heathen would hack her to bits with his axe, or take her against her will, or both. She knew not which death would be worse, only that either fate would surely bring her overdue end.

Two more savages stormed into her chamber, eyes wild, axes raised above their heads.

Her sobs became a living, breathing thing she could no longer suppress.

*Why have you forsaken me, Father?*

The first barbarian barked something, and they stared, then muttered and left, closing the door behind them.

He removed his helmet and went down on one knee before her, studying her with a strange, unsettling expression.

Outside, the sun began to rise. Its first uncertain ray filtered through the window and illuminated his features. It took all her will not to scream, for it was as though a heathen from her Rathlin wood had slipped from her nightmares into her waking world. His head was shorn at the sides and densely covered with heathen marks that spilled onto his cheeks. What hair remained was plaited close from forehead to nape in thick flaxen braids that tumbled down his back. His broad face appeared stripped of expression, and his cold blue eyes pierced hers like two shards of ice. A dark, long-haired pelt of some beast cloaked his massive shoulders. He seemed a beast himself—savage and wicked as a wolf.

Brigit's prayers of repentance had never done her any good, for her mind always summoned the boy Reidar. And for one wild, desperate moment, she yearned with all her bruised heart and all her wretched soul and every part of her being for this man to be him. For despite his thick sandy beard, she judged he'd seen no more than twenty-some winters. Reidar would be this age now and would have grown this tall and this broad. And this detestable.

Her lips stopped trembling. She felt them curl as her Great Scorn drowned out such folly. Like his accursed people, the boy Reidar would now surely wear his hair in this barbarian manner and would have these heathen marks branded into his flesh. For he would be what he'd always been—a savage, bound to the abominable ways of his race.

She came back to her senses as the man gripped her forearm and jerked her up to stand. Her shawl slipped from her shoulders and fell to the floor, leaving her in her husband's cursed shift that concealed nothing.

With a gasp, she wrenched her arm from the savage's and hugged herself. The man scoffed, then grabbed her arms and pulled them down her sides with such force she staggered. She dared not move as he looked her over with an expression of profound displeasure that seemed to mask something she knew too well, thanks to her husband—the unchecked lust of a beast in heat.

"The Lord is my shepherd... I shall not want," she whispered. "He makes me lie down in green pastures. He leads me beside the still waters..."

A cold calm settled over her, and she lifted her chin and met the heathen's eyes, daring him to act. This man was twice her husband's size, and it wouldn't be misery and self-pity, but a slow, painful death. Yet no doubt, death it would be—overdue and much welcome. Fair wages for her daft fancies.

"Have at it then," she spat, humming like a fiddle string, burning like a flame. "See if I give a whit!"

With a derisive huff, the savage stuffed his hands beneath Brigit's arms, then slid them down.

She sucked in her breath, wishing he would just slit her throat.

He patted her down, as if searching for something.

"I have no weapons," she breathed.

The savage ignored her. Mouth set in a hard line, he moved his hands beneath her breasts, down to her abdomen. Not in a lewd way. Not yet.

"Stop," she panted. "Stop it."

His hands traveled to her hips and legs, then along her ankles, as if feeling for something through the thin linen.

Satisfied, the heathen straightened.

With all her might, Brigit called on her Great Scorn, sharpening its edge. She squared her shoulders and met his dispassionate gaze. "I loathe you," she mouthed under her breath, too low for him to hear should he understand.

With a strange, tight expression, the heathen scanned the chamber. He charged at her bed and shoved it against the wall with force enough to shatter it to bits. Somehow, the bed held fast. He glared at it with a look of murder, then grabbed it again and pulled it toward him, leaving a narrow gap at the wall. Rigid as a board, he grabbed two fistfuls of fleece pelts from the bed and hurled them into the gap.

He barreled toward her.

Brigit's anger faded, and in its place rose the fear that surely seizes a rabbit trapped by a foaming, ravenous wolf. She swayed on her feet, whispering her futile Lord's Prayer, wishing she had something to strike him with.

With neither warning nor ceremony, he gripped her arm and pulled her behind him toward the nook between the bed and the wall.

The notion of that small strip of floor becoming her deathbed made Brigit's insides roil.

"You—hide," he grunted out, pointing at the space with a large, stiff forefinger, his voice the low growl of the sea, the Irish words strange and wrong-sounding. "I—come back."

She stared, the thought of being spared not quite fitting in her head. Yet it fit.

"Come back for what?"

The savage threw back his head and spat out what could only be Norse curses, rough and sharp as daggers. He fixed her with a hard stare. "I—" he bumped his chest with a fist—"master. You—" he gestured toward her—"thrall."

*Thrall.*

They peered at each other in the silence that fell, his eyes burning holes in her face as if seeking something. How could such pale eyes blaze with so much fire? To escape it, Brigit darted a glance at the window. Maybe she could climb out while he was gone and run where her sight carried her until her strength failed.

But she should have kept her gaze steady, for the savage appeared to have read her thoughts. With a low growl, he reached into his belt and produced the longest, thickest rope she'd ever seen.

She went cold with an unbidden flash of memory: pain and terror, gentle thumbs brushing her mangled wrists, sky-blue eyes filled with remorse. Not with this flint-hard discontent, weighted by the taste of evil.

"I'll hide, I swear it—" Very slowly, one step at a time, she backed away from him.

Fast as lightning, he grabbed her at the waist and sat her on the bed. Then he went down on one knee, seized her ankle with his enormous hands, and studied it.

Breath hitching, Brigit peered at the tight, wheat-colored plaits at his crown as he traced the very spot she'd sprained on Rathlin Island with a warm thumb. She swallowed against a dull ache at the back of her throat. She always knew she was wicked deep down, and here was all the proof laid bare.

For her heart never raced—save with revulsion—at her lawful husband's touch the way it did at this heathen's.

As if in answer, the Norseman lifted his head and locked his eyes with hers.

She froze as all air caught in her chest. The clear blue ponds glittered with something resembling shame.

She shook herself. Surely, terror had played her false, and the shame was hers.

"Let me go," she breathed.

The savage snapped his gaze back to the rope in his hand. Jaw set, he slipped a hard knot over her ankle and tied another complicated one on top, tightening the rope. He blinked at her yelp of pain and swiftly loosened the knot—not enough to free her, only to ease the bite. With a deep groove between his brows, he tethered the other end to the bed leg, using the same knot. Then he took her by her upper arm again and steered her to the gap between the bed and the wall.

"You—hide," he bit out. "You—wait."

Brigit sank her teeth into her lip. The fear of being ripped to shreds or worse had drained out of her somewhere between his thumb sweeping her ankle and the emphatic "you—wait."

The heathen crossed to the door.

With a shuddering breath, Brigit slumped onto the fleece pelts.

Abruptly, the savage turned and headed back to her. He removed a chain from his neck and tossed it over her head, swift and precise. The charm that hung from it struck her square in the chest.

"Men—" He gestured at the door. "Show—" He pointed to the charm, then to the top knot at her ankle. "Safe."

Without waiting for her reply, he marched to the door but turned once more before leaving. "Hide."

Numb, she rolled into a ball. She was free of her husband at last, and the price of her freedom was new slavery.

# Chapter Seven

## Shame
***Reidar***

*She is more dear to me than any*
*Maiden has ever been to a man,*
*But no one among the gods or elves*
*Will let us be together.*
— Skírnismál, stanza 7

Reidar shut Ingrid's door behind him. Then he stood outside her chamber, pleading with all the gods of Asgard for strength and wisdom. But neither came, and in their place reigned gloom and confusion.

After Rathlin, he'd gone on many profitable voyages to Éire—Inishmurray and Skellig Michael, Inishbofin and Innishkea, Tyrconnell Bay and Connemara. Spoils piled high in the longships' holds: gold and silver, fine cloth and keen-edged blades. Each raid earned him renown and increased the number of his sworn men. Yet only he and his *fostra* knew the true reason for his relentless fixation with this faraway land, though he never truly believed he'd find Ingrid in any of those Odin-forsaken places. Still, he joined and later led the raids, searching for her despite his better sense.

He'd been a witless boy when he committed the unforgivable folly of leaving her to perish on that ruined, desolate island, grievously injured and with neither food nor water to survive. Recklessly and without any thought, he'd all but sentenced her to death for the daft promise of taking her home. He'd long since understood he should have brought her aboard his father's longship instead. If she hadn't survived the crossing, he would at least rest in knowing he'd done all he could for her. And if she had, she'd have been his for seven winters. Now, in punishment for his stupidity, his nights swarmed with twisted dreams of her starving and cursing his name until her last breath.

Shortly after arriving home from Rathlin, he heeded his father's counsel and claimed a thrall among dozens of young women they'd brought to sell at Eastlands slave markets. His concubine looked nothing like Ingrid, but she was of age, comely, and always willing to share his bed. And best of all, she spoke Ingrid's tongue. He loved hearing her talk in that lilting, beguiling way and had her teach him, telling himself it was only for war and plunder. Irish was lovely but bewildering, and though his learning was slow, he grasped nearly all her words, even when his own tongue stumbled over them. Still, he'd acquired skill enough for Ingrid.

Yet for all his daft, clandestine searching of her, he half-hoped to never find her, for that would spell a greater curse. He was Reidar Valorborn—a name won by spilling a sea of heathen blood in honor of his father, the late Harald Fairblade. And Reidar Valorborn's sole purpose was *blodhefnd*—avenging his father's untimely, dishonorable death.

Reidar was but seventeen winters when the gods turned their backs on him, after Vargr Bloodgale's second wife died of a broken neck. Enraged, Harald declared his brother a wild, uncouth beast unfit to sit on his Althing. Vargr responded he was not to blame for marrying women who took such poor care of their necks, then demanded single combat to restore his besmirched honor. It was strange how one blow from Vargr's axe to his father's leg had robbed Harald of all his strength. For three days, he lay in bed, unable to sit nor eat. On the third day, the pain worsened, the skin around the wound mottled purple-black, and the chamber filled with a foul smell of rotting flesh. Then came the fever, and with it, the slow, ghastly pull of death.

All suspected Vargr had coated his blade with wolfsbane, but none dared say it aloud. After Harald Fairblade departed for Valhalla, Reidar had neither might nor support to claim the jarl's title, and it went undisputed to Vargr.

From that day, Reidar measured his every thought and deed against his *blodhefnd* and mercilessly disposed with anything that stood in its way. Even as he sought Ingrid, he knew if fate cursed him with finding her, she would only draw him from his steadfast purpose. Worse yet, she'd stand between him and his betrothal to Astrid, if yet unsworn. And that would not do.

Astrid was a fierce shield-maiden, skilled with her axe and loyal to Reidar, if not a bit consumed with him. To wed her was to bind her father's power and her brothers' strong blades to his cause. Besides, save for his muddled thirteenth-winter ritual, Astrid was a girl of his firsts—first touch, first kiss, first lovemaking—first everything a boy dreams. And while they both knew she wouldn't be his last, she was a patient kind. She followed him on every raid and shared his bed when he wished it without a word of reproach, ignoring all his other fancies—thralls and Norse women alike—and told anyone who would listen they'd wed after this raid.

Still, while Reidar made no effort to disprove her words, neither did he offer confirmation. Much to his chagrin, he couldn't remember when he last burned with passion for Astrid—or if he ever had. In truth—and it pained him to admit this—she clung to him like sap to a tree, vexing him to no end with her lack of pride. But he'd likely wed her all the same, and with her unwavering loyalty and her family's great strength, he'd rally every man in his jarldom and cast Vargr the Blasted from his rightful seat.

Something cut through Reidar's ill-timed reverie—the unmistakable peals of weeping behind the chamber door. He clenched his fists and marched away, toward the great hall.

Soon after his return from Rathlin, his *fostra* declared him enchanted, for she alone knew his shameful secret. She called it his Great Flaw, though she always added he was not to blame, for even the strongest warriors fell prey to a sorceress' spell. She was likely right, for after that voyage, he was never himself again. For one, he developed a strange, unbecoming fascination with wild strawberries. He often ventured into the forest with the single purpose of being in their proximity. There, he would pick a whole sprig and study it as if searching for Ingrid in its tiny red berries and bright green leaves.

As he traced the leaves' veins with his fingertip, he'd uncovered a wonder most curious. The three prominent lines in the center of the leaf lay in the exact shape of the Algiz rune—a stick figure of a man, stretching his arms toward the sky. Like the twig he found in Ingrid's hair. It was then, as he stared into those lines, that her small wooden cross appeared in his mind's eye. The Algiz rune and the cross were nearly the same. Only the arms of the cross stretched outward, as if reaching to embrace.

After that, the notion remained jammed into his head, refusing to let go, much like his memory of the girl and the shame that came with thoughts of her. Even his *fostra*, who knew everything about him, could not fathom the extent of his enchantment. Neither the Irish thralls, nor Astrid, nor any woman contented him, for his true Great Flaw was not what his *fostra* called "softness of heart." No, his cold, Norse heart was forged from iron. His true Great Flaw was measuring each woman against his vision of Ingrid in her full bloom and finding each lacking.

Reidar shook himself and headed for the great hall. The raid was done. Better yet, the rising scent of roasted meat and his men's boisterous exchanges told him he'd arrived in time for a nightlong celebration. They would not soon depart from Dalaradia, for this time, Reidar's purpose was to claim the land and leave half his men here to tend it as their own.

Reidar shook off his shameful brooding, squared his shoulders, and lifted his chin. Vargr Bloodgale may have ruled Ljosstrond, but Reidar Valorborn ruled the seas. The fate of his *blodhefnd* hinged on his conquests and ironclad resolve. He'd learned well the lesson his father had taught him: men followed a strong leader to the ends of the earth and gladly did his bidding to bask in his glory. And so long as he lavished them with the thrill and riches of the raids, they'd eagerly march with him to unseat Vargr Bloodgale when the time was ripe.

A heart-wrenching wail cut through the mounting din as Reidar stepped toward the great hall. By Thor, he could swear it was another fit of sobbing in Ingrid's chamber, but that was as impossible as it seemed.

He clenched his jaw and shut his eyes, struggling to shake off her mighty spell. In all his wild imaginings of her as a woman grown, he never dreamed she'd be so dazzling. Still small and delicate, especially compared to Astrid, she was so perfect it was maddening. Through her thin shift, her every line, every curve, every dip seemed made just for him. Her emerald eyes, sparkling amidst dark lashes, drew him in like a tide in which he felt himself drowning and didn't want to come up for air. Her supple lips, the color of wild strawberries, set his blood on fire.

He nearly took leave of his senses and kissed her when she fixed him with a stare that made his stomach turn. And then, he was glad for the dark flames of fear, loathing, and defiance in her eyes, for they burned away his Great Flaw and ground it to ash. The very eyes that haunted his dreams glared into his, untouched by any trace of recognition. It was then Reidar's chest turned into a hard, tight cage. Like a fool, he'd searched all of Éire for her, dreaming of her each night, replacing every woman he bedded with her specter, mourning her death and endlessly blaming himself for it. And now that he finally found her, she looked at him with revulsion deserving of a filthy beast.

*I loathe you.*

The fury that rushed through him upon hearing this was so bright it nearly consumed him. But it was only fitting, for he bore no trace of what he'd been. He was no longer a simple boy trembling with the excitement of drawing his first heathen blood. He'd drawn plenty of it since he met her—his densely inked skin displayed the glory of his triumphs. Triumphs over her weakling race of heathens.

Surely, it was Loki who'd played this trick on him again, dangling a shiny trinket, then taking it away in one fell swoop. And it was Thor who'd slapped him upside his head to shake him free of this crippling folly. The time to shed his boyhood dreams and the hopes unworthy of his name had long passed. This foreign girl was naught but his spoils, as she had always been, and the moment to rid himself of his Great Flaw had finally arrived.

By Thor's favor, his first kill had taught him to stifle the unseemly, shameful ache in his chest. He soon grew skilled at disposing with the knots in his stomach at the terror in the thralls' eyes. For the Christians weren't like his people, and so they weren't deserving of his pity. And neither was this girl he'd named Ingrid—a beautiful goddess. She was no goddess, but a fearful, hateful thrall, like the rest of them.

Reidar tightened his fists. If he still suffered any qualms at his over-rough handling of her, it was only due to his Great Flaw. Before long, he would pluck it from his heart like the weed it was. A brief encounter, and already he'd gained ground. The look in her eyes as she sank onto the fleece pelts had proved he'd subdued her. And he was glad of it. Yes, glad and relieved, too.

There was much work to be done in this Odin-forsaken place called Dalaradia, and his only remaining concern with his thrall lay in keeping her unspoiled for him. For he, Reidar Valorborn, would not tolerate another man fouling his plunder. That was the only reason he'd stashed her behind the bed and given her his *Mjolnir* amulet—Thor's Hammer—to ward off both men and ill fate. And that was the only reason he'd tied his own Thor's Braidknot at her ankle for any prowling brute to see.

Reidar blew out a slow, steadying breath. It would do for now. There was time enough to have pleasure of her, and he hoped to Odin she'd prove poor company in his bed, so he could rip her from his heart at long last.

He lifted his chin and barreled into the blasted Irish great hall.

"By the gods, well done!" His thunderous hail echoed off the walls. He hoped it shook up what Irish wretches still lingered in this house, praying to their useless Christ for phantom mercy.

"Thanks be to the gods!" His younger brother, Thorsten, returned his greeting, reaching for something on the floor with a knowing smirk.

"Meet Cearbhall mac Bressal, the late chieftain of Dalaradia!" He lifted the Irishman's severed head to the roar of laughter. "This good Christian was sadly cut down while plowing a woman who—" he winked—"was not at all his wife."

# Chapter Eight

## Captor
***Brigit***

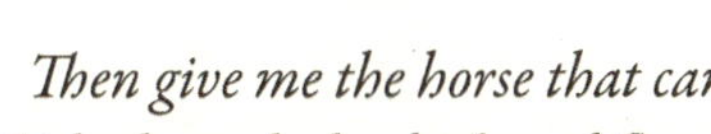

*Then give me the horse that can*
*Ride through the dark and flames,*
*And give me the sword that can*
*Fight on its own against giants.*
— Skírnismál, stanza 8

Brigit spent the day hiding beneath the fleece pelts. She rose but once—to relieve herself in the chamber pot and grab her flagon from her dressing table, all the while keeping an eye on the door. The savage had left plenty of slack for her to move around the chamber, but her maidservant had not come with fresh ale, so that proved of little use. Still, Brigit had all day to think, and she resolved she was weary of heathen Norsemen, lascivious husbands, and cruel masters. And she was bone-tired of living in dread of an encounter with the next man who would hold her freedom in his hands. But most of all, she was drained to the marrow by her ceaseless and ever-mounting Great Scorn. So after praying and begging God for guidance, she vowed to kill her new captor the first chance she had. Or perish in the trying. This was not the Christian way, but she could take no more of this ghastly life. And if that earned her a place in hell, then she would see the Norseman there.

Seeing as Brigit's imaginings never veered far from the boy Reidar, she thought of him, too—yet innocent of the world and unmarked by its wickedness. Throat tight and chest aching, she remembered the kindness and regret in his striking eyes, the way his warm arms had shielded her from the pillage, and how his gentle voice made the savage words sound like the murmur of a creek. And after thinking all that, she buried her crumbling face in the fleece and wept the bitter tears of bereavement for what time had wrecked beyond mending.

After getting her fill of sorrow, she studied the strange trinket her captor had tossed over her head—some heathen amulet shaped like a hammer and inlaid with a network of intricate swirls. She disliked the feel of it beside her cross. But if the savage believed it powerful enough to safeguard against men like him, who was she to argue? So she let it be and lay still, awaiting her fate.

By the time the door creaked open, Brigit had wearied of hiding, thirsting, and starving, so she sat up, intending to say so. The words froze on her lips as a new barbarian stepped into the chamber. He was shorter and infinities uglier than her captor, and the look in his eyes spelled every conceivable indignity.

Before she could utter a sound, the man was beside her, pulling her up by her hair and spitting low, hoarse words that had the tone of obscenities into her face. His glassy stare and the amalgam of stale sweat and rotting meat made her gorge rise, but she formed a tight fist and buried it in his fleshy jaw.

In an instant, her back slammed against the floor. Her cheek rang with a vicious blow.

Brigit blinked away the tears and balled another fist. "May God strike you and all your kind dead!"

Grunting like a pig, the man grabbed her neckline. He froze.

Trembling, Brigit followed his gaze. With widened eyes, the swine stared at her captor's amulet at her throat, then at the knot at her ankle and back again.

He dropped her neckline as if it had caught on fire. Muttering something in Norse, he stood and drew back. Then drew back some more until he reached the door. With a wince, he whispered what sounded like an apology and maybe a plea, and left, closing the door behind him with utmost care.

Brigit's cheek throbbed with pain, but she scarcely felt it as she collapsed onto her fleece pelts. The barbarian's response meant only two things: her captor was a man of high standing, or they were all ignorant savages who worshiped charms and knots made by the human hand.

She remained in her hiding place until it grew dark, then stood and lit the candles. Her belly grumbled in earnest now, and she tossed a grim glance at the door. Would her captor have enough sense to bring food and drink? Or did he, like the boy Reidar, fancy women survived on air alone?

The night fell, but her captor didn't return. Face sore, lips parched, and stomach empty, Brigit turned on her side and tried her best not to weep with self-pity. But just as she lost the fight with herself, the door creaked open.

She froze, heart pounding like a *bodhrán*.

"Thrall." Her captor's deep, guttural voice pierced the silence of the chamber.

Brigit threw back the fleece and sat up, squinting in the falling darkness. He didn't come alone. Caoimhe, one of her husband's servants, trailed behind with a heavy food tray in her trembling hands.

Alongside the supper, her captor brought a large pile of fresh fleece pelts. He tossed them onto the bed, then fixed his gaze on the paling Caoimhe and gestured toward Brigit with a low, "Food."

The tray contained a helping of venison fit for two men, an entire loaf of barley bread, and an overflowing flagon of ale.

*Fattening me up for the spit, are you?* A sudden dizzying urge to laugh or weep—whichever came first—filled Brigit to the brim. She grabbed the flagon and drank deep to drown it out.

"Och, all our menfolk are gone...dead or put to work, I know not..." Caoimhe breathed. "Och..." She pulled in her breath at the sight of Brigit's face. "Lord, rescue us from these heathens—"

"Go." The captor's command cut through her frantic whisper.

Eyes wide, the woman bolted from the chamber.

Brigit's captor blew out all candles save one and returned to the bed. Paying her no mind, he set his ghastly battleaxe on one side of the bed, then unsheathed his sword and placed it on the other. Unhurriedly, he divested himself of his many garments: black furs, leather jerkin, chainmail, belt, leg wraps, and woolen tunic. Clad in nothing but a white linen undertunic and trousers, he tossed everything to the foot of the bed. Then, in one smooth motion, he pulled off the linen over his head and sent it after its companions.

Brigit sat motionless, unable to look away. A multitude of heathen marks covered his broad, muscled torso from neck to waist, spilling over his shoulders and dripping down his arms to his wrists—so bold, they didn't vanish in the night.

Heart fluttering, she nudged her tray away. Her hunger was gone. Given his savagery and powerful build, it would be a terrible death. Her daft schemes of killing him faded along with her clearing mind.

She pressed a shaking hand to her small wooden cross and closed her eyes.

*Even though I walk through the valley of the shadow of death,*

*I will fear no evil, for You are with me—*

"Eat."

Brigit's eyes flew open.

Her captor stared at her with an unreadable expression, his eyes dark pools in the dim.

"Eat," he repeated.

She lifted her chin. She wasn't a beast to be fed and butchered. And neither would she succumb to fear and cower before this savage again.

Fighting against the tremor in her knees and the heat in her cheeks, she stood. "Have it done with," she spat in the most menacing voice she could muster, "and may your nights be haunted by my tears."

The heathen flinched as if struck. Rigid as a spear, he sank onto the bed with his back to her and remained there without movement.

Abruptly, he stood. "You—bed? I—floor?"

It took Brigit a heartbeat to comprehend his words. He'd sleep on the floor while she took the bed? And—she studied his face and found nothing untoward there—there would be no plunder? Wordless, she shook her head. Better he be the first thing the "men" see if they entered in the dark of night.

He nodded, then lay down between his sword and axe and turned to face her. "You—safe." His voice softened, incongruous with his heathen marks and tugging at a fragile, aching place inside her. "Eat."

When she made no reply, he sprawled on the bed and fell into a steady, silent slumber.

Brigit didn't know how ravenous she was until she tasted the roasted venison and washed it down with ale. She peered at her captor as she ate. How did he sleep so well with her not a foot away? How easily she could kill him right now, if she wished it. She studied his sword—nearly three feet of steel beyond her strength to wield. Lips pursed, she craned her neck to look upon his heavy battleaxe resting at his other side. Maybe not so easily, for she'd likely not lift it with one hand.

Outside, a sliver of the new moon peeked from behind the cloud, washing the strange symbols on his cheeks in its silvery light, making them fade. He looked different without the stark marks. His brows were cleanly arched, strong and neither too high nor too low. His broad cheekbones—Brigit swallowed—they were just like the boy Reidar's. With a glare at her tethered ankle, she forced the notion down. The Norsemen all had such cheekbones.

Sated, she pushed away her tray. His straight nose curved up at the end in a way that was, begrudgingly, almost appealing. His lips, parted amid his thick beard held a lovely shape, almost sensual. Brigit scoffed. Were he not a vile Norseman, he might have been handsome.

His left hand, nearest to her, was concealed in the fleece pelts, but his right hand lay splayed on the axe haft. As men's hands went, it was sizable and well-proportioned, not hairy like her husband's, but smooth and shimmering with a dusting of fine golden hair.

She pulled herself up to have a closer look. Without warning, she lost her balance and tipped against the bed with a loud gasp.

It happened so fast, she didn't understand how she was suddenly on her back beneath her captor, his breath ragged like a workhorse fresh from the field. His giant body pinned her to the floor. His axe blade hovered a fingerbreadth from her throat.

Her scream tore through the air, freezing him mid-step. Eyes wide, he straightened and shook himself. Then, with a familiar-sounding oath, he tossed his axe onto the bed—near to the edge.

Brigit hoped he would rise, but he remained.

The moonlight faded as he trained his pale gaze on her and traced her jaw with a large, warm fingertip.

Her heart was the wild beat of the *bodhrán*. Here it was then. This heathen hadn't tied her to the bed to keep her fed and safe. But though she wasn't born a warrior, she would die one. And she would take him down with her, too. For heavy or not, she would grab his axe while he took her against her will, and she would strike him for all she was worth.

*Father, help me meet my end with gladness in my heart, for I am on my way to You at long last.*

The Norseman withdrew his hand, studying her with an unreadable expression. "Why?"

"Why what?" She choked out.

"Why you—touch—?" He gestured to the bed.

Brigit shifted beneath him, his weight taking her breath.

He didn't stir.

She set her jaw, ready. "I wanted to look upon my captor." *Before I kill you*, she added silently.

A small groove formed between his brows, and he lifted his shoulders as if to ask, "And?"

She compressed her lips.

"I—kill." He echoed her thoughts, nodding to emphasize his point. "I—sleep—wake—kill. Do not—touch."

She had nothing left to lose, so she stared into his eyes with all the scorn she possessed. "I'll not touch you if you don't touch me." She made her voice carry through the chamber like a bell. "Do not ever touch me or I—kill."

He scoffed and slowly extended his hand. "Ever?"

Brigit shrank back, but he only smoothed an errant strand of hair away from her face.

"Sleep—thrall." He stood and returned to the bed, his voice tinged with a strange, bitter edge.

Brigit didn't expect to sleep, but she must have, for she woke in the morning light to the telltale tinkling of water against the chamber pot. For an instant, she feared it was her husband. But the man in her chamber was twice his size and half his age. Sufficiently awake, she clenched her jaw and sat up.

The heathen remained where he was with his back to her, as if lost in deep thought. After a time, he tied his trousers, went to the basin, and splashed water on his face. Something was different about him as he turned, and Brigit didn't like it.

He flicked his hand toward his clothes at the foot of the bed with a scornful breath. "I—master. You thrall." He sounded odd, as though he was saying it more to himself than to her. "You—dress I."

Shivering in her thin *léine*, Brigit stood. By all accounts she'd been dispossessed of her maidservant, and therefore of her gowns, for it was the woman's duty to clean and press them for her. It mattered not. Even if she had the lady's kirtles her husband insisted upon, she wouldn't know how to put them on. The intricate lacing alone was entirely beyond her.

She curled her lip. Her captor would soon learn she was ill-suited for the task. With a scoff of her own, she grabbed her shawl and wrapped herself in it. Then she stepped to his heap of fur and leather and heaved it up. It weighed at least four stone.

The heathen froze as she dumped the heavy bundle, his gaze trained on her bruised cheek. "Who?" The word emerged in a low growl.

Brigit retreated a step. The bruise only hurt if she touched it, so she forgot about it. But it must have looked a sight in the daylight.

"I don't know. A man." She dropped her gaze, wishing she'd angled her face away before he saw the ugly mark.

Eyes flashing, he balled his giant hands into heavy fists. "He—uh—he—" The savage shook his head with an exasperated Norse oath. "What—he—? He—force?"

"He did not." She studied the floor, face burning like a blaze.

The heathen tipped her chin with a hard finger and peered into her eyes. "Do not—fear. He—hurt—you. I—know."

Brigit blinked against his piercing gaze. "I tell you true, he did not—not like that." She drew back another pace. "He saw your daft trinket and your daft knot." She pointed to his amulet at her chest, then to her ankle. "Are you their chieftain?"

The ill-timed, impudent question slipped out before she could stop herself. It hung like a thundercloud as her captor fixed her with a cold, mute stare.

He pointed at the heap that was his garments. "You—dress I."

# Chapter Nine

## Heathen
**_Reidar_**

*I will give you the horse that can*
*Ride through the dark and flames,*
*And the sword that can fight on its own,*
*If you are a worthy hero.*
— Skírnismál, stanza 9

Reidar didn't believe Ingrid's help with his attire would bring recognition. But it was all he could think of drawing near to her without too many objections. And without appearing lewd. He suppressed a scoff. He'd meant it when he resolved to treat her as nothing more than his spoils, but his Great Flaw had always been mightier than his firmest resolves.

Her shawl began to slip as she haltingly dropped his linen undertunic over his head. To his disappointment, she abandoned her task and pulled it around herself tighter. She managed his woolen tunic and rawhide belt without a snag but couldn't hold up his chainmail even with two hands. The effort made the shawl loosen again; it fell to the floor. She dove after it, but not before he saw her.

After all these winters, his longing for her was something from the realm of Freyr and Gerd. Reidar winced. Much like Freyr's servant, Skírnir, he'd threatened Ingrid for his own ends, though lucky for them both, he had no power to cast curses and kept his daft wrath mostly to himself. Yet neither did he have golden apples and magic horses, though he possessed considerable wealth, as well as his longships.

Ingrid's cheeks turned the delicate shade of wild roses as she straightened, scrambling to cover her lovely figure with the blasted shawl again.

Reidar's heart squeezed as she glared at his chainmail with a look of murder. Everything he did seemed destined to end in her degradation. But that was only as it should have been.

He stood and put on his chainmail, then finished his wardrobe of leather and furs as she looked on with a frown that somehow made her appear even lovelier.

"Done." He fixed her with a long stare.

He was well and truly lost. Not once when he searched for her, had he considered she might be wed. That was the first thing he'd learned from the skittish servant woman, Caoimhe. Yet he couldn't comprehend how a peasant girl from a raided fishing village had become a chieftain's wife, save that her beauty must have driven the man out of his senses. By Thor, he understood that all too well. Still, it was an unwelcome complication, seeing as his men had killed her husband. He didn't blame her for loathing his kind. That was all she knew of them—raiding her home and murdering her loved ones.

Reidar's chest tightened as he pulled on his boots. Did she care for her husband? His brother found him in another woman's bed before he removed his ugly head, but Ingrid may not have known that. Or likelier, the woman was one of the chieftain's proper concubines, and Ingrid loved or at least admired him for rescuing her from what had surely been the life of squalor and hunger. If so, she'd despise him all the more when she learned the truth.

He looked up at her bitter scoff.

Jaw set, she hugged herself. "Will that be all, *master?*" The way she spat the word, dripping with loathing and scorn, made him want to dive into the sea and wash himself clean. It also made his stomach harden. He should never have sought this girl—she bore his doom as plain as his *fostra's* runes.

"I—not—master?" He pointed at himself with a stiff hand, then looked around the chamber with cold, exaggerated curiosity. Lips pinched, he crossed to the window and peered out. "Where—master?"

She didn't reply. She only watched him with eyes made of hard, cold emeralds; the bruise on her cheek a silent indictment of everything he was to her.

Reidar locked his jaw. The time to execute his plan was upon him. He would present her in the great hall, publicly claim her, discover the oaf who'd wronged her, and mete out punishment on the spot. But she couldn't very well come before his men in her shift and shawl.

He went to her chest of drawers and opened each one, sensing her glare on his back as he rummaged through her shifts, underclothes, stockings, head coverings, ties, pins, and jars of scented oils. He found no gowns there. Beside the chest stood a trunk, and he threw it open. It contained fur-lined cloaks and goatskin shoes, as well as jewelry wrapped in linen, but not a single gown.

He turned to her with his palms up. "You—dress?" He remembered the Irish word. "Kirtle?"

She frowned. "My maidservant has my kirtles," she muttered. "I know not where she keeps them."

He didn't know which of the heathen wenches was her maidservant, but he passed from chamber to chamber until he found a stack of finely woven gowns laced with intricate embroidery. He grabbed the top one—green with gold thread—and returned to Ingrid's chamber.

"Dress." He tossed it to her.

She bit her pretty lip, crushing the gown in her hands with an odd expression. "I need my maidservant."

"Why?" He lifted a brow. Was she playing games?

Her face flooded a furious shade of pink, save for the bruise, which he would shortly redress. "I'm not good with the laces," she mumbled.

Reidar kept his expression impassive though he wanted to chuckle. She'd just reached for his lone golden apple.

He approached, allowing himself a half-smile. "I—help."

She recoiled, but he had no intention of giving her a choice. He tugged at her shawl. "Off."

The pink in her cheeks deepened to red. She didn't move.

He grasped the corner of the shawl and unwrapped it. Thor must have been watching, for the chamber flooded with light, putting every curve, every dip of her lovely body on display through her thin shift. But Loki was never too far, for the sight of her filled Reidar with such ache it made him ill.

"Raise—" He pointed to her arms, struggling to keep his voice under command.

With a look of alarm, she scanned the chamber as if seeking aid from the walls. She squeezed her eyes shut and raised her arms.

"Only—dress," he bit out, gruff.

He slipped the gown over her head, letting it cascade down the length of her body. It had a calming effect: the green sparkled in her eyes, the gold lit her hair on fire. She was like a vision from a dream, an Asgard goddess come to the human realm to bring ruin to any man reckless enough to gaze upon her. Stilling himself, Reidar placed his hands on her lovely shoulders and turned her away from him.

While he spent ample time in the company of Westland women mastering the art of removing laces, not once in his life had he fastened them.

"By Thor's hammer," he murmured in Norse, lifting her thick, silky hair of gold-tinged bronze and draping it over her lovely shoulder. "How is it I am dressing this girl when every part of me longs to undress her?"

She stood still as he worked the laces, her heat searing his hands through the gown. Her nearness made him dizzy; it turned his wits to mush. But he kept at his task, taking in her willowy neck, graceful waist, and the supple, blood-stirring curve of her hip. As if enchanted, his fingers moved over the laces, pulling and threading. With each tug, he called on the Æsir to make her know him, to speak his name, to confess that she, too, had been consumed by the fire of his memory. But she remained mute and rigid, her body stiffening with his every touch.

It was only when he reached the midpoint that he noticed her breathing—an uneven clip that cut through the clamor of heartbeat in his ears. Sickened, he dropped his arms. Her chest rose and fell like a restless tide, and though she struggled to contain it, she'd failed. Did she loathe his touch so much it made her weep?

Heart heavy as lead, he tilted his head and stole a glance at her face.

He straightened. She wasn't weeping. She was biting her lip as if to stall a gasp, yet one still escaped, along with the gooseflesh that seemed to flood her from crown to heel.

Reidar's body thrummed like thunder as he bent to her ear. "Tight?" he breathed, fruitlessly searching for the Irish "should I loosen?"

Without turning, she shook her head.

It was on the tip of his tongue to call her Ingrid, but he stopped himself. If Loki was watching, he was surely laughing all the way from Asgard, for here was his Great, Irredeemable Flaw for all the gods to see. All his hollow proclamations of letting go of his folly, of treating her as befitted a thrall weren't worth a raven's cry. For here stood the woman he'd pined after for seven long winters, trembling beneath his touch, and his only thought was how fiercely she'd loathe him once she knew he was the same one who left her for dead on her ruined island after his people killed and enslaved everyone she loved. And how her eyes would flood with scorn when she learned he'd added her husband's murder and her new home's plunder to his ledger. And how she would rebel against what he had to do next.

Heart sick, Reidar finished the lacing, then bent to her ankle and removed Thor's Braidknot and the slipknot. He crossed to the bed and untethered the rope.

Ingrid seemed to have stopped breathing as she peered at him, her gown turning her eyes to emerald flame and hair to molten sun. She looked unearthly, as if spun from old forest magic, weaving her spell and drawing him deeper into her shimmering web of green and gold and soft curves and pink lips.

Reidar shook himself. He hadn't a clue how he was to gently fasten the iron slave collar around her neck to present her in keeping with her station. So he shut his eyes and promised a great sacrifice to Odin for a scrap of wisdom. The memory of their first meeting washed over him, distant and bittersweet. He grasped her wrists, bound them in front of her, and tied a new knot.

She'd kept her gaze on her hands as he did so. But now, she raised her head, her eyes filled with such ice, he shuddered.

Reidar blinked. *I will always be of my people, as you will be of yours. Receive me as I am or lift this spell from me.*

Their eyes caught, and it became a staring match of sorts—wondering, seeking, glaring. He looked away first, unable to abide her enmity.

Ingrid jerked at her bonds and lifted her chin in a gesture that was becoming too familiar for its unchecked defiance. "Where are you taking me now, *heathen?"* she spat.

A chill slithering down his spine, he stared at her for a long, silent moment. Did she know sputtering such a slur in his men's hearing would earn her a hard flogging or worse if he were to keep their fealty and allegiance?

Teeth clenched, he closed the distance between them.

She didn't stir. The all-consuming loathing returned to her eyes. It seemed to flow in her veins in place of her lifeblood, comforting and sustaining as a hot stew on a cold winter night.

"Heathen?" he barked, trembling like an oak in a thunderstorm. "You—say—heathen. You—" He didn't have enough accursed Irish to tell her. "You—flog." It came to him at last. "You—ears cut. Nose cut. You—work. You—starve. You—die." He shoved his palm against her mouth. "Quiet."

All color drained from her as she stared up at him with still, wide eyes.

He dropped his hand and cursed long and hard—until his folly faded into the blasted Irish mist and gave way to a new, unshakable resolve. He'd been a bumbling halfwit to think she'd ever feel for him a shred of what he did for her. For even without knowing him, she despised him no less than she had when he was but fifteen winters.

Heathen! To her, he wasn't even human.

Shaking, he barreled toward a wall, formed a hard fist, and punched it with all his might.

She shrieked behind him, but he felt nothing save a tearing, urgent need to rip her from his heart once and for all time.

"Thank you for this gift, Odin," he spat, wiping his bloody hand on his wolf's pelt. "I will sacrifice greatly to you today."

Ignoring the blood and the pain, he bound the slack around his wrist so tight it bit into his flesh. Then he marched from this blasted chamber, giving the foul-mouthed, peat-digging bog witch no choice but to follow.

# Chapter Ten

## Debts
***Brigit***

*It's dark out, and I think it's time*
*To go through the wild,*
*(To go through the giants' stronghold;)*
*We will both come back, or the*
*Terrible giant will get us both.*
— Skírnismál, stanza 10

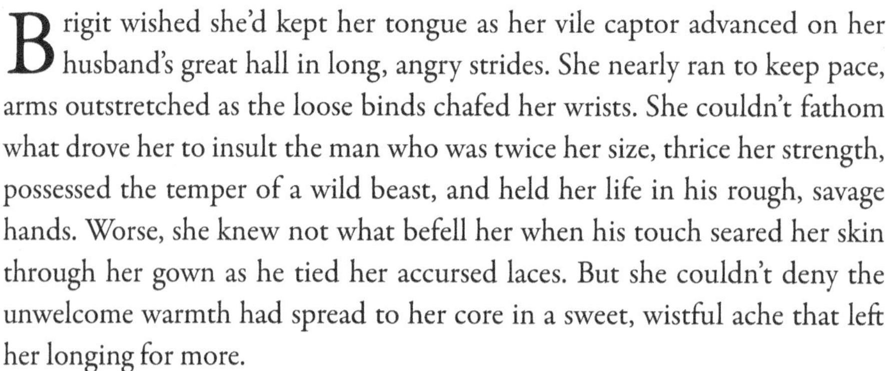

Brigit wished she'd kept her tongue as her vile captor advanced on her husband's great hall in long, angry strides. She nearly ran to keep pace, arms outstretched as the loose binds chafed her wrists. She couldn't fathom what drove her to insult the man who was twice her size, thrice her strength, possessed the temper of a wild beast, and held her life in his rough, savage hands. Worse, she knew not what befell her when his touch seared her skin through her gown as he tied her accursed laces. But she couldn't deny the unwelcome warmth had spread to her core in a sweet, wistful ache that left her longing for more.

She'd never known such wicked yearning before, never fathomed a touch could make her feel so much. And she wondered, despite herself, if that was how it should have felt with her husband.

None of it mattered now, for she'd likely never again lay eyes on Cearbhall mac Bressal. Brigit stared ahead as she scurried behind the

Norseman's towering bulk. She would soon be flogged, mutilated, starved, and killed—all for the indiscretion of calling the heathen what he was.

She choked back a wild shriek of laughter. So this was how she'd meet her end—not plundered to death by her captor, but at the hands of his henchmen. A bile of sorrow and self-pity rose in her throat, replacing the strange laugh. None remained in this world who loved her. None would weep when she suffered and died. None would hold a wake. Her anguish streamed freely now—warm, salty, and unashamed. What did it matter if she set her misery free or swallowed it whole? The Norsemen had no souls, so they felt no mercy.

Still, at this darkest hour, she only feared the means by which she would die, not death itself, for surely, after such torment, God would lift her up into Heaven. Her only regret was that she hadn't tried to kill the depraved savage in his sleep, for even if she had failed, he'd end her on the spot—as he'd promised—and she wouldn't have to endure the forthcoming agony and degradation.

The vile Norseman came to a halt at the hall's entrance, sparing her a single backward glance—cold and dispassionate as a winter sea.

Brigit loathed him with everything in her—his tall, broad frame, moving with effortless grace, his sure, lusty gait, his long, flaxen plaits, flanked by heathen patterns and streaming down his back. His large, brutal hand leading her like a heifer to slaughter. And she resolved once and for all that if by some miracle she should survive the day, she'd not rest until she killed him. And while she awaited her chance, she'd never speak to him again.

Cold all over, she stalled at the entrance. The only proof the hall had belonged to an Irish chieftain was her husband's crest banner, torn to shreds and clinging to the wall by some fluke of fate. Inside, the faint scent of freshly baked barley bread mixed with the nauseating stench of male sweat, polished iron, and brutality.

"Come—thrall," her captor tossed over his shoulder, jerking her rope so hard she staggered.

The place teemed with Norsemen, all in a state of idleness, which undoubtedly boded ill for her. Some still broke their fast on mutton, cabbage, and bread. Others sprawled across pallets, densely strewn all over. A few were sharpening their axe blades. Everyone looked up when her captor entered, dragging her, stumbling, behind him.

Heartbeat pounding in her ears, Brigit drew back as dozens of foreign eyes fixed on her—with curiosity, interest, apathy.

Her captor's gaze swept the hall, then he pushed her in front of him and said something in his ghastly, heathen tongue. Still, his voice boomed like the beat of the *bodhrán*, deep and commanding. Those who lazed about sat up and paid heed.

Brigit blinked. He was indeed their chieftain.

Jaw hard as a rock, the Norseman reached for her throat, and she shrank away with a gasp. But he only grasped his amulet and lifted it for all to see, forcing her head up with it. Then he barked something in a tone so filled with fury and menace, the hall fell silent.

A strange sight caught Brigit's eye. She could hardly believe it. A woman—dressed like the men, with hair plaited in the same fashion—sat on a pallet, holding a battleaxe, her piercing eyes fixed on Brigit. The ice in them made Brigit's hair stand on end, and she felt in her bones—if given a chance, this woman would hack her to bits with her blade.

Lip curling in a vicious sneer, the woman took her gaze off Brigit and fixed it on her axe, as if to offer confirmation.

Beside her, the Norseman spat something in Irish. Brigit flinched as he grabbed her face and turned it for all to behold like a groom displaying a prized horse. "I ask—who?" he growled in her ear.

Heart thudding, she stared at the throng of heathens, their faces a blur of hard eyes. If she even recognized her attacker, would he not return to exact retribution were she foolish enough to mark him—if she lived after this?

Her captor gave her a shake that made her teeth chatter. "Tell. Now."

Brigit swallowed, schooling her mind to order. She spotted him outright. He was the only man with his head down, drawing back as if trying to vanish behind the others.

She pointed with a stiff hand.

Her captor nudged her out of the way and widened his stance. Then he spoke to her attacker in such a soft, low voice Brigit shuddered.

The man rubbed the back of his neck and muttered something that sounded like a plea of defense. Her captor didn't answer outright, but when he spoke, his tone dripped with mockery and the promise of swift, unbridled violence.

A vein bulging on his neck, her attacker approached. In her chamber he seemed large, but now, compared to her captor, he looked puny and pitiful.

Her captor turned to her and spoke a question in Norse—no doubt meant to confirm this was the man.

She nodded.

Those who were near them stepped back a few paces. Breath held, she followed suit.

Without so much as a word, the Norseman formed a tight fist and delivered a crushing blow to her attacker's face. A bright rivulet of blood trickled down the man's cheek, but he neither flinched nor tried to defend himself. Another strike sent him to his knees. He shook his head as if to clear it and made to rise. But he didn't get the chance, for her captor charged again. And again, dealing his punches with cold, calculated precision.

The man's face was a sickening, bloody mess when he tumbled at last.

Brigit's stomach turned at the sight, but she quelled it and, by some miracle, didn't retch.

Her captor wiped his hands on his pelt, then pointed to her and said something low to the mute gathering. Everyone, save for the woman, nodded. She only glared, her eyes like two shards of ice.

Without warning, the Norseman grabbed Brigit's rope and marched to the exit. She followed behind as if in a daze. She wouldn't be flogged and killed. Instead, he'd punished her offender. She lifted her gaze to the rafters. If only the Lord would guide her through this bewildering dark valley.

In the chamber, her captor left her standing by the door, then went to the basin. He washed his hands, splashed water on his face, and dried himself with the linen. The rage seemed to have drained from him as he approached her. Silent, he unbound her wrists. He froze, gaze fixed on the pink marks etched by the rope.

He peered at her with a strained expression. "Hurt?"

She shook her head, then squared her shoulders. Did he want it to hurt?

Jaw clenched, he took her wrists and ran his thumbs over the marks. Brigit stopped breathing as he bent his head and pressed his lips to them, shockingly soft and warm. Slowly, he straightened, his face tight as a fiddle string.

She stood, reeling, her heart thrumming with something too tangled to name. She shoved it down. Dug her fingernails into her palms. Slammed the door on her weakness. Braced it. Barred it.

Her captor stepped behind her and touched her laces. "I—help," he muttered, voice low and hoarse.

Brigit compressed her lips. She was hoping to remain in her gown, but she'd resolved to never talk to him again, so she remained mute.

He took his time, tugging and loosening, running his fingers through the lacing, pulling the gown apart. And once again, Brigit's pulse raced beneath his touch. She drew a long, shuddering breath, failing to still herself. This was how she imagined the boy Reidar's touch when he became a man—a skin-tingling mixture of warmth, firmness, and tenderness.

Sickened, Brigit stared ahead. The degradation this heathen had been putting her through must have taken its toll, breaking her and bending her to his will. So she lifted her chin and made herself recall how seven winters past, she found her mother vanished, her father slain, and her village strewn with ruin and corpses. How she licked drops of soured milk from broken shards, and how Rathnait worked her to the bone with an empty belly and her back afire, and how Cearbhall mac Bressal's touch drove her to want to flay herself alive.

The savage pulled the gown down her right shoulder, then her left. Her skin flooded with gooseflesh. The vile memories faded away, and in their place, a sweet, achy longing filled her to the brim, rushing through her like an unstoppable tide. The dress slid to the floor, leaving her once again in her thin *léine*.

For a long moment, her captor remained motionless, then placed his hands on her shoulders and turned her to face him. He stood a foot away, still as an oak, save for the racing pulse at his throat. Their eyes locked, and despite her better judgement, Brigit found herself unable to look away. His gaze on her coaxed and beckoned like a bright ray of sun on a gray winter morning, calling her and pulling her in against all sense.

Slowly, he reached for her cheek and breathed something in Norse that sounded half a thought, half a question. Eyes boring into hers, he smoothed an errant strand away from her face and tucked it behind her ear.

His touch sent thunderclaps throughout her body. And on their heels, shame, bright and searing, cut through her like a blade. This was much worse than the self-loathing in her marriage bed, for her unbecoming yearnings for the boy Reidar in her husband's repugnant embrace were but fleeting fancies. On the other hand, the unbridled sensations storming through her now were as real as the large, patterned heathen standing before her, looking upon her as though he'd been riding for leagues in the summer heat, and she was a bubbling creek.

Brigit bit hard into her lip. She would not succumb to her baser nature, for her mortifying stirrings burned as true as the memory of his people torching her monastery, enslaving her mother, slaying her father, and razing her village. As real as the certainty that if he—she bit her lip harder—that if the boy Reidar had taken her along instead of leaving her, a girl of thirteen winters, to starve and fend for herself, she might have been spared the torment and despair that often made her long for death.

So she dropped her gaze, gathered the little left of her vanishing reason, and forced out a prayer under her breath:

"Our Father in heaven...

Lead me not into temptation...

But deliver me from evil..

Deliver me, Father..."

Her longing ebbed and breathing slowed as she lifted her head, surprised to find the Norseman's gaze no longer filled with things that made her lose her wits. In their place hung a question.

"What—you—say?" He studied her with a quirked sandy brow.

She kept her mouth shut, honoring her decision.

Something like a smile played on his lips. "What?"

"The Lord's Prayer," she bit out.

He drew back a pace. "What—the Lord's Prayer?"

Brigit blinked. Maybe the Lord wished her to tell him.

"It's a prayer asking for God's love, guidance, and protection."

He narrowed his eyes. "Ah—" he fell silent, searching for a word —"spell?"

Brigit widened her eyes.

He gave a slow nod, as if thinking of a word. "Magic."

"Not magic." Brigit shook her head. "A prayer."

He lifted both brows. "Say—prayer."

Brigit swallowed. This marked heathen with no soul wished to hear the Lord's Prayer.

"Our Father in heaven," she began.

"Our Father in heaven," he echoed in his strange way.

"Hallowed be Your name," she continued. "Your kingdom come, Your will be done on earth as it is in heaven. Give us this day our daily bread and forgive us our debts as we forgive our debtors..."

Gaze fixed on her, he repeated every word, including Amen, then closed his eyes and stood still.

"It—Christ magic." He opened his eyes. "But—I like."

Speechless, she drew back a pace. Perhaps her path had been set all along and was only now coming to light. The unbearable truth that had been clawing at her chest lodged in her throat. She feared his answer as much as she craved it, the hope and the dread of it coiling inside her like the swirls on his sword's blade.

She braced herself and met his eyes. "What do they call you?" she breathed.

For a moment, he stared ahead with a faraway look, like one measuring his choices. Then he fixed her with a still, unreadable stare. "They call me—Our Debtors," he said at length.

A strange sensation spread through Brigit. It filled her lungs with too much air and her heart with too much light.

Jaw set, he picked up the rope from the floor and sank to one knee before her. "What do they call—you?"

"Brigit," she whispered, holding her breath.

Without a word, he tied the rope around her ankle, then tethered it to the bed. And in that moment, this unapologetic, practiced act of stripping her of freedom seemed to shatter whatever spell he'd fallen under.

But now that she was asking, Brigit wanted answers.

"I didn't see my husband, chieftain Cearbhall mac Bressal, in the great hall." She struggled to keep her face impassive as her heart thudded with unseemly, wicked hope. "What has become of him?"

The Norseman kept his gaze on his knot, then stood with an expression that brooked no questions. "I—come back, thrall." He made a curt gesture toward her hideout, then headed to the door and went out.

Brigit couldn't quell the sting in her eyes and the ache in her chest as she climbed into her cramped nook. Inexplicably, the heat of his fingers still lingered along her spine, and his fleeting kiss still clung to her wrists. It burned all the way to her center like a brand. But surely, such feelings belonged to her husband, not to a heathen who thought so little of her, he kept her bound and refused to speak her name.

It was then she knew she'd just added another link to her Great Chain of Scorn—his degrading insistence on calling her thrall.

# Chapter Eleven

## Sacrifice
***Reidar***

*Tell me, herdsman, sitting on the hill,*
*Watching all the paths,*
*How can I talk to the maiden*
*Past Gymir's hounds?*
—Skírnismál, stanza 11

Reidar returned to the great hall, pondering Ingrid's "Lord's Prayer." It was a lovely sort of magic, and powerful, too, for it cooled his blood—a fortunate turn. It seemed to salve her also, but not before he saw the tremor his touch left in its wake and the fierce battle she waged against it. He furrowed his brow at the memory of the strange green flame in her eyes when she asked his name. He'd hoped the question wouldn't come so soon and was not at all prepared to answer. But she'd have surely spat in his face had he been reckless enough to reveal it. Luckily, he owed Ingrid neither answers nor courtesies.

He found his men still sprawled about the great hall, awaiting his orders. In the corner, away from everyone, Orm the Oaf lay on a pallet, his thrashed face covered with wilting cabbage leaves. *Fool.* Did he think a stunning girl had been stashed in a lovely chamber amid fine fleece pelts for his pleasure?

"We ride to see land today, to judge if it will bear crops," he declared, sitting at the long wooden table. "Those who would claim it will remain here. The rest will sail home with me in a fortnight."

He broke his fast with Irish porridge, enjoying the way they poured a creamy layer of milk over the top. Finished, he beckoned the skittish servant, Caoimhe.

"My thrall—" He gestured at his bowl. "Bring breakfast, supper—each day."

"M'lord," the woman choked out, trembling like a leaf.

"Help—my thrall—wash, dress hair, new tunic. No gown. Clean—bed, basin, chamber pot, floor."

The servant nodded eagerly at his every word.

"Go. She—hungry."

They set out soon after, riding the horses from Bressal's stables. Fine, handsome steeds, some of which he would bring home.

Reidar led his men in silence, eyes fixed on the lush, green valley in the distance. Perfect for farming.

"Reidar." Brow furrowed, Astrid rode up beside him. "That little heathen of yours must be skilled in bed." Her voice emerged too bitter for his liking. "Seeing as you no longer seek mine."

Reidar kept his gaze on the land. It was unlike Astrid to grudge him thralls and whores. Besides, he had no mind to speak of Ingrid with her—or with anyone.

She urged her gelding near, softening her voice. "I miss you, Reidar."

He risked a glance. She sat slumped in her saddle, eyes shiny and wide.

Reidar grunted out an oath under his breath. "There is much to be done here, Astrid." He kept his voice dispassionate. "And not much time to do it."

She reached to touch his arm. "We are soon to be wed, my love. I wish to share my betrothed's bed tonight."

Reidar thought on this. He hadn't been with a woman since they arrived in Dalaradia, and his body was feeling the strain. But Astrid was not who he wanted. Besides, the notion of Ingrid alone at night in her little hideout filled him with unease. Claimed or not, when his men grew fuddled with drink, they couldn't be trusted with lovely thralls.

He fixed Astrid with a long stare. "Are you jealous of my thrall?"

"No!" The answer came too fast. "Why would I be? That heathen is not worth my little finger. I would never be jealous of her!"

"Good." He nodded. "Neither would I be of yours if you were to claim one."

The afternoon air, fresh from rain, smelled of peat and heather. Reidar drew in a lungful, reveling in the lush beauty of the valley. A hint of salt drifted inland from the sea, mingling with the rich scent of wet grass and the faint, sweet tang of crushed clover. The wind shifted in restless gusts over the hills, carrying the distant smoke of turf fires from scattered dwellings.

He reined in his steed, jumped down, and grabbed a fistful of the soil at his feet, watching it crumble between his fingers. Smiling, he raised it for his men to see—rich, dark loam, begging to be tilled, plowed, and seeded. Unbidden, the memory of Ingrid's soft skin and the way her chest rose and fell at his touch rushed through him, stark and piercing.

"Reidar." Astrid dismounted with him, as his men did, and now stood a foot away, staring at the soil with blank eyes. "I do not want a thrall. I want you, my love." Her voice emerged thin with pleading notes. "Come to my bed, and I swear I will content you no worse than she does. I will give you all you desire."

"Will you now?" The words slipped out before he could halt them, but he found himself not caring. "What do you know of my desires, woman?

"We will grow barley and rye here." He turned to his men to a murmur of approval. "Enough grazing for cows up by the stream, and space for grain to spare."

They mounted again, traveling to the edge of a small wood thick with oak, ash, and rowan. Plenty of timber to build homes, even a proper longhouse.

Astrid rode among his men, stooped and sullen, her haunted eyes fixed on him with a wearying, consuming fervor. And in that moment, Reidar knew in the hollow of his heart he would never wed her—even if it meant foregoing a wise alliance, even if their union improved his chances of unseating Vargr Bloodgale. For the notion of sharing her bed and hearth weighed his stomach with lead and ground his bones into dust.

He shifted his gaze back to the valley. "We can make a home of this place—put our mark on this fertile soil, as the Irish have done." He turned his mount around to face his men. "We will sacrifice to the gods today for the abundant gifts they have bestowed upon us."

Thorsten rode up, grinning wide. "A fine land and a bountiful loot to bring home, brother. Gold, silver, and livestock. Handsome women for slave markets and enough strong men to leave behind to tend to the land. The gods are smiling on us indeed."

Reidar's scalp prickled, and he nodded to halt the sensation. It remained. He turned to his brother. "Which heathen would please Odin today, Thorsten?"

His brother stroked his beard, then pointed toward the castle. "The wench we found in the chieftain's bed. She knows sacrifice, for it was neither love nor passion that led her to a man old enough to be her father."

After a day of threading the rugged Irish hills, with a brief rest to eat salted venison, barley bread, and wild apples they'd foraged near a stream, they returned at eventide. The castle stables bordered a small wood, and it was in its quiet clearing, surrounded by trees and strewn with wildflowers, that Reidar gathered his men. The place held the air of their sacred grove back home, and in the middle stood a circle of age-worn stones, calling for great flames.

He forced a smile, ignoring an uneasy flutter in his gut. Why should he feel anything but content and gratitude? It was as if Odin himself had led them here to honor him and seek his favor for what lay ahead.

The day had been warm, and now the night sky stretched high above, bursting with stars. Though Reidar had looked forward to the fire, he found no comfort in its blaze—only heat, thick and suffocating. Restless, he stripped off his pelt, tossed it aside, and wiped the sweat from his brow. Then he crushed the wild tumult inside with all his might.

By the time Astrid brought the girl, he and his men had painted their faces with coal and placed their shields around the stones. The girl stood a whole head shorter than Astrid, staggering behind her with a wild look in her eyes, her body quaking with vicious tremors. Like a bolt of lightning, the flames fell on the thrall, illuminating her with a flickering, fiery glow.

Reidar's limbs tensed, as they had in winters past, before he carved weakness from his bones with heathen blood. The girl appeared ill-used. The front of her gown was torn, and she clutched at the ruined bits of wool to cover herself. Her nose was broken, and an ugly pattern of bruises covered her left cheek and jaw. Gritting his teeth, Reidar forced down the vision of Ingrid's bruise as Astrid pushed the girl toward the flattest of the stones.

With a loud gasp, the thrall fell to her knees, releasing the tatters of her gown. Her hand fluttered to her throat, and Reidar assumed it was to cover herself again. Instead, she grasped at a small cross.

Despite the heat, a cold shiver crept up Reidar's neck. He drove it down like a hammer and approached the kneeling girl.

The men raised their battleaxes above their heads. They began to chant: "Odin, Allfather, hail! Wise one, we call upon you. Guide us and strengthen us, favor us with victories and riches. We await the day we feast with you in Valhalla..."

Reidar dug his fingers into Shadowbane's smooth pommel. He lifted it. "In the presence of the gods—" He urged his voice to carry deep and powerful, like a battle drum, but it came forth low and strangled. He cleared his throat. "Allfather, may the blood of this heathen be pleasing to you—"

The girl raised her head and peered into the night, unseeing. She was moving her lips, and to his shock, he made out the words—the familiar Irish words of the Lord's Prayer:

*And lead us not into temptation*
*But deliver us from evil:*
*For Yours is the kingdom, and the power, and the glory...*

The hair on the back of Reidar's neck stood on end as something happened to his sight. The girl vanished, and in her place knelt Ingrid, her eyes fixed on him with bleak pity and damning accusation. He grasped at his throat as a vicious cut appeared on hers. It grew wider and darker. A spray of blood burst from it, flooding the stone, covering him like a sea tide, soaking him from head to foot.

He shut his eyes, shaking with an ill fever. *Odin, Allfather, do not forsake me. Give me strength to offer you this sacrifice. Keep me from this Christ magic. Do not abandon me now.*

But Odin was silent, and Ingrid still stared at him with her wide, glittering eyes the color of spring leaves, fresh grass, and all that made life worth living.

Swaying as if with drink, Reidar went down on one knee and buried his head in his hands. Still, Ingrid's gaze pressed upon him.

He stopped breathing. It was no longer Ingrid. In her place, stood a Man with a crown of twisted thorns, weeping scarlet tears.

Reidar wheezed through his searing chest, screamed against the blinding light that burned worse than a thousand fires. *Our Father in heaven... help me... deliver me from evil...*

The light softened to a warm glow. Trembling, Reidar lifted his head. The girl's eyes were closed. She stopped shaking and knelt before the stone with hands folded in silent prayer and face serene with the stillness of one at peace.

Reidar took in the gathering. The men stared at him with furrowed brows and set jaws. Astrid stood with her arms crossed, glaring at the girl.

"Are you trying to make Odin angry, Reidar?" Sveinulf the Querulous muttered to the din of growing hum of disapproval.

Reidar's trembling ceased, and he straightened to his full height. He fixed the man with a heavy stare, choosing his words with care. "Odin granted me a vision." His voice boomed in the falling night, strong and sure as a battle drum, piercing the air and what remained of the chanting. "The gods do not wish for the blood of this Christian. Bring me a fine, fat sheep."

He placed a hand on the girl's shoulder with a soft Irish, "Stand."

She opened her eyes and looked at him.

"Who claims this woman?" He turned to the men as she rose, pressing both hands to the front of what had been her gown.

"It is I, what of it?" Sveinulf stepped forward, chin lifted.

He was a fine warrior and a loyal man, though he suffered greatly from lack of composure, which served him well in battle but earned him scorn in the hall.

"Lest you are called Vargr the blasted Bloodgale, the Althing would not look favorably on such mistreatment of a thrall." Reidar paused, letting his men scowl and spit at the sound of his uncle's name. "Take care to keep her clothed, fed, and free from injury henceforth."

They feasted on roasted mutton later, the meat succulent and bursting with flavor. To his utter vexation, he found Astrid following close behind as he headed to Ingrid's chamber for the night. It had grown late, the sacrificial blood had dried on his face and neck, tugging at his skin, and he wanted nothing more than to rinse it off in Ingrid's cool basin and drop onto her soft bed.

"The gods will be well pleased not to have the foul Christian blood marring their halls." Astrid caught up with him. The crimson streaking her cheeks lent a vicious edge to her words, twisting her features into something nearly repulsive. Strange that he'd never noticed before.

"The men value your wise counsel and swift judgement, Reidar Valorborn. As do I."

He said nothing and quickened his stride.

She followed suit.

"Reidar." She stopped feet away from Ingrid's chamber door, then darted before it, blocking his way. "Come to my bed, my love." She searched his eyes. "Let us honor the gods with our lovemaking tonight. Let us bask in their favor."

Reidar kept his voice low lest Ingrid hear him and think to investigate—he'd left slack enough in her rope to step outside. "The day has been long, Astrid," he muttered. "I am tired and wish to sleep."

Her face tightened like a bowstring. She closed the distance between them. "Please do not go to her, Reidar. Do not taint yourself with this heathen woman on such a night."

Her voice shook as she spoke, teeth biting into her lip so hard they left marks.

"You look tired, Astrid." He steadied her with his hands upon her shoulders. "Go to bed."

Eyes swimming with blue, she placed her hand on the back of his neck and stood on her tiptoes. "Do not shame me so, Reidar," she breathed. "Kiss me like you used to do, my love."

Reidar shot a glance at the door. It was closed and would remain so. One kiss and he'd be rid of Astrid—at least for tonight. Then he would bide his time until they reached Ljosstrond. There, with her mother to cry to, he'd tell her to stop spreading the falsehoods she nearly made him believe. They'd never wed, nor would they be lovers again, for he did not love her as a man should love his wife.

"I am falling off my feet," he grumbled, bending to her parting lips. "Would a single kiss content you, Astrid?"

# Chapter Twelve

## Hate
### *Brigit*

*Are you doomed to die or already dead,*
*Rider who came here?*
*You will never be able to talk*
*To Gymir's daughter.*
—Skírnismál, stanza 12

"The heathens' chieftain said 'no gown...'" The servant woman reddened, handing Brigit a freshly pressed *léine.*

Scoffing, Brigit pulled it over her head. For the first time since the Norsemen's arrival, Caoimhe brought porridge and buttermilk to break her fast, cleaned her chamber, and filled a small wooden tub with warm water for bathing. It appeared the savage had tired of his games and now prepared her for her imminent demise.

"Will Saoirse return to see to me?" Brigit inquired half-heartedly. She liked Saoirse—not for her skill as a maidservant, which Brigit cared nothing for—but because she alone in her husband's domain was kind to her. None of that mattered now, however.

"Och...poor Saoirse had fallen to a ghastly heathen with a long, forked beard and face marred by scars." Caoimhe dropped her gaze. "Their chieftain bid me to wait on you, m'lady. It's a mercy I'm old and homely." She shrugged. "Youth and beauty are a bane when none stand to shield it."

Brigit squared her shoulders, swallowing a bitter retort. "What's become of my husband?"

"He'd not been seen since the fiends fell upon us." Lips pursed, the woman picked up Brigit's hairbrush. "The heathen bid me to dress your hair."

An angry wave of heat rushed from the pit of Brigit's stomach and landed in her ears, pulsing and pounding. "Tell him I've no need of a maidservant, and least of all if 'no gown!'"

"Please don't banish me, m'lady." To Brigit's shock, Caoimhe fell to her feet. "He would surely bring horrors upon me, should he learn I'm not needed here."

After the servant woman left, Brigit stood by the window, looking out into a bright, golden day. She ran a cold hand over her untangled hair, dressed with strings and jewels. Courtesy of her husband, who'd never been her shield, she knew precisely what horrors the savage would bring upon *her* once he came back. She bit her lip, fighting an unseemly thought—it wouldn't be horrors if the scandalous heat beneath his hands consumed her again. Either way, her obscene wardrobe surely spelled disgrace. So Brigit closed her eyes and prayed for defiance and a swift end instead of falling to temptation that dragged her soul into darkness.

Caoimhe arrived in the evening with a tray of stewed mackerel and cabbage for supper and word of the heathens. After roaming all day, they'd dragged in a fat slaughtered sheep and now roasted it in the courtyard, the barbarians.

Soon, the castle filled with a foreign din that made Brigit's gut turn—they must have entered the keep. The night wore on, but her captor didn't return. So she climbed into her hiding place and held a wake for her wretched life.

A long while had passed, yet the vile heathens' voices and ribald laughter still echoed from the great hall, along with the scents of roasted mutton and sweat-drenched men.

Brigit stood and crossed to the table for her ale flagon. She froze as footsteps approached her chamber—two sets, drawing near. Heart pounding, she made for her hideout but came to a halt at the sound of a woman's voice outside. The woman spoke Norse, and from her thin, sorrowful notes, she appeared to be pleading.

Brigit raised her brows. This was not how she imagined the voice of the dreadful woman with the battleaxe. Wary of making a sound, Brigit padded toward the door. She stood still, listening to her captor speaking to the woman in a hushed, vexed tone. It was her captor—of that she was certain, for even changed so, his cadence remained deep and commanding.

A moment later, they both fell silent. If they left, they must have done so very quietly.

Breath coming fast, Brigit pressed her hand to the door. She eased it open just a crack.

She went still at the sight. The woman stood with her back to Brigit. Her captor faced the chamber but wasn't looking at it. He was too busy kissing the cursed daughter of Balor, his arms wrapped around her hale frame and head bent to her lips. Melting into him, the woman stroked the column of his neck and moaned something into his mouth.

Brigit's heartbeat thudded in her ears like thunder. A hot, red tide rushed through her, scorching everything in its path. They were like beasts in heat, ready to mate for all the world to see, heedless of discovery and unaware of propriety. If she clenched her teeth any harder, she would have shattered them. Trembling, she lifted her chin and grabbed the door. But instead of shutting it, she continued to watch as if rooted to the spot.

The woman was a fit for him, tall and stately, her lovely hair, the color of bleached bone plaited close to the scalp, and the side of her smooth face free of marks and blemishes. Brigit swallowed against a sting of tears in her nose. Her throat ached something fierce, and eyes burned and itched. She never knew a kiss like this. Her husband never kissed her at all—a mercy—and the only kiss she had a claim to belonged to...to the boy Reidar. Chaste, worthless, and false as it was!

Dizzy, Brigit swayed on her feet as the skerry beneath her carried her into an angry tempest. As the tall man with his wheat-colored plaits, broad cheekbones, and pale blue eyes drifted farther off—oar-lengths, then boat-lengths, then leagues away.

The tears came despite herself, along with a small, strangled gasp. She didn't think it loud, yet it must have been, for his eyes flew open. Swiftly, he dropped his arms and pulled away from the woman. His eyes widened, then locked with Brigit's, raw and stricken. But it must have been the trick of the light, for what was her misery to him?

Heart racing, Brigit stepped back into her chamber and closed the door with a trembling hand. She glowered at the bed, suffocating on her breathing. If she had a dagger, she would cut it to shreds. She would burn it to ash.

She tried to listen through her sobs. The woman spoke in a pleading tone again. Her vile captor kept silent, then said something low and soothing.

Brigit bolted to her hideout and threw herself onto the fleece pelts. The filthy savage, the soulless heathen wretch! That woman—dressed as a man and carrying a battleaxe Brigit couldn't lift—was his lover! And all the while, he kept her tethered to his bed and made her sleep beside him on the floor like a hound!

A small voice reminded Brigit he'd offered the bed from the start, but she told that voice to go to hell and remain there. Gulping down her misery, Brigit curled into a ball and buried her face in the silky fleece. Something burned inside her chest, hardened in her stomach. But why should she concern herself with her foul captor and his wicked lover? Why should it matter what these heathens did at all? Yet her breath came faster, and tears grew hotter, spilling in a furious deluge. The heathen knew little of the scorn she harbored for him. It was enough to drown all of Éire beneath its dark, heavy tides.

The moon rose to the top of the sky and slipped behind a cloud when her weeping ceased. Brigit lay on her side now, numb and drained, staring at the small twig she'd retrieved from under her pillow. It seemed smaller now. Much smaller than when the boy Reidar placed it in the palm of her hand—delicate and innocent. Brigit's chamber didn't have a hearth, but if it did, she would have hurled it there and watched it burn.

She wrapped it back in its cloth and buried it in her fleece pelts. She'd done so in time, for the door opened, and the Norseman entered the chamber. He stood at the threshold for a beat, then went to her hideout.

Her muscles tensed so hard, they cramped. But she didn't stir.

"Thrall." His voice held an odd, strained edge.

Pulse pounding in her ears, Brigit stood.

A groove between the heathen's brows appeared to have been etched there. "She—" He shook his head and fell silent.

Wordlessly, Brigit prayed for the Lord to give her guidance—to not let her succumb to her boiling rage, to her daft, misplaced hurt, to say what He wished, or better yet, nothing at all.

Instead, as if propelled by some invisible force, she approached him—with his plaits, and cheekbones, and eyes—and trained her gaze on him. Then, she sputtered the most ill-conceived words she could: "I hate you!"

The heathen flinched as if struck.

He swallowed. Swallowed again. "You—hate I?

"Me!" she spat, casting off what little sense she had left. "You hate *me*, not *I*! *That* is how we say it in Irish!"

He trained his eyes on her, and she couldn't tell if the frost in them was for her mockery or for her unchecked loathing of him.

The moon broke from the cloud, and its light revealed his face painted with coal and streaked with blood. With a gasp, she drew back.

He stepped closer. "*You* hate me? You hate *me?*" His voice was like a fiddle string about to snap. "I—looked...searched... I—food, drink, care—you!" His breath came in fast, rugged huffs. "I—work—you? I—beat—you? I—force—you?"

Brigit dropped her gaze, her mind a tangle of red-hot detestation, searing degradation, and something she never knew until today. The vision of his hands on the woman's waist flew back at her like a fling of muck from a cartwheel. Her chin trembled, sight blurred, and as if taken a life of its own, her hand rose, then connected with the heathen's cheek with a resounding slap.

Fast as lightning, he caught her wrist.

"I'm sorry," she breathed, shrinking back. "I..."

Eyes wide, he held her wrist as he closed the distance between them. He bent to her, so near his pupils flooded with black, and his scent of sea, fur, and man filled her head. He stood before her—a wall of muscle and sinew, his lips a breath from hers. And for a heart-pounding moment, Brigit thought he would kiss her, like he did the woman.

Instead, he shoved her away with such force she staggered.

"You hate me." Jaw clenched, he nodded as if to himself. Then he stared at her with such a wretched expression, she shuddered. "I hate—*you!*" He thrust a trembling finger in her face. "I hate you!"

Brigit clasped her hands together so tight they hurt. Her head spun as she shook it, struggling to think of something to say. But no words came—only shame and self-loathing that made her wish she'd never been born.

Abruptly, her captor turned on his heel and marched to the door. For a heartbeat, he stood there swaying, then charged toward her, face tight as a knot, eyes shooting daggers.

Shaking like a great ash in a squall, he removed his battleaxe from his belt.

Brigit's back slammed into the wall behind. Her shriek pierced the chamber as he raised his axe with a berserk look in his unblinking eyes. But it died on her lips as a flash of clarity sliced through her, cold as ice. She'd prayed for a swift end—and now it had come.

With all his might, the heathen struck the rope at her ankle.

Brigit's scream drowned out the whack of the blade as it buried itself in the floor, reverberating into her marrow.

Her captor pulled it free and straightened. "You hate me? You—no longer bonded to me!" He spat something in Norse, then reached for her neck and ripped off his trinket. "Go!"

The world reeled, closing around her like a casket. It tilted as if the floor might give way beneath her.

"I—" She parted her lips, but nothing emerged.

The heathen didn't wait for her reply. Without a backward glance, he stormed from her chamber, slamming the door so hard it nearly fell off its hinges.

Brigit stood frozen, heart racing in pace with her swiftly clearing mind. She slid to the floor in a motionless heap. She thought she loathed him, but he loathed her—so mightily, he didn't even wish to kiss her. And now he was gone, and she might never see him again.

The notion slowed her heart to a dull, lifeless flutter. It formed a hard lump in her throat and filled her stomach with knots. He took away his shield of protection and left her to fend for herself. Soon, his men would swarm in and drag her off to a life of cruelty and defilement, and he would not be there to save her again, for he hated her. And why shouldn't he? She was a detestable, bitter creature filled with venom.

Brigit dropped her head into her hands—this was no less than she deserved.

Limbs heavy, she climbed into her hideout, removed her twig from the cloth, and brought it to her trembling lips. Then she knelt, fixing her gaze on the large bronze crucifix mounted on the wall, and closed her eyes.

"Please forgive me this sin, Father, for I cannot help it," she whispered against the twig as she'd done every day since the boy Reidar left her. "Please return my soulless Norse heathen to me."

# Chapter Thirteen

## Wrath

***Reidar***

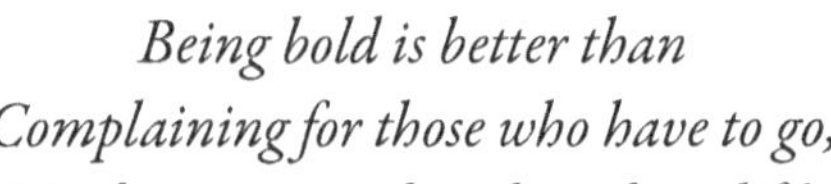

*Being bold is better than*
*Complaining for those who have to go,*
*My days are numbered, and my life's*
*Span has been set.*
— Skírnismál, stanza 13

Reidar's heartbeat pounded in his ears like Thor's hammer, blurring sight and taking reason. He didn't know where he was heading, only that he needed to put distance between himself and the accursed Irish girl.

The world shrank to a dark, narrow cave that had no beginning and no end. And he would march through this cave until he dropped dead. How repulsive he was to her. Through all his summers of war and plunder, he'd never seen such all-consuming loathing and detestation in anyone's eyes—neither from the Norse nor the Irish. Her bright green gaze lacked even a trace of fear when she slapped him. It bordered on madness.

The full moon rolled out from behind a cloud, revealing a small creek. Reidar shook himself and barreled toward it. What bordered on madness was his shameful, unflagging infatuation with her. Why, by Thor, did he feel, as he stepped into her chamber, like he'd been caught breaking the bonds of wedlock? Ingrid was neither his wife, nor his lover, nor even a free woman. He'd made her no vows and owed her no explanations.

*What in Odin's Hall was all that howling, brother? These Irish wenches are like wild beasts. Best you break her before she breaks you...* Thorsten's words echoed dully in Reidar's mind as he dipped his hands in the creek and washed his face clean of coal and the sheep's blood. Unsatisfied, he thrust his head into the rushing current and held it there until his fury mixed and mingled with the stream and finally drained away.

He reemerged with a long, trembling breath. The water was cool and fresh, so he closed his eyes and drank until he could drink no more.

His *fostra* spoke true—Ingrid was no ordinary woman. He knew it in the marrow of his bones. Even as a girl, she must have been a powerful enchantress, skilled in Christ magic as none other. Reidar shuddered as the bloodcurdling memory of the sacrifice pierced him like a blade. How mighty was her sorcery to have eclipsed all the gods of Asgard? To make him see things that weren't there, bend him to her will, and force him to utter falsehoods before Odin and his men? Unless the gods took heed, she would soon break him wide open.

With a steadying breath, he closed his eyes and buried his dripping head in his hands. "Odin, Allfather, do not turn your gaze from me," he breathed. "Do not let your favor wane. Shield me from the foul arts that bind me, break their spell, and fill me with your strength and wisdom."

Reidar stood and shook himself free of water, then continued on his path, sure and calm, until he reached the shore. At the top of the sky, the moon shone like a jewel amid countless stars. Along the beach, his stately longships, with their splendid carved dragonheads, awaited his call to sail. His mind cleared at the welcome sight of them. He would be setting sail in two days' time and bugger Éire and his designs for it.

His plan had been to settle half his men here as a foothold. And if his rebellion against his uncle failed, and Thor spared his life, he would return to Dalaradia to claim a jarl's seat here.

*No longer.*

Reidar scoffed and turned back to the castle, thanking Odin for knocking sense into him at long last. He was done with this accursed land, with the little spell-weaving witch, and with his daft designs, all. Soon, he'd set sail with those men who wished to return and leave behind the others to carve out their own fate. And if their settlement failed, they'd have his longship to sail back to Norway.

A twinge of unease tugged at his heart as he walked back through the hush of the night. After raiding Ingrid's new home and enslaving her new people, he would be leaving her alone yet again. But such notions were mere remnants of his Great Flaw—more habit than reason. For he needed not concern himself with Ingrid any longer. She had done well for herself since the last time he left her—wed a chieftain and became the lady of the castle. How cunning and resourceful was his enchantress and filled to the brim with scorn that sustained her better than food or drink. She'd find a way to thrive once more. Would put a spell on another hapless fool and make him share his hearth, wealth, and bed with her!

Hands cold as ice and stiff as a tree limb, Reidar wrenched his battleaxe from his belt and hurled it into the ground with a loud thwack.

A few paces away, a rustle broke the stillness, followed by the sharp crack of snapping branches.

Reidar went to his axe and pulled it free, squinting into the dim. The moon had cast strange shadows that made his hair stand on end. What evil creatures inhabited this Odin-forsaken wood?

Something stirred to his left, then to his right.

"By Thor..." Slowly, he removed Shadowbane from its scabbard and straightened. He cursed under his breath. His shield wasn't with him. He'd left it behind when he stormed out of the blasted castle with his blood boiling in his veins.

Like a bolt of thunder, Irish battle cries shattered the quiet wood, feral and sharp as crows descending on carrion. Five armed Irishmen erupted from the trees, their javelins gleaming in the moonlight.

Fast and precise, a spear flew, cutting the air with a vicious hiss.

Reidar ducked.

The spear hissed past his ear and struck a tree with a dull, bone-deep thunk.

Its thrower lunged, an Irish guard by the shape of his boiled leather jerkin and his practiced thrust.

Unflinching, Reidar threw his battleaxe. It spun end over end and plunged into the man's chest. Mouth agape, the Irishman staggered, then crumbled to the ground with a soundless gasp.

With a roaring cry of his own, Reidar surged forward, wrenching the axe free as another charged at him with a hideous string of Irish curses. Reidar swung hard, catching the second man in the neck. The crack of bone filled his head; a gush of the man's lifeblood sent a spatter of warmth across Reidar's face. The Irishman dropped like a stone.

Reidar's nostrils flooded with the scent of cold iron and damp soil. His ears rang with the rush of his breath and the telltale snapping of the branches behind. He whirled and brought Shadowbane clean on his attacker's neck. The head separated from the body. The body swayed, then collapsed in a heap.

The two remaining men hesitated. They retreated, then closed around him like wolves stalking a stag.

"Prepare to meet your gods in hell, where they fester with demons," one snarled as the other drew nearer.

Reidar tightened his grip on Shadowbane's smooth hilt. His heart pounded like a war drum, limbs strained with battle rage. These two were larger and better built than the others, their powerful shoulders and arms a match for any of his men. But maybe not for him.

They moved as one, stepping closer in calculated unison. Reidar's muscles coiled and hummed. He raised his battleaxe once more. The man on his right lunged. Fast as a northern wind, Reidar turned and drove his axe clean into his chest. The man's cry tore through the air as he crumpled, hands clutching at Reidar's axe haft.

Four dead Irishmen.

*I hate you!* Ingrid's eyes stared into his, burning him to ash.

But he shouldn't have let his focus waver, for he lost a precious moment as he turned to the last man and struck him with Shadowbane. All at once, pain, hot and crushing, exploded in his shoulder as the Irishman's javelin found its mark, cleaving through Reidar's chainmail and biting into his flesh.

Reidar's sight burst into a fiery haze. He staggered and fell on one knee, the world tilting and spinning. A tang of blood filled his mouth as he gritted his teeth, struggling to rise.

With a grimace of fury, the Irishman loomed above and pulled his javelin free. Then he dropped it and fell beside him.

The edges of Reidar's sight darkened, and he felt himself floating down to the rich Irish soil.

*And now you have killed me, my love.* The thought flickered as he closed his eyes. He lacked the strength to fight the Valkyries when they would sweep in to carry him to Valhalla.

# Chapter Fourteen

## Anguish

***Brigit***

*What is that loud noise*
*I hear in my house?*
*The ground shakes, and Gymir's*
*Home trembles around me.*
— Skírnismál, stanza 14

As Brigit was no longer under her Norseman's yoke, she had Caoimhe help her into her kirtle. She would not remove it for anything now and would tell him so when he returned. For he surely would, with so much left unsaid. And when he did, she might summon her courage and tell him true what dwelled in her heart. Come what may, she might even admit that her scorn of him was of a strange sort, for it often took the shape of something quite the opposite. And if she dared, she might even question his claim to hate her, for she resolved it was cut from the same cloth. While she wasn't certain what merit such confessions would have, she was past caring, for everything in her world had turned to ash with his leaving.

Two days had passed, yet he didn't come back. Caoimhe still brought food and drink and performed her household duties, such as they were, but she knew nothing of his whereabouts. Like everyone in the castle, the servant woman had heard the racket in Brigit's chamber and concluded the heathen had taken his fill of the lady, then left her for dead. Seeing that she was miraculously unharmed, Caoimhe only shrugged in response to Brigit's questions and said she'd mercifully seen no sign of him.

For two days, Brigit lay on her fleece pelts, scarcely touching the food. She knew well where he'd gone. And the visions of him and the terrible woman made her stomach harden until it hurt and her chest squeeze until she couldn't breathe.

The morning of the third day, Caoimhe entered with a tray in her hands and a thoughtful expression on her face.

"Och, praise the Lord, our troubles may be nearing the end." She set the tray on the bed and straightened. "I bring good tidings, m'lady."

"What tidings?" Brigit sat up in her hideout, heart picking up the pace.

"At dawn, they found your tormentor half-dead in the wood, they did. Our guards—those who fled during the raid—fell on him while he strolled there in the dark of the night, the heathen. Five fine lads, and he murdered them all, yet they dealt him a mortal blow, too. And it festered!" She crossed herself. "May the Lord forgive me for my wicked gloating, but if he departs to hell where he belongs, maybe the rest would leave too, seeing he is their chieftain."

Brigit shot to her feet, the world flickering at the corners of her eyes. "Festered...?" Her heart pounded against her chest, delivering painful blows and making it impossible to speak.

"Och...the joy of it is more than you can bear, m'lady!" The daft woman petted her head with a grimace of motherly love. "Do not fret so. He is not coming back here now!"

Cold all over, Brigit recoiled from Caoimhe's hand. "Where is he?"

"Too far from here to cause you more harm. Last I heard he was in our lord's chamber, tended to by their witch doctor."

Heart thundering, Brigit waited for Caoimhe to leave, then sank on the bed and hugged herself. With all her being she longed to run to the lord's chamber, to lay eyes upon him, to see for herself that he still lived. Yet the notion frightened her. The castle crawled with savages, and what was to halt any of them from taking her before she ever reached him? Her Norseman's amulet was gone, and even though his knot at her ankle remained, would these barbarians pay heed with their chieftain so weakened?

She froze at the sound of heavy, unfamiliar footsteps outside. Before she could move, the door creaked open, and a man stepped in, leaving it ajar. He winced at the sight of her, then marched forward, his expression hardening.

Brigit lurched with a shriek. The tray crashed to the floor, porridge and buttermilk splattering in every direction.

The man spat something in Norse and pointed to the door. He was young—younger than her Norseman—and a bit shorter and leaner. Her new master.

"I have a master." Trembling from head to foot, Brigit gestured to the knot at her ankle. "I am claimed."

"Come." His voice grave, the man set his jaw and pointed to the door once again. He had no Irish, and the word mangled on his tongue.

Brigit shook her head. "I won't go with you. I await my master here."

The man frowned and stepped closer. Without a sound, he stabbed his fingers into her arm and drew her to her feet. She hardly felt the pain as he dragged her after him, for her heart was but an instant from leaping from her chest. Every terror and indignity she dreaded loomed dark and inexorable, devouring what little remained of her.

The castle was in the state of chaos—worried faces, hushed tones, disordered halls. Yet hope soared, wild and glittering, as the man took the familiar path toward the lord's chamber. Breathless, Brigit heightened her pace, but she came to a screeching halt at the threshold. The chamber teemed with heathens. They didn't see her. Not yet. Brigit's breath hitched as a terrible realization crashed down like a blow. Her Norseman wasn't there at all—only these brutes who would no longer abide his orders to let her alone.

She squeezed her eyes shut. *The Lord is my light and my salvation...whom...shall I fear?*

Her new master pushed her inside, his hand on her arm like iron. She lurched back, seeking escape, but he shook his head, his expression grim.

"Let me go..." she breathed. "Please let me go."

A deep groove formed between his brows as he shoved her forward, harder this time. She recoiled, and he spat, then barked something in Norse, raising his voice above the din. Every man in the chamber turned.

Her knees buckled.

But the men only parted to make way.

It was then Brigit noticed the air hung thick with smoke. It stung her eyes and clogged her throat. The sharp tang of blood and the cloying scent of burning flesh filled her nostrils. It made her stomach churn. Someone had draped a fleece pelt over the window and lit nine candles in place of daylight. Their shadows danced on the stone walls like beasts and licked the man lying on her husband's bed.

At the sight, Brigit forgot the smoke, the shadows, the stench, and the fear. On her husband's loathsome bed lay her Norseman, stripped to the waist, his skin the color of soured milk and slick with sweat. Across his shoulder gaped a brutal flesh wound, charred and oozing with festered blood. All around him, crumpled sheets glistened with crimson. On the night table, in place of the ornate crucifix, stood a carved wooden idol with a wicked expression in his one eye, the other gouged out.

She gasped, and the Norseman opened his eyes, dull and hooded, and fixed them on her. They appeared strange, lighter than before, his pupils sunk deep into the pools of blue. He said something in Norse, his voice low and strained, then looked away and closed his eyes.

On the side of the bed stood an old woman, her long gray hair left wild and tangled. Coal darkened her face, and beneath it sprawled etched patterns of heathen symbols. The woman began to chant—a low, rhythmic invocation that made Brigit's skin crawl. She worked as she chanted, spreading a thick, foul-smelling paste onto a strip of linen.

Brigit gulped. "Is he dying?"

The woman covered the wound with her poultice, then wrapped it tightly with a long strip of fresh linen. She stopped chanting. Eyes dark and piercing, she peered at Brigit. "What are you to him?" The Irish words emerged clipped and strange but properly formed.

Brigit hugged herself. "I'm his thrall."

The woman stared, her eyes gleaming amid the coal. "Thrall, yes, you are that. He asked for you, thrall. Not his brother. Not his sweetheart. You! After what your accursed people did to him."

Brigit dug her fingernails into her palms but didn't look away. "Will he live?"

The healer kept her disconcerting gaze on Brigit's face. "Your people wanted his heart. But the gods spared him and gave them his shoulder instead. I do not know whether he will live or die. I did all I could for him. The rest is up to the gods." Lip curled in a sneer, the woman wiped her hands on a clean linen. "He wanted you here. But I gave him a tincture to ease his pain and bring sleep. Soon, he will not know you or even himself."

Brigit stood without movement as her Norseman opened his eyes again and muttered something in his tongue, his voice nearly a whisper. One by one, the men filed from the chamber, leaving behind the witch doctor and the one Brigit thought her new master.

Her Norseman turned toward the man and spoke in the unmistakable tone of an order. The man protested but left after her Norseman's voice deepened with warning.

Like all their kind, the witch healer was tall and towered over Brigit. "What he tells you, he will not mean," she murmured, staring down at her. "He will not even remember this if he lives." She shook her head with a look of disgust. "Your Christ magic is nothing compared to mine."

# Chapter Fifteen

## Truth
***Brigit and Reidar***

*There's someone outside*
*Who's dismounted his horse,*
*And set it free to graze.*
— Skírnismál, stanza 15

Brigit stood feet away from her husband's bed, her heart clenching with so many tangled feelings she nearly swayed. She detested this bed so much, the sight of it sickened her. Hands tightening into fists, she darted a glance behind her, half-expecting to find the wretched man standing at the door in a state of undress. But they must have killed him if he was no longer in his lord's chamber, and she scorned herself for her lack of remorse. Yet she loathed this bed even more now that it had become her Norseman's deathbed.

"Are you in much pain?" she squeezed out.

Reidar opened his eyes, the chamber rising and falling like a longship's deck in a storm. Before him stood a Valkyrie, her lovely face streaked with tears. He shut his eyes, then opened them again—he wasn't dead yet, and she wasn't a Valkyrie. She was his Ingrid. Weeping. For him.

Groaning, he pushed off the bed with his right hand, pulled himself up, and swung his legs down, settling on the edge. The world tilted. The Irish chamber morphed into a peaceful wood—the one on Rathlin Island.

Ingrid—a woman grown—lifted her small basket of wild strawberries. *Take it, it's yours.* He raised his hand and beckoned her to come nearer.

She didn't stir.

"How is it mine when I cannot touch it?" Reidar scoffed. "When I cannot taste it."

It was freeing to speak Norse to her. He should have done so from the start, for he could tell her his deepest longings, and she would never know. He laughed at the notion, the wood flooding with sun rays. They fell on her face and turned her eyes to real emeralds. They brushed her arms and made her gleam with light so bright it illuminated the skies and the seas.

"Gerd." He chuckled. "You are Gerd, and I am Freyr, vying for you like a lovestruck oaf. But your kin are hostile to the gods, and neither do I have a loyal servant like Freyr did. Who would woo you in my name?"

Ingrid grasped her little cross and shut her eyes. "Father, heal him, don't let him die. Don't take him from me, save him—"

"Save your prayers, my love." Reidar reached for her hand and placed it on his injured shoulder, where it was bandaged. The pain subsided. "I doubt your Christ would intercede on my behalf for I do not sacrifice to him."

Brigit stared, breathless, as her Norseman drew her to stand between his legs. The heat bounced off him in waves, flooding her. He was burning with an ill fever, yet he smiled—a flash of white that made his broad cheeks ride even higher and turned his eyes to bright blue slits. Brigit's heart clenched tighter. If it kept squeezing like this, it would surely shatter to bits.

"Are you dying?" she choked out.

Her Norseman murmured in his tongue again, then leaned forward and pressed his burning head to the spot above her heart. She kept her hand where he'd placed it, the linen beneath her fingers warm and damp. It smelled of garlic and honey, mixed with something woodsy. He muttered into her chest, and for the first time in her life, Brigit wished for at least some Norse. Yet even without understanding a single word, she knew he mistook her for someone else.

Limbs weighted with lead, Brigit dropped her head and stared at his flaxen plaits. He demanded to see her, wanted her to be here with him. But now, with his mind benumbed, he must have thought her his "sweetheart." What other reason had he to speak Norse to her?

"Please don't go." She tried again, squeezing out the words through a tightening throat.

Reidar let himself drown in the sweet scent and the soft feel of her. Surely, he was dreaming. Why would she care whether he lived or died? Why would she pray for him? She hated him. Doubtless, while he dwelled in this hazy new realm between Midgard and Valhalla, she sat in her chamber, smiling and glad to be free of him.

Still, it took Freyr nine nights to earn Gerd's love.

Reidar shook his head, and the movement sent a wicked shot of pain into his shoulder. He clenched his teeth. Maybe he would yet gain her consent.

In that same trembling voice, Ingrid repeated her plea for him to live. What a sweet dream.

Reidar forced a smile. "How could I die now, knowing you want me to live?"

Brigit nodded, thinking it strange that she understood he'd just assured her he wouldn't die. Uncertain, she lifted her free hand and stroked his flaxen plaits—soft and silky to the touch. A flash of crimson drew her gaze to his shoulder—the blood had seeped through the linen bandage. Brigit swallowed against a growing ache in her throat. If the Norsemen were anything like her people, he would not remain their chieftain if he became a cripple. And such a fate would surely crush him.

"D'you think you will be whole...after?"

Reidar tucked a loose strand behind her ear. "It heartens me to know you want me whole, even if this is only a dream." He brushed the back of his hand along her jaw.

Ingrid trained her gaze on him, running her trembling fingers along his plaits.

"Tell me what they call you," she whispered.

Reidar took her hand and brought it to his lips. "Your mouth asks my name, yet your heart refuses to say it."

Brigit searched his eyes for any sign of comprehension. They looked even stranger now—dark pinpricks of pupils swallowed by the frozen pools of blue. Did he even hear her question?

As if in reply, he closed his eyes and tilted his head to one side. One moment longer, and he would tumble. Quickly, Brigit slid both arms beneath his uninjured shoulder, straining to hold him steady as he eased himself into a lying position. It must have hurt him terribly for he grunted and paled another shade, though he neither screamed nor cursed.

Biting her lip, Brigit covered him with fleece pelts and sat on the edge of the bed. His breathing grew quieter; it soon steadied into a calm, even rhythm. She studied him as he slept. In the candlelight, his brows were the same flaxen gold as his hair, but his lashes appeared a few shades darker and longer than she would have guessed. They nearly brushed his broad cheeks.

His lips parted, and she stared at them for a long moment. Even with these heathen marks, he was beautiful. Without thinking, she leaned in and pressed her mouth to his. All at once, every part of her flooded with light, and she wished he was hale and awake, and would kiss her back, and would never let her go.

He didn't stir.

*Please don't let him die, Father.* She breathed into him. *Please heal him—*

Without warning, the door flew open.

Brigit lurched a moment too late. Her heart drummed a furious roll as her Norseman's "sweetheart" marched in, battleaxe tucked in her belt and eyes shooting daggers.

She charged at Brigit and stopped short, trapping her against the bed. For a long moment, she stared at Brigit's Norseman, then shifted a cold gaze to her.

The woman's eyes held a new feral gleam that made Brigit recoil.

"Rise, thrall," the woman said in serviceable Irish.

Fists clenched at her sides, Brigit stood. Better to face the wretch standing.

The woman drew near, closing the gap between them—so near Brigit smelled the ale on her breath. "He is mine—" She spat into Brigit's face. "Keep away, thrall. Or I rip heart with bare hands. Eat it while you watch."

Brigit stood rooted to the spot, spittle dripping down her cheek.

The woman slammed into Brigit so hard, she nearly tumbled. "Get out!"

Brigit's heart thudded like a *bodhrán*, and her hand trembled like a leaf as she wiped her face with her sleeve. This woman—almost a head taller and at least three stone heavier—might very well kill her with one bare hand, to say nothing of her axe. But Brigit straightened to her full insignificant height and squared her shoulders.

"I doubt he'd thank you for eating my heart when he recovers," she said as calmly as she could, thrusting the woman to the peak of her Great Scorn. "In the event, see that you don't choke on it, for it's full of thorns and venom."

Eyes widening, the woman opened her mouth, but nothing emerged.

Scoffing, Brigit walked around her and went out, affecting not to see her would-be new master standing outside with a hand on his axe haft.

*Thank You, Father, for interceding...* Her thoughts came fast and ragged as she ran to her chamber. *Thank You for such a timely reminder...*

She rushed in and shut the door, then threw herself onto her bed.

# Chapter Sixteen

## Unbound

***Brigit***

*Tell the man to come in and drink some mead*
*Here in our hall;*
*Though I fear that the person outside*
*May be my brother's killer.*
— Skírnismál, stanza 16

Brigit knelt before her crucifix and closed her eyes. It had been a fortnight since she'd last seen her Norseman, and with each passing day, she prayed. Without flagging, she prayed three times each day—upon awakening, at midday, and before bed. Yet she feared she was asking God too much, for her list of pleas seemed endless. And to make amends, she always ended her prayer the same way: "Father, if You grant me but one thing, let it be his healing and the grace to know You."

What little Brigit knew of her Norseman came from Caoimhe. By the woman's reckoning, his fever broke two days after the witch healer's ministering, and his "sweetheart" had moved into the lord's chamber to tend him day and night. To Brigit's questions of how he fared, Caoimhe usually replied with an oath and a curled lip, followed by a swift sign of the cross and a prayer to undo the dark thought she'd let slip.

The door opened as Brigit whispered, "Amen." She didn't turn, for she no longer feared intruders. It seemed everyone, save for Caoimhe, had forgotten about her. Still, she had no stomach for the servant woman's curses and ill wishes now, so she remained where she was.

The motion at the door ceased.

Brigit blew out a surreptitious breath. Could Caoimhe not put the tray on her bed and leave her to her prayers? Lips pursed, Brigit turned. She blinked, half-wondering if her tormented mind had conjured up a vision.

At the threshold stood her Norseman. His left arm and shoulder were bound with leather straps that wound around his torso, and the sides of his head were newly shorn. But while he appeared somewhat leaner and paler than before, he looked hale, strong, and keenly aware.

He peered at her for a long moment. "I—come—later."

"I'm finished." Brigit stood and smoothed her skirts, suddenly uncertain what to do with her hands.

He entered but didn't close the door.

"Are you...in much pain?" she mumbled, her heart pounding with one agonizing question—did he remember her in his sick chamber?

"Your people—" With his free hand, he pointed to his bandaged shoulder, his gaze cool and steady.

Brigit bit her lip, trying and failing to stay her wild breathing. "They don't want Norse masters. Can you fault them for wishing to be free?"

He inclined his head the smallest amount. "I—sail back—eleven days." Nothing moved in his face as he studied her with clear, piercing eyes. "You come with me—thrall. You stay—free. You—choose."

Brigit took one small step toward him. She stopped. His eyes betrayed no memory of her standing between his legs and stroking his hair, and of him pressing his head to her chest and murmuring to her in Norse. What a fool she'd been to pray he'd recognized her in his stupor. What a dullard to care if he had.

She shrugged, gulping down her folly. It was just as the witch healer foretold. Besides, if he remembered any of it, by now he surely thought she'd been his "sweetheart"—the same one who'd nursed him back to life. Brigit suppressed a scoff—and the same one who had vowed to eat her heart. Since Rathlin, Brigit had little regard for that raw, aching knot in her chest, yet she still wished to keep the shattered pieces of it in one place until the Lord called her home.

The Norseman contemplated her with a dispassionate expression, awaiting her reply.

Brigit lifted her chin and met his eyes. As if to torment her, the words got wedged in her tightening throat, but she pushed them out all the same: "I don't wish to be your thrall."

For a moment, he stilled, then shook himself, and dropped to one knee before her.

Pulse hammering, she stared as he lifted the hem of her skirt and untied the knot at her ankle with his free hand. What was left of her rope slipped to the floor. His fingers brushed her skin, and Brigit froze, breath catching, as he bent to the place where it had been bound and pressed his warm, firm lips to the spot. A rush of bright, searing sparks shot up into Brigit's very soul. She bit into her lip to steady her quickening breath. With everything in her, she longed to stroke his plaits as she did in the chamber, to talk to him as she did then. But for all her pining, the courage to lay herself bare left her.

He rose, his body tense as a coil, bright blue gaze trained on her.

Brigit stared into his eyes. She knew him. She always knew this beautiful stranger, this man above men, who came to her in the dark of the night as surely as he'd come at dawn's first light. She clenched her jaw. Who came to take her land, murder her people, and enslave her.

"You—no longer bonded to me." He turned and headed out. "Or—any Ljosstrond man." His voice came forth as a growl, low and hoarse, before he closed the door. "Do not fret. I—whole."

Heart racing, Brigit stared at the door, but it remained shut. She imagined pushing it open, dashing outside, calling for him, demanding to know why he gave her a choice instead of taking her as his spoils, why she must remain his thrall, and how he could keep leaving without a fight. And she imagined telling him all the things they'd left unsaid, then kissing him as she did in the chamber, and telling him he was a fool, and that she would follow him to the ends of the earth, free or bound, for she'd been waiting for him all her life.

She clapped a hand over her mouth and dug her heels into the floor, lest her feet carry her against her will. Her mind and heart were at war—two vicious foes fighting for her soul. She told her mind it was a fool. She told her heart it was a jester.

Someone rapped at the door, and Brigit's heart gave a thunderous, excruciating jolt. But it was only Caoimhe, for her Norseman never knocked. He entered and left, and left again as he wished, forever leaving her to pick up the pieces.

"Are you unwell, m'lady?" Caoimhe set the breakfast tray on the bed. "Och, don't I bring tidings to lift your heart! The cursed heathens sail back to whatever icy cave they came from in eleven days' time!" She curled her lip. "Och, some will remain, but not here, they won't. They'll be settling the land down by the clearing, you see. They've taken who they need—men and women both—but not me, nor you, m'lady. Word is, Flann mac Eochaid, our lord's cousin, will claim the title of chieftain. Lord be gracious, he may take you as his wife."

Brigit touched neither breakfast nor supper after Caoimhe finally left her chamber, threatening to fetch a healer and clucking her tongue at the harm the Norsemen had wrought upon her poor lady. She'd met Flann mac Eochaid when he came to stay a winter past. Young and powerfully built, he bore no resemblance to her husband, save perhaps for the eyes. But even then, where Cearbhall's gaze overflowed with greed and unconstraint, Flann's glinted with something hard and cold—especially when he trained it on her with a tight, icy smile.

Caoimhe had it right. He was yet unwed and, as custom demanded, would make her his wife. Then she would have a new master again—one who was likely as dishonorable as he was cruel.

Heart sick and head pounding, she knelt before the cross and closed her eyes. "Father, I ask for Your guidance, for I am well and truly lost. Is it Your will for me to remain enslaved to the heathen and live a life of sin, or wed another counterfeit Christian and dwell in misery and shame for the rest of my days?"

# Chapter Seventeen

## Thrall
***Reidar***

*Are you from the elves*
*Or the offspring of gods,*
*Or from the wise Vanir?*
*How did you come alone*
*Through the leaping flames*
*To see our home?*
— Skírnismál, stanza 17

It was the break of dawn, and soon Reidar and his men would set sail for home. All was readied for their departure—the loot stowed in trunks and hauled to the longships, the thralls bound and waiting on the shore, provisions made for those who would remain to tend the land.

Reidar lifted his left arm, bent it at the elbow, and flexed his fingers. His shoulder still ached, though less with each passing day. The wound—once perilous for its festering—would leave him with another scar, not a lasting weakness. He gave a bitter scoff. After all Ingrid had said at his sickbed—stroking his hair and, he was sure of it, kissing him as he drifted into sleep—he believed she would come willingly.

Blasted woman. She had always been his Great Flaw in the flesh. If his men discovered he'd granted her—a foreign thrall—a choice, his *blodhefnd* would fade into distant memory. They'd surely think him mad, mock him out of the village, and refuse to follow him on any raid thereafter—let alone aid him in overthrowing his uncle and claiming the jarl's seat. She had bewitched him after all.

But bewitched or not, he was still Reidar Valorborn, Harald Fairblade's son, and he would stand no more of this madness. Jaw tight, Reidar shrugged on his wolf pelt, seized his rope, and cast one last glance around Ingrid's dead husband's chamber. He'd had enough of doubt and the same old folly.

Struggling to shove aside all thought, he strode to Ingrid's chamber. He'd likely find her kneeling before her crucifix again. He frowned. How was it that while his true gods kept their distance, this unseen Christ hovered so near, even his Norse soul stirred when she prayed? And how could this Christ be called unseen when on the night of the sacrifice, He revealed Himself, as undeniable as breath? Reidar scoffed. He might learn in time, for time may soon be on his side.

For a heartbeat, he lingered at the door, then pushed it open.

Ingrid gasped, and he flinched as they bumped into each other. She stood at the threshold, clutching her shawl in her hands. Was she aiming to seek him or run? It made no difference whatsoever.

"You—sail with me," he barked, unable and unwilling to soften his voice.

He'd been half-hoping she would recoil in terror, weep, and plead to stay in Dalaradia—and set him free. He'd prayed to Odin she would not, for the notion of frightening her stung worse than sea water in an open wound. But she did nothing of the kind. Instead, she held his gaze for a long moment, then squared her shoulders and demanded, "Why?"

"Why." He scoffed to mask his relief. "I—your master. You—my thrall. I say—you do. You do not question—*me*."

"You freed me!" She glared at him, hands curling into small fists at her sides. "This is my *home!* I wish to remain here!"

"By Odin, Thor, and Freyr," he bit out in Norse. "I have tried, but I cannot give you up. You have made your blasted *home* in my heart, in my soul, in my bones."

A small groove formed between her dark brows. And owing to some powerful sorcery, it set his blood on fire. She straightened, adding scarce more than a fingerbreadth to her diminutive height. "You said I am no longer bonded to you!"

Reidar envisioned taking an axe to his Great Flaw and hacking it to pieces, then hurling them into the sea. In his mind's eye, the fragments knit themselves together and surged back into him.

Heart thudding, he drew nearer to her. "I changed my mind!" It was uncanny how her mother tongue was coming to him easier each day.

"Did you now!" She lifted her chin, eyes shooting lightning bolts straight into his wretched, damaged heart. "And if I refuse?"

He closed the distance between them. "Then I take you by force."

Ignoring her shrieks of protest, he grabbed her wrists and quickly bound them with his rope.

"Curse you—" Her tears came, fierce and burning. "And all your people, and all the idols you bow to, so you can cloak your wickedness in their names!"

Reidar widened his stance, fighting words bubbling at his lips. She was one to talk, when all her precious Irish chieftains did was raid and slaughter one another while asking their Christ to aid them in strife and bloodshed. By Thor's hammer, her own blasted husband's hands had been stained to the elbows with his own countrymen's blood. But Reidar lacked the Irish words to make such declarations hold weight and had no desire to quarrel with her over gods. Besides, when he brought her to Ljosstrond, she would see reason. When she saw how the gods worked in their lives, she would surely abandon her heathen ways and hail the Æsir as the only true ones.

Ingrid lifted her fettered hands and wiped away tears, her glittering eyes fixed on him. "I do not wish to be your thrall."

They stared at each other in the taut silence that fell.

He brushed an errant strand from her face and tucked it behind her ear. "It—way of my people." He searched her eyes. If she could come as a free woman, would she follow him willingly?

She dropped her gaze, her voice faint as a whisper. "And what of your sweetheart?"

Wordless, Reidar studied her flushed cheeks and pinched expression, a tingling warmth coursing through him at the sight. Was that the true cause of all this storming?

*You are my one true sweetheart.* He swallowed such folly down. "I do not have—sweetheart. Astrid—only old friend."

Ingrid lifted her face to him, biting her lip as if struggling to hold back an entire flood of emotions.

Reidar arched a brow. Now that they stood so close, the girl could not conceal her true feelings to save her life.

He tipped her chin with his forefinger, unable to tear his gaze from her lovely mouth, unwilling to look elsewhere. He hadn't been with a woman since Ljosstrond, having spurned Astrid's advances in his sick chamber. A blunder. He should have let her do as she pleased and come to Ingrid sated and content, instead of standing here like a fool, humming with longing at the sight of all he dreamed of for seven long winters.

Deep within his heart, Reidar knew Ingrid would not be claimed this way, but all reason slipped away as her sweet scent filled him to the brim—crisp morning dew, fresh grass, and ripe wild strawberries. His skin was on fire. His whole body was on fire, pulsing and aching for her. He bent his head—only two fingerbreadths away.

She stopped biting her pretty lip. She stopped breathing altogether.

It would be so easy to kiss her now, to lose himself in her—in the true flesh and blood of her—not a mere shadow conjured by his unslaked yearnings.

Their lips touched, and a jolt of thunder rushed through him, wild and exhilarating. Unchallenged. By Thor's hammer, despite everything, he must have made his home in some part of her, too.

"I am wed," she said very clearly against his lips, "and not to you."

He drew back, her words crashing down on him like a bucket of cold water. For all his daft hopes of never having to broach this subject, here it was, and at the worst moment imaginable.

"You—love your husband?" he muttered, struggling to steady his breathing.

She clenched her jaw, staring off into the distance. "Am I a widow?"

Reidar nodded, a cold weight settling in his chest and driving out the remnants of lingering warmth. Unaccountably, she had loved the old chieftain, and now, he added yet another crime to his growing ledger.

She was silent for a spell, then peered into his eyes with a wary, turbulent look. "Tell me..." She cleared her throat. "D'you...do you know...Reidar?"

His name left her lips, soft and lilting, shining onto him like a thousand suns, but he stood very still, keeping his face perfectly blank. "Reidar?" he echoed to buy time. Perhaps she suspected it all along. But if he told the truth, would he find scorn or relief in her face?

He lost the fight with himself before it began, for he could not abide any more of her loathing. Feigning indifference, he shrugged. "I knew Reidar—once. But no more." He scoffed. "He—changed."

He'd made a blunder, for she dropped her shoulders and studied her bounds with such a wretched expression, it drove his Great Flaw to the very top and filled his heart with a dull, heavy ache. Briefly, he considered telling the truth, but the voices and clamor outside brought him back to himself. This was neither the place nor the day for such a talk. There would be time enough to lay it all bare when he returned home.

"We leave now." He scanned the chamber, then headed to her chest of drawers. All her possessions would fit in the trunk that stood beside it, so he emptied it out and filled it to the rim with everything but her warmest cloak and boots.

"Sit," he pointed to the bed.

Shoulders slumped and eyes downcast, she did as he said.

Heart pounding anew, he pulled the fur-lined boots on her feet—small and delicate like the rest of her. If he could do away with all that constrained him, he would dress her in the finest furs. He would give her all his possessions. He would go to any length to banish her dejection.

*How the gods must be laughing at me now.*

He said nothing as he draped her in a fine fur-clad cloak, fastened it at her throat, then grabbed all her fleece pelts, and made for the door, rope in hand.

"Wait, please," she breathed behind him. "I must bring something along."

He shook his head. "No room—in trunk."

She glanced toward her bed. "It's very small."

Reidar released the rope as she bent to her pillow and removed a tiny bundle from underneath. Quickly, as if not wishing for him to see, she brought her hands to her belt and tucked it in.

He glimpsed none of his men until they'd gone out. The remaining two carried what appeared to be the last trunk from the lord's chamber.

"Is there room for another?" he asked.

"No, my lord. All ships are full, space left only for this one."

"Leave it," said Reidar. "Go to my thrall's chamber and bring her trunk instead."

# Chapter Eighteen

## The Crossing
***Brigit***

*I am not from the elves,*
*Nor the offspring of gods,*
*Nor from the wise Vanir;*
*Though I came alone*
*Through the leaping flames*
*To see your home.*
— Skírnismál, stanza 18

The surf broke and retreated in pace with Brigit's heartbeat pounding in her ears. It drowned out the harsh shouts of the Norsemen, the anxious murmur of the women beside her, and the resounding thuds of the trunks against the decks. Her knees, which had only wobbled during the walk to the beach, now trembled so fiercely they threatened to buckle. The longships she'd glimpsed on Rathlin, seven winters past, had been but faint outlines shrouded by the mist. Now a dozen lined the shore, looming larger than doom, their towering prows reaching for the sky, grotesque dragonheads sneering down at her like beasts on the hunt.

The sand shifted beneath Brigit as her Norseman vanished into the throng of men without a backward glance. And with his departure, her blunder broke over her like dawn, laying bare her unforgivable folly. Moments before he entered her chamber, she'd nearly resolved to seek him out and follow him across the sea. She swallowed a lump in her throat—fool! He remained a savage with neither scruples nor honor, and now he'd taken her as his thrall—a trinket, a possession, a thing to be used and disposed of when no longer pleasing.

Brigit knew enough of men to see the truth, plain at last, for it had been no different with her husband. Yet when he grew weary of her within the sanctity and protection of her marriage, she still maintained the dignity and freedom of her rank before the world. As his thrall, her Norseman would likely pass her on to the others or sell her at one of their degrading slave markets.

Brigit clasped her bound hands together, suffocating on her breath. Something was terribly wrong with her to have grown warm when he brushed his lips against hers. Worse still—to have kissed him in his sick chamber of her own free will. Her broken, wicked nature ran too deep to fathom, yet at least she knew it and repented. But he? He was a heathen with no mercy in his heart, accustomed to leaving misery and ruin in his wake. He hadn't even looked at her as he roped her with the other women, like cattle, and left her standing here!

In a cruel twist of fate, her own maidservant, Saoirse, stood beside her, sobbing like a small child. Her normally neat hair hung in matted strands, gown appeared torn in places, and she wore neither cloak nor shawl over her coarse homespun.

"May the Lord call me home before I set foot on their cursed land, m'lady," she whispered. "May they all meet their end in the tides before they reach it."

"*M'lady,*" Brigit's good-sister Mairead bit out with a sneer. She had the look of a commoner now, dressed in rags befitting a kitchen wench. "I wager *she* doesn't wish for such things, having traded my noble brother for that big heathen wretch." Her voice turned shrill. "I wager *she* indulges him readily in exchange for her fine boots and warm cloak!"

The other women kept their heads down, but a young chambermaid darted a frightened glance at Mairead. "By your favor, hold your tongue, m'lady, lest we all get the lash."

Brigit shifted her gaze to the longships, shutting out the vile woman's bitter tirade and the servant's impertinence. Her good-sister never concealed her disdain for Brigit, for a peasant had no place at her brother's side. But Mairead, who'd earned a hefty link in her Great Scorn chain, seemed to forget Brigit had no choice in the matter.

It made no difference now. Brigit's stomach churned as she watched the Norsemen secure their loot and prepare to set sail. She couldn't grasp how she'd gone willingly at all, or why she hadn't fought it. All she wanted now was to run from here until her legs gave way.

A large barbarian with cold eyes strode toward them and grabbed their ropes. Brigit's stomach dropped and throat closed as he marched them across the wet sand to one of the longships. A steep, narrow gangplank stood at its side, and that was where the Norseman pointed as he spat his order. Brigit was the first to climb in and nearly slipped, but by some miracle remained upright. Her erstwhile maidservant wasn't so lucky. After taking two trembling steps, Saoirse stumbled. With a terrible curse, their overseer seized her around the waist like a sack of grain and hurled her into the ship. Screaming, she landed at Brigit's feet. The rope pulled tight at Brigit's wrists as the women swayed with impact. Quickly, Brigit clasped Saoirse's hands and helped her up, trying not to notice a pool of scarlet above her lip.

A handful of heathens waited aboard the longship, yet her Norseman was nowhere in sight. A blade twisted in Brigit's stomach, sharp and cold. She was naught but plunder to him, as was her due—proper penance for her daft hopes and wayward longings, and for the darkness that lurked within her heart. For she should have been cloaked in grief for her murdered husband instead of harboring forbidden fancies for a shorn, marked savage who had carved his way into her life with blood and fire.

The rest climbed in without incident, driven by fear and the mounting stream of Norse curses and barked commands. Without delay, the man seized the ropes and hauled the women toward the stern. With a rough gesture, he pointed to the cramped space between the trunks. Before they all settled in, he knotted their bindings, secured the slack to the ship's side beams, and stalked off.

Brigit affected not to notice Mairead, who sat beside her, glaring ahead. She turned to Saoirse instead. The woman was praying fervently, begging God to end her torment. Brigit cast a glance about—still no sign of her Norseman.

The wooden planks beneath them gleamed dark with salt and age and smelled of brine and destruction. The air reeked of tar, sweat, and sea. The interior of the longship resembled the mouth of some terrible beast that had swallowed them alive. The oars hung at the sides, long and menacing, awaiting the rough hands that would carry her away from Éire forever.

Like a ray of light, tight flaxen plaits flashed before Brigit, and her whole body slackened, awash in unwelcome warmth. As tall as these heathens were, her Norseman towered above them all as he tossed her pelts aboard and jumped in after them. He stuffed them beneath his arm and headed toward the stern, his gaze fixed on her. He reached it in a few long strides, then dropped to one knee and wrapped her in the soft fleece.

"You go—*home*," he murmured in her ear.

Heat, fast and fierce, flared through Brigit in pace with her racing heart as he strode away.

The women grew quiet, staring at her with widened eyes.

"Oh, would you look at that!" Mairead spat through her teeth. "Our *lady* has taken a lover, and what a lover he is!"

Brigit closed her eyes and asked the Lord to blot out her Great Scorn, to replace it with His words, with any words that weren't her usual venom-filled spitting. But the darkness that dwelled within her was too strong.

"Aye, I have." She turned to Mairead with a long, cold stare. "And he is, by far, a better lover than your vile, lascivious brother ever was." Brigit glared at her good-sister in the shocked silence that fell. "And from the looks of it, I'm still above you and have the Norse chieftain's ear, besides, so you'd do well to keep your mouth shut in my hearing."

Mairead paled and shrank back, but this didn't bring Brigit any joy. It only made her wish to leap into the waves and wash herself clean. Yet none would grant her such mercy, for within moments, dozens of men boarded the ship and took their places at the oars.

A shiver crawled up Brigit's spine as her Norseman's sharp command split the air, followed by the creak of the wood and the groan of ropes tugged tight. With a heave of muscle and timber, the ship lurched forward.

The fleece pelts grew suffocating, but Brigit couldn't remove them for her tied wrists. Suspended between stifling heat and prickling cold, she watched as her Norseman unfurled the sail with practiced ease. It was terrible and beautiful, its blood-red and yellow-gold stripes glinting in the early morning light like flames.

Brigit's chest locked; her breath came thin and sharp. He said she was going *home*. Home! Plundered and fettered like a heifer and swaddled like a babe in the height of summer into the bargain.

The shoreline shrank. The gentle, green hills faded into a gray blur, then vanished. Brigit stared at the horizon until her eyes burned, but her one true home was gone, and with it, everything she'd ever known.

The wind rose, pulling at her hair and whipping at her face, and despite herself, Brigit felt a grudging gratitude for the fleece. Time stretched as the longship cut through the waves. The steady splash of water and the rasp of planks dulled her thoughts. The sun climbed higher; its warmth seeped through the wind and mingled with the softness of the pelts wrapped around her. The gentle sway of the ship turned soothing. The ceaseless horizon blurred her heartbreak into a haze. The haze morphed into a beckoning darkness.

She was back on Rathlin, a girl of thirteen, running through her beloved forest. Running as fast as her small legs carried her. Away from herself. Toward herself. Running home.

*For I know the plans I have for you,* the leaves whispered.

*Plans for welfare and not for evil, to give you a future and a hope,* the birds sang.

At the clearing stood the boy Reidar, armed with his strange sword and ghastly axe, and draped in a black wolf pelt.

You go—*home.*

An icy chill pierced Brigit's skin and spread through her lifeblood. She came to a screeching halt, unable to take another step. His eyes were the stark color of winter and of depths so frozen, it seemed they never knew warmth.

*Your light is like ice, Reidar—dazzling yet cold.*

The ground shifted. The world flipped upside down. A great roar filled the air and swallowed Brigit's forest and the boy Reidar with it.

Around her, the sky and the sea became one—a raging, heaving beast bent on the annihilation of all that dared disturb its lair. The longship groaned and lurched. The men at the oars chanted and cursed at the heavens, but their cries died in a deafening rumble of thunder and a furious hiss of rain.

A lightning bolt split the world in two, illuminating the chaos into which they all had been cast. The oarsmen strained against the raging sea. Their oars plunged and surged, but the ship bounced like a child's plaything against the storm. A sickening jolt slammed Brigit into Mairead. An icy wave crashed over the longship. Its force struck her down, then drove her head-first into the unmoving Saoirse.

Her Norseman's frantic command drowned in the maelstrom as the ship tilted on its side. An angry deluge of cold black abyss surged over Brigit. Then it engulfed her. It forced its way into her nose and mouth. It seared her throat and burned inside her chest. Gagging and choking, she dug her nails into the slick wood. It slipped from her reach.

The wave retreated as abruptly as it came. The longship righted its keel with a gut-wrenching shudder. The impact hurled Brigit forward, crushing her against Mairead's limp body. Brigit lay where she landed, gripped by a cold unlike any she'd ever known. Her fleece pelts and cloak had vanished into the sea. Her soaked kirtle clung to her, heavy as iron. If she hadn't been lashed to the side beams, she would've surely been thrown overboard. And then, this living nightmare would have ended.

Another arc of light pierced the sky, revealing Saoirse's glassy, sightless gaze. Beside her, Mairead curled into a shuddering ball, her drenched rags plastered to her body like a shroud. A short distance away, lay a single sodden pelt. Shaking like a leaf, Brigit reached across the heaving deck as far as her bounds allowed. Each jolt threatened to tear them off; the planks beneath her palms scraped her skin raw. But the fleece was only an arm's length away. She lunged for it.

There it was—a pathetic, sodden mass caught against a beam. She pulled hard, and it came loose. The wind howled, and the unrelenting spray whipped her face, but she dragged herself back to the trunks. To her good-sister, who stared at her with a wild look. Clumsily, she rolled near to Mairead's meager warmth and heaved the fleece over them both. It made no difference. The fleece was drenched; its weight only added to the chill.

Brutal, relentless ice seeped into Brigit's bones. But she knew what she must do to survive this, too. So, with everything in her, she pushed this wretched crossing and the man who plundered her to the peak of her Great Scorn. This served her, as it often did, and all at once she wanted to scream, to rage against the cruelty of being dragged from her home to endure this new torment. But her voice caught in a jolt that made the sea howl like a great pack of wolves. The ship moaned and pitched beneath her. It threw her against the trunk.

Brigit's breath came in ragged, pained gasps as another wave approached, its tattered edges lit by a flash of lightning as if by the fires of hell. And for the thousandth time in her pitiful life, her Great Scorn failed her.

*Listen to me, Lord, and answer me,* she sobbed.

*For I am helpless and weak.*

*Save me from death,*

*For I am loyal to You...*

*Save me,*

*For I trust in You...*

A wall of water surged over the ship and crashed down upon her. The sea's icy grip sank deep into her flesh like the merciless blade of a Norse battleaxe, sharp enough to carve through her skin and to freeze the very marrow in her bones. The pain was too great to fathom, too vicious to bear. Another agonizing moment, and she would fade away at last—this time, into a dream that would never end.

A roaring flash of lightning illuminated sodden flaxen plaits and aching blue eyes, laying everything bare. Begging her to live. With all her waning strength, Brigit clung to that naked gaze, but the truth she finally glimpsed came too late to save her.

*Home is love, but your longing is not, my Reidar.*

# PART TWO

## Nine Nights From Now

*Ljosstrond, Norway*
*803 A.D.*

# Chapter Nineteen

## Storm

***Reidar***

*Eleven apples,*
*All made of gold,*
*I will give you, Gerd,*
*In exchange for your promise*
*That Freyr will be*
*Considered your dearest.*
— Skírnismál, stanza 19

"Hold fast to the oars! Pull, by Thor!" Reidar's order cut through the chaos, raw and hoarse like a battle cry.

All along the benches, men strained shoulder to shoulder. Two dozen backs bowed and heaved in a frantic rhythm. Some grunted through clenched teeth. Others howled curses at the wind, their words swallowed and flung back by the storm. The oars plunged and rose like ravens' wings.

Reidar stood fast against the curve of the hull as another icy wave burst over the gunwale and slammed into him with brutal force. The ship groaned, every plank shuddering as if it might tear loose. He dug his fingers into the slick wood. He and his men had faced many hard seas together aboard these longships.

*By all the gods, it had to hold.*

He stared into the raging storm, commanding himself to pay no mind to the stern. It contained nothing but spoils—trunks and thralls. Valuable but replaceable, unlike his ships and men. Such reasoning fled him as the next flash of lightning revealed no sign of Ingrid's cowering form.

Reidar's hands tingled and heart raced with the all-consuming need to see her.

*Mighty Thor, forgive this frailty within me.*

Another flare of lightning shattered the darkness, striking feet away from the longship.

For the hundredth time, he glanced at the stern.

*Your wrath is just, but punish me alone—not my men, nor anyone else on my ships. Allfather Odin, I will purge my Great Flaw. Show me the way.*

As if mocking him, the light caught the scattered trunks and the spaces between. Reidar's heart dropped at the sight. The women lay strewn about like dead fish, Ingrid among them. A chilling thought stabbed him like a blade. It crept into his lifeblood, cold and final in its clarity. This was neither Thor's rage nor Loki's tricks. Such precise, relentless fury could only belong to Ingrid's unseen God—her Christ. He was the one punishing him for tearing her from Éire against her will.

The longship pitched beneath his feet. The timbers creaked under the strain. His men clung to the ropes, poles, side beams—anything solid to keep the longship upright. He swallowed against a mounting weight in his chest. He had never seen such a vicious tempest. How much longer before the ship shattered and they all perished?

With another glance toward the stern, Reidar shut his eyes. *God of Éire and all Christendom, if it is Your wrath I face, know this—I took her not from malice but because I cannot breathe without her. Let her live, and I swear to you, I will love and care for her as my own wife until my last breath.*

A crack of thunder answered him, followed by the surge's cruel sting that struck his face like a whip.

The oarsmen leaned into their oars with every muscle, pulling the ship back on course with pleas to Njord, Thor, Odin, Freyr—any god who would heed them. But the waves mocked them, rising and crashing down, pouring into the longship.

"Bail!" Reidar grabbed his helmet.

The others followed, scrambling with helmets, wooden bowls, bare hands. Yet the harder they bailed, the faster the sea poured in.

The throbbing in Reidar's shoulder became a flame, trapped beneath his skin. A merciless ache spread down his arm, leaving it leaden and numb. His men's strength unraveled with each punishing wave. Sagging shoulders, raw hands, slackened faces, hollow eyes. They no longer called to the gods, nor cursed them.

Reidar's helmet slipped from his grasp, snatched away by the hungry sea. If Odin faltered before such wrath, what hope had mere mortals like them?

Trembling, he dropped his head into his hands and breathed the Irish words into the tempest:

*Our Father in heaven...*

*Forgive us our debts...*

*Deliver us from evil...*

He couldn't tell how long it went on. Time dissolved into a blur of crashing water and roaring wind. Every heartbeat felt like his last. Each moment stretched thin by the storm's relentless pounding. But when all seemed truly lost, God's fury ebbed as abruptly as it had begun, leaving the longship adrift on a quieting swell.

The sky brightened with the first light of dawn. The wind dwindled to a ghostly whisper. The rain softened to scattered drops that pattered against the sodden wood. Silence descended, thick and unnatural, broken only by the ragged breaths of his crew and the slap of waves against the hull.

Reidar scanned the sea. All his ships had weathered the storm. They bobbed behind like restless shadows. Breath held, he trained his gaze on the barren stern. His shoulder wound had likely split open, but the pain scarcely touched him as the sight between the trunks pulled him like a lodestone, carrying him forward.

The women lay huddled together, save for one at Ingrid's left—limbs frozen in place, face drained of color, lips parted in an unmistakable scowl of death.

*But Ingrid.*

Reidar's chest filled with frost, sharp-edged and suffocating. Her hair clung to her brow in dark, wet tendrils; her eyes were shut. He struggled to draw breath. It got wedged in his throat. He'd never seen her look so pale.

Not even when she crouched against the wall, frightened by his ill-wrought arrival. Nor when he brought her to the Irish hall to name her attacker.

Reidar's heartbeat raced like a tide. It surged into his throat. It thundered in his ears. The world held still. No wind, no sound. Only deafening, pulsating silence, as if her God Himself had paused to measure the cost of His wrath.

One of the women gasped. Her eyes flew open in a wild, mute alarm and locked on the corpse beside Ingrid. The scream that followed—piercing and raw—jolted others to life.

*But not Ingrid.*

Shutting out all but her, Reidar crouched before her small shape and placed a rigid hand upon her forehead. It was cold as ice.

The sea, the longship, the men, the panicked thralls—all faded without a trace. Insignificant, useless, inconsequential. He dropped to his knees beside her, pulled out a dagger from his boot, and sliced through her bindings. As if watching himself from elsewhere, he saw his stiff fingers press against the cold, damp skin of her dainty wrist. Nothing.

*Please, no.*

Swaying, he shifted his fingertips to another spot and pressed harder. He felt it then—a faint, fragile pulse, weak as a wren's wing fluttering against a cage. He tore his wolf pelt from his shoulders and wrapped her in it. Tight, tighter.

"Ingrid." His voice came through gruff and ragged. "Ingrid, wake up."

She didn't stir.

He dug his fingers into her arm—so hard, she would have recoiled if she weren't dying. But she remained unmoving.

"Odin, Thor, Freyr...Christ," he breathed, pushing away the unbidden memory of his father's face before he departed to Valhalla and the tearing grief that came in its wake. "Do not take her from me. Not now. Not when I have so nearly brought her home."

The sky, streaked with dawn's pale light, revealed a familiar line in the distance. The hard and jagged coast of Ljosstrond. They weren't far. A few leagues, perhaps—no more.

Reidar's shoulder screamed in protest as he slid his arms beneath Ingrid, but he lifted her all the same and cradled her against his chest.

"By the gods." His brother's voice cut through her faint breathing, noticeable only when held near. Thorsten stepped forward, casting a glance at the lifeless woman beside them. He hefted the corpse over his shoulder, then walked to the gunwale, and dumped it overboard.

Numb, Reidar watched the body slip beneath the waves. He pulled Ingrid closer.

*Thank You for not letting it be her.*

Thorsten wiped seawater from his cheek. He scanned the rest of the ragged bunch, cowering between the trunks, then trained a steady gaze at Ingrid. "Any others to feed the sea?"

Reidar made his face blank before meeting his brother's eyes. "My thrall yet lives."

"Careful, Brother." Thorsten gave a slow nod, lowering his voice. "Our uncle will surely take notice of her. Do not let him see where you bleed."

Reidar eased Ingrid back onto the planks, jaw tightening. "I bleed only for my seat of power, the one our uncle wormed himself into after murdering our father. You—" He gestured at the nearest thrall as his brother squared his shoulders and spat. "See to—her."

The woman stared, clutching her pitiful rags about her with chattering teeth.

Reidar leaned in, making his voice low and soft. "She dies—I—kill you."

He headed to the bow, wary of the fleeting terror in the thrall's eyes, followed by too-eager submission.

"Raise the sail!" His order thundered across the deck—firm, commanding, and betraying nothing of the relentless pull to turn back.

The men scrambled, hoisting the soaked sail. It billowed weakly in the light morning breeze, yet the longship cut through the waves as Ljosstrond's coastline rose to greet them in earnest.

Soon, dark cliffs gave way to green slopes dotted with longhouses, the faint glint of smoke curling into the dawn. Reidar stood at the prow, gaze fixed on the restless ripple of the sea. It must have been the cold, mixed with the fright, yet she lived, and his *fostra* would tend to her. Gyda would know what to do—she always did. Surely, she would bring Ingrid back.

The men leaned into their oars, guiding the longship toward the shallows. The hull scraped against the sand as it beached. The reassuring jolt reverberated through its frame.

At the water's edge, the villagers awaited as they always did, some shouting greetings, others gasping at the bedraggled state of the crew.

In a cool, deliberate manner that made Reidar's blood boil, a tall figure draped in fur and silver stepped forward. His uncle's hand, Asbjorn, was as mild as Vargr Bloodgale was feral, yet no less ruthless beneath his stillness.

"The jarl awaits," Asbjorn murmured in a voice calm as a summer breeze, "to look upon the spoils and thralls."

Reidar widened his stance, holding the man's gaze in a deadlock. "Tell my uncle we have met with a storm. I will go to the mead hall after I rest."

"Hmm." Nothing stirred in Asbjorn's features as he stepped aside to make room for Reidar's men carrying trunks. "He will not be pleased to hear this."

Reidar watched Asbjorn melt into the crowd, the skin on his face growing taut as a newly stretched war drum. He stilled himself. Composure. Patience. Restraint. When the time came, he would unseat Vargr with all his strength and men, as precise and unforgiving as his blade's strike—not the rash impulse of a boy ruled by anger.

*Ingrid.*

Jaw clenched, Reidar marched to the stern. The thrall tasked with keeping her alive held Ingrid's head in her lap, stroking her hair and whispering something that sounded like one of their Christ incantations. She flinched as his shadow fell upon her.

Reidar knelt before Ingrid—still motionless but no longer pale. Her cheeks flared crimson; her brow shone slick with damp.

Ignoring the throbbing in his shoulder, he lifted her once more against his chest. His heart sagged beneath the weight of mounting dread. She burned like a forge.

"Ingrid." His voice quavered as he brushed a lock from her face. "Ingrid, you—*home.*"

Her eyes fluttered open, dull and glassy, then slipped shut again.

Holding her as though she might shatter, Reidar rose to his feet and turned to his men. "Carry the spoils to the mead hall. I will not be long."

He paid no heed to the villagers' whispers and lingering gazes as he stepped off the longship and strode toward his longhouse, trailed by six of his most trusted *hirdmen* who dwelled there with him.

"Go with the rest." He tossed over his shoulder. "Do not give him cause to punish you."

His stride never faltered even as his stomach twisted into hard, cold knots.

# Chapter Twenty

## Malevolent

***Reidar***

**First Night**

*I will not take*
*Any man's gifts*
*These eleven apples ever;*
*Nor will Freyr and I*
*Find a shared home*
*For as long as we live.*
— Skírnismál, stanza 20

Stillness wrapped around Reidar and the limp girl in his arms as he stepped into his longhouse. The familiar scent of woodsmoke and timber hung thick in the air. The steady crackling of the fire carried on as if nothing were amiss. A sound of life while it slipped from Ingrid's grasp with her every labored breath.

Smiling, his *fostra* turned from the hearth. Her smile vanished at the sight of Ingrid.

"She is to claim my bed," Reidar bit out before Gyda could speak. "She burns with fever. Cover her with cooling cloths. Give her your medicines, tend to her as you would to me."

His *fostra's* sharp gaze flicked between him and Ingrid. "Your uncle will want to know why you did not feed this ill thrall to the sea."

Ingrid's heat seemed to have surged into Reidar, blazing hard and furious as he marched to his chamber, Gyda trailing behind. With great care, he laid her down upon the fresh furs.

Her pulse quickened, racing under his fingertips, then slowed, growing faint.

"She is my thrall," he barked, straightening, "and not a concern of my uncle's."

"She is your Great Flaw, breathing and aching in plain sight." Gyda placed her hands on her broad hips and lifted her chin, her gaze cutting to the axe at his waist. "You must staunch it before he catches wind of it, for blood is the tongue he speaks best, my boy."

Reidar stared at Ingrid, thoughts dark and heart full of misgivings. She slept the heavy sleep of the deathly ill, her lovely skin burning up, the otherworldly, elfin features of her homeland sharpened by the journey that had been past her bearing. He sucked in his breath. A big, thick-skulled oaf. He should have known she wasn't made for the rough Northern Sea with its brutal storms and bone-deep cold. He should have understood tearing her from home was akin to uprooting a tender sprig and thrusting it into hostile, foreign soil.

He clenched his jaw. He'd scarcely touched her—not even when he loosened her laces, and her mask slipped for a heartbeat, revealing longing beneath the loathing. He ought to have taken her then, warm and willing. And he ought to have left her in Éire instead of succumbing to his accursed Flaw and enfeebling himself with this daft, unbecoming infatuation. How could he have allowed his heart to stray from the fortress of his body and dwell in his eyes, naked and bleeding for all to see? How could it no longer drum to its own beat, but to the faltering cadence of a sick girl?

"Reidar."

He tore his gaze from the lovely figure on his bed and gave his *fostra* a reassuring nod.

The groove between her brows resembled a cleft in the mountain slopes. There was no fooling Gyda, weathered as she was by the years, sharp-eyed as a hawk, and steadfast as the fjords.

"If you will not dispose of her, you must rule your heart lest it betray you." Her voice rang with the same concern as when he was small and reckless. "You must bury it deep down."

"Only here," he said, standing straighter.

Gyda shook her head. "One look at you, and Vargr will make you Ljosstrond's laughingstock. There will be no coming back from that, let alone claiming what is rightfully yours."

Reidar compressed his mouth against the dull ache in his chest. "Will she live?"

Gyda stared long and hard, then heaved a weary sigh. "I will bring the Irish sorceress back to life for you, my boy."

"This girl is no sorceress." He gave a bitter laugh. "And my boyhood faded long ago."

His *fostra* lifted her chin. "Yes, your boyhood is long gone, Reidar. But a girl who brought a great warrior to his knees? Who, even in her half-death, is unravelling your might and seeping your strength? This 'girl' is a mighty enchantress, if ever I saw one."

Stomach hardening, Reidar took Gyda's old, weathered hands into his and squeezed so hard she sucked in her breath. "I'll give you a large deerskin, two gold amulets, and dress you in the finest wool if you swear not to harm a hair on her head."

He regretted his words outright as the woman's gray eyes filled with hurt. "I need no bribes to cherish what you love, Reidar. Even if I see the error of it."

He knelt before the bed and brushed his fingertips across Ingrid's forehead. It burned with a damp ill fever he knew too well to fool himself.

*She's dying.*

She opened her eyes, bright and unseeing, and mouthed his name.

He snatched his hand away.

His. Name.

"I'm here," he breathed. But her eyes closed. Her small fingers lay weightless in his as he brought them to his lips, longing to breathe life into her. "Seep all my strength, my love. Take everything from me. Only live."

His *fostra's* gasp cut through his anguish like a blade.

"You are done here, Reidar Valorborn." Her voice took on the stern note he hadn't heard in so long, he forgot the sound of it. "You will now go to the mead hall and tell your uncle what he wants to hear."

He stood and went to the door but slammed to a halt. *She thinks she knows best.* He peered at Gyda over his shoulder. "I will burn you alongside her, still breathing, if she dies by your hand."

Reidar would do no such thing to his beloved *fostra*, but the silent scream in Gyda's eyes proved his words had reached her. His stomach clenched as he turned on his heel and went out without a backward glance. Out of her sight, he squared his shoulders and let out a long, steadying breath. Gyda was in no peril. Unlike Ingrid. His heart drummed a thick, sluggish beat at the thought, but he pushed the image of her small helpless shape away and marched to Vargr's hall. To *his* rightful hall.

Outside, his uncle's men were penning the thralls deemed worth keeping. From the still forms stacked just beyond the path, those judged useless had already met the edge of a blade.

They had all been hale before the storm.

Sickened, Reidar peered up at the heavens. *Odin, Allfather, I'll sacrifice to you each day if you spare her.* No answer came, so he straightened and entered the hall with a sprint in his step and a smile on his lips.

Inside, the air reeked of sweat, seawater, and the cloying tang of mead-soaked timber. In the center—carved with knotwork and beasts and draped with rich, soft furs—loomed the jarl's high seat. Reidar's rightful seat. And there reclined his uncle, Vargr Bloodgale, ringed by his *huskarlar*—a vicious band of killers famed for unflinching loyalty to their jarl and unspeakable brutality toward any who defied or stole from him.

Vargr sat unmoving, watching closely as Reidar's men hauled in heavy chests, iron bands glinting in the firelight, the weight of silver and gold making the wood groan. Amid low murmurs and barks of laughter, thralls scurried, stacking trenchers high with meat and bread and pouring mead into drinking horns. Some of the men dropped onto the benches, wolfing down their fare. Others lingered near the fire, gripping their horns, eyes glazed with weariness. The rest stood by, awaiting their turn.

"Nephew." Nothing moved in Vargr's face as he shifted a heavy gaze to Reidar. "You have taken something from me."

Reidar never stole from his uncle. He had neither cause nor desire to feast in Valhalla before his time. But the jarl never missed a chance to turn suspicion toward Reidar.

"I'm heartened to see you too, uncle." He scoffed to mask his racing breath. "I bring you such spoils that we nearly drowned beneath their weight, yet you greet me with charges of thievery?"

Vargr licked his lip with a thoughtful expression. "What of the girl you carried off into your longhouse?"

As one, all heads snapped toward Reidar. The din faded away.

He scanned the mead hall—only Vargr's men and his. A spy in his midst, then. One of his own men stealing off to curry favor with Vargr. And after all he had done for them: skin-tingling adventure, countless women, unspoken riches!

His blood boiled, turning his sight to bursts of hot, bright flashes. But this was neither the hour nor the place for battle rage. With all his might, he unclenched his fists and quelled the pounding in his ears. He would learn the traitor's name in due course.

With a small shrug, Vargr turned to his *huskarlar.* "Will he speak before the next thaw?" A cold smile twisted his thin, bloodless lips as he locked his darkening gaze on Reidar. "The girl, I said."

Reidar's heart dropped to the pit of his stomach, then shot into his throat in uneven, painful thuds. "She is my thrall," he said low, casting a cold glare at Asbjorn, who stood at his uncle's right side. But the troll-spawn had gone before Reidar carried Ingrid toward his longhouse.

A muscle twitching in his jaw, Vargr stared at Reidar as if seeing him for the first time. He surveyed the hall with rounded eyes and raised brows. "*His* thrall!"

Someone snickered. The *huskarlar* gripped their axe hafts.

Reidar tossed a glance at his *hirdmen*. They sat still as a cliff, faces hard and grim.

"Ah!" Vargr slapped himself on the forehead with his meaty hand. "I must have given Reidar leave of this thrall and—" he turned to Asbjorn with a frozen, wide-eyed look—"forgot!"

Asbjorn curled his lip. Two of the *huskarlar* drew their axes from their belts and stepped forward.

Vargr straightened in his high seat. He spat. His wide-eyed look was gone, and in its place hung a grimace of wrath and bloodlust. "Remind me, nephew," he murmured in a voice soft as the hiss of a blade. "When did I give you leave of this thrall that you claim her as *yours*?"

From the hearth, smoke curled like so many vipers, its hungry flames licking at the runes carved into the firestones.

*Odin, hear me.* Reidar stared into the fire, heart thudding like a hammer against an anvil. *Calm my blood and seal my lips against foolish words, Allfather.*

"Forgive me for acting without your leave, uncle, but she is no good to you now." He uncurled his hands and raised his head. "Nor will she be good to any man for a time."

"No?" Vargr pulled a dagger from his belt and hurled it at the floor. It bit into the wood with a low whistle. "Bring her here outright, or do you hunger for a branding iron, young thief?"

Reidar glanced over his shoulder at a sharp gasp. At the fire sat Astrid, pale as soured milk and straight as a rod, her haunted gaze trained on Vargr.

"Uncle." Reidar approached the high seat, scarcely containing the white-hot rage that, despite all his efforts, rolled through him like the blaze in the hearth. But this wasn't the hour for uprising and rebellion. Not with his men bone-weary from the passage. Not with Vargr's *huskarlar* armed and ready to do battle.

"Yes, I took her." He spread his arms with a sharp look at the gathering. "It was a long, bitter crossing, bringing all this here, hmm? We met with a storm that nearly sank us." His men nodded as one. "Make me this small allowance for serving you well."

Reidar lifted his chin and held his uncle's dead gaze. He had backed the vile wretch into a perilous corner. The crew's bedraggled state spoke louder than any claims of storms. And while Vargr ruled by fear, if he failed to honor the sacrifices made, the loyalty given, and the rewards earned, none would raise a blade for him again.

"Hmm." Vargr pushed himself off the high seat and leaned forward. "I think you found the lovely heathen girl you had forfeited your first raid for, when you were only Reidar the Sapling." He pursed his lips and sat back.

"The same one you have crossed all of fair, green Éire for, these past seven winters."

Reidar stood rooted to the spot. Ice, sharp and merciless, spread through him and froze his blood.

"You did not think I knew?" Vargr's hard features twisted into a condescending grin as he rose. It sent Reidar's heartbeat straight into his ears. "Nephew." He scoffed. "Nothing evades my notice. I would bet she is the one you have hidden away from me, your rightful jarl!"

Reidar blinked against a sudden darkness as the walls advanced on him and the hall shrank to the size of a chest. This was not how he'd envisioned his rebellion. His men might even refuse to fight, drained and famished as they were. His heart sank. He must have lost favor with Odin for his reckless entreaty to Christ during the storm.

He gave a hollow chuckle—light and carefree, and not at all tinged with his blood. His anguish surged so close to the surface, another moment, and it would spill into rancor that would surely end in his death. And in Ingrid's.

Every muscle locked, Reidar blew out a long, steadying breath. "My uncle has a good memory!" He addressed the crowd in a voice edged with amusement. "And better imagination! Lovely as she was, the girl had been seven winters dead." He shrugged. "I would know. I was the one who killed her."

"I might die of thirst and hunger if this goes on a moment longer," someone grumbled in the back.

Vargr nodded and waved his hand toward the tables. "Yes, you all are sea worn and hungry. Sit, feast, and drink with me!" He shot Reidar a cold smile as everyone rushed to the benches. "You have done well, nephew. The spoils you brought are plentiful and will enrich us beyond measure. And tomorrow, you will bring the rest of what you owe—of no use or otherwise." He grabbed a cup from a thrall and drained it. "Then I will see for myself if she is the same girl." He winked at Asbjorn. "It is not soon a man forgets a face like hers."

Reidar's mind raced like a gale before a tempest. He had no time to craft a reply. "I cannot bring her." He shook his head. "As I said, uncle, she is no good to anyone now."

Vargr gave a bark of laughter. "Have you plowed her to death then?"

Reidar fell silent. The village had no use for morbidly ill thralls. But with Vargr's keen interest in Ingrid, her life would be forfeit even if she recovered. The untimely deaths of his three wives had been dressed well. The first one fell and broke her neck. The second drowned in the fjord, her neck snapped like a twig when they found her. The third got lost in the wilds, and none could fathom why she'd gone there.

The women shared two things in common—neither was a native of Ljosstrond, and each died soon after the wedding. And though none spoke of it openly, all knew his uncle's dark gaze upon every woman he chose had much to do with it.

"No." Reidar settled on a half-truth, bidding for time. "She fell ill during the storm, but Gyda is seeing to her. She will be restored soon. Are you pleased with the bounty, uncle?"

"I am. And I will have *my* thrall once she is—" Vargr's icy smile made Reidar's stomach churn— "healthy."

The feast was long and generous: roasted boar, fish stew, fresh cheese, honeyed berries, hearth-warm bread. But while Reidar ate and drank no less than the others and jested as well as he'd always done, he hardly tasted his food and couldn't make sense of words.

When it was finally over, and he walked back to his longhouse, trailed by his overdrunk *hirdmen*, he wondered not for the first time if Vargr possessed the power to peer into men's very hearts. For even when Reidar was a boy, his uncle seemed to know his every innermost wish. A chill pierced him at the thought. Perhaps some unknown, malevolent god ruled over Vargr, bending him against all that was good and decent. And at the image of his fevered, dying Ingrid falling into Vargr's hands, Reidar grew cold as a winter sky.

# Chapter Twenty-One

## Rival

***Astrid***

*Then I bring you*
*The ring that was burned*
*In the past with Odin's son;*
*From it, eight rings*
*Of equal weight fall*
*On every ninth night.*
— Skírnismál, stanza 21

Astrid was grateful to be seated, for her knees had gone weak when the jarl threatened Reidar with the branding iron. His pelt hung heavy and drenched, skin chafed raw by salt, and plaits fell wind-frayed about his shoulders. Even so, Reidar Valorborn stood tall and broad like a god, and the thought of fire laid to his beautiful face turned her stomach.

She should have waited for another to mention his wretched thrall, but the urge to be rid of her rival had burned too hot. By the time she placed her plunder chest before Vargr Bloodgale, and he asked what became of Reidar, it blazed like a cursed Christian monastery. So she told him Reidar couldn't attend his jarl, for he'd gone to his longhouse with his new Irish whore.

Now, despite her wobbling knees, Astrid's stomach hardened into a solid, unbreakable mass. A branding iron would serve Reidar right. He hadn't so much as wanted her on the same longship, and she spent the storm in terror of never laying eyes on him again, for deep in her heart she wasn't entirely certain of Valhalla. For all its professed glory, Odin's Hall with its greasy feasting and ceaseless fighting offered little to tempt a woman. Even a shield-maiden.

Astrid curled her lip. When they finally beached in Ljosstrond, Reidar didn't once look in her direction nor ask how she fared during the worst tempest of their lives. No, he was too busy fawning over his accursed thrall, who looked dead to all the world. Astrid's chest had flooded with warmth at the sight of her limp form, and she half-hoped he'd toss the harlot overboard. Instead, he'd carried her to his longhouse!

Reidar's man Ulf scoffed beside her. "Has the storm soured your belly? Not mine. I will eat this mutton if you will not." He winked, reaching for the meat cooling in its grease on her trencher. "My bed awaits tonight, Astrid, since *another—*" he raised his brows—"is warming Reidar's."

She glared into the flames. "Find someone else. I have no taste for anything tonight."

Seven winters past, all had heard the strange tale after Reidar's return from his first voyage. But though he claimed to have killed the girl, Astrid didn't believe it. It wasn't in Reidar's nature to harm lovely, powerless women—or anyone who wasn't a match for his strength. Besides, the girl would have been his first blood, and surely, he'd not boast of such meager prey. Of all in Ljosstrond, Astrid was the first to grasp why he returned time and again to Éire and explored no other shore. For it was after that voyage that he had changed toward her.

While Astrid always burned with passion for Reidar, she was no fool. She understood he was a man she could never keep to herself. Yet none of his other entanglements troubled her. All his thralls and free women alike had only been passing fancies, for he returned to her each time. Yet day by day he grew cold. After a time, he no longer seemed present during their lovemaking, as if lost to another place, with another lover. And in her heart, Astrid knew who it was.

"Come, Astrid." Ulf bent to her ear. "We have always fared well together."

"Leave me be." She nudged away from him. She'd used Ulf before to wound Reidar and might do so again, but not tonight.

She couldn't even be sure Reidar ever loved her. Worst of all, she felt in her marrow he wouldn't wed her, no matter how often she spoke of it. For she never saw the love in his eyes for her that he had for this wretched thrall.

Astrid marked her rival the moment she saw the girl in her hideous husband's hall. Thorsten had done her a great favor when he killed him, though now Astrid wished he hadn't. But it was when Reidar stormed in with murder in his eyes that she knew he'd found his precious harlot at last. Orm the Oaf had truly earned his name then. Did he not realize what he'd dared to touch?

Now, with Odin's favor, the heathen would die, and Astrid would finally be free of her. Then, she'd love Reidar back to her and make him forget the specter who kept them apart. Maybe they would even wed, and with her father and brothers, she'd rally everyone to unseat Vargr, and Reidar would become jarl. It would take time and patience, for she saw the storm in his eyes as he ate without tasting and joked without laughing. But she was a patient kind.

Her heart leapt when Reidar and a few of his *hirdmen* stood and headed to the door.

"There he goes." Ulf chuckled. "Come, Astrid. We have shared worse nights."

Paying Ulf no mind, she followed Reidar out of the mead hall as he made his way home, shoulders slumped and head down.

"Reidar—" She caught up with his long strides, ignoring his men, who swayed with drink, shouted nonsense, and burst into bawdy songs.

But he only shook his head and kept walking.

"Reidar." Astrid bolted in front of him, forcing him to halt.

He may have laughed and jested in the hall, but now he wore his true face—wretched, hopeless, desperate.

"I wish to be alone, Astrid." He walked around her. "You have done well. Go rest."

Hot tears burned her eyes. She tightened her jaw so hard it hurt. "Come to my bed, Reidar. I will make it better—you know I will." She sought his gaze, nearly running to keep up with him. "The girl is ill, is she not? She is no good to you now—you said so yourself." She tried to reach for his cheek but missed. "Come, my love. I will make you forget, even if for a moment."

He came to a halt, and her heart soared with hope.

"Astrid." He took her hand, making her stomach flutter.

"I am a lost man." He squeezed her fingers, his eyes so glum she shuddered. "I do not even know who I am anymore, nor if our gods are the true ones. Forget me, Astrid. Find someone who can give you all you deserve."

An icy chill crept along Astrid's spine. She pushed it down.

"Do not speak so, my love." She gripped his fingers. "You know well who you are. You are Reidar Valorborn, the son of Harald Fairblade. The rightful jarl of Ljosstrond!"

He shook his head and made to withdraw his hand, but she held on tight.

"It is obvious you have been charmed." Her words burst through in a hot whisper. "That girl, lovely as she is, is a powerful sorceress! Anyone can see she cast her dark Christ magic to confuse your thoughts and pull you away from your people and from me. But our gods are the true ones, and look how they are punishing her for daring to take our best from us! Let her go, my love. Come back to me."

The gloom left his eyes, and bright, weightless tingles fluttered in Astrid's stomach.

He gave a faint scoff. "It may be she had charmed me, even when I was a boy. For it is as though some great power is pulling me away from all I once held sure. But that power fills me with light, Astrid, not with darkness." He dropped his hand. "I am sorry this brings you unrest. It is not what I wish. But you would do well to heed my words and forget me. My heart has been taken for a long time now."

He turned and walked away, leaving her trembling and gulping against the thickness in her throat.

"What does that daughter of rot have that I do not?" she spat when Reidar's large form vanished from sight. Jaw clenched, she glared at the sky. "I will sacrifice to you greatly tonight, Freya, to rid me of the troll's whelp in my beloved's bed. For I see she will not go willingly. She had made her defiance clear in Dalaradia. But if it is your will that she lives, Freya—" Astrid balled her fists—"then, let it be my life's work to bring about her ruin, no matter the cost."

# Chapter Twenty-Two

## Fever
***Reidar***

**Third Night**

*I don't want the ring,*
*Even though it was burned*
*In the past with Odin's son;*
*In Gymir's home*
*There is no shortage of gold*
*With the wealth my father holds.*
— Skírnismál, stanza 22

A swift movement pulled Reidar from a thick, tangled dream of bloody axe blades, crushing waves, and dimming eyes filled with reproach and defeat.

"By Odin..." Relief, light and tingling, rolled through him at the sight of Ingrid seated in bed and staring ahead.

She still wore her Irish gown, tattered from the storm, but he'd told Gyda to leave it on. If the gods spared her, the last thing he wanted was for her to awaken undressed in his bed when he hadn't so much as breathed on her. Now, her gown slipped from one pale shoulder, and the thin light of early dawn caught in her hair and eyes. A flare of burnished bronze and emerald fire against his carved wooden headboard.

The straw mattress creaked beneath his weight as he rose onto one elbow, allowing himself a grin and seeking the right Irish words.

For the last two days, fever battered and ravaged her, burning through her lovely body with such relentless fury, he felt consumed by it, too. She'd surfaced once, when Gyda placed cold linen cloths on her head and chest. With eyes trained on him, glassy yet searching, Ingrid mumbled something in Irish. But when the cloths grew warm, the fever had dragged her under again, leaving her trembling and drenched in sweat.

But she looked healed now.

The knot twisting in his chest gave way. "Better?" he ventured in Norse, failing with his Irish.

She fixed her gaze on him, steady and unblinking. And full of the familiar loathing.

He winced as she sank back onto the bed and shut her eyes. If she loathed him before, she'd likely want vengeance now. But he would sacrifice to Odin and Thor all the same for sparing her. The gods had been silent long enough.

He brushed a hand along her shoulder, damp and warm to the touch. "Ingrid."

Her lashes fluttered.

"I swear to you I will think of something," he said in Norse, free to lay bare his heart without risking scorn. "I will burn this whole land to cinders before I let him near you. I will lay waste to all he holds dear—"

Reidar fell silent as Ingrid peered at him with eyes that looked like two green lakes in her wan face. He drew back. She wasn't looking at him at all.

"Ingrid!"

She didn't reply. The fever returned with brutal force, her body shuddering and skin blazing, her sense slipping away.

Reidar stood and charged outside, cursing his ill fate. There was no need to wake Gyda—he could soak linen in cold rainwater as well as his *fostra*. He returned in short order and placed the cooling cloths on Ingrid's forehead, chest, arms, and legs. Her body softened against the furs, but he kept vigil through the night lest she take a turn for the worse.

The fever still burned on Ingrid's brow when the sun climbed into the restless, cloud-torn sky. But the worst of the heat ebbed, and her breath steadied.

Chest weighted with lead, Reidar dressed and went out. Since his return to Ljosstrond, he threw himself into the familiar rhythm of homecoming—ensuring the spoils were accounted for, inspecting his longships, seeing to the blades dulled by salt and battle. For two nights he sat in Vargr's mead hall, forcing his thoughts away from his chamber. And though his dutiful feasting with his men and listening to their boasts and laughter brought no relief, he thanked all the gods for turning his uncle's eye from the ailing girl and for pressing Astrid to loosen her hold on him.

She'd appeared cheerful enough as she drank and laughed with his man Ulf, then left with him at night. But today, she sat beside Reidar with a wry smile and a sly twinkle in her eye.

"How does our thrall fare?" She brushed her fingertips along his arm. "Still fevered?"

He knitted his brows with a glance at the high seat. Vargr spoke with the visiting Danes, but his uncle's hearing was sharper than most knew.

"Oh, do not worry, he is too busy with the Danes." Astrid lowered her voice and leaned in as if to plant a kiss. "They are speaking of alliances and military support," she murmured into his ear. "Now we are back, it is time to return to our plans, Reidar. Neither I nor your men can suffer his rule much longer. Or have you grown so soft for your bed-warmer that you would let your rightful claim slip through your fingers?"

Heat surging through him, Reidar pulled Astrid close with a rigid arm. "Bloodgale's spies are everywhere," he bit out, fighting the urge to give her a good shake. "Have you lost your wits to speak of such things here?"

"They hear nothing—look how gone in drink they are." She pressed her lips to his neck. "It is time to awaken from your enchantment, Reidar Valorborn."

He released her so fast she swayed. "Who are you to order me around, woman?"

Stiff as a post, he went out and marched back to his longhouse. Astrid was becoming a real pebble in his boot. Her will had always been strong and her stubborn streak fiercer still, but her refusal to heed his words wearied him. Could she not see his interest had waned?

Yet Reidar's troubles with Astrid fell away the moment he stepped into his chamber. A steaming cloth lay draped across Ingrid's fevered brow. The sharp scent of meadowsweet mingled with the faint bitterness of yarrow and willow bark. Beside the bed stood the source of the smell—a wooden bowl half filled with muddy liquid. But the brew had been prepared in vain, for dark stains marked the front of Ingrid's shift and the furs beneath her limp form.

Kneeling at her side, her back to the door, Gyda murmured the steady chant of *galdr*. With careful fingers, she traced healing runes over Brigit's wrist, smudging the damp sheen of sweat. Head bent, she poured a slow stream of mead from a cup into a shallow bowl at her feet, the amber liquid gleaming in the candlelight.

"Heal this wretched stranger, Eir," she whispered, "even if you see the error of it, for Reidar's heart is bound to her beyond all reason."

Reidar pulled in his breath, coming back to himself. Ingrid was out of her gown, wearing only her sweat-soaked shift that clung to her every breathtaking curve as if to mock him with what never was and likely never would be.

Startled, Gyda whirled around. Reidar had never seen his *fostra's* eyes so wide and face so pale.

Ice, sharp and punishing, filled his veins and froze him to the spot. "Is she...dying?" He forced out, his voice coming as if from elsewhere.

"I would not wager on it." With a strange, choked sound, Gyda reached for a small bundle on the floor and lifted it toward him—a scrap of linen with something hidden inside. "She yet lives and will likely outlive us all, for she is indeed a great sorceress."

His poor *fostra* stood and approached, holding the cloth at arm's length. "Look what I found on her when I undressed her!"

He took the bundle from Gyda's trembling hand and unraveled it. Like the brightest ray of sun, a burst of warmth shot through him at the sight.

"This was in her belt!" His *fostra's* voice emerged thin and shrill. "Tell me, Reidar, what is this Christian doing with a twig in the shape of our Algiz?"

Reidar traced a fingertip along the little twig. It appeared even smaller now—a tiny, fragile remnant of Éire in his large palm, like the girl who kept it all these winters. He wrapped the twig in linen and closed his trembling fingers around it. She kept it despite his unforgivable desertion, despite being bound to another, despite drowning him in loathing and scorn. It had meant so much, she'd tucked it into her belt and carried it across the sea.

A mournful sob escaped from Gyda's lips. "She will bring bad luck on our heads! Even now Vargr sees through your game. This enchantress will give him cause to see you ruined!"

Reidar slid the cloth beneath his pillow. Ingrid's cheeks glowed as if lit from within, bright against her pale lips. The heat radiating from her lovely shape would be enough to melt the ice in anyone's heart.

*It is obvious you have been charmed.*

Unbidden, Astrid's words flew back at him. Two women in his life thought Ingrid a sorceress. Likely, she was. But what did it matter now she was dying? He swallowed against his tightening throat. Despite his *fostra's* fears, the girl was half-gone.

"Ach, you are hexed!" Gyda stared at him, stricken. "I shall call upon the *volva* for aid!"

Trying not to frown, Reidar took the old woman's hands into his. She was only steeped in superstition and frightened out of her wits. "Do not fret for me, Gyda. I am not hexed." He forced a smile. "When I met Ingrid in Éire seven winters past, I found this twig in her hair and gave it to her. She kept it all this time—do you understand?"

"Oh, I understand!" His *fostra* wrenched her hands from his. "She kept it and worked her evil Christ magic on you, luring you to her and making you a fool for her. Please, Reidar, let me burn it. Let me save you from her dark charms, my boy!"

Reidar straightened. "It will remain beneath my pillow until her last..." He gulped. "Until she is healed. And you will continue to gather your herbs, and make your salves, tinctures, and poultices to tend to her until she does."

After Gyda left, he sank down beside Ingrid, staring at her wasting form. He'd seen sixteen winters when the *volva* came to his father's longhouse—old, bent, and smelling of ash and earth. Frightening Gyda, she'd come to a halt upon seeing Reidar. Without asking leave, she'd dropped to the floor and cast her runes by the fire. "Your fate lies in a strange land," she muttered through her thin lips, "with a stranger to Norway, but not to you." A deep, fierce shiver shook her, stilling her daft words. "This person should have been here from the start, for your paths have long been bound," she'd choked out. "Yet this stranger bears a great threat to our gods—how they writhe and tremble at the might buried within."

The *volva* was a fool and a fraud. His fate lay here in Ljosstrond, in his rightful seat of power—with Ingrid or without. As for the threat—Reidar gave a bitter scoff. What threat was Ingrid to the gods when she couldn't even save herself?

# Chapter Twenty-Three

## Wages
***Reidar***

**Fourth Night**

*See, maiden,*
*This sharp, bright sword*
*That I hold in my hand?*
*I will chop off your head*
*From your neck*
*If you don't do as I say.*
— Skírnismál, stanza 23

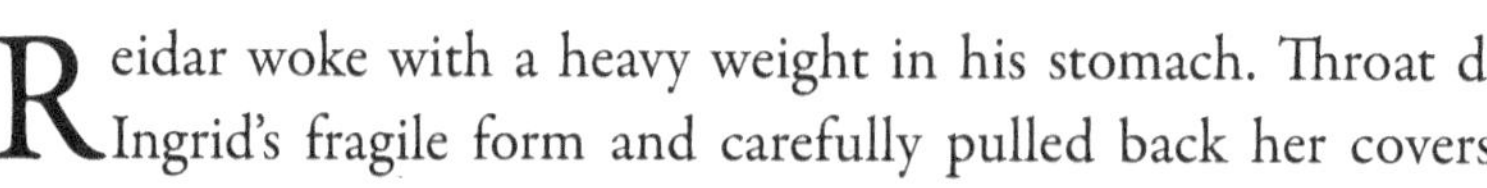

Reidar woke with a heavy weight in his stomach. Throat dry, he eyed Ingrid's fragile form and carefully pulled back her covers. A wraith made of moonbeams and morning dew, she was no longer of this realm. A creature of her native otherworld—her hair a tangle of dark seaweed, cheekbones sharp upon her breathtaking face, two bright red spots burning through her pallor. In all the world, there was no one like her, nor ever would be.

He closed his eyes. *Odin, grant her health, and I will honor you with my every breath. Grant her life and take mine in her stead if you must.*

No answer came, and she lay as still as before. Abruptly, her chest rose, and her fevered breathing became wheezing.

Heart racing, Reidar shot to his feet. "Gyda!"

The old woman stumbled over to the bed, rubbing sleep from her widening eyes. "Cold wraps," she choked out, the whites bright around gray irises.

Reidar wore only his undertunic, yet the biting night air barely touched him as he burst outside and grabbed an overflowing rain bucket, water sloshing over his bare feet like ice. By the time he returned, Gyda had pushed the furs aside and spread a clean sheet across the floor.

Ingrid weighed next to nothing as he lifted her and laid her down, wheezing and choking. In an instant, her ill fever heated the wraps Gyda had packed over her, long rivulets running down into the floorboards. The wheezing ceased, and Ingrid's breath faded to a whisper. So faint he could scarcely hear it.

His hands curled into fists until his knuckles ached. She'd kept his twig. The chamber narrowed to the thinning sound of her breath and the terror of coming silence. He should have laid everything bare while there was still time. Then she would have fought to live.

Gyda sank down beside Ingrid. "I have done all I could for her, my boy," she squeezed out through trembling lips. "In the name of your mother, who loved me well, I beg for a clean death before you set fire to me alongside this wretched creature."

A tearing, skewering ache pierced Reidar through the core and robbed him of his own breath. The ground shattered beneath him as he plummeted into a pitch-dark hollow, from which he'd never find his way home. How cruelly Loki laughed in Asgard. The sound scraped through his heart like a blade, leaving blood and ash in its wake.

He knelt beside the dying girl and buried his face in her chest—damp, soft, and smoldering with heat. *Save her, Odin.*

The small cross she wore around her neck dug into his forehead. He clenched his jaw. Even here, among the true gods, her unseen God reigned supreme, for He was taking her from him.

Reidar raised his head to be met with his *fostra's* unblinking eyes.

"My poor Gyda." He softened his voice against the spreading emptiness inside. "You have grown old and foolish to think I would ever hurt you, let alone kill you. Pay no mind to what is spoken in fear and grief. You have done all you could. Now, leave me."

He stared ahead as Gyda left his chamber, whispering unnecessary words of love and gratitude.

Jaw locked, he closed his eyes. "Odin, Allfather, forgive me."

His heart pounded like a death knell as he traced the sign of the cross over Ingrid's chest and then across his own.

"Save her, Christ, God of Éire, for she loves and worships you." He bowed his head low as he'd seen Christians do. "If you let her live, I swear I will sacrifice to you, and I will love her always and forever, and I will die before I let any harm come to her."

But like Odin, Christ was silent, so Reidar picked up Ingrid's limp body and eased her back onto the bed.

At his ear, Loki gave a dark snicker. *How many times do you mean to kill her, fool?*

Reidar covered his face with his cold hands, but Loki's words rang like a blow. He killed her three times: when he left her for dead on Rathlin, when he took her freedom in Dalaradia, when he ripped her from all she'd ever known and hauled her to Ljosstrond. And though he worshiped and sacrificed his whole life, no god ever stopped him in his foolish pursuit of her destruction. Not Odin. Not Thor. Not Freyr. Maybe they weren't even there. Or maybe they were and did not care a whit for him.

"Ingrid—" The numbness spread into every part of him as he sank onto the bed's edge beside her small, still shape in its soaked-through shift. Her chest no longer rose and fell, but when he leaned in, a faint puff of air brushed against his cheek.

Her last breath—just for him.

A crushing ache cleaved through him, folding him in half. Rocking, he grasped her cooling hand and pressed it to his lips. "I would have loved you well, my Ingrid. I would have burned this world for you, and if that were not enough, I would burn it again." A strangled sob burst from his throat, terrible as a wolf's howl. "But your God is a jealous kind, and who could fault Him? Were I Him, I would want you all to myself, too."

Something warm and contemptuous rolled down his cheek, and he tore at it with the rage and viciousness he could neither spill nor swallow. "You will not feast with me in Valhalla, my love, for you are surely on your way to your daft Heaven now." He staggered to his feet, wishing to kill, maim, and plunder all that still breathed in this miserable world.

The bed shifted as he stumbled against it. Ingrid's body tipped with the motion, lips drained of color, fingers stiff upon the furs.

The wages of his reckless longing struck the air from his lungs. The fruit of his covetous heart crushed the strength from his limbs. The walls pressed in. The chamber tightened like a fist.

Something was wrong with his hands as he struggled to dress. He dragged his pelt over his shoulders askew. He wrenched it straight.

"Forgive me if you can," he choked out before lumbering from the chamber. "I loved you the only way I knew how."

Reidar found the mead hall free of the Danes and abuzz with the same tall tales and bawdy laughter he'd heard countless times before. How could anyone laugh and jest on such a day?

From the hearth, smoke curled thick with the scent of pine pitch and roasting fat. A tang of sweat and damp wool clung to the air, stirred by the shuffle of boots on packed earth. At the high seat, Vargr contemplated the gathering with sharp eyes, hand resting on the hilt of his blade.

"Ah, at last my nephew deigns to appear among us." He pinned Reidar with an unblinking glare. "I trust my thrall has recovered by now."

To his right, Asbjorn scoffed. The *huskarlar* fixed Reidar with dark stares.

Reidar felt his chest caving in. Why did he keep returning to the very place that fed his ruin? He squared his shoulders and tightened his fists.

"I said, bring her!" Vargr's voice strained, like a plank about to snap in half. "I will not ask again."

Trembling, Reidar stumbled out of the hall. He ached to sink his axe into Vargr Bloodgale's ugly head. He longed to throttle and kill him with his bare hands. He wished he'd never been born. But those were dreams, so he would bring Vargr Ingrid's corpse, then take her deep into the wilds and bury her there as was the Christians' way. He would mark her resting place with a cross and go back to his empty life to live it out in senseless strife and plunder until the Valkyries came to take him to the equally empty Valhalla, where he would wither for all eternity.

The thought of lowering her into the cold, hard earth made his sight go black at the edges. Then it struck him that Gyda would have found her unbreathing in his bed, and for fear of her spirit, weighed her down and sunk her in a bog.

# Chapter Twenty-Four

## Mercy
***Brigit***

*I will never suffer for anyone's sake*
*To be moved by power;*
*But gladly, I think, Gymir will seek*
*To fight if he finds you here."*
— Skírnismál, stanza 24

Earlier that day, an unsettling dream haunted Brigit. It stole upon her, thick with misgivings and hot with unrelenting fever, as all her mind wanderings had been since she found herself in this strange, heathen place. In her dream, she was back in the wood of her girlhood, picking wild strawberries with the boy Reidar. It was a stifling summer day. The great red sun smoldered her skin through her gown and burned her flesh with its sharp, fiery rays. But the forest was free of savages, and oddly, Reidar wore a white *léine* and Irish sandals. Still, his hair was styled as a Norseman's which, for reasons unfathomable, only made him more beautiful.

Despite the punishing heat, they laughed and fed each other wild strawberries, talking freely in the same tongue.

"Ingrid—" He reached into her basket for another berry, but they'd eaten them all, so he put it aside and bent to kiss her. His eyes were just as she remembered—the lightest shade of blue and sitting above high, broad cheekbones.

"Ingrid," he said into her mouth, his lips warm and tasting of strawberries.

"Reidar," she echoed. "You ought to call me Brigit."

He ignored her, deepening the kiss, his beard soft against her skin. An unbidden glimpse of his rough, patterned cheek tore her from her stupor. Reidar had vanished, and she found herself in the arms of her captor. Beside her basket lay his hideous rope and gruesome axe. She flailed against his hard bulk. How did she not see it before? Her heart raced like a wild steed as she tried to push him away, but he didn't budge.

"Do not fight it, Ingrid. Let it be."

She peered into his eyes, stunned. They belonged to the boy Reidar. But Reidar, with his kind eyes and warm lips, had always been a heathen barbarian. She heard more of them now. Soon, they would set fire to the monastery, murder her father, and drag away her mother.

Her captor's breath at her neck burned hotter than the sun, searing her to ash. And yet she would have rather turned to cinders than be parted from him now. Her stomach dropped. This was wrong, wicked, sinful.

"Where is Reidar?" she breathed, fighting the longing that carried her away like a wild reel. "What have you done with him?"

"Reidar is gone." The savage with Reidar's eyes reached for his rope.

"Let me go." But Brigit pulled him closer instead, her body ablaze.

"Never." He tied her wrists. "Never again."

Brigit's voice rose in her throat, raw with the need to demand her freedom from his hold. But she had no breath left in her lungs, so she thrashed, panting and wheezing. Another moment and she would suffocate.

She gasped, no longer in a dream. Through the thick, dizzy haze, her captor said something urgent to the older woman. The fleeting thought returned—she couldn't be his mother, for they looked nothing alike. But none of it mattered now, for her very breath had failed Brigit, and at last, death stood waiting.

To her bitter disappointment, Brigit did not die. Instead, she stirred to find herself prostrate on something rough and unyielding, at once burning up and rigid with cold. In a flickering light, a flash of two pale-blue pools trained on her with a fierceness she once found life-giving. But no longer. She'd had her fill of this life that had always been too much and not enough.

How bone-weary she was of struggling, fighting, fearing, and loathing. How deeply she despised the very weight of living. Mercifully, the ague that struck her must have been the sort that would have felled her father—had the Norsemen not beaten it to the task.

At long last, the Lord was calling her home, and she yearned to bow to His will. But she'd left one thing undone—or rather, unsaid. So, she continued to fight, struggle, fear, and loathe.

Another flash of her Norseman's haunted eyes. Another glimpse of his large, helpless hands. Another stroke from his kinswoman, who was neither beautiful nor mild in speech but had the gentlest touch and, in truth, the kindest eyes Brigit had ever seen. It had been so long since anyone was gentle or kind to her, and for that alone, she was forever indebted to her.

A pity Brigit would never repay this debt, for her fever seemed to worsen with each heartbeat despite her relentless fighting. Now it burned so fiercely, it twisted every bone in her body and stole her remaining breath. This new agony was too great, and as the woman packed her with cooling cloths while chanting her futile incantations, Brigit understood it was her fate to leave that one thing undone. So she asked the Lord's forgiveness for her many sins, and then she stopped fighting.

The pain receded, along with struggling, fearing, and loathing—all that made up her pitiful life. And in its place sprouted a thin thread of light. Delighted, she took hold of it. The thread grew wider and brighter. It turned into a path.

*I'm on my way, Father—*

"Ingrid—"

The light receded.

The loathing returned. Why did he insist on calling her by this heathen name? She wished to tell him she was christened Brigit, after the great Kildare saint, famous for her many miracles. She longed to say she was a woman grown, not his to name as he pleased. She ached to declare it was she who kissed him in his sick chamber and not his awful "sweetheart." She yearned to whisper the one thing she would now never say, for not a wisp of air remained in her chest.

The thread of light reappeared as her Norseman leaned in, his heart-breaking eyes wide and naked.

An instant left—a final mercy. Brigit parted her lips one last time. *Loathing you was a lie I told myself to survive your cold farewell, the bitter winters that followed, and your return clad in blood and plunder. But I cannot help it. I love you, my Reidar.*

The light swelled, replacing all that ever was. It lit her path and filled her with peace and joy she never knew before. She ascended higher and higher, carried by its gentle warmth, awed by its amazing grace.

"But what of him—down below?" Her words were at once thought and sound, soft, sorrowful, pleading. "Now, he would never find hope, nor shall we ever meet again."

The light dimmed. Her journey came to a halt.

"Your quest is rife with heartache and torment." The voice was of a Father—of thousands of fathers. "Come home."

Brigit didn't see the Speaker, but she knew Him, so she sank to her knees and bowed her head. And as she knelt there, she thought of the young Norseman with cool eyes and a warm heart, of being parted from him for all eternity, and of his soul—for he surely had one—never knowing God's boundless love.

So she bent lower still and let the truth spill from the depths of her soul. "Father, I thank You for this mercy, but I'd been too rash to ask it. Lead me in Your ways and teach me to do Your will."

# Chapter Twenty-Five

## Power
***Reidar***

**Fifth Night**

*Do you see, maiden, this sharp, bright sword*
*That I hold in my hand?*
*The old giant will bend before its blade—*
*Your father is doomed to die.*
— Skírnismál, stanza 25

Head swarming with dark visions of Ingrid's body sinking into the bog, Reidar barreled back to his longhouse and burst into his chamber like one in the thick of a battle rage. He stopped short at the threshold, struck mute at the sight within. In his bed, reclining against the pillows, sat Ingrid—damp strands plastered to her forehead, but eyes open and clear. Beside her stood Gyda, wiping her brow and patiently feeding her rich mutton broth with bits of marrow mixed in.

*She lives.* This irrefutable truth rang through his lifeblood like a victory horn over the fjord.

Ingrid's stare pierced him to his core, draining the remnants of his rage and anguish.

"Tell her I can eat myself," she said in Irish, dropping her gaze. "I'm not a child."

Reidar shot Gyda a look. "Give her the spoon," he said stupidly in Norse.

"And let her have leave of her hands?" Gyda scoffed. "So she can make that Christian sign over me and hex me, too? I might be old, but I am not yet senile!"

As if in a daze, Reidar studied Ingrid. Her fevered flush and unhealthy pallor had vanished without a trace. Though thinner, she looked as well as when he found her in Dalaradia. And while he was certain he'd imagined it, he could have sworn a fleeting smile brushed her lips.

"How does she yet live?" Mind fuddled, he turned to Gyda. "When I left, she was not...breathing."

Gyda sat the bowl on the small table beside the bed. "Odin must have heard your prayers," she muttered, keeping an eye cast on Ingrid as the girl tried to lift her hand. "No!" Gyda's voice emerged shrill as a gull's cry. "You will not charm me, sorceress!"

An incomprehensible small giggle escaped from Ingrid's lips—a sound sweeter than anything Reidar had ever heard. He'd never seen her smile until now, and all her pretty frowns and scowls paled beside this rare, unguarded glow.

His *fostra's* eyes widened. "She is laughing at me!" Gyda drew back. "She has already set upon her evil work!"

Reidar stifled a long sigh. The old woman had lingered long enough. "You are in no peril, Gyda." He pointed his chin toward the door. "I had begged Odin—it is true—but he was not the one who answered. It was her God, and I did not even sacrifice to him."

Ingrid made a strange sound—something between a scoff and a snort.

They both stared at her. Did she suddenly find Norse funny?

"She may well be an enchantress," he continued, trying his best to ignore Gyda's deepening frown, "but if her God is so powerful He brings people back from the dead, then such enchantment would be a gift of fate."

"Powerful, hmm..." Gyda compressed her lips. "I see you wish to be alone with her." She headed for the door. "I will leave you then. Surely, she cannot hex you worse than she already has."

Reidar turned to Ingrid as Gyda stepped out, fighting to keep his face still. Ingrid's cheeks flooded with color—not the furious crimson of all-consuming fever, but the delicate hue of rose petals.

"I—think—" He couldn't form the Irish words, for his body responded in the most inconvenient way. "I thought you—dead."

She pursed her lips as if considering her reply. "I was," she said in perfect Norse.

Reidar blinked hard. Blinked again. The joy of seeing her alive, mixed with his unbearable longing, must have played a trick on his ears.

"How—?" He spread his arms. "You—living?"

She studied her hands. "Do not ask this. I cannot tell you."

Reidar drew back a pace. Her response to his crude Irish was in Norse—there was no mistaking it. She spoke it as well as anyone in Ljosstrond, her lovely voice stringing each word into a birdsong.

A misgiving, thick as the mist over the fjord, filled Reidar to the brim. Gyda may have been right all along. The girl was likely a powerful sorceress, and he was doomed to lose his mind and fate. Already, he'd let go of reason to allow her stand between him and his *blodhefnd*.

He squared his shoulders. He should seek the *volva's* aid to break the enchantment. He should retreat into the wilds and seclude himself until her power faded away. And above all else, he should never lay eyes on her again.

He ran a stiff hand down his plaits. Her enchantment was the sweetest joy he'd ever known. To be rid of it was to live without breath.

"How is it... How do you speak my tongue?" he choked out.

"I do not know that either." She glanced up through her thick, dark lashes. "I had died—this I know. But with Him all things are possible."

"Him—?" Reidar cast a wild look around.

A sharp knock on the door made them both lurch. It swung open, and in stepped Gyda, her eyes cold.

"The accursed Asbjorn is outside." She wiped her stiff hands on her skirts. "Vargr wants to see the thrall—now."

Reidar's fingers bit into his palms. "Does he, then?" A searing wave of heat swept through him, straining muscle and sinew. With all his might, he pushed it down. Not yet. But soon. In due time, he would rise up against the dog-born oath breaker and make him pay in blood.

"Who is Vargr?"

Ingrid's faltering voice brought him back to himself. He stiffened, catching sight of Gyda's face with its slackened mouth and unfocused gaze.

"By Freya..." The old woman leaned against a wall, gasping for air. "By all the gods of Asgard, how does she speak our tongue?" Her eyes flashed. "And why did you not warn me, Re—"

"Learned it from the Danes," he cut in. "The ones who were there—before."

Both women stared at him with rounded eyes.

"Help her with washing and dressing," he bit out before Gyda blurted the name he'd guarded like his blade since the day he found Ingrid.

He knew it in his marrow—she had to speak it first. For even if his face and soul had changed beyond all knowing, some part of him must remain. And it wasn't whether she recognized him that mattered, but whether she wanted to. It had to come from her—clear, certain, and unclouded by fever or doubt.

"Make haste, Gyda, for I am to bring her before the *jarl*." Reidar spat the word as if it were poison.

With great effort, he closed the door behind him instead of slamming it. Then he paced the length of his empty hall, blood afire and gut clenched like a stone. The time to unseat Vargr was fast upon him. Though he'd likely lost Astrid's backing—and with it, the strength of her father and six brothers—he could yet win most of his men to his side, given the right words. Still, the weight of knowing lay heavy in his chest—the winds did not blow in his favor. While Reidar's warriors were fierce and battle-tested, Vargr's men were many and vicious. They fought like ravening beasts, with savagery and bloodlust. Not to conquer but to destroy.

He needed a clear mind, a careful plan, and more time. But fate offered no such mercy, for he'd meant it—he'd sooner die than let Vargr touch one shining hair on Ingrid's head. Reidar tightened his hand on the fine gold inlay of his Shadowbane's pommel. It might be today that he would raise his father's gift in vengeance.

His chamber's door creaked open, and Gyda peeked out with a thoughtful expression.

"The sorceress is ready—" she dropped her voice—"and may she hex your uncle so he would at last plunge into madness that stalks him since birth."

With a scoff, Reidar entered his chamber. Ingrid sat on the bed, dressed in one of Gyda's thick woolen gowns that now looked fit for a queen. On her feet were her own fur-lined boots, and her hair, as well as a good part of her face lay hidden beneath a long, trailing scarf.

Frowning, he searched Gyda's eyes.

"It is to make her appear less bea—" Gyda blinked and fell silent.

Ingrid lifted her chin. "I do not wish to go before this jarl." She met Reidar's gaze. "I thought *you* were the jarl!"

Reidar's stomach clenched so hard it hurt. "I am not the jarl," he ground out. "And you will go whether you wish it or not. You may speak our tongue, but you know nothing of our customs if you think you have a choice."

The girl shrank back as he neared the bed, but he lacked the strength for gentleness while bracing for a fight to the death. He seized her hand and drew her up to stand. His throat closed as she swayed like a reed in the wind. If he hadn't caught her, she would have surely tumbled to the floor.

They stared at each other as he held her in his arms—small, soft, and living. And for the second time this day, the fight drained out of him like mead from a cracked horn. He wished never to let her go. He longed to carry her out, put her in a fishing skiff, and sail until they were so far from this place it ceased to exist.

But such notions were for children and fools. So he slid an arm beneath her knees and swept the other round her shoulders, fighting the memory of the Rathlin Island wood as it rose within him, warm and tingling. Then, struggling to ignore her sudden pallor, he walked out of his longhouse and marched to his uncle's—to do his bidding for the last time.

The din in the mead hall receded as Reidar entered with Ingrid cradled close. He stopped at the entrance, scanning the gathering. All his *hirdmen* were there, their faces relaxed and contented with food and drink. His ribs tightened like a vise. They would not wish to fight on a full stomach and without notice.

"Ah, at long last—" Vargr leaned back in his high seat, licking his lip—"I am granted the rare pleasure of beholding my own thrall!"

His words drew a handful of chuckles and a single long whistle.

Reidar froze as Ingrid dug her small fingers into his arm. She was staring at his uncle, her face white as snow.

Heart hammering, Reidar crushed her to his chest.

"Put her down." Vargr's order struck him like a whip.

Reidar let out a long, steadying breath. "She is not well enough to stand."

"Then why was she not dragged to the midden with the rest of the scraps?" Vargr scanned the hall with widened eyes. "Oh, I know why! She has recovered, and you have been keeping her from me!"

Ingrid went limp in Reidar's arms, releasing her frantic hold on him. Her gaze traveled beyond the timber walls, to a place unknown.

An ugly, cold smile spread over Vargr's face. "Bring her here, nephew."

The menace in his uncle's voice sent a sharp ache through Reidar's hand, making it long for Shadowbane. One leap, one strike, and he would silence the vile scum forever.

Reidar scanned his men, locking eyes with each in turn—the time had come.

Back straight, he approached the high seat. "Stand," he said to Ingrid. "I will help you."

He knew precisely what would happen next. Vargr would try to take her from him or see her slain. Either would ignite the bloodshed.

Ingrid stared at Reidar with still eyes as he planted her down on her feet, trembling and wobbling. Then he held her by the waist, propping her up from behind. It seemed Gyda had dressed her in two of her gowns to hide her thinness.

Vargr's dead gaze bored into the girl. "Let her stand on her own."

Without warning, Ingrid wrenched from his arms. She floated to the floor in a flurry of skirts. The scarf slipped off her head, revealing her wan face and a cascade of long, bronze coils of hair.

"By Odin's blind eye, my nephew has lied to us all!" A tight muscle jumped in Vargr's jaw. "How could he have killed the girl if she is here?" Lips pursed, as if in deep contemplation, he stared at the gathering. "Lying, cheating, stealing—so many offenses, I fear Reidar can no longer be my trusted *hersir.* No, certainly not..." His face brightened. "Ah, he will pay me restitution, but each of you will vote! Is it flogging and banishment for our young thief? Or branding iron and exposure in the stocks?"

Silence settled over the hall like a shroud. Only the rasp of breath. Low, tight, expectant.

Reidar's every muscle hummed as he picked up Ingrid and carried her to the nearest table. The woman he planted her beside stiffened and drew back.

"Pray," he breathed in Ingrid's ear in Irish, but she only stared ahead, like one deaf and blind to the world.

With a heavy stare at his *hirdmen*, Reidar barreled toward the high seat. Nostrils flaring, he stopped a foot away. "Is it I who have stolen from you, Vargr Bloodgale?" Reidar's voice boomed throughout the hall like a battle horn. "Nothing here is yours—" heart thundering, he unsheathed Shadowbane—"for it has always been mine!"

Behind Reidar rose the scrape of cups and the thud of benches. He glanced over his shoulder. A handful of his men had risen, his brother Thorsten among them. But they were too few. If it came to blades, it would be a short fight, and none of them would live to tell about it.

Vargr peered past Reidar, eyes raking the hall. The *huskarlar* grabbed their axe hafts.

Suddenly, Vargr barked a laugh. "Ah, this Christ magic is powerful indeed. Look how my young nephew has fallen under this Christian's spell. She has robbed him of wits and sense! It was a jest, Reidar." His smile died. "All the more reason to feed her to the hogs."

The benches creaked behind Reidar—his men settling back down.

Reidar's chest tightened. He swallowed against a bitter taste in his mouth.

With a dismissive nod to his *huskarlar,* Vargr stood, ignoring Shadowbane. "I am your rightful jarl and uncle, Sapling—" he spat loud enough for everyone to hear—"and nothing moves my pity more than the sight of green youth. So, I grant you one more night with her."

He fixed Reidar with a dark, heavy stare, dropping his voice into a low whisper. "Upon my word, you will live to regret your unwise outburst, nephew, for it is your last."

# Chapter Twenty-Six

## Twig
***Brigit***

**Sixth Night**

*I strike you, maid, with my magic staff*
*To make you obey my will;*
*You will go where no human*
*Will ever see you again.*
— Skírnismál, stanza 26

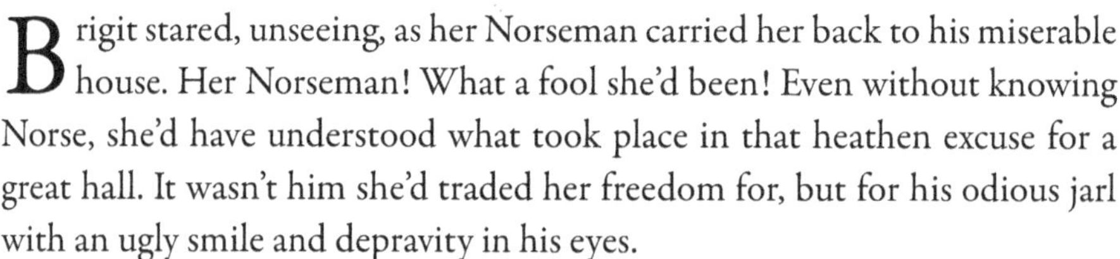

Brigit stared, unseeing, as her Norseman carried her back to his miserable house. Her Norseman! What a fool she'd been! Even without knowing Norse, she'd have understood what took place in that heathen excuse for a great hall. It wasn't him she'd traded her freedom for, but for his odious jarl with an ugly smile and depravity in his eyes.

She clenched her teeth to stop them from chattering. Oh, she remembered him well from the Rathlin wood. He'd already been a man when she'd first had the misfortune of crossing his path—when the boy Reidar brought her into the midst of his savage horde. She remembered the glint in his beady eyes as he tried to buy her for a necklace and a bracelet. Time had done him no favors. He'd thickened into a barrel and curdled into a lump of malice, for it seeped from his every pore, pooled in his dead gaze, and curled around his cruel mouth. A Fomorian of the old tales—a face like his was fit to keep children meek for a fortnight.

Brigid startled—without warning, her thoughts slipped back into Irish. Strange how the Norse tongue had grown familiar since she returned from the dead. Stranger still, she couldn't explain how she lived again—only that the Lord had answered her plea. A shame. She was already regretting her unforgivable folly. For even before the Fomorian spoke, she grasped his men's blank stares and the meaning of his plundering gaze stripping her of her borrowed gowns as her captor stood her up before him like a prized steed.

*You come with me—you thrall.* Brigit bit her lip, fighting hot tears and wishing to deal her captor a blow. What a dullard she'd been. He never said she'd be *his* thrall. And even if he'd changed his mind and wanted her for himself, his claim ran as hollow as a bell with no tongue. He was not the jarl and had neither men nor power to keep her. Nor to save her.

They'd returned to the house. Mute, the savage laid her on his bed, then sat at the far end, his broad back turned to her. She shut her eyes, struggling to still her thundering heart. Tomorrow, she would be given over to the Fomorian to be defiled, then slain, and thrown to the swine.

She rolled onto her side and curled into a ball. *Forgive me, Father, for not heeding Your warning. Heartache I have, and torment is soon on its heels.*

She flinched as a large hand brushed her shoulder. These heathen barbarians were worse than beasts. For all the jarl knew, her Norseman had been using her from the start, and he saw no wrong in it. A bitter scoff escaped her lips. Perhaps they viewed female thralls as wild horses—to be broken for the lord.

"Ingrid."

She lurched upright so fast, her head spun. "My name is Brigit!"

Her heart raced at the sight of his clenched jaw, and in that moment, the truth struck her, cold and bleak as this forsaken land. This man could not be Reidar. He was a changeling who took his place. For he hadn't claimed his name when she offered him a chance. Moreover, the boy with kind eyes would never hand her over to that hideous beast. A pity she hadn't died when the end was so near. Better death than the vile degradations planned for her all along.

Out of habit, Brigit reached beneath the pillow for her twig. She stopped breathing—there was no twig in this new bed. Frantic, she grasped at her belt, but this gown wasn't hers.

"Where—" A chill coiled in her belly and crawled up her spine. "Where is my—"

The savage contemplated her with a deep frown as she threw back the pelts, patting down the bed with stiff hands. *Gone!* The old woman must have thrown it out when she found it.

Brigit pressed an icy fist to her waist. "It was mine!" she choked out. "It belonged to me!"

His bitter scoff brought her up short. Lips pinched, he reached beneath his pillow and pulled out her cloth. "This?"

Brigit's hand shook as she snatched it from him. She clutched it to her chest and glared at her captor. "Did you know—" her voice cracked against her tightening throat—"I had decided to follow you here even before you stormed in to take me by force. But I did not come here of my own will for your *jarl!* I made that perilous journey for someone who once saved me! And who would keep me safe from the likes of you and your 'uncle!'" Her fingers curled into fists; her whole body trembled with the effort not to weep. "I came here for Reidar, but you are right—he is gone!"

The words died on her lips at the change in the savage's face. He'd gone so still, he might've been carved from stone. His eyes became two frozen lakes—trained on her, drifting to the small bundle in her hand.

"Don't." She needed to run—or crawl—as fast as her weak legs would allow her. Away from this house. Away from these piercing, pale-blue eyes.

Suffocating on her breath, she jerked back. Her spine met the bed's hard wooden frame.

Her captor drew near. His gaze never leaving her face, he seized her hand—the one clutching the cloth with the twig. Without a word, he flipped it over, pried her fingers open, and took it from her.

"Don't." Brigit bit into her lip so hard she tasted blood.

She knew what he would do next. Maybe she always had. Even when he tied his daft rope around her ankle. Even when he kissed his cursed "sweetheart." Maybe her heart was too fragile for such calamities, but he'd leave her no choice now.

Her pulse rushed into her ears. It surged into her fingertips. "Don't," she breathed, hugging herself so tight her fingers dug into her flesh through the layers of wool.

Their eyes locked as he lifted the tiny twig, holding it between his thumb and forefinger.

"Give it back," she choked out. "It is mine."

She cast a wild glance around the chamber. Perhaps she could summon enough strength to rush past him, flee into the night, and keep running until her body gave out. Then she wouldn't be so near this savage, who brought her here for his jarl. And wouldn't grieve the burning hope in his eyes that surged through her like a blaze, twisting her insides.

"Don't," she sobbed, sorrow filling her to the brim.

Pale as freshly fallen snow, the Norseman placed the twig upon her head.

She was burning with fever again. It tossed her into the air and left her floating in a new, feverish dream. In this dream, there once lived a girl who went into the forest to gather wild strawberries for her ailing father. There, she met a barbarian boy who beneath his rough, savage exterior was kind and gentle. He was a blessing and an answer to her desperate prayer. The boy had kissed her with a chaste kiss that tasted of wild strawberries and everything that was right in the world, and then he saved her the only way he could. The barbarian boy left, and she never saw him again, but the memory of him remained with her. It lived in her heart, in her bones, in her soul, and not a day had passed when she didn't see his beautiful, fair face in her mind's eye. Not a moment slipped by when she didn't feel the warmth of his hand on hers. Every glance, every touch, everything in her life, the girl measured against him and found lacking. His very name was so dear and familiar to her, it was like the air she breathed. Then, as a woman, not a day went by when she didn't imagine him grown, her heart sick and body aching with bittersweet longing, for surely, she'd never again look upon the blue-eyed boy Reidar, for as long as she lived.

"*Home*," he whispered in Irish. "You are home, Ingrid," he said in Norse.

Brigit tumbled back into this foreign chamber, into this cold, dismal world. When she sought her heart for him, envisaging him as a man, she saw him with his wheat-colored hair falling to his shoulders, his beautiful mouth curving up amid a fair, silky beard. Like a fool, she never dreamed he'd become one of his people with long plaits, shaved sides, and wicked marks that ran from cheek to waist. It never crossed her mind he'd return to take her as plunder, then procure her as spoils for another man.

"Home!" she spat the word like a curse. Like a vile obscenity he'd made it. "You dare profane the notion! Maybe your name is still Reidar, but you are not him! You could never be! You have changed beyond imagining—"

"Shh—" He silenced her with his lips upon hers, his arms holding her hostage against the wall that was his body.

She had neither breath nor flesh nor sinew. She only floated on a heart-breaking tide of air that shifted into the creasing blue eyes and lips tasting of wild strawberries. But it was a memory better left to the past, for his lips tasted of bitter betrayal now. Yet while her mind knew it, her body turned treacherous in his arms. Her fingers skimmed his soft blond plaits and dug into his powerful neck. Their eyes locked, and something strange happened to her mind and body as the two drifted apart. For while her mind remembered the fire, the corpses, the rope, the jarl, her body responded as if none of it mattered.

His hand found the curve of her back. Swift as an anchor dropping, reason returned, and she recoiled and put space between them.

"Do not fight it, Ingrid," he breathed, drawing her close. "Let it be."

Brigit flinched. What did it matter that he'd been the boy Reidar all along? What did it matter that in some hidden part of her mind she'd always known? She knew nothing else about him, save that he always was and forever remained her enemy. Perhaps even as a boy, his first aim had been to lure her in for someone else. A sweet boy to confuse her until it was too late. A handsome man to blind her until she lost her freedom.

She thrashed against his deepening kiss, trying to wrench free, screaming into his mouth. But he was too fast and too strong. He was what he'd always been—her captor.

The world dimmed. It turned into a ceaseless night where she would dwell until her dying breath. A darkness with no hope, and therefore, no future. She ceased her struggle as her soul mourned what had never been.

"Forgive me, Ingrid." Chest heaving, Reidar broke the kiss and released her. "The nearness of you strips me of reason."

With trembling hands, she wrenched the twig from her hair and hurled it onto the floor. Then she dropped her swimming head into her lap and held a wake for the foolish dream of her youth.

"Do not weep." His arms encircled her again, holding her prisoner. "I swear I will make it right."

He pulled her in so tight, her cross dug into her skin through the wool.

*What have I done to deserve such a cruel fate, Father?*

Yet if this was the Lord's will for her, who was she to question it? So she grew still and let her weak, heavy limbs rest in the hug made of iron and savagery.

# Chapter Twenty-Seven

## Light
***Reidar***

**Sixth Night**

*On the eagle's hill you will always sit*
*And look at the gates of Hel;*
*Your food will become more loathsome to you*
*Than a pale snake is to men.*
— Skírnismál, stanza 27

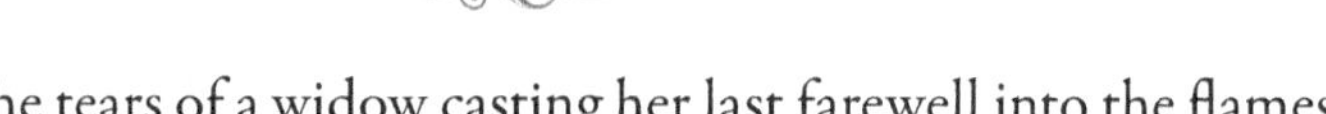

Ingrid wept the tears of a widow casting her last farewell into the flames of her husband's pyre.

Reidar released her and crushed his hands together in a white-knuckled grip, lest he paw her again. He expected fear, disbelief, even wrath. He hoped for relief and for the end of her unendurable denial. But not this dark despair. Not this utter devastation, this bitter disappointment in him.

He shook himself as if from a vile dream, reached for her hands, and peeled them from her face. Now they were touching again, restraint was akin to taming a wildfire with a whisper. He said nothing as he brought them to his mouth—small, warm, and salty—and kissed each finger until she stopped weeping. Until she lifted her lovely, tear-stricken face and peered at him.

She knew all along and never said a word, yearning to see the boy he'd been. But she was right. That boy had long been claimed by war and bloodshed, and no earthly power could bring him back.

"Ingrid." Her name on his tongue made him tingle. He brought his thumb to her cheeks and wiped away her tears. Very slowly he pressed his lips to hers once more—a chaste kiss, like the one on Rathlin. "I swear by all the gods of Asgard and Éire, I will keep you safe," he whispered.

He meant it, for he would never give her to his uncle. He knew too well what Vargr did to every lovely thrall who caught his beastly, ravenous eye. Even as a boy, Reidar saw the girls' stooped backs and vacant eyes after he'd used and discarded them—those who, by the gods' favor or cruelty, lived.

But he chased such thoughts away. There would be time enough for strategy or grief, yet their time together was slipping away. Unbidden, his body responded to this simple kiss as it did seven winters past. And in a heartbeat, he was back in that light-filled, green forest, standing face to face with this otherworldly, elfish vision. Her honeyed scent, her wild-strawberry mouth that had never been kissed, her wide, shiny eyes the color of spring leaves, fresh grass, and all that made life worth living.

Fighting his longing for her was akin to holding his breath beneath a wave—he had to come up for air lest he suffocate. Despite himself, he gathered her back into his arms. He was plunging into a sweet, aching yearning he had neither strength nor will to resist. It rushed through his lifeblood; it sang in his bones—fierce and unyielding. "My Ingrid." He twined his fingers in her silky hair, pulling her closer. Nothing in the world rivaled the feel of her small, soft, pliable body. Reckless, he deepened his kiss once more, silencing her weak protest.

As a child, Reidar discovered there were languages beyond speech. There was the language of the eyes, where a single glance cut deeper than any words. There was also the language of the body, especially of the hands, where one gesture replaced a stream of words. The language of silence was perhaps the mightiest—it roared when words only fell short. And when he first lay with a woman, Reidar learned the language of love, where words only stood in the way.

This time, Ingrid didn't pull away as he pressed on. She responded in kind—a soft, willing surrender to his escalating advance. The sort of language he liked best. His hand slipped to the front of her gown.

The world came to a grinding halt as she drew back, staring at him with large, naked eyes. Her chest rose and fell like a rolling wave as she parted her lips. But no sound emerged.

She swallowed hard. "Reidar."

He let out a slow, shuddering breath. His name on her tongue kindled the air and lit it on fire. The way she said it at long last, in her sweet, lilting voice, it sounded new and magical. A name for him alone.

"You are mistaken if you think I would let that man touch me," she forced out, pressing her hand to her cross. "For while you took me away from home under false pretenses, I can still leave here—" She gulped. "Even if it earns me a place in hell."

Reidar froze, blood draining from his face. He'd spent enough time among Christian thralls to understand her meaning.

Her gaze flicked to the dagger at his belt. "I would rather take my own life than let him near me."

He flinched, chilled to the bone. "He will not touch you." With a rigid hand, he reached for an errant strand falling over her eyes and smoothed it behind her ear. "Neither the jarl, nor any other man will lay claim to you while I draw breath."

She pulled away from his hand that lingered despite his better sense. "I was there, in the great hall, when you presented me like a prized horse," she choked out.

"Is that what you think I did? You do not understand—" He drew back, speechless, as she glared at him. "We live by oaths and bindings. You are a thrall, Ingrid, and his property, for he is the jarl. Still, I am telling you, no man—jarl or otherwise—will touch you while my hand can lift a weapon."

Her eyes locked on his face, filling him with light. "No man? Yet you have already touched me."

"I—" He rubbed his forehead, lost in the tangles of her incomprehensible ways. "I thought—"

Her eyes bored into his. "How long, Reidar?"

He blinked, unable to make sense of her question. There was yet another sort of language—one where words carried unspoken thoughts. He turned her question over, searching for its true meaning. The light dimmed as he fell back to the cold, dark earth. At long last, she was here, alive and well—in

Ljosstrond, in his house, in his chamber, in his bed—and he had no more claim to her than when she lived leagues away, in her misty homeland.

Reidar shut his eyes, sealing in a furious storm that crashed through him. He wished to take her now before Vargr altered her beyond recognition. He ached to march to the mead hall and throw his axe clean into his uncle's head. He longed to be back in Éire where Vargr held no sway, and neither allegiance nor fealty bound and shackled him.

"You do not understand." Her voice pierced through him like a blade. "Even if you contrive to claim me now, how long until you tire of me and hand me over to...someone else?"

The candlelight flickered with her words, casting shadows across the chamber and glinting in her steady gaze. This language stung worse than her challenge, for it carried the weight of knowing, laced with despair too dark to fathom. Reidar's thoughts raced, clogging his mind with the image of her stooped back and mute, vacant face.

He stood and shook his head, trying to clear it. It stayed clogged. Soon daylight would ebb, and night would fall. Then the morning would rise, and with it, the time to act. Beyond Ljosstrond, men followed him on voyages and offered their loyalty, but here, they knew well who held the reins. Most would not bleed for him—proof enough in how readily they had returned to their feasting. And tomorrow he would face two choices—kill Vargr and meet certain and immediate death from Asbjorn and the *huskarlar,* or hand her over and live a bit longer. He knew his uncle. His words were no idle threat. Vargr would see Reidar dead for his impudence, and soon.

Either path ended with Brigit in his uncle's beastly grip.

Numb and hollow on the inside, Reidar dug his hands into his plaits. He needed air. He needed silence. He needed solitude.

"I must leave now. To think." He tried to soften his voice. Failed. "I will return soon."

Her glittering gaze cut him to shreds.

"You should have never brought me here." Her words emerged thin and clipped. "But when in your selfishness, you did, and God wished to spare me the forthcoming indignities, I should have let Him do His will." She scoffed. "And, Reidar, you know nothing of me if you think I would lie with a man who is not my husband—you or any other."

Rigid as oak, he headed to the door. "I will come back," he muttered before leaving.

The clouds hung thick and low as he neared the edge of the wood. Rain began to spill, cool and soft, trailing down his face like tears. He swiped at his cheeks. Dullard. What made him think she would fall into his arms once all lay bare between them? She hadn't then. She wouldn't now. She was cut from different cloth than all the countless women he'd mindlessly taken to his bed. Maybe it was her unseen God who gave her restraint and bid her to guard her love for a husband. Or maybe she had more mettle than was her rightful share.

Either way, without knowing, she'd given him a third choice. He could save her by marrying her, for even a jarl would not dare defile his *hersir's* wife.

Reidar threw his head back and shut his eyes. In the thick of the storm, he'd sworn to make her his wife if only she lived. And she had.

He clenched his jaw until it ached. Yes, marrying her would save her, but what of him? He would become the laughingstock for binding himself to a thrall. His *blodhefnd*, his birthright, his carefully planned strategies—all would fall by the wayside. Marrying Ingrid would forever doom him to remain at Vargr's mocking beck and call—until his uncle found a way to get rid of him. And then he would have Ingrid anyway.

Reidar squared his shoulders and walked on until he reached the large boulder he used to climb as a boy. Brown lichen clung to its rough surface, and rain gathered along the edges, running in slow, steady streams. Reidar glowered at it, his thoughts an angry torrent, his chest a breaking storm, pounding with the weight of his impossible choices. Marrying would save her and ruin him. Not marrying would ruin her and save him.

He lifted his chin to the sky. "Thor, show me the right path."

But Thor stood idle when the sea nearly swallowed him and death reached for Ingrid.

He widened his stance and clenched his fists. "Odin, do not leave me alone in this. Lend me your wisdom."

But Odin never heeded him.

For a breath, he thought to plead with Freyr, but what was the use? It was Ingrid's God who was so powerful, he brought her back from the dead.

Yet his father's faith in the true gods ran as deep as the fjord and as constant as tide and wind. Harald Fairblade never wavered. He sacrificed at the sowing and the reaping, when setting sail, before battle, and after victory. He honored the solstice, the dark of midwinter, and generously poured blood for protection, strength, and vengeance. He trusted the gods to answer and said they had.

But they stood aside when Vargr struck him with a poisoned blade. And they turned their backs when he died a slow, agonizing death. And they abandoned Ljosstrond altogether when Vargr seized the jarl's seat and loosed tyranny on its people.

*The gods give victory.* Harald Fairblade's voice reverberated in Reidar's mind, low and steady as the day his father tried to pull him free from the haze of the Rathlin voyage. *But they never give peace. That, a man must win for himself.*

His father had been right. Every battle Reidar won was by Thor's favor as the god's strength surged through his limbs and his rage boiled in his chest. But those victories weren't worth a raven's cry if he failed in the one that mattered—to avenge Harald's murder. And if he denied his father's gods, did he turn from his father, too?

Reidar gritted his teeth. His *blodhefnd* was no longer the only battle that held sway. After dragging Ingrid from her home and bringing her here, small and defenseless, it was his duty to keep her safe. Peace was for children and fools. He needed Thor now more than ever. For while Christ was mighty, He shunned bloodshed and offered no vengeance. Instead, He asked for the unthinkable—to turn the other cheek.

Scoffing, Reidar peered skyward once more. The rain clouds sagged low, gray and heavy as lead. Such sermon reeked of fear and defeat, and Reidar Valorborn was no coward.

*Turning the other cheek is not cowardice. It is refusing to let hate rule you.* He froze at the strange thought as it rose from within yet rang from without.

*But when evil comes for the innocent, you must stand.* The words came like wind through a crack, slicing clean through to his soul.

Reidar buried his pounding head in his hands.

This unseen God saw his every wound and shadow.

This unseen God spoke clearer than thunder.

This unseen God echoed the beat of Reidar's own heart.

He could deny it no more than his own sight—this unseen God was no longer unseen.

With a long, steadying breath, Reidar traced the sign of the cross on the rain-slicked boulder, struck as ever by its likeness to the Algiz rune. As a boy, he loved studying the runes—each one perfect, precise, and loaded with meaning. Yet this one was something more. Not a rune, but a door.

"God of Éire, Father, Christ, I cannot give her up," he whispered. "Help me, for I am lost."

He wondered if he should say the Lord's Prayer but found he couldn't recall all the Irish words. Still, he tried.

*Our Father in heaven*
*Your name is hallowed*
*Your will is done*
*Forgive my debts*
*Deliver me from evil*
*For Yours is the glory*
*In Christ's name,*
*Amen.*

He waited—for what, he didn't know. A feeling. A stir in the air. A sign. But nothing happened, so Reidar drew a dagger from his belt. All gods demanded sacrifice, and Ingrid's had to be no different, for power always came at a cost. Her God was only slower to claim it.

Shoulders squared, Reidar pulled up his sleeve and brought the tip of the dagger to his forearm.

"Christ, I call upon You with my blood. I offer this sacrifice in Your name. Guide my heart in wisdom. Show me the path to deliverance. Look upon me with favor."

Reidar went still as the clouds broke, and a column of sunlight struck the boulder, setting it aglow. He shrank back, dropping the dagger. But he shook himself. It was only a shift in weather, nothing more.

Yet when he looked up, the rain still fell everywhere else. Only above him did the sky open, as if offering a path.

Heart thudding, he stared at his trembling hands—pitiless tools of death and destruction. Had he any right to plead with Christ for favors? If Ingrid's

God knew all the horrors he'd done to those who worshipped Him, He would surely smite him. Yet, strange as it seemed, the only road forward was to spill all that churned within him.

The sunbeam brushed his face, warm and tender like his father's hand, and Reidar felt in his marrow he didn't need to utter a word. But if Ingrid's God knew his unspeakable shame, He showed no anger toward him.

Chest hammering, Reidar knelt as he saw Ingrid do.

"Forgive my failings, Father. I have not known You," he breathed, lifting his eyes to the light. "My strength falters, my soul drowns in turmoil. The mire pulls at my feet, and the dark draws near. Lift me from this pit. Set my feet upon a rock. Show me the right path. My faith is in You alone." He closed his eyes, shaking from head to foot. "Come swift as the storm and mighty as the sea. Deliver my beloved from evil."

If anyone happened to be there, they would think him a madman, for Christ was a foreign, silent God. Yet He spoke louder now, even if His words only rang in Reidar's heart and not in his ears:

*In the heart of the storm, you vowed to love and care for her as your own wife until your last breath.*

And in those words, lay the only choice this God would accept, making it no choice at all.

"You have all my praise, Father." Reidar stood, awestruck by the light and the sense of rightness that coursed through him as he let go of his *blodhefnd*, birthright, and carefully planned strategies.

Tension melting from his shoulders, he bowed his head, then turned back toward his longhouse.

Ingrid lay facing away as he entered. Despite the clamor of his arrival, she didn't stir.

He didn't mind—she'd stir soon enough. His step light, he went to the bed and reached for the little twig on the floor. By some miracle, it remained unscathed.

"Ingrid." He touched her shoulder. His wife's shoulder. The notion made him want to laugh with joy.

She turned to him, eyes dry and dull, hands limp and lifeless. Her lips parted, then closed again. She gave a bitter scoff. "Do not torment yourself so over a *thrall*." Her voice grew brittle and faint. "Take me to him and have it done with."

"Never." His breath caught in his chest at the freedom that flooded him, pure and true. He took her hand and pressed the twig into her palm. "My uncle will not touch you because no man—not even a jarl—can lay claim to my wife."

Light, warm and bright, welled up inside him at the sight of her widening, glittering eyes. What he said next, he must say in Irish, for it would strike deeper.

"Do not fret—my Ingrid." He smiled his first carefree smile in seven winters, finally remembering the Irish word that joined two things together. "It is you—and—me now."

# Chapter Twenty-Eight

## For Good

***Brigit***

**Sixth Night**

*If you come out,*
*Hrimnir will stand and stare at you in fear*
*(People will marvel at you);*
*You will become more famous*
*Than the watchman of the gods!*
*Come out of your prison, then.*
— Skírnismál, stanza 28

Brigit blinked after a silence, unsure what startled her more—his bewildering proposal or the mysterious new calm in his eyes.

"Ingrid?" He shrugged off his fur and sat on the bed beside her.

She dropped her gaze, thoughts heaving like the waves in the open sea. True, she hadn't been here long and knew little of Norse ways, but she understood Reidar was a *hersir* and a man of means. When he carried her to the jarl's great hall, she saw people in rags shoveling mud—wan-faced, hollow-eyed, and worn down to the bone. As she herself had been before Cearbhall mac Bressal took it into his head to wed her.

Yet Reidar wore a cloak of rich fur, a belt adorned with silver buckles, and owned a fine blade inlaid with gold and silver. He lived in his own longhouse and commanded his own *hirdmen*. He was a Viking warlord and the jarl's own nephew. And while Brigit didn't know Norse ways, she knew enough of life. A man like Reidar would never wed a thrall. His union would be one of wealth and politics, carefully arranged for gain and power. Taking her as his wife would ruin his future and defy his jarl in one reckless, irreversible blow.

His voice grew tight. "Ingrid?"

She lifted her head to find him motionless, save for a vein that pulsed along his powerful neck.

"You would wed me—a thrall?" she choked out.

He trained his pale-blue gaze on her. "By taking you as my wife, I would set you free."

Brigit's pulse surged into her throat. She swallowed against it. The strain in his jaw spoke louder than any words. He was in earnest—determined to wed her, unbind her, and deliver her from the looming terror that was his uncle.

She dug her fingernails into her palms. Most women would weep with joy and fall at his feet in gratitude. They'd spend the rest of their lives pleasing him in all things without complaint. And she wished with all her heart she were like those women, but the damage done to her over the years must have been too great. All she could think was that he meant to wed her not out of love, but out of necessity. If not for his uncle, he would happily keep her as his thrall.

She stared at her hands, struck by another harsh truth.

"Reidar..." The words clawed their way up, and Brigit bit down hard. But anguish overpowered sense, and out came the daftest thing ever uttered in this heathen place. "Would we be wed by a priest?"

"A priestess." His face grew tighter. "There are no chapels in Norway, my Ingrid."

Her heart thudded like a hammer at a forge as she stared into his unblinking eyes. He couldn't help who he was, nor the ways laid upon him at birth. It wasn't his fault that no holy halls stood in this savage land, nor that he worshiped idols made by the human hand.

She clenched her jaw until it hurt. True, his reasons lay bare, but she'd been baptized in the name of the Lord, taught the way of truth, and sworn to walk in it. What excuse had she to stumble? None. And now she stood at a crossroads. *Heartache and torment.* Only now, it was heartache or torment.

Wed Reidar without the Lord's blessing and live in sin—or be handed to his uncle for pillage and death.

Brigit clasped her hands until they hurt. Perhaps Reidar's very offer of marriage was the Lord's blessing and His way of keeping her from harm. She glanced at Reidar and flinched at his pained expression. He was still the boy from her girlhood. And he still offered out of mercy what he could not give out of love.

He chose her only when death forced his hand.

"I—" She cleared her throat, squeezing out each word. "I thank you, but—" She glanced away at the sight of his widening eyes. "You would grow to resent me for stealing your future."

She didn't dare meet his gaze in the silence that fell.

He tipped her chin with his forefinger, making her look at him. "And this alone holds you back?"

"You would grow bitter with time," she breathed. "You would regret marrying me."

Gentle as summer rain, he traced her jaw with his thumb. "I have searched for you for seven long winters. I would never regret marrying you, my Ingrid, let alone keeping you safe."

She pulled away at the unbidden memory of his face, painted with coal and streaked with blood, and Caoimhe's frantic whispers of human sacrifice that followed. Even if he meant well, even if his every word were true, where it mattered most to her, they stood worlds apart.

"How can we wed—" she gulped—"when we are not equally yoked?" She winced at his blank stare. "We do not pray to the same God, Reidar."

She stopped breathing as his brilliant smile made his broad cheeks ride even higher and turned his eyes to bright blue slits.

His boy Reidar's eyes searched hers, creasing in the corners. "You pray to Christ." He touched the cross at her chest.

His words hung between them, thrumming like an overwound fiddle string.

"You know I am a Christian," she whispered, "and you—"

He pressed a finger to her lips. "Now, I am one, too."

Brigit shrank back with a gasp. This beautiful heathen had no notion of the blasphemy he just spoke. Her eyebrows knitted, and she didn't care to halt them. "Faith is not a mantle to put on when it suits you!"

His lips twitched. "I have never seen a woman wear a frown so beautifully. It is not a mantle, my Ingrid." He took her hand in his. "When you lay ill, then...dead—" he swallowed—"I called upon my gods and begged them to spare you. But they turned their backs. Then I pleaded with yours. We are both witnesses to His miracle." He stared at their joined hands. "And just now, my Ingrid, when I sought solace, I prayed to your God again. And though His reply flies in the face of all I know, I left with a heart lighter than it has ever been."

A soft drumming rose in Brigit's chest and spread through her, filling her with a bright, steady glow. She clasped his hand, breathless, speechless, and floating on a warm, salty tide. She never felt so completely awake.

"Reidar—" How dazzling it was to call him thus. How wondrously freeing to be unburdened of her Great Scorn.

He gathered her into the safety of his large, warm hug. "I will never let you go again—I cannot give you up," he whispered into her hair. "Maybe He meant for us to meet and for me to love you."

Brigit heard herself speak, but the sound was lost to her, replaced by a bubbling, breathless laughter that escaped her lips. Her head swam as if with wine, knees wobbled beneath her, and ears rang with his words, deep and rich like the toll of a distant bell. *To love you.* No man had ever spoken such words to her. One man alone could make her want to hear them. She never wished to be free of his arms. She longed to fuse with him and never part.

"The time is short." He pulled her closer. "I must see to our wedding, for it is to be today."

Brigit shut her eyes, afraid to let him go lest she awaken from this lovely, impossible dream.

"Yet before I go, I must ask you something that weighs heavily on my heart."

She blinked at a sudden somberness in his voice.

"When I prayed to your God—to our God—I wanted to offer Him a blood sacrifice, but He refused it." He peered at her with a deep groove between his eyebrows. "Teach me your ways, Ingrid, tell me how to do it, for surely I must sacrifice to Him greatly if He is to bless our union."

Brigit ran her fingers along his shoulder, smoothing the hard leather of his jerkin. She was neither wise in Scripture, nor fit to speak of holy things. Indeed, she was the least suited to teach the Word. And yet, here sat her kind-hearted Reidar, her gentle Norseman with his fledgling faith, and none but her to turn to for answers.

*Father, help me with this insurmountable task.*

"Long ago, in a land east and south of Norway, God revealed Himself to a people," Brigit ventured. "He is a loving Father who longed for them to live and thrive, so He gave them laws to guard and draw them near Him. But they bore the weight of the Fall, and their hearts were sick, always reaching for life apart from God. Our hearts are no different. We are born into a broken world, far from the garden He made for us—where we once walked with this faithful Father. Look around: greed, envy, corruption, strife, betrayal, pain, murder. This is not how it was meant to be."

Reidar made no reply, so she took it as a sign to go on.

"So when it became clear we could not reach Him on our own, God did what only He could—He came to us. He stepped down from Heaven into our brokenness by sending His Son to bridge the divide. At Passover, the time of ancient sacrifice, Christ became the sacrificial Lamb. He was offered for our sins, once for all. So we do not sacrifice to Him. He is the sacrifice. And through Him, we are forgiven. Through Him, we return *home* to the Father."

Reidar broke the embrace and dragged a hand down his plaits. "Odin is the Allfather, and like Christ, he hung on a tree before he returned. He sacrificed himself for nine days and nine nights, and in the end, he acquired a great, secret wisdom." He shrugged. "Maybe they are not that different?"

The words came to Brigit at once; so effortless, they rolled off her tongue. "Christ did not die on the cross for wisdom. He died for love."

The soft taps of rain returned, pattering against the turf roof. A gust of wind slipped in through the smoke hole, carrying the scent of damp earth and wet ash into the chamber. The drizzle thickened, swelling into a steady drumbeat that spattered against the timber walls.

"I once believed love was for children and fools." Reidar shook his head with a faint scoff. "Then I met you on your island." His gaze lingered on her, bright and unguarded. "Gyda called you my Great Flaw, but she was wrong. You are my Great Strength." He stood. "I must go now and speak with the priestess if we are to be wed before tomorrow's light."

"Reidar, you should know," Brigit called after him, breathless, as he reached the door. "When your people came to plunder my island, I prayed for help. And after, when misery swallowed me whole, I begged God to save me. Even here, in this strange land, when all hope fled, I cried out for deliverance. And each time He sent *you*."

Her Norseman, who had so recently discovered the boundless joy of God's love, tossed her another achingly familiar smile over his shoulder. And as he closed the door, and Brigit lay down, warm and content, she recalled the young monk named Padraig teaching her that God, in His unfathomable wisdom, worked all things for good for those who believed.

# Chapter Twenty-Nine

## Nostrum
***Brigit***

*Rage and longing, chains and wrath,*
*Tears and torment will be yours;*
*Wherever you sit, my doom will be upon you*
*With heavy heart*
*And double pain.*
— Skírnismál, stanza 29

The soft rain veiled the forest in mist, shrouding the half-naked branches and the falling leaves. The ground lay mottled with damp earth and scattered gold, as if summer and autumn grappled for rule, neither yielding to what must come next. Shivering with new misgivings, Brigit stood near a plain standing stone. No chapel. No priest. No Christ to bear witness. Still, Reidar had arranged the wedding with astonishing haste, and soon she would belong to him. And remain beyond his uncle's reach.

In preparation, a somber Gyda had brought her a hearty meal and helped her cross the chamber—first with the help of her arm, then alone—to be certain she could stand at her own wedding. And though meant in kindness, all of it struck Brigit as wrong. Too fast, too grave, and steeped in dreadful foreboding she couldn't shake.

Now, the chilling air made her heart clench and her fingers go numb. Yet she resembled a proper bride in her white, fur-edged gown, procured somewhere by Gyda. Her hair had been braided and crowned with a wreath of twigs and rowan for protection, thyme for fertility, and wheat strands for abundance. So Gyda said as she scrubbed and dressed her, then arranged her hair, muttering something about its lovely but unnatural color.

Flanked by a handful of his men, Reidar stood steps away, but his eyes dwelled elsewhere as he scanned the edge of the wood with swift, sharp glances, hand gripping the pommel of his blade.

Without warning, a hushed voice stirred the air beyond the trees, and he stepped forward, taking his place beside her. His dark wolf pelt rippled like a living thing as he drew his sword and laid it across his palms.

Brigit flinched as a tall woman emerged from the shadows like a wraith. Her long, white hair hung plaited with bones and bits of cloth. Dark marks curled along her broad cheekbones, temples, and beneath her eyes, stark against her pale skin. Her cloak—rough-spun wool dyed the color of dried blood—dragged through the wet ground behind her, and a string of animal teeth clacked softly at her neck with each step.

Brigit shut her eyes. *Lord, have I made a grave misjudgment in my confusion of despair, joy, and longing? Surely, this is not what You want for me and not what I wish for myself—to be wed to my beloved in a heathen ritual.*

Stone-faced, the priestess raised her arms.

"Who brings this woman to stand beside this man?" The low, flat drip of her voice died in the falling rain.

Gyda stepped forward, frowning and drawing her drenched pelt tight about her. "She comes of her own will."

The priestess nodded, then turned to Reidar. "You come armed."

Reidar lifted his sword toward Brigit. "This is Shadowbane, a gift from my father, Harald Fairblade. I offer it in trust."

At the sound of his voice, unease spread into Brigit's fingertips as it had seven winters past.

The priestess looked to Brigit. "Will you keep it safe, even if your heart should turn?"

"I will," Brigit choked out.

"Hold—" Gaze trained on her, Reidar passed her the sword, the Irish word startling instead of soothing.

She staggered beneath its weight, unprepared. Reidar lunged for the blade as it tipped in her hands, sliding across her palms. But she caught the pommel before the sword sank into the ground, a breath from her feet. Trembling, she gripped the hilt, leaning on it lest she tumble. Even if the blade drew no blood, this was wrong. Ill-fated. Marked for ruin.

The priestess raised her brows with a sharp look at Reidar. "Do you want to be man and wife in the sight of Freyr and Freya?"

Face tight, Reidar scanned the wood, then nodded with a curt "Yes."

The priestess studied Brigit for a long, weighty moment. "Do you agree?"

*Father, forgive me.* Heart thudding, Brigit dug her fingers into the carved hilt.

The priestess drew back. "Think carefully, for the two of you will be bound henceforth."

*Give me a sign, Father.* Brigit lifted her eyes heavenward. *Is this what you want of me?*

The raindrops fell on her face, cool and gentle. But she received no other answer, save a stifled breath from Reidar beside her.

"I agree," she squeezed out.

With another long look at Reidar, the priestess drew a small dagger from her belt. "Join hands."

"You—safe," Reidar whispered in Irish, placing his large, warm hand over hers on top of the pommel. "You—*home*."

Brigit's heart swelled at the sight of their intertwined fingers and the warmth of his words. *A handfasting!* But her joy died as the woman swiftly pricked their thumbs with the blade and pressed them together.

"By iron and blood, we call upon the gods to bless this marriage. You are bound."

The sight of crimson on their skin made Brigit's hearty meal rise to her throat. But she should have saved her queasiness for what came next. With a low, guttural incantation, the woman took a ring from her belt and reached for something on the ground, beside the standing stone. She lifted a small wooden bowl filled with a liquid thick as sap and dark as a moonless sky.

Brigit's throat tightened as the woman dipped the ring into the bowl, then pulled it out, dripping with blood, and handed it to Reidar.

The wood spun, and if not for the sword, Brigit's knees would have surely buckled. *Heartache* and *torment. Heartache* or *torment.*

"Nearly done," Reidar whispered in Norse, sliding the bloody ring onto her thumb, crimson mixing with rain and dripping onto the sodden earth.

"Before these witnesses, now you are wife," said the priestess with an expectant look.

An icy chill rolled down Brigit's spine, making the world go dark at the edges.

The priestess rolled her eyes. "Put the ring on him."

Hands trembling, Brigit removed the bloody ring from her thumb. Was she to slide it onto his? It would never fit.

Lips pressed together, Reidar took her hand and guided the ring over his little finger.

At the edge of Brigit's vision, Reidar's men eased their hands from their axe hafts.

The priestess heaved an exasperated sigh. "And now you are husband. Let none unbind what the gods have seen and sealed."

Reidar kept the ring on as he sheathed his sword, picked Brigit up, and carried her from the wood without a backward glance.

"You are weary. You are not yet healed," he said, quickening his stride. "For that I am sorry, but I must announce our marriage at the mead hall before the day is done. Then we will go home, and you can rest at last, my Ingrid."

His grip softening, her Norseman pulled her against his warm, solid chest and whispered, "You are free now."

She closed her eyes, unable to fight the contented warmth that spread throughout. And like long ago, she settled her head on his shoulder, wishing they could stay this way forever and longing for him to carry her back to the wood of her youth, where they were once young and innocent.

# Chapter Thirty

## Despair

***Astrid***

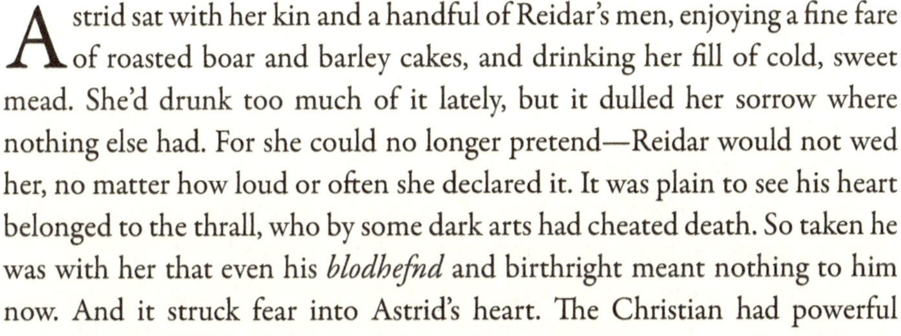

*In the giants' home, vile things will harm you*
*Every day with evil deeds;*
*You will get grief instead of happiness,*
*And sorrow to suffer with tears.*
— Skírnismál, stanza 30

Astrid sat with her kin and a handful of Reidar's men, enjoying a fine fare of roasted boar and barley cakes, and drinking her fill of cold, sweet mead. She'd drunk too much of it lately, but it dulled her sorrow where nothing else had. For she could no longer pretend—Reidar would not wed her, no matter how loud or often she declared it. It was plain to see his heart belonged to the thrall, who by some dark arts had cheated death. So taken he was with her that even his *blodhefnd* and birthright meant nothing to him now. And it struck fear into Astrid's heart. The Christian had powerful magic, mightier than anything she'd seen in all her days.

Still, aside from the comely lamb she'd offered Freya to rid her of her rival, Astrid found comfort in one thing alone. Reidar would not refuse the jarl. And when Vargr was finished with the girl, she'd no longer be fit for any man—least of all for Reidar, who liked his women whole and fair.

Astrid was on her third mead horn when Reidar entered with the accursed thrall in his arms, followed by his most trusted *hirdmen*. Why did he insist on carrying her everywhere like some treasured bride? He'd never so much as raised Astrid off her feet—

Heart leaping, she gasped. Jealousy had blinded her to the truth. Freya had heard her plea, for Reidar was delivering the thrall to Vargr before her time!

A strange hush swept the hall.

Astrid blinked, the weight of her error crashing down like a thousand boulders. In her mead-clouded haze, she didn't notice what she saw now—a wedding wreath of twigs and weeds upon the Christian's head.

The hall swayed. It grew small and suffocating. The horn slipped from Astrid's hand and crashed onto the table, knocking over a bowl and spilling the mead all over.

Back straight, Reidar pulled the harlot closer and approached the high seat, where Vargr stared with hard eyes. Carefully, he set her down. This time, she stood on her own—pale and trembling like a frightened rabbit and wearing a fine wedding gown trimmed with rich fur.

Astrid blinked. She blinked again. It could not be.

"Uncle. Dear friends." Reidar's deep voice boomed throughout the still hall as he faced it. "This is Ingrid, my wife." He grabbed a horn from a slack-mouthed *huskarl* at Vargr's side. "Skol!"

"Skol!"

Astrid lurched as someone to her left thrust his horn into the air, spilling the drink.

"Skol!" The hall roared, relief palpable in every corner.

Laughing, Reidar turned back to Vargr, who sat stiff and silent as a stone. "Apologies, uncle, but I fell in love with this girl, and so I wed her!"

Without waiting for the jarl's reply, he took his bride's hand and led her to a table where they sat amidst low whistles and crude taunts. And lewd as they were, Astrid choked down a lump the size of a goose egg. She would have given everything to have them aimed at her.

Vargr snapped from his stupor with a violent twitch of jaw. "Skol." He lifted his horn, face locked in an ugly, cold rictus. "May the gods smile upon your happiness."

Astrid sat motionless as everyone returned to their noisy jesting, greasy feasting, and the careless spilling of mead. She strained to recall a time Reidar told her he loved her, spoke of a future together, or even kissed her of his own will. She couldn't—for he never had. And why would he? She'd all but leapt into his bed at the crook of his finger, giving away what should have been a battle hard-fought and a prize hard-won. Chest pounding, she glared at the Irish whelp beside him, sitting demure and proper and sipping her dainty sips of Norse mead.

A terrible knowing crept through Astrid, cold and sharp as ice. Christian women often demanded marriage before lying with a man. The first time Astrid heard of it, she laughed. Foolishness—to deny the gods their due. She gulped, unable to fathom that Reidar—*her* Reidar, who'd bedded so many women he'd lost count—would wait until marriage to claim a thrall!

"You must be heartbroken," Astrid's cousin, Sigrid, said from across the table. But Sigrid knew nothing of heartbreak—not with her strong husband and three handsome sons. "What a shame to wed a heathen thrall when he could have had a fine woman like you. He is not worth your spit." Sigrid scowled into her mead. "Find one deserving of you."

Reidar draped his arm around his so-called wife, laughing at some jest, while the girl drank from a horn so large she needed both hands to lift it.

"Yes, I shall," Astrid muttered, staring ahead. She didn't want another. She wanted Reidar. She loved him since they were children, and she'd want no other as long as she lived.

Slowly, she fixed her gaze on the heathen daughter of rot, uncaring if anyone saw.

*Freya, goddess of love and war, heed my pleas and strike her dead. Let her beauty fade like frost in the sun. Let her womb be barren, her breath stolen in sleep. Loki, trickster, tear the heart from her chest and twist it in your fist. Let her choke on her good fortune. Let her suffer as I do. I gave him everything. I bled for him. And still, he chose her. Let all the Æsir see it and make her pay.*

Ingrid, he'd named her—beautiful goddess! Astrid would have laughed if she weren't so close to tears. A false name for a false woman! The thrall wasn't Norse, and she was no goddess, beautiful or otherwise. The images slashed through Astrid's mind like a rusted blade. This wedding night should have been hers. Reidar loving his wife for the first time should have been hers. Offering their union to the gods should have been hers.

She flinched, as if burned, beneath the weight of an unseen stare. And before she knew how it came about, she'd locked eyes with the jarl. He peered at her for a beat, then lifted his chin toward the door. So slight a movement she would have missed it, had she not marked the flick of his gaze. Then, he turned to Asbjorn, and it was as if it never happened.

The evening wore on. All around her, the hall swelled with drunken cheer—raised horns, slurred songs, careless laughter. And Astrid played the merry fool, boasting and laughing even as her stomach turned from food and mead alike. Still, her eyes clung to the high seat, so she saw the moment the jarl rose and left without so much as a glance in her direction.

Her heart pounded like a hammer striking iron as time slowed to a dreadful crawl. She'd likely lingered too long, wary of drawing attention. But at last, she stood, and making a show of stretching and stumbling, went out. She spotted him outright—a large, hulking shape standing in the shadows and watching the night.

The rain stopped falling, and the earth lay heavy and dark beneath the dim glow of the half-moon. Slowly, Astrid crept forward, careful to muffle the sound of her boots in the mud.

"How utterly humiliating," Vargr said without turning, "to have a thrall steal your betrothed. "How terribly it must sting."

His gravelly voice made Astrid's skin crawl. She drew her shoulders up, struggling to suppress a shudder that ran the length of her body.

"It is true, my lord," she forced out.

"You wished to have a word." He turned to face her. "Speak."

Astrid blinked as her thoughts scattered like leaves in the wind beneath his dead gaze. "I—" she shivered—"I better return to the hall—"

He tilted his head, as if measuring her and finding lacking. "I see I had been wrong about you, Astrid. You are just as the rest of them—beautiful but not too proud. A pity, especially after being discarded like a used rag."

Astrid curled her hands into fists. The way Vargr put it—humiliated, discarded—that was the truth. Reidar hadn't just chosen another in her place. He had shamed her.

"I seek your help, my lord." Astrid's voice trembled despite her effort to steady it. "I ask that you intercede on my behalf and...return Reidar to me!"

The jarl's gaze upon her lay dark and heavy, like a wolf sizing up its prey. "Hmm." He clasped his hands behind his back. "No small charge it is to tear a man from his wedded wife and drive him into the arms of the woman he cast aside."

A thick lump rose in Astrid's throat, near dragging the unshed tears with it.

"A bold request, shield-maiden." He held her gaze. "And not easily granted."

Her stomach knotted at the way his eyes raked her—like a rabbit trussed for the spit. A sensation too terrible to name swept through her. She needed to leave before he stepped closer, before more words passed between them.

She straightened, suppressing a new tremor. "Apologies for the bother, my lord."

He drew so close, she nearly gagged from his scent of sharp sweat, old mead, and stale urine.

"I did not say it would be impossible." He bent, murmuring into her face. "I only said it would be difficult."

Astrid was tall and hale, but the jarl towered over her, his bulk twice hers.

"I could help you—" He licked his lip, and it took all her strength not to flinch at the low, feral notes in his voice. "But you must prove your loyalty to me first, shield-maiden. The choice is yours."

Astrid stood very still as he withdrew a pace with a scoff. Vargr was the jarl. Nothing in Ljosstrond lay beyond his reach. She stared at her clasped hands, forcing her misgivings away, replacing them with a bright flicker of hope. "I thank you, my lord," she heard herself say.

"Good." He closed the gap between them, his face a blade's width from hers, eyes boring into hers like two hot coals. "I will rid you of your rival, but I will take something of yours as a bargain."

"My lord," Astrid whispered, pushing down a belated alarm.

He reached for her lip, dragging it down with his hard, cold thumb. "I warn you, woman. Lying with me will be like standing bare in the clash of steel, for I am no gentle lover." His dark gaze traveled down her body, then returned to her face. "Do you still wish for my help?"

Astrid's heart thudded so hard it hurt her chest. Like everyone in Ljosstrond, she knew about his dead wives and his way with women. But she wasn't a pathetic, helpless thrall or some foreign, weakling girl given to him in marriage. She was a shield-maiden—the best of her kind—and he just said it would be like a battle. Astrid had no fear of battles, nor of rough lovemaking.

This didn't mean she wanted to lie with Vargr.

"Must it be so, my lord?" she breathed.

"It must." He shot her a tight, mirthless smile. "And you would play another part in our little plot. Are you agreeable?

Astrid nodded. "I am, my lord, as long as you promise to remove the heathen whore from Ljosstrond."

"Yes." His cold hand slid to her neck, stroking. "Once the thrall is gone and you wed our grieving Reidar, you will bring me word of his designs. I know he seeks to unseat me." He scowled, lips curling. "If I harm you, Astrid, I will also reward you handsomely for your knowledge. You shall have Reidar as your husband and me as your patron."

Astrid's limbs grew heavy as iron. She did not wish to betray Reidar, yet if it meant claiming him, it would be worth the price. Especially if she told only half-truths and not for a long while.

"My lord—" she tightened her jaw—"how will you rid me of her?"

Vargr's smile was the kind that haunted children's dreams. "I will tell you in time. Do you agree to my conditions, Astrid?"

She swallowed against her racing heart, not daring to question the jarl further. It didn't matter. The gods had finally smiled upon her. Even if she didn't know the means, she knew enough of Vargr to be certain—the wretched thrall would not survive him. And when the girl was gone, Reidar would be hers. Free of the Christian's charms, his mind would clear, his focus return, and together they would overthrow his uncle. Nothing would stand in their way then.

"I do," she forced out as his hand trailed to her chest, hard and heavy as a battleaxe.

"Good." He removed it abruptly, like a wolf snapping its jaws. "I will await you in my chamber tonight."

# Chapter Thirty-One

Fire

***Brigit***

**Seventh Night**

*You will live forever with three-headed giants*
*Or never know a husband;*
*(Let longing grip you, let wasting waste you.)*
*You will be like the thistle*
*That was thrown into the loft and crushed there.*
— Skírnismál, stanza 31

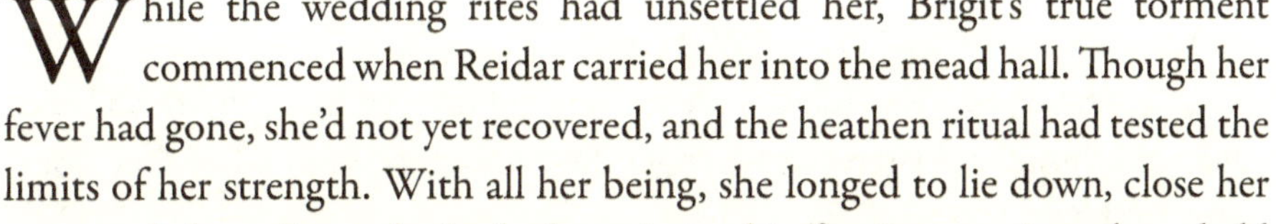

While the wedding rites had unsettled her, Brigit's true torment commenced when Reidar carried her into the mead hall. Though her fever had gone, she'd not yet recovered, and the heathen ritual had tested the limits of her strength. With all her being, she longed to lie down, close her eyes, and sleep. Instead, she had to sit in this foreign, roaring place, held steady only by Reidar's arm at her back.

Someone placed a hammer in her lap—larger than the one Reidar wore on a chain around his neck. Thor's hammer—to bless their union with fertility and abundance of children. Through the thick haze, she listened to ribald taunts, blind to her fragile state: "I hope the bed is stronger than Reidar's back. Wouldn't want the bride to break two things in one night!" and "If she walks straight tomorrow, we will all know he is no warrior where it counts!" and "May their night be long, their furs warm, and their voices hoarse by morning!"

At last, it was over, and she lay still in his arms as he carried her home. While she knew nothing of Norse customs, all marriages must be consummated. And now that it was upon her, she dreaded what was coming with all her heart and soul. But not with her body, which made it all the more unbearable. She'd worn no veil and saw no cross—only sky and rain and blood. No priest had blessed their union, no holy sacrament sealed it. No vow had been sworn before the Lord. Surely, this was not a marriage in His holy sight. It was a mockery of vows—a wife in flesh only, and her baser nature only too eager to comply.

Brigit held her breath as her new husband opened the door of his longhouse and strode to his chamber. The bed stood newly made, untouched and expectant, a red cloth dyed with crush berries draped across.

He laid her down in her white wedding gown, then sat beside her and smoothed an errant strand away from her face with a gentle hand.

"Reidar, please forgive me—" she swallowed, "I—"

"Shh." He brushed a finger across her lips. "We are together now. Rest easy, my love."

Brigit slept all night and most of the following day. When she woke, she found herself alone, the chamber dim and quiet, save for the muffled thrum of voices and laughter drifting in from the hall. She sucked in her breath—she still wore her wedding gown.

All at once, her nose filled with the smell of roasted meat and fresh bread, and her stomach twisted with hunger. Stretching, she pulled on her boots, went to the door, and eased it open.

The hall was full of men. She remembered most from Dalaradia. She retreated.

"...by Thor—" A bench scraped across the floor. A hoarse voice rose above the din. "I split him from shoulder to hip!"

A fist struck wood. Cups jumped. "You could not split firewood straight last winter!"

Strange how the same words that once filled her with fear now wrapped around her like an old cloak. Stranger still, how dull and crude they sounded as the men boasted of past raids, their laughter loud and bragging louder.

She entered the hall.

Reidar sat at the head of the table with a drinking horn in his hand and a frown on his face. As if sensing her, he turned. In an instant, his eyes lit up.

"Come and join our wedding feast, wife." He stood. "You must be hungry."

"Ah, there she is, the bride who barely survived her first battle!" The man to his right laughed.

Wide-eyed, Brigit drew back. He was the same one who entered her chamber in Dalaradia—the one she'd thought her new master. Heat surged up her chest and into her cheeks, and she fixed him with a glare.

Reidar shook his head, a groove deepening between his eyebrows. "She speaks our tongue, brother, but she is not one for these jests." He motioned to her. "Come, wife, do not mind these drunkards. They are harmless."

The man shrugged and upended his horn.

They looked anything but harmless, but Brigit pasted a tight smile on her face and took her place on the bench beside Reidar.

The scent belonged to a roasted boar, so rich and tender it melted on her tongue. The mead, sweet and golden, warmed her from within. Her gaze fell on the coarse loaf, its crust dark and steam curling from the broken edge. Her heart gave a jolt against her chest. It looked just like the barley bread her father brought from the monastery after trading his catch with the monks.

She reached for it, tore a piece free, and raised it to her lips. In a heartbeat, the years fell away. She was a girl again, sitting barefoot on the rushes, sun on her face, sea salt in her hair, her father's laughter filling the hut as she bit into that same warm bread.

Dazed, she turned to Reidar. "Who bakes this?" she whispered.

But he only shrugged. "You like it? I will have them bring more."

Hunger eased and heart quieted, Brigit leaned back and studied the hall. Laughter rang off the timbers, voices rising as the men swapped tales of plunder and storms, past glories, and journeys yet to come. None spared her a glance.

A tight squeeze gripped her ribs. She was alone with this heathen horde, her unsanctified husband's faith new and untested, half-shaped by belief, half by her presence. Worse, he had let her rest, but now that she was whole and fed, he would expect her to act the wife in full. A blazing wave of heat surged through her, followed by a sinking in her gut. The undertow dragged her down no matter how hard she fought it.

Just then, as though summoned by some ill wind, Reidar stood and took her hand, ignoring a new burst of lewd jests.

"Off with you two now!"

"If the bride needs help, I will gladly show her how it is done!"

"May the gods grant you sons!"

They stepped into the chamber together, but Reidar left her by the door as he strode to the bed. Mute, he shed his furs, belt, and trousers. She'd been helpless when he first did this in Dalaradia, and she clung to that excuse, telling herself the blame would not be hers. Now, standing free at this threshold, she would be complicit.

A strange thought seized Brigit as Reidar pulled off his white tunic, revealing his powerful torso—beautiful but for the multitude of heathen marks. This mockery would be no different from her first marriage, only now she was taking part willingly. While her wedlock with Cearbhall mac Bressal had been a binding contract of power and lechery, this was a union forged in foreign ritual of blood and necessity. Did it matter that it was also born of love, even if twisted at the start?

Reidar turned and approached.

She smoothed the soft weave of her wedding dress with a rigid hand.

"My Ingrid." He bent to her mouth, brushing his lips against hers. As if sparked by unseen magic, warmth bloomed through her limbs, the fire in the torches mixing and melding and wrapping her in their brilliant glow. He deepened his kiss, and she wanted to weep with joy. The walls, the bed, the flames—all fell away. Impermanent, unimportant, inconsequential. Only this kiss, scented with sea, rain, and for the first time—with freedom—the one she waited for her whole life.

He withdrew, and the loss of him made her knees wobble. Without a word, he took her hand and led her to the bed but didn't lay her down. Instead, he moved to stand behind her.

"Ingrid?" he said, low.

She closed her eyes, trembling in his nearness, disbelieving that he was asking her permission while he could take all he wanted now she was his wife. This man—her new husband—was the boy Reidar she'd longed for through seven long winters. And he was still as she remembered—kind, strong, and handsome. Better yet, he loved her enough to wed, and though his faith was new, they were now equally yoked.

If only their first meetings weren't so warped and shadowed.

Until this moment, Brigit had been too sick, frightened, and overcome by all that life had thrown at her to gather her wits. Now, a treacherous knot tightened in her belly as an unbidden memory of her ruined island, burned monastery, murdered father, and enslaved mother flooded her like a riptide.

The sparks died away. The chamber grew cold.

Owing to his people—and him—she'd become a slave who worked from dusk to dawn for a measly meal that always left her hungry and with nothing but thin, moldy straw for a bed. Owing to his people—and him—she was sold to the man who defiled her while hiding behind the sanctity of marriage. Owing to him, she was now a stranger in this strange land, forever sundered from her home.

Heart sick, Brigit closed her eyes, willing to rid herself of the visions better confined to the past. But they lingered. Every evil thing done to her lay at the feet of Reidar's people—and his own—for he left her when he could have taken her along. And now, she was moments from committing the sin of the flesh in a bed that wasn't blessed by a proper marriage.

He walked around to face her, his eyes searching hers. "What troubles you, my love?"

She dropped her gaze. "Though you proclaim your faith—" her words emerged faint and shaky despite her best efforts—"you still think all that sword passing and blood spilling make you my husband, but our union is not blessed by the Lord."

Mute, he reached for her face and wiped away her sorrow with his thumb. A big, patterned savage seeking Christ and drying her tears. Her cheeks burned as if aflame, and she lifted her eyes and peered at him.

"You still loathe me." He stood unmoving, his large hands hanging at his sides, shoulders drooping as if weighted by boulders.

Brigit bit her lip until it throbbed, searching for the right words to tell him she loathed what his people stood for, what they had done, and what they would continue to do. But never him. She yearned to tell him she loved him with all her heart and soul. But the gap between them yawned too wide, and she needed his aid to cross it.

She parted her lips. "I—"

A long horn blast outside made her hair stand on end. It was followed by a loud banging on the door.

"Reidar, come out!" a man shouted. "Grain is on fire!"

"By the gods." With a wild look, Reidar whirled around. "I must go, Ingrid. Our grain..." Quickly, he pulled on his tunic, trousers, and boots. "I will come back as soon as—" He stared at her with wide, stricken eyes, then charged toward the door.

"Reidar—" Heart thudding, she bolted after him, out of the chamber and down the emptying hall. "I don't—"

"I will make it right—I swear to you," he tossed over his shoulder before rushing out.

She peered outside as his broad form disappeared into the darkness. In the distance, a large hut stood engulfed in flames, the air reeking of scorched grain, dark smoke curling in the moonlit sky. Brigit strained into the night, imagining him caught in the blaze, his tunic aflame, his cries swallowed by the roar of burning timber. The vision coiled in her chest, twisting until she could hardly breathe. The fear of losing him, of never hearing his voice again, rushed through her limbs colder than the winter wind.

Brigit withdrew inside. Everyone had gone—even Gyda—leaving her completely alone for the first time since her arrival. The thought landed like a stone. She sat on the bed. Maybe the fire was a mercy, sparing her from the sin she'd come so close to committing. Sickened, she shook herself—how selfish and daft to fancy the entire village would go without grain all winter for her unstained soul. More likely, this was the work of some evil spirit. This place teemed with them like an anthill with ants.

She lurched at the footfall outside the chamber. Strange that he returned so soon.

Before she gained her feet, the door crashed open, and in walked Reidar's erstwhile "sweetheart," Astrid, with a rope in her hand and a scowl on her face.

# Chapter Thirty-Two

## Heartbreak
***Astrid***

*I am going to the wood,*
*And to the wet forest,*
*To find a magic wand;*
*I have found a magic wand.*
— Skírnismál, stanza 32

For a night and a day, Astrid remained in bed, feigning illness and refusing all food and drink, for she could stomach neither. Vargr had lied when he said lying with him would be like a battle without weapons, for Astrid had the mettle for a true fight. In battle, she fought with axe and shield, and when those failed her, she bested her enemies with her bare hands and brute strength. But she had been as powerless as a blade of grass against the beast that was Vargr—the vicious, bloodthirsty Fenrir, set upon chaos and destruction. For what took place in his chamber was not a battle at all. It was plunder—a depredation the likes of which the most brutal berserkers reserved for thralls and whores.

Astrid knew pain and didn't fear it, but this was another kind altogether. Worse, never in her life had she been so humiliated, for she'd found herself stripped of all dignity and nearly pleading with the jarl to let her leave. But he'd only sneered, and for one terrible moment, she thought he would kill her. Instead, he pushed her away and sat up.

"You fought well. I expected no less from a shield-maiden." He yawned as she scrambled to pull on her tunic with shaking hands.

He fixed her with a cold stare. "Now remember our agreement. Tomorrow, when darkness falls, I will see to the fire, and you to the girl."

She didn't reply for fear of sobbing, but bent her head low, wrestling her boots onto her feet.

He stood, and despite herself, she shrank back with a stifled gasp.

Swift as a striking blade, he grabbed her chin and pushed it up, forcing her to look at him. "If you so much as dream of other ideas, I will say you started the fire, then abducted and killed the girl. No one would question it, for you—not I—have the most to gain from her death." He gripped her neck, squeezing so hard she broke into a coughing fit. "Do we have an understanding?"

"Yes," she choked out.

"Good." He tightened the vise, making her sight blur. "And when it is done, and you wed Reidar, you will report all he says against me—lest you wish to be found out. Answer me!"

"Yes," she croaked.

"If you do not obey my orders as they come, I will take another night from you, and this one will seem a lover's first kiss by comparison."

He'd laughed in her face before releasing her, trembling and gasping for breath.

Now, her body ached as though she'd come back from the most vicious fight of her life. Worse, Vargr's defilement had done something awful to her, for she hardly cared for Reidar's betrayal now and even less for delivering the Irish witch into his uncle's rabid clutches. Vargr said once he'd had his fill, he would cast her body into the wilds for wolves and crows. There wouldn't be a shred of her left by the time a search party went looking. The notion filled Astrid with revulsion and a hatred for Vargr that burned hotter than her love for Reidar ever had.

But she was no longer free to love or hate, so she kicked open Reidar's door and limped into the chamber where they used to make love.

Still wearing her accursed wedding gown, the daughter of rot sat on the bed, where at the height of passion, Astrid asked Reidar to wed her, and he locked his lips with hers and kissed her deep in reply.

The harlot shrieked and sprang to her feet, but everyone had gone to put out the fire, so her screams reached no one's ears. Slowly, Astrid impounded on the whelp of Hel. Everything that befell Astrid was this girl's fault. If not for her, she'd have been wed to the beautiful, strong Reidar instead of becoming a whore and a game piece of his beastly uncle.

With a vicious war cry, Astrid pushed the detestable thrall onto the bed and stuffed her mouth with a rag she'd stashed into her belt. She rolled her into the pelts to disable her arms and quickly looped her rope around the writhing bolt, wrapping it a few times and pulling tight. The jarl's command was clear—bring her alive. Cursing him, Astrid yanked the furs from the girl's face.

Ignoring the pain that flared through her, Astrid grabbed the mute, still bundle and headed outside. She spared a glance at the grain store. It stood engulfed in flames. Shouts and screams echoed through the smoke-choked air, breaking against the wail of children. The stench of burning wood and grain filled the night like some evil spirit. They likely lost all their stores and would have no bread all winter. It served Astrid right. But what had her people done to deserve such a fate?

Groaning, she dragged her burden a distance away, where her steed stood sniffing the air, his nostrils flaring against the smoke. Teeth clenched, Astrid hoisted the Irish whelp onto her horse's broad shoulder and used another rope to tie her down. Then she mounted herself, landing onto the hard saddle with a pained gasp. She should have padded it with furs, but how could she think of everything when her body was failing her?

The full moon laid bare her path and her living, breathing curse. Save for her round, staring eyes, the cunning fox remained still as a post. For all her injuries, Astrid had done a fine job with the rope. Quickly, she urged the horse into a gallop toward the wilds, biting her lip to keep from screaming as each jolt tore through her with agony she never knew before. It grew unbearable with every step, and despite her need to hurry, she stopped several times, teeth clenched and tears streaming down her cheeks.

At last, she reached the old hunter's lodge. A clever choice—the place was no longer in use, for its timbers rotted from disrepair. Cursing hard and loud, Astrid yanked the unmoving bolt down from her horse, dragged it into the hut, and hurled it onto the floorboards. The impact had to hurt, but the harlot didn't make a sound, nor spared a look at Astrid. No, the witch's face was a picture of perfect serenity, her eyes leagues away.

Panting, Astrid wiped her tears and sank onto the floor beside the accursed thrall. All of Ljosstrond buzzed with talk of her Norse, smooth as a native's, so Astrid did not bother with Irish this time.

"I have changed my mind," she spat, steadying her voice. "I will not rip out your heart and eat it while you watch. No, what I have in store for you is much worse, for you will soon be devoured by a ravening beast of Hel, then torn to shreds by a pack of hungry, rabid wolves."

Astrid stared at the pale, wan face. Nothing moved in it. The talk was false, of course. The thrall hadn't understood a word.

"Your soon fate—ravage and mangle by beast," she tried again in Irish, "then eat by wolf."

Astrid received no response. The viper didn't seem to be there—working her heathen spells, no doubt.

A white-hot riptide swept through Astrid, and she shook the harlot so hard, her head bumped against the floor. "Your Christ magic will not help you now," Astrid shouted in her face, "for it is powerless against our true gods! Reidar has always been mine and will remain mine while not even a trace of you will be left in Midgard." She pulled the rag from the harlot's mouth. "What do you say to this? Speak!"

The thrall licked her lips and swallowed. "Thank you for removing the rag. It was hard to breathe," she said in perfect Norse. "I am sorry you are in so much pain."

Though it hurt her mightily, Astrid bent to the insolent foreigner and locked eyes with her. "Very soon," she said in a soft, low voice, "you will know agony and humiliation you had never dreamed of. And you will suffer like I suffered. But you will die, and I will live, and I will bear Reidar's sons while even the memory of you will vanish."

A sob bubbling in her chest, Astrid stood and turned on her heel, then stumbled out, and shut the door. She dragged herself a distance away from the lodge, then collapsed onto the cold, hard ground, and wept like she did when she was small. She'd hoped her angry words would ease some of her sorrow, but they didn't—not in the face of such unfathomable courage.

Though it rankled to admit this, the Irish thrall had more mettle than was her due.

*See that you don't choke on my heart, for it's full of thorns and venom.*

Astrid still couldn't believe she'd dared defy her in Reidar's sick chamber. She scoffed. It would be a grave error to try it with Vargr—not that it mattered. The girl wouldn't survive the jarl, even if he meant her to, which he didn't.

The thought turned Astrid's stomach. She rolled onto her side and curled into a ball. When she was nursing Reidar back to life in Dalaradia, and he was consumed by fever, it wasn't her name he breathed again and again. She would never forget his wince when the fever finally broke, and he found her there instead of his "Ingrid." A low, gutted wail burst from Astrid's bruised lips. Though he'd been well enough to receive pleasure, he refused it. It was a terrible thing to admit to herself, but she couldn't remember when Reidar last said he loved her. Or if he ever said it at all. All their talk of marriage and future belonged to her; he only listened. Each time they drew close, it had been by her lead. He never asked her to come on any of his voyages—she tagged along of her own accord.

Moaning, Astrid rocked against the cold earth. He'd let her go long before he found his Irish harlot. Maybe he was never hers to begin with. And if she didn't have Reidar, what did she have? With all her being, she wanted the answer to be the gods, but her only reply was silence. Hollow, aching, and vast.

Her lip twisted. Either the gods were a lie, or they were no gods at all, but evil spirits bent on inflicting harm. For not once when she prayed and sacrificed to Freya, did the goddess answer. And though Astrid believed she'd been heard this time, the reply proved a cruel, bitter mockery. In truth, too often, Astrid sensed all that worship was folly turned inward. She had taken on the look and might of Freya, convincing herself to believe in something that wasn't there.

Astrid wiped her tears and sat up. Even the Irish harlot was better off with her Christ magic. In the face of life's worst horrors, she held a peace beyond Astrid's knowing. What mighty God gave her such courage to meet a grim fate with clear eyes and an unshaken soul?

Far off, a wolf's cry tore through the dark, thin and mournful. Deeper in the wilds, another howl answered. Shivering, Astrid rose and mounted her horse. She rode slowly, for every jolt hurt like a thousand axe wounds. She would not fight the wolves if they fell upon her, for if they dragged her down, her torment would end.

The night stretched dark and indifferent, save for the faltering moonlight that lit her path. By the time she reached the village, the fire would be out, and everyone—tired and disheartened by the devastating loss—would be abed, falling into an uneasy slumber.

Astrid huffed a bitter breath and lifted her eyes to the uncaring expanse above.

"I no longer believe in you, Freya," she spat, "for I would not feel so utterly alone if you cared for me."

# Chapter Thirty-Three

## Torment

***Brigit***

**Seventh Night**

*Odin is angry, the best of the gods is angry,*
*Freyr will be your enemy,*
*Worst of maidens, who has earned*
*The magic wrath of the gods.*
— Skírnismál, stanza 33

"Make haste, oh God, to deliver me! Oh Lord, make haste to help me!"

Brigit's voice scarcely sounded like her own, thin and muffled against her aching head. The throbbing began when she bounced mercilessly atop the galloping horse. It turned into pounding after Astrid slammed her to the floor like a sack of peat. Though the furs had softened the blow to her body, her head had struck bare. Now the world tipped and twisted, a sick churn in her gut rising with it. But that was nothing compared to the ice clawing up her spine. The shield-maiden had gone, and soon, the "ravening beast of Hel" would come to devour Brigit before throwing her body to a pack of rabid wolves.

Her blood ran cold, and she closed her eyes to shut out the horrors. They remained.

Though the night blinded her, the lodge reeked of neglect. The air about her hung thick with the scent of damp wood, laced with the musk of nesting rodents and the sharp tang of rot. Brigid's heart raced so fast, the thuds in her head reverberated into her fingertips. She was bound and alone in an abandoned hut in the dark of night. Reidar wouldn't know to look for her here, and even if he did, the beast was likely on its way. Or was it Astrid herself who would return to torment and then kill her?

Something small scattered a foot away, then another. A wild hope flittered—if the rats chewed through her bonds, she could flee before it was too late. But that was daft, for the rats didn't want the rope. They were only after what all living creatures wanted—nourishment. So Brigit squeezed her eyes shut and fought against the mounting terror with the only weapon she had.

"Answer me quickly, Lord; my spirit fails." The words emerged thin and feverish. "Do not hide Your face from me, or I will be like those who go down to the pit. Let the morning bring me word of Your unfailing love, for I have put my trust in You."

Brigit drew a long, steadying breath against her racing heart. She needed to take stock, to think, to focus. Even in the dim, it was clear something dreadful had befallen the shield-maiden. Her lip was split as if from a savage blow, her neck beneath the slipping pelt mottled with dark bruises, and her strange new limp betrayed excruciating pain. Even her viciousness, though genuine enough, seemed lacking in heat. More posture than heart. Her state was so strange, at first Brigit half-believed she was doing someone else's bidding. The notion dissipated when Astrid spoke words of rage and enmity to her.

*Heartache and torment.* Brigit would have both. Unless she freed herself and ran from this place as far as her eyes could see.

Once again, she jerked inside her tight encasement. Despite her grievous injuries, Astrid had made an unyielding prison out of furs and rope. Brigit's breath came fast as she tried to roll from side to side to loosen her bindings. With all her strength, she pushed her elbows through the furs. She'd gained a fingerbreadth. One more attempt—hardly the breadth of a knuckle. For a long time, she rocked, pushed, and writhed but hadn't gained enough span to free one arm.

A low, ominous howling pierced the night, making Brigit's hair stand on end. Ravenous wolves. There was no use freeing herself, for where would she go? She was much too far from the village, didn't know the way back, and the wolves would fall upon her as soon as she wandered into the darkness. Chest pounding, Brigit ceased her struggle, trying her best to ignore several pairs of small eyes gleaming in the faint moonlight. Hungry rats. Her heart stopped, then came back to life like a hammer, leaving her covered in cold sweat. If the rodents were numerous enough, would they feast on her?

"Go away!" she screamed, ignoring her aching head. "There is no food for you here!"

She steadied her breath as the critters scattered. Astrid was wrong, but she was right, too. While Ljosstrond crawled with evil, God ruled everywhere—even here. Strange how she came so close to having what she desired most in this world only to have it wrenched from her before she succumbed to her weakness.

Brigit dug her fingernails into her palms, trying to halt her reeling mind. But it pushed back, filling her head with notions too terrible to fathom. Upon his return, Reidar would find her gone. After what she told him, he'd think she'd fled. Why wouldn't he? She'd made it clear she didn't see them as truly wed. He thought she still loathed him.

Her breath caught fast and shallow, rising too quickly in her chest, suffocating her. Surely, once healed, Astrid would find her way back to him, and that was only as it should have been. Brigit pretended not to notice the warm, salty rivulets slipping down her cheeks and stinging her lips. With her fierce, striking beauty, Astrid matched Reidar's strength the way Brigit never could.

The ache in Brigit's heart eclipsed the pounding in her head, clenching her chest like a fist. She'd lost him for good this time. How different life might have been if only he'd taken her along those seven winters past. Then he would've kept her as his concubine, cloaked in his love and protection. He'd likely never taken Astrid to his bed at all. And while that would have been sinful, she wouldn't be lying now in this forsaken place, bracing to be ravaged and mangled by the "beast of Hel."

The world reeled and tilted. Her sobs filled the miserable hut to the brim, hoarse and mournful against the stillness of the night. A wake for what never was and would never be—

She froze at a telling warm trickle beneath her wedding dress—her flow couldn't have come at a worse time. The scent of blood would surely draw the wolves. Then, they would tear through the crumbling logs that made up the lodge's sorry walls and rip her to shreds.

"Turn to me and be gracious to me, Father, for I am lonely and afflicted," Brigit whispered through trembling lips. "Free me from my anguish!"

She said other things, some pleading and some too angry to count as a prayer, then she closed her eyes and wished for oblivion. But sleep never came, and soon the dawn unfurled like a shroud, bleak and pitiless. It banished the rodents and brought about thirst, made crueler by the soft pitter-patter of rain outside.

Brigit swallowed against her parched throat and scanned her prison. The place lay in shambles, its timbers blackened by the scorch of old fires, the roof sagging beneath the weight of age and neglect. A cold draft swept through the many cracks, stirring the scattered remnants of pelt and bone and carrying the pungent scent of mildew and earth's decay. Yet thanks to Reidar's furs and her own boots, the chill touched only Brigit's face.

She went still—Astrid wanted her alive. Brigit's sight blurred at the edges, flickering and fading; her breath exploded in painful thunderclaps. Of course, it wouldn't be Astrid—the woman would have already killed her. No, it would be darkness that ruled here above all. The beast not of Hel, but of hell, and perhaps there was no difference.

The walls rushed toward her, twisting and menacing. They swallowed her whole.

She came back to herself as dusk claimed the day, stealing what scant light filtered through the cracks. Yet the beast hadn't come. And as the night fell—colder and thirstier than before—Brigit understood. There was no beast. Astrid had left her here to a slow, horrific death.

Her heartbeat roared in her ears, drowning out thought. With all her might, she thrashed against her bounds, then screamed a bone-chilling cry of a banshee that echoed for none but the scurrying rodents.

Sharp as a lightning flash, a loud neighing outside shattered the night. Brigit's scream died. Panting, she fixed her gaze on the door, praying for Reidar to cross the threshold.

Her heart soared as the ground trembled with heavy footsteps. "Reidar!"

The door opened, and in walked the jarl with a torch in his hand.

Brigit's sight shimmered with bright wee spots, but she dared not blink. For a long moment, all she heard was the mad reel of her heartbeat in her ears. He'd appeared menacing enough in the great hall. But now, as he loomed above her, a cold smile twisting his hideous face, eyes dark and lifeless beneath a low brow, he resembled a beast.

An icy chill rushed through Brigit. It left her limp and numb.

"Ah," the jarl gave a sharp, ugly laugh, driving the torch into the half-ruined hearth. "And I feared I had waited too long! You simply refuse to die, hmm? Do not fret, you will surely die this time." He licked his lip. "But not very fast at all."

Brigit's heartbeat thundered so fiercely in her head, it drowned out his words. Her breath wedged in her throat as the trick of the night turned the jarl's mouth into a snout and lit his cruel eyes with a dark, restless flame. Strange how her mind wandered. It was hard to fathom this creature had once been a small boy, loved and tended. What sort of darkness had he welcomed in to twist him so?

Her terror ebbed, leaving behind a hollow, glum stillness. He believed himself lord over life and death, yet he was the one who stood condemned.

*Our Father in heaven...*

The beast squatted beside her. "You must be not only beautiful but very skilled in bed to charm such a man as Reidar. My nephew had known many beautiful women, but none of them grabbed him enough to wed."

*Hallowed be Your name...*

He leaned in, breathing rot and depravity into her face. "I will learn just how good you are, and I will make you better."

*Your kingdom come, Your will be done...*

He pulled a dagger from his belt.

*On earth as it is in heaven...*

He brought the blade to her bindings and slashed through them.

*Forgive us our debts as we forgive our debtors...*

He threw back the furs. "Stand when I talk to you." Fast as a lynx, he grabbed her wrist and pulled her up.

*...deliver us from evil, for Yours is the kingdom, and the power, and the glory, for ever and ever...*

His gaze skimmed her trembling body, and his face contorted into a mask of revulsion mixed with something resembling fear.

She glanced down. In the center of her white wedding gown spread a dark crimson stain the size of a splayed hand.

"By Loki!" The jarl's face turned the color of bog fire. With an awful obscenity, he spat and aimed to kick her but whirled and brought his foot to the wall instead. The logs creaked in protest, low and mournful. "What spell did you cast to time your bleeding so?"

Brigit lifted her head and met his eyes. "In Jesus Christ's name. Amen," she said very clearly in Irish.

He drew back. "Save your curses, I will not touch a bleeding witch. Your magic will not work on me!" He spat on the floor. "Run if you wish. You will never find the way back, and this forest is teeming with hungry wolves."

He barreled to the door but halted before leaving. "Still, you did not go completely to waste. You did me a fine favor by hexing Reidar the Sapling." He scoffed. "Marrying a sickly thrall when he could have had the beautiful and strong Astrid, along with the might of her father and brothers. No one will follow him now, and his foolish plans to unseat me will fade like ashes in the wind!"

Brigit sank onto the dirt floor as he slammed the door shut. Outside, the creak of a saddle gave way to pounding hooves that faded into the night. Shaking like a leaf and dizzy with thirst, she wrapped herself in a pelt, pushed the door open, and staggered out. A short distance away stood an old rain bucket, and she fell to her knees and drank from it long and deep.

When she'd drunk her fill, she stumbled back inside with tangled words of praise and gratitude. Then she rolled the remaining furs about her. And she slept.

# Chapter Thirty-Four

## Doubt
***Reidar***

*Listen, rulers of frost, hear, giants,*
*Sons of Suttungr,*
*And gods, too,*
*How I forbid and how I ban*
*The meeting of men with the maiden,*
*(The joy of men with the maiden.)*
— Skírnismál, stanza 34

Reidar sank onto the sand and shut his eyes, listening to the murmur of the waves lapping against the shore. After three days of searching, his men gave up. They'd combed well beyond the village—much farther than Ingrid could have ventured on foot—and found no trace of her. It was then he knew she'd thrown herself into the fjord, for if she'd gone anywhere else, they would have tracked her—or what was left of her.

He dug his fingers into his brow. At the very least, they would have spotted the fine wolf and fox furs she'd taken along. Chest hollow and aching, Reidar stared sightlessly ahead. She'd seized too many to carry. Thick, heavy bundles no delicate girl like her could have managed with ease. And why take them, only to cast them into the sea? It defied reason, yet no answers came.

He scanned the fjord for the thousandth time. He'd been guarding this shore since first light, murmuring what he remembered of the Lord's Prayer, watching the waves ebb and flow, and hoping against hope that her body didn't wash up. Numb, he dropped his head into his hands. He had no power over his cursed fate, for he was his people. And as his people spelled death and destruction to Éire, so he'd always been destined to destroy Ingrid. Defying fate never ended well for anyone. Even the wise and prophetic Frigg, who made every living thing swear not to harm her son Baldr, had overlooked the modest mistletoe, which Loki used to kill him. Even the all-powerful Odin, for all his hanging on Yggdrasil, sacrificing his eye, and seeking the dead's counsel, couldn't prevent Ragnarök. Even the brave Brynhild found nothing but heartache and ruin after defying Odin, for her beloved wed another.

Astrid's face flashed before Reidar, still and pale, making him wince. He'd done her wrong—there was no denying it. He should have stayed with her and never reached for what lay beyond his claim. Reidar swallowed hard against the knot in his throat. Ingrid had never been for him, nor he for her, even if they longed for each other during the few unguarded moments granted by his gods. Maybe it was that longing that doomed her in the end, for it was the very thing forbidden by hers.

Reidar knew enough of the Christian ways to understand her need to wed in a chapel. And after her God talked to him, he'd wished for one himself. But none stood in Norway, and he couldn't give her the sacred rite that would bind them before Christ. For he was his people.

He lifted his gaze heavenward. Maybe her God had seen him clearly at last—the man who'd torn through life with neither mercy nor remorse in his heart, spilling Christian blood with wild abandon. He gulped—and the man who'd repaid a loyal friend and lover with apathy and scorn. And for his sins, He took her from him. Or maybe her God was just like his gods—toying with mortals for pleasure, dangling new, shiny things, then ripping them away, bleeding and weeping. Or likelier, He didn't reign here, where the gods of Asgard ruled since the beginning of time. And now, Loki was having his revenge on Reidar for spurning his fate.

He traced a finger along the smooth carvings of his arm ring—the one he received when pledging his sword to Vargr, not a day after his father's send-off. His ears still rang with the memory of blinding rage as he knelt and spat the oath. Reidar clenched his fists. In his mind's eye, his father's pyre still smoldered in the wind, the *blodhefnd* that took root on that day coiling in his chest and spreading like the flames that consumed Harald Fairblade's corpse.

Reidar lifted his chin and glared at the tides. Instead of sitting here and praying to a foreign God, he should sacrifice generously to Odin. He should appease Loki. He should beg for Thor's revoked favor. But to what end? Save for Thor's strength and rage in battle, the gods never answered him. Now, strength served no purpose, and rage burned him hollow.

Heart slamming against his chest, Reidar grabbed a fistful of small rocks at his feet and hurled them before him with all his might.

"Whoever You are, I have had enough." He glowered at the clear, blue sky. "Strike me dead instead of tormenting me!"

No answer came, not that he'd expected one. He grabbed the *Mjolnir* charm at his throat. He ought to rip it from his neck and hurl it after the rocks—and Vargr's arm ring along with it. Then wear a cross to spite the gods.

He squinted. In the distance, a boat appeared, drawing near the shore. A small fishing skiff to carry a day's catch of haddock, pollock, and herring. It skimmed over the water, growing larger with each swell. The skiff slipped onto the sand with a soft scrape, and a single fisherman dragged it ashore. Gaze trained on Reidar, the man strode toward him.

Reidar fixed the fool with a cold stare. "What do you want?" He'd meant to pack all his fury and sorrow into his words, but they came out flat and brittle.

"Forgive me, my lord," the man bowed low, "but you seem to be in distress."

Reidar lifted an eyebrow, a bitter castigation bubbling in his throat. But it died on his lips. The fisherman—neither old nor young—looked strange, his silver hair shining, his thin tunic no match for the sea and dry when it should have been drenched. Yet he didn't seem cold as he stood before Reidar in his bare feet.

"Do not concern yourself with my distress," Reidar muttered. "Go back to your nets."

"I will, my lord." The man's eyes creased with a smile, shining as bright as his hair. "And you go back to yours."

Reidar dragged a hand over his face. "To mine?" The fisherman must be mad to order him around.

The man regarded him with a sure, steady calm. "Do not lose faith."

Gooseflesh, warm and tingling, covered Reidar from head to foot. "Who are you?" he whispered.

"My name is Gudbrand." The man touched Reidar's shoulder, his hand at once heavy and weightless. "None is to be found here. Go home and wait."

Mind racing, Reidar stared after the man as he walked away, then vanished into a wall of mist that hadn't been there before.

"Wait!" Reidar shot to his feet, rushing after him.

But when he reached the water's edge, the skiff was gone.

# Chapter Thirty-Five

## Confession
***Astrid***

*Hrímgrímnir is he, the giant who will have you*
*In the depth by the doors of Hel;*
*To the frost-giants' halls you will go every day,*
*Crawling and craving in vain,*
*(Crawling and having no hope.)*
— Skírnismál, stanza 35

Astrid dragged herself from her bed and stood in the gray of late morning. At long last, she'd made up her mind. At nightfall, she would mount her gelding and ride to the hunter's lodge beneath the cover of darkness. Then she'd know for certain whether the girl had perished or—

Astrid gulped, unable to keep this line of thought. But her thinking didn't matter. If by some twist of fate the foreigner still lived, Astrid would bring her back to Ljosstrond. The image of the small Irish thrall alone with Vargr had become all-consuming, like a sickness that devours from within. A strange affliction—for even as some part of Astrid hoped the jarl had forgotten the girl, another part of her wished just as fiercely that he had rid Ljosstrond of her for good. These warring notions burned hot as fever, and the only cure was to learn what became of the thrall. But she couldn't bear the idea of facing the hunting lodge alone.

Astrid's hands felt numb and heavy as she splashed her face with water from the basin and twisted her braids into a tight crown at the top of her head. Cold and rigid, she slipped into her finest woad-dyed gown and tugged on new cowhide boots, still smelling of the tannin and smoke.

She reached for the length of wool she wore to cover Vargr's marks. Though her flesh was mending, the bruises yet showed. Worse, inside she felt as bent and withered as an ancient crone and as foul as the muck beneath a midden cart. Neither woolen shawl, nor lovely braids, nor finery masked what she had become. Still, she took the wrap and wound it snugly about her neck.

The world swayed as she stepped into the gloom of autumn, heavy with clouds and unrelenting rain. She hadn't slept much since her night with the jarl, for when she shut her eyes, she saw hideous beasts with teeth like daggers and bloodied claws like swords. In her night terrors, they never touched her; instead, they ravaged the girl hidden away in the abandoned hunter's lodge. They attacked, mangled, and tore her to shreds while Astrid screamed, bound and helpless. But even as they murdered her, the girl remained silent, keeping her wide, unblinking eyes fixed on Astrid.

In these dreams, Astrid wanted to run, hide, cover herself from that accusing gaze, but it followed her everywhere she went. And when she woke, trembling and coated in cold sweat, she still saw those strange green eyes, full of reproach and reprobation. Yet no matter how many times she tried to summon the old hatred and disgust for the accursed foreigner and cast off the unbearable weight pressing on her chest, she always failed.

There were other visions, too—so vile they turned her stomach and left her gasping for breath in the dark. She buried them deep, telling herself they were nothing but the rot of a broken mind. Still, they came. In those dreams, she caught her reflection in a pool of clear water, lurching with a cry of horror. For the face staring back wasn't hers. From the pool, Vargr's dead eyes gleamed with triumph, his mouth twisting in a cold corpse-smile, as if he'd slipped beneath her skin and made a home there.

It was all those dreams that roused her yearning to return to the lodge—each more powerful than the last. Twice, she nearly mounted her horse—only to stop short, gripped by a dread of what she might discover. Yet discover it she must, for she was powerless to stop the compulsion. It was as if some dark part of her needed to face it, just to taunt her.

*You deemed yourself the finest shield-maiden in Ljosstrond? You are nothing but a vengeful woman with neither true strength nor honor. You believed Reidar would love you for handing his wife over to the beast who stole his birthright? He will hate you, despise you for all eternity, and if there is Valhalla, he will make sure you never set foot in it.*

For a moment, Astrid wrenched free of this unceasing torment. She hadn't yet made up her mind, and much rode on Reidar's response. But maybe today she would cast off her terrible burden. For today—right now—she would go to Reidar and throw herself upon his mercy.

So she clenched her fists and headed to his longhouse.

She hadn't seen him since his wedding day but heard from her brothers of the search party's failure to find even a trace. Their idle talk twisted her stomach into painful knots. It made her want to scream. She blew out a long, shuddering breath. It would all be over soon.

One of Reidar's men opened the door, staring at her for a long moment with stunned eyes. Yes, despite all her efforts, she looked a sight. But she was past caring.

"Astrid." He shuffled his feet. "You look unwell."

"I am fine." She crossed her trembling arms. "I need to see Reidar."

The man made an inarticulate grunt. "He is in his chamber... Suit yourself."

Nearly swaying, Astrid stumbled past the man, then, with a stiff hand, pushed the familiar door open.

She froze at the sight. At the bedside, on a night chest, stood a large, ornate crucifix. And before it, knelt Reidar, bowing low, deaf and blind to the world.

Breath held, she approached. "Reidar."

He lifted his head and looked at her. His face was like the ashes in the hearth. His eyes were etched with shadows. But worst of all, something new and terrifying marked his eyes—a strange calm, tinged with resignation.

He studied her with a groove between his brows. "What happened to you, Astrid?"

She stood rooted to the spot, arms cold and limp at her sides. "I was...very ill," she whispered, the chill inside spreading into her lifeblood. "I am getting better, but...what is all this, Reidar?"

He rose. "My father gave me this crucifix as a keepsake—after Rathlin Island." His frown deepened. "I heard you were ill. I asked you what happened."

Did he already suspect her? She'd seen him in the fury of the fray. None survived his blade—or fist, if it came to it. And while Astrid was a fierce shield-maiden, she chose her opponents with care. Never would she take on such a warrior as Reidar. But now, though she couldn't fathom it, he might strike her in rage or rush her in sorrow. Or worst of all—tell her who she was. And while she would recover from Vargr's pillage, she would not survive Reidar's scorn.

Astrid swallowed the confession bubbling like hot oil on her tongue. "Nothing—an ague," she forced out against her trembling chin. "But why are you kneeling like a...a Christian?"

Reidar turned to the crucifix and ran his large, beautiful hand along the bejeweled wood. "Because I am a Christian, Astrid."

"No, you are not!" She shrank back as his terrible words bounced off the walls like the crack of a whip. "You are Reidar Valorborn, the son of Harald Fairblade! You are like all those who came before you, and you belong to the..." Astrid wanted to say true gods, but she didn't believe in them anymore, so she fell silent.

"Why are you here, Astrid?" Reidar crossed the chamber to her.

"I—" A scorching heatwave rushed through her, then receded. And in its place descended cold no sun could touch, and a darkness no flame could lift.

She took a steadying breath. Another. "I was passing by and thought I'd see how you...fare."

He drew near, his gaze lingering on her face, traveling down to her split lip. "I ask you again, Astrid, what happened to you?"

"I-I still love you, Reidar—" Her heartbeat surged into her ears. "And I—" Never. She could never speak the truth to his face. "Your wedding... It made me very ill."

Eyes frozen, he raked his plaits.

Long ago, she used to braid his hair for him in this very chamber. An ugly, hoarse sob broke through her lips.

He took her hand. "By my sword..." He compressed his mouth. "We had not been true lovers in a long time, Astrid, but I should have spoken. I should have told you sooner." He raised his free hand as she tried to speak. "None of this is your doing. My heart has been Ingrid's since the day I met her, seven winters past." He let go of her hand, watching it drop, lifeless, to her side. "You never said a word about other women, nor shied away from taking other men to your bed. I thought you saw our bond as I did—that it served us both." He winced. "I have caused you pain...I am sorry."

Astrid's eyes stung and burned. Her sight blurred. She shook her head, and the tears spilled, hot and abundant.

He wiped them away with the back of his hand. "We could wed now she is gone," he choked out, his face a mask of unutterable agony. "I owe you that little."

Eyes wide, Astrid stumbled back. Was Loki real, after all, or was the wretched girl's God mocking her? She stilled. Perhaps it was all madness, and the only truth was this miserable world, brimming with shame and despair.

"I do not need your pity." She shook her head, envisioning a heavy boulder at her neck and the cold fjord tides closing over her. "You should have spoken sooner, but so should I, instead of pretending your affairs did not touch me or filling my loneliness with loveless bedfellows. But do not fret, Reidar. I will not burden you with my troubles."

"It is no burden." He scrubbed a hand over his face. "I remain by your side, Astrid, no matter the storm." A new shadow passed over his eyes. "Will you be attending the Althing today?"

"Today?" she echoed, a terrible idea creeping inside her like smoke. No, she would not face the boulder and the cold tides. She would choose something far more dreadful for herself—and far more just for Reidar. She owed him that little.

"Yes, I will." Despite all her efforts, she trembled from head to foot, but Reidar only stood unmoving—a world apart. She wished he would gather her in his large, warm arms. She ached for him to kiss away her sorrow and banish the crimes she'd committed. She longed for him to tell her he loved her. But he would do none of those things, so she squared her shoulders and became the shield-maiden she was always destined to be.

"I have loved you too much, Reidar." Her scoff emerged as a wail. "And I wanted you to love me in return, but now you will hate me more than even your uncle." She turned to the door, ignoring his stricken look. "To say I am sorry is to say nothing at all," she spat without a backward glance.

Back in her chamber, she sat on a bench and waited for the evening to fall and for the Althing to commence.

# Chapter Thirty-Six

## The Althing

***Reidar***

*There, base creatures by the root of the tree*
*Will give you horns of filth to drink;*
*You will never find a fairer drink,*
*Maiden, to meet your desire,*
*(Maiden, to meet my desire.)*
— Skírnismál, stanza 36

The Althing was well underway when Reidar stepped into the mead hall, head heavy as a rock and chest hollow as a drum. If not for mourning Ingrid, he would have set things right with Astrid before letting her leave his longhouse. But he had nothing left to give. Still, her illness and madness both lay at his feet. His father used to say women's hearts were unlike men's, often impossible to understand. He knew the truth, yet like a fool had believed Astrid was different. Almost from the start, they'd made no secret of their other lovers, and until Ingrid, she hadn't rebuked him once. She even made light of his straying affections and jested about it with others in his presence, drinking and laughing as though it amused her. He'd been certain her talk of marriage was for the sake of his *blodhefnd* and birthright—and the power that came with being a jarl's wife. If he'd known the depth of her feelings for him, he would have ended their entanglement long ago.

Reidar clenched his jaw until it hurt. Maybe he'd always suspected the truth, but she'd made it too easy to carry on. And what did that say about him? He was a fool and a failure—letting the woman he loved slip through his fingers and wounding a loyal friend. He balled his hands into fists, wishing to deal himself a well-deserved blow. What *blodhefnd?* What birthright? He should be content with being his uncle's *hersir*. Even that was too lofty for the oaf who wrecked everything he touched.

The hall overflowed with petitioners and onlookers, the scent of old mead and wet fur hanging thick in the rafters. At this late hour, all seats had been claimed, so he stood at the back, longing for solitude. But a *hersir* answered the Althing.

The fire popped behind the Lawspeaker as he came forward, his long cloak edged with fine white fox. "Let those with cause speak," he croaked in a voice rough as old timber.

A woman in a dark shawl stepped out, the hem of her dress damp with rain. She didn't bow. "My brother's field lies flattened where Hroald's oxen broke the stone markers," she spat. "They ate what feed was left. He refuses to answer for it."

Hroald, thick-necked and red with drink, raised a hand. "The beast wandered. No man can leash hunger."

The Lawspeaker shook his head. "And no man can trample his neighbor's land without cost."

Next came a karl with a young woman at his side, hands clenched into fists, shoulders rigid as a longship's prow. "My daughter was promised to Bersi's son. Now Bersi wants coin to settle the matter!"

A weighty pause was followed by laughter from a corner.

The Lawspeaker held up a hand. "Coin may settle debts. But promises weigh heavier."

Vargr leaned forward from his carved jarl's seat, his voice cold as winter. "Bersi, do you trade your word like fish in a barrel?"

"No, my lord." Bersi looked to the gathering, then to the girl standing beside her father. "I will honor it."

The line dragged on—neighbors bickering over stolen cattle, broken fences, and wounded pride.

Limbs heavy as iron, Reidar leaned against the wall and let the noise wash over him like wind-blown ash. What did any of it matter? God, or maybe the gods—he no longer knew the difference—they hated him.

He fingered Shadowbane's useless pommel. Once, he believed he was meant to avenge his father, take his place as jarl, and rule with strength and honor over Ljosstrond. Now, he was halfway to becoming a jest—a tale told over spilled mead. The ill-fated brute who wed a thrall, only to have her flee into the wilds. Or throw herself into the tides.

He stared at the flames flickering in the hearth. All gods were alike—cruel and capricious, laughing as they shattered men's lives for sport.

The hall rustled as Astrid approached the high seat. She looked unwell in the gray daylight, but now her decline hit him like a blow. She seemed shrunken beside the others, her once-hale frame thinned, her back hunched as a crone's. She still wore the same fine gown, but only now did he see how it hung on her, where once it clung to every curve.

The way she spoke in the morning—about the hate he'd have for her or some other nonsense—she might do something foolish before the gathering. Reidar pushed off the wall, ready to step in. He could save her from shame, even if it was too late for the rest.

"My lord." Her voice came forth in a trembling croak. With a wild glance in Reidar's direction, she cleared her throat.

He froze with belated clarity. She meant to speak out against him and demand retribution. In her mind, he'd promised marriage—even if he never spoke the words aloud. Then he'd strung her along for the fleeting comfort of her company in his bed, and his silence passed for assent in her heart.

He scoffed, bracing for the blow. It served him right, even if Vargr would never honor an unspoken vow—especially when their union threatened his rule like a crack in a shield wall.

"My lord." Astrid lifted her voice, making it ring in the hall. "I bring a complaint against a man who had done me great harm and grievously wronged every person in Ljosstrond."

The jarl stiffened.

Reidar rushed forward, fighting his way through the throng of onlookers. The illness must have eaten at poor Astrid's wits. While he'd wounded her pride and bruised her heart, he'd harmed no one else in Ljosstrond, save himself.

"As all here know—" pale and trembling, Astrid turned to address the hall—"it grieved me greatly when Reidar Valorborn took the foreign thrall to wife and broke his promise to me."

Head thudding, Reidar pressed on, no longer caring what became of him. He had to stop her before she shamed herself. He owed her that little.

"It hurt me so much that I lost all reason and sought someone's help," she choked out. "This man offered to rid me of my rival, but at a price."

Reidar came to a grinding halt, nearly knocking a young boy off his feet. The hall fell away, floating about—hearth, tables, and faces spinning and blurring into something as inconsequential as mist.

A low murmur stirred. Someone coughed near the entrance.

Reidar shook himself. Clenched his fists. Her words didn't fit together. They swirled and scattered, refusing to settle.

Astrid clasped her hands, shaking like a reed. "The price was a night with him. And he would—"

"This woman is unwell." Vargr's voice cut through the thickening silence like a rusted blade. "We will hear no pleas from her until she is fit to stand before this hall."

Nostrils flaring, Astrid turned toward the jarl. She stopped shaking. "I am well enough," she spat. "For the price of one night—" her voice cracked—"he promised to set fire to our grain stores, so all, including Reidar, would rush to the flames and leave the girl unguarded—"

Reidar choked on his breath. Swallowed down bile. Pulled in a ragged, burning draw of air.

Vargr shot to his feet. "Remove her at once!"

No one stirred. Not even the *huskarlar*.

"While they battled the fire, I was to seize the girl. Take her to the old hunter's lodge in the wilds." Astrid's voice rose, thin and shrill, as if scraped raw. "He would use her, then leave her for the wolves."

Low, horrified gasps rippled through the crowd, swelling into words.

Reidar blinked against the pounding in his ears, drew another aching breath against the ice in his veins. He couldn't feel his hands. He took a swaying step forward, heart slamming against his chest.

*Ingrid—*

"I did not see Astrid at the fires," someone whispered.

"No, she was there. I saw her!" said another, louder.

He had to get to the lodge. He stumbled, catching himself on a table corner as the crowd turned in waves of indignant rumblings.

*This whole time—*

He doubled over in agony.

*Alone and helpless. In terror and pain. In torment and despair.*

The agony gripped his gut and tore through every bone and sinew.

*She is gone.*

A great hush fell over the hall.

Vargr scoffed. "A fine speech, though it barely holds weight." He sat again. "From now on, we shall have a new law: ill folk are not welcome at the Althing."

Reidar caught a sight of his hands: fingers digging into the table, knuckles bloodless against sun-bronzed skin.

Astrid lifted her head. In a swift, vicious move, she tore the wool from her neck.

The crowd recoiled as one at the sight of ugly, dark bruises smearing her neck.

"This was the price he demanded," she breathed.

"Enough!" Vargr pounded the side of his chair with the haft of his axe, the sound ringing through the hall. It faded in the deathly stillness.

Eyes wild, Astrid seized her neckline with both hands and tore it straight down. The front of her gown split open.

A deafening silence descended as she stood there, half-exposed, her chest marked with dark bruises and cruel, half-healed cuts.

Reidar blinked hard. Blinked again. "Astrid..." He didn't recognize his voice, torn and raw, like a madman's.

"I will strip what remains if any among you still doubt me." Her words fell hoarse and clumped together. "My whole body bears the marks of his savagery."

Reidar's sight blurred, then filled with bright sparks. A cold, hard undertow surged through him. It swept into his limbs. It curled around his ribs. It wound tighter with each breath and stilled his thoughts. He'd brought his Shadowbane, he remembered.

"Who is this beast?" some dull soul whispered.

"Hang him from the ash tree!" a woman shrieked.

"No! Break his bones and throw *him* to the wolves!"

"Tie him to the sea rocks at low tide!"

Mind clearing, Reidar scanned the hall for his men. They stood at the ready, faces hard, hands gripping weapons.

"Silence!" Vargr barked from his high seat. He sat stiff as a post, thick fingers clenched on the armrests. "Face me, Astrid." His voice came out too low and too even. "Who is this man, this beast, who beat you, lay with my nephew's bride, and robbed the people of Ljosstrond of their winter grain?" He rose with great purpose, scanning the assembly. "I will do all in my power to find him and make him pay in blood!"

Stone-faced, Astrid turned. "It is you, Vargr."

The crowd ebbed back as if a foul wind had swept through the hall.

"Of course it is." Vargr laughed, the sound grating like the screech of a raven's talon on stone. Then, as abruptly as it came, his laughter ceased. "How sad it is to watch a fine shield-maiden wither, lost in madness from a broken heart." His gaze swept the gathering, cold and searching, before landing on the table where her family sat. "One of you, take her home. Tend to her and see that she is made better."

The crowd shifted uneasily, eyes darting between Astrid and Vargr. Astrid's family didn't stir.

"No, it cannot be him," someone murmured.

Another spat. "Yes, it is him, dullard!"

Astrid's eyes locked with Reidar's, clear and still.

"Ride to the lodge," she forced out, each word heavy as if carved from stone. "No doubt she is long gone. But you will find your fine furs there. Along with sure signs of struggle, torment, and murder."

The veins in Vargr's neck stood out as he drove his heel into the floorboards. "I will not allow madness to rule here." He shot a cold glance at his *huskarlar*. "I said, take her away. She is ill by her own admission."

The *huskarlar* looked at each other, then at the crowd. They didn't move.

Reidar quelled the storm inside. Narrowed it to a blade's edge.

From the corner of his eye, his man Ulf pushed to his feet. He approached Astrid, shrugged off his heavy fur, and draped it over her shoulders. He took his place among Reidar's men again.

"We ought to..." Chin quivering, Astrid's mother rose. She turned to her husband and sons, their hands locked tight around their axe hafts. She sank back into her seat.

Reidar shut his eyes. In one corner of his mind, he mounted his steed and galloped for the lodge. In another, he drew Shadowbane and drove it clean through Vargr's thick neck. The vision faded as Vargr heaved a long sigh.

"Very well then..." His voice emerged low and mournful. "Let us entertain this tale a moment longer. I have no objection, Astrid. But mark this well—you will never crawl out from under this shame. Say I did rut with you all night, and in return for such questionable pleasures, I torched our grain stores—only to slink off to a ruined, rat-infested lodge to enjoy a thrall in the cold muck, when I have a dozen finer at my beck and call? It is not just madness—it is fevered fantasy! Why would I do such a thing?"

Shoulders squared, Reidar barreled toward the high seat. "Because you've coveted my woman since Rathlin, when you offered trinkets to feed whatever darkness festers in you." His words cut sharp and cold as a newly forged blade. "Because you thought her death would shatter me—" a bitter laugh cracked loose—"and wrecking Astrid would finish me." He trained a steady gaze on his uncle, hand tightening on Shadowbane's pommel. "You moved your pieces too well, Vargr—though blind to One who bends the sky and the sea. Now, stripped to the bone, I come for reckoning."

"Nephew." Vargr shook his head, as one speaking to a child. "Ah, youth—so much fire, so little sense. Very well. Let us say every word is true, though the gods alone know why I would waste my time destroying my brother's foolish but dearly loved son." His voice hardened. "Tell me, Astrid—do you bring witnesses to this tale spun of fever and grief? Surely someone saw you at my longhouse that night." He spread his hands. "I do not deny the marks. Someone hurt you. And by the Allfather, I will find him."

"It was done in secret, as you well know." Astrid drew Ulf's fur close, her gaze sweeping the hall. "You told me to come by night, so no one would see!"

"I saw," a feeble voice said at the back.

# Chapter Thirty-Seven

## Blodhefnd

***Reidar***

*I am writing you a charm and three runes with it,*
*Longing and madness and lust;*
*But what I have written I may yet erase*
*If I find a need for it.*
— Skírnismál, stanza 37

Reidar turned with the crowd toward a slight man standing at the edge of the gathering.

Vargr raised his brows. "I am unpleased with this mockery of the Althing, yet by all means, let the fool speak." With a bitter scoff, he leaned back in his seat. "What is there to lose, now that we have turned this sacred council into a spectacle fit for thrall fights and drunkards' tales?"

Gaze on the ground, the man shuffled his feet. "Thank you, my lord. My wife, Kelda, has been unfaithful to me with two of my neighbors—Ebbe the Boar and Knut Meadgrip." He cast a glance toward a girl barely old enough to be his daughter. "That is the complaint I bring, my lord. I have been nothing but kind to her, even helping with housework. She is young and inexperienced, and I have taken to the loom myself...yes, even that, to my shame. And yet she has always claimed she missed her mother and went to visit her."

A few chuckles rumbled through the hall.

With effort, Reidar unlocked his jaw, a stabbing jolt of pain shooting from neck to brow.

"But what did I find? One night, I caught her kissing one man, and later, another. And I said to her, 'Kelda, you have hurt me deeply, sneaking about behind my back. Have I not been kind to you, working your loom and tending to the hearth? Is this how you repay my trust?'"

"We have heard enough." Vargr rolled his eyes, lips twisting in a faint smile. "Thank you for your unhelpful witnessing. I will deal with this matter when this farce is behind us."

"Oh, but I am not done yet, my lord." The man's voice cracked. "Apologies for being long-winded, but my wife hurt me worse. That night, once again, I woke to find her place empty beside me. I went to Knut Meadgrip's hut, and there I found her in his bed. I begged her to return home, but she refused. My heart was heavy, and I could not stay inside. So I wrapped myself in fleece and came here, hoping to ask my lord for aid. But it was the dead of night, and the hall stood empty. I did not wish to intrude upon my lord's house. So I sat in the shadows and wept."

"The poor fool," someone muttered. "The little harlot should pay."

The man winced, but as Vargr tried to cut in, he continued. "And that was when I saw Astrid Eldarsdottir, creeping like a shadow beneath the cover of night, slipping into the longhouse. I knew it was her—tall and stately, and with a face that stops a heart in its tracks. At first, I thought nothing of it, lost in my sorrow. But at dawn's break, I saw her again. Bent and broken, she emerged from the house, and I mistook her for another at first. But the light of day revealed it was her. She sobbed, her back hunched and her steps slow as if she carried the weight of the world. She limped like an old crone, she did, dragging herself toward her home."

Everyone's gaze locked on Vargr. He pursed his lips and studied the carvings on his chair's armrest as one bored.

"I thought she had taken ill..." Astrid's mother's voice trembled in the stillness that fell. "How would you explain that away, my lord?"

"Little wonder, with all his wives dead!" a woman called out from the back.

"And all the thralls he had ruined!" another echoed.

Burning with a steady, cold flame, Reidar stepped closer to the high seat. "Did you set fire to our grain, Vargr?" His voice emerged in a low, menacing growl.

The heavy thud of Reidar's men closing in behind him pounded through the hall like a shield wall locking into place.

"Why, it is true!" someone shouted. "He was already there when it burned, and I smelled the tar, thick in the air. Why would the jarl be at the grain store in the dead of night?"

"Seize him!" came the roar from the crowd.

Two *huskarlar* grabbed Vargr by the elbows, their grips ironclad.

The assembly surged forward.

"Unhand me!" A vein twitching in his jaw, Vargr shook off his guards. "I am still your jarl!"

"Not much longer!" someone screamed.

"Justice for Astrid!" shrieked another.

"I have something to say! And all of you will listen to your jarl!" Vargr's eyes flickered over the crowd, bright against his sudden pallor. "Though you do not yet understand, I have done what is best for this place! But Astrid's fate does not rest in my hands. You will see that soon enough."

Muscles straining like longship ropes in a storm, Reidar scanned the gathering. Tight faces, frozen eyes, clenched fists. He widened his stance and crossed his arms.

*Wait for the scum to soil his own leg.* "Let him talk," he said aloud.

The guards exchanged a glance. They didn't attempt to grab the jarl again, but neither did they retreat.

"I did set fire to the grain," Vargr bit out.

A deep hush fell over the hall, then it erupted like a thunderous cloud.

"But I always planned to buy it from Hvitvik! I have enough wealth to buy three times what we have lost!" Vargr raised his hand, his voice growing louder. "What fool here thinks I would let this place starve through the winter? I did it to create a diversion—to rid Ljosstrond of the Christian sorceress! Look how she had charmed my poor nephew!"

A low, rumbling anger, like a gathering storm, simmered through the hall.

Reidar pushed down a dark swell rising in his chest. *Patience.* He gave his men a reassuring nod.

"I had no hand in Astrid's wounds." Vargr's eyes darted from face to face. "It was not me she went to see that night. Many dwell here in this longhouse. I do not know who harmed her."

"I have a cousin in Hvitvik," a woman cried out, her shout slicing through the din. "He is a farmer. They have no surplus to sell. The harvest nearly failed there too!"

"I am a farmer," a man joined in. "Grain was poor this summer. We fell short by half. No one in Norway has enough to spare!"

A new ripple rolled through the crowd, rising like thunder.

Reidar trained his stare on Vargr, his voice cold as the wind that howled off the fjord. "Who took my wife?"

Silence fell, then cracked with Astrid's brittle words. "I spoke true, Reidar." Her gaze on him lay still as winter. "It was I."

Reidar did nothing to halt his heartbeat as it surged into his ears. He drew his sword, his voice a growl of all he'd been holding back: "Seize Vargr Bloodgale for his crimes against the people of Ljosstrond!"

The crowd erupted in a scream. The *huskarlar* reached for Vargr.

But he jerked free again.

"You insult me, nephew." He smoothed down his tunic with trembling fingers. "Before you bind me like a thief, I challenge you to a single combat!"

Reidar's skin crawled with thousands of fire ants; hands throbbed with the need to fight, to strike, to punish. "Gladly," he spat.

"Tomorrow, then," Vargr stood. "Everyone, go to your homes now."

No one moved. Behind Reidar, more men rushed to join his *hirdmen*, their bodies a wall of stone.

Reidar's chest became a cage filled to the brim with a raging tempest. It pounded in his head and thundered in his limbs. But he tempered his voice to a cold, sharp blade. "So you can prepare your sword with poison?" He closed the remaining distance, his face a fingerbreadth from Vargr's unsteady, darting gaze. "As you did when you murdered my father?"

Gasps broke like waves, surging and crashing over the hall.

"We have suffered the tyrant long enough," a man howled. "Let it end."

"Reidar!" Someone pounded on a shield. "Reidar! Reidar! Reidar!"

Reidar drew Shadowbane, his hand aching with the urge to drive it through the vile snake. "We fight now, or you meet the same fate as the grain you took from us." He tossed the *huskarlar* a nod. "Take him outside."

Reidar didn't wait to see them drag Bloodgale from the longhouse. He hardly noticed the crowd parting with deference as he stepped into the biting wind. The cold struck him like the edge of an axe. If he lived, his *blodhefnd* would be done, and his birthright won. He would be jarl, and he would never feel the warmth of Ingrid's soft skin or drown in her shining green eyes again.

All was dust and ashes now.

He stared into the night, struggling to picture her glad and at peace in her Heaven. But he knew nothing of such realms, and the vision fled him.

*Lord, I do not wish for Valhalla. If I am to meet my end now, forgive my many debts and reunite me with my beloved.*

The entire Althing spilled out into the hall-yard, the voices rising like breakers over a rocky shore.

"Death to the traitor!"

"Blood for blood!"

Reidar scanned the ground. It had grown slick with rain; the soil lay uneven and scattered with rocks that rolled beneath his boots. The scent of grain smoke still clung to the air, bitter and acrid. The moon hung high, casting long shadows that danced in the flickering torchlight.

At the edge of the crowd, Astrid stood straighter now, her eyes, frozen and hollow, locked on Reidar. Beside her lingered Ulf—whether as guard or friend, Reidar could not tell.

*Blood for blood.* He stared at his hands. Would spilling more only drag him back into the shadows he sought to leave behind?

*He meant evil against you, but God meant it for good.* The thought moved through him, sure and steady. And in its wake came stillness, like his father's long-forgotten embrace. *Justice over revenge.*

He tightened his grip on Shadowbane's pommel as the *huskarlar* pushed Vargr into the center of the yard. At his full height, he stood as tall as Reidar and carried greater bulk. Slowly, his uncle cracked his neck and hefted his sword—a massive, crude thing that had tasted more blood than a butcher's floor.

"Reidar is the jarl!" someone shouted.

"Silence!" The Lawspeaker raised his staff in his weathered hand. "This combat shall be fought clean and witnessed true." He looked from Reidar to Vargr. "You have both chosen your weapons. Give them shields," he said to a *huskarl*. "You will not be getting a second shield if your first is shattered. This is a fight to the death—only one of you will come out of it alive. If Vargr Bloodgale dies, Reidar Valorborn becomes the new jarl. This is the law."

The crowd fell silent as a priestess stepped forward, her face smeared with white ash and eyes rimmed with coal. In one hand she carried a bowl, and in the other a fir branch. She dipped the branch, then lifted it high. The firelight caught the red droplets as she cast the blood over Reidar and Vargr with a sharp flick. "Let Odin mark your worth."

The crowd grew restless again.

"Kill him, Reidar!"

"Kill him!"

"You think you can best me, Sapling?" Vargr's laugh emerged in a low growl, silencing the din. "When the Valkyries, out of pity, swoop down to carry my fallen nephew into Valhalla, all of you will remember who your rightful jarl is!" His gaze swept the crowd, cold and feral. "Who the strong, clear-minded leader is. The one who made Ljosstrond thrive and saw you through lean winters, fed and unharmed! All of you will see your folly, but I will forgive those who spoke out against me, for I am a just and merciful ruler! And I, your jarl, claim the first strike—"

Vargr's charge was as swift and powerful as it was abrupt. But Reidar blocked the blow with his shield, his feet steady on the sodden earth. The ground beneath his boots groaned as Reidar charged, Shadowbane cutting through the air, fast and precise.

He'd missed.

Vargr pressed forward. A wall of muscle, his strikes like thunder. Reidar blocked again. Brought his blade down.

It rent the air as Vargr shifted to the right.

He'd missed by a hair.

A roar split the night as Vargr swung again, a move too sudden and unexpected. The blade scraped Reidar's sword arm, sparing his weak shoulder. Still, the force of the blow sent him stumbling backward. His arm grew numb. His back hit the earth, the shock jolting through his spine.

The crowd gasped.

Reidar's mind raced like rain clouds. Only the God of justice could save him now.

The crowd's voices rose. They burst into chaos.

A woman's frantic shriek pierced the air. "Get up, Reidar!"

For a heartbeat, Vargr loomed over him, grinning like a wolf, his breath heavy and labored. "Tell your arrogant father that taking your life gave me none of the pleasure I took in ending his," he murmured, raising his sword. "I will settle that in Valhalla."

The throbbing in Reidar's back vanished along with the numbness in his arm. And in their place reigned white-hot flames, roaring through him like a thousand war cries. Reidar rolled, coming up on his feet as Vargr's sword slammed into the dirt where Reidar's head had been a moment past. With a howl of rage, Vargr turned, but Reidar had already lifted Shadowbane. Mightier than the storm, faster than the wind.

It cleaved through the night. It struck before Bloodgale could lift his shield. It cut through the thick of his side.

Time stopped. It stood still as Harald Fairblade whispered his last words in Reidar's ear. *Avenge my death, Son.* It shifted as Astrid ripped her gown to bare her battered body. *This was the price he demanded.* It crumbled into ash as Ingrid trained her emerald gaze on him in farewell. *Our union is not blessed by the Lord.*

Vargr's eyes widened. His lips parted, but only blood came.

"It is not Valhalla you are going to." Reidar twisted his blade, then pulled it free in one swift move. "But hell."

Breath coming in ragged gasps, Vargr staggered. He fell to his knees.

A great hush came over the crowd as Vargr collapsed with a thud.

"Hel..." He locked his gaze with Reidar's, then grew still.

Chest heaving, Reidar straightened. How many nights he'd dreamed of this reckoning, how often he'd seen it play out in his mind's eye. But he felt nothing now. Only a hollow void where vengeance should have roared, and a chill colder than a winter sea. Still, while Ingrid was lost and Astrid beyond saving, the people of Ljosstrond deserved a future founded on justice and fair rule.

He lifted Shadowbane, battling the crushing gloom coiling in his chest.

From the corner of his eye, Thorsten approached the trembling Asbjorn and drove his blade clean into the wretch's throat.

His men's shouts faded beneath those of the overeager *huskarlar*: "All hail Jarl Reidar!"

Like one, the gathering erupted: "Reidar! Reidar! Reidar!"

The cries rose, splintering the air, bursting into a wild roar. A thunderous drumbeat of fists and axe hafts against the shields filled the night to the brim, mixing and melding with flaring torchlight.

Reidar sheathed his blade and forced his shoulders back. The effort near broke him, flooding him with such bleakness it crushed his bones and froze his blood. With a single stroke, the Lord granted one favor and claimed another. He must have seen into his wretched soul at last. And as reckoning, Reidar would not be reunited with Ingrid, for he was now doomed to rule over this empty place until old age. Just wages for all his terrible debts.

"I will take up my duties tomorrow." He made his voice boom over the gathering, bleeding out each word. "Tonight, I go to the lodge to bring home...what remains of my wife." He swallowed the tearing ache in his heart and nodded to Ulf. "Take Astrid inside. We will decide her fate later. Who rides with me?"

# Chapter Thirty-Eight

Grace

***Brigit***

**Eighth Night**

*Accept this welcome instead,*
*And take the frost-cup filled with mead;*
*Though I never believed that I would love*
*Anyone of the Wanes.*
— Skírnismál, stanza 38

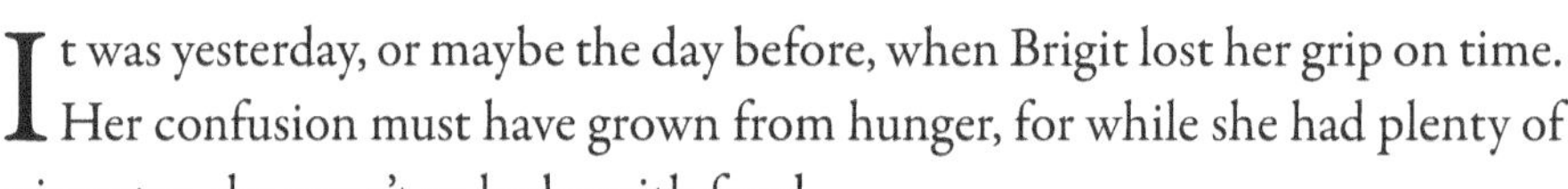

It was yesterday, or maybe the day before, when Brigit lost her grip on time. Her confusion must have grown from hunger, for while she had plenty of rainwater, she wasn't so lucky with food.

A distance away stood a lone hazelnut tree, but when she shook its branches with all her might, only a few clusters fell. After cracking the shells open with a rock and eating what little there was, she found no more. Farther out sprawled a bush of red, tart berries, but they soured her belly and left her curled in pain. Yet as the cramping gave way to hunger pangs, she dared not stray far from the lodge, for this foreign wood crawled with gloom and rang with the howls of prowling wolves even in the light of day.

At first, the hunger gnawed dull and slow. But with time, it bit deeper, swelling into a sharp, twisting pain. It was as if her body had turned inward, devouring itself from within. Soon she grew too weak to rise. Only recently, she'd dragged herself outside for water. Now her limbs no longer obeyed her. Even lifting a hand felt like something done in a dream, not in flesh and bone.

The world blurred into a strange, muted daze. She drifted in that in-between place, neither living nor gone, and slipping closer to the end with each shallow breath. It wouldn't be long now, for the hunger had passed. Strange how in its wake lingered a heavy stillness, like her body had hollowed itself out and left nothing behind but the ache of mere existence. Stranger still, the pain spread not like fire, but like weight—the kind that crushes slow, until it steals the final breath. Her body, once quick and capable, now lay crumpled like a broken wing. Even her sight faltered, for the world swam in and out of shadows, and twisted shapes moved at the edge of her vision. Whether angels or ghosts, she knew not.

Doubtless, the end pressed close, for time itself had gone still, stretching thin like a thread about to snap. And if it pleased the Lord to take her home now, then she was ready—save for one thing.

Through the dimming haze, she saw Astrid find her way back to Reidar. Surely, they were together, as they always should have been, for Brigit—with her unceasing Great Scorn—was never fit for a man as noble and kind as him. Even after all he'd done for her, she hadn't found the courage to tell him what he meant to her. Her time must have well and truly come, for she never scorned herself more than she did now. She would have scoffed if she had the strength. Her disdain had always been for herself alone, and not for anyone else.

The back of her nose stung, faint and distant, but no tears came, for there was no water left in her for weeping.

"Ingrid!"

She listened as Reidar's deep voice called for her in her dying mind—a beautiful, faraway specter. Too beautiful for the likes of her. Still, she wished it would never stop, not until she slipped from this world.

"Ingrid!"

How she loved these rare spells of madness, when he almost seemed near—his eyes alight with sky-blue sparks, his arms strong and warm as they pulled her close. In her tangled mind, she heard the door crash open, followed by urgent footsteps echoing through her fading senses like a far-off drumbeat.

"Ingrid!"

Reidar's voice drew nearer, as though he stood beside her.

*Thank you for this last mercy, Lord.* How sweet was this end, to leave with the thought of him at her side.

"Ingrid, by the gods..." he breathed—so close, his warm breath brushed her cheek. "By Heaven, my love..."

Madness, yes, and most welcoming, as he flung aside the furs and gathered her into his trembling arms.

"Do not leave me." He buried his face in her chest, his words spilling out fast and fevered. "Come back to me."

With all her remaining strength, Brigit opened her eyes. The hunter's lodge faded, then vanished altogether, along with its cracked timbers, sagging roof, and the stench of mildew and decay. She was thirteen again, lying on the forest floor with a twisted ankle and a scraped knee, still tasting the stolen strawberry kiss she would have now given freely for all the world's riches. *Home.* She was still feeling his hands, too large to be so gentle, pressing a bit of moss to her wound. His unfathomable pale-blue eyes searching hers for a sign she felt it too—*home.* His strong, sure arms lifting and settling her against his warm chest. *Home.* Then, a crash of iron against wood, a distant burst of vicious laughter, a heathen savage from her girlhood's wood—with his eyes, with his hands. And Thor's hammer charm, and a special knot at her long-ago healed ankle. *You—safe.* And his skin-tingling fingertips running through her lacing, his burning head pressed to her chest, their lips touching. *You go—home.* His kiss, scented with sea, snow, and freedom.

Her savage, her heathen, her Norseman, her boy Reidar, her forbidden beloved, her unbaptized husband, whom God unfailingly sent each time she begged Him for help.

She floated between heaven and earth, safe in his faithful arms, tucked into his solid chest. She had to tell him before she perished, but when she parted her lips, only a rasp escaped.

"Do not talk, my love." His deep voice cracked in the cold night air. "You are going *home.*"

Vaguely, she recognized the Irish word. *It is so, my heart—but not your home.*

The dryness in her throat and the twisting in her belly burned so fiercely she scarcely held on. The joy of seeing him again must have drained what little life still clung to her. But while time was short, enough remained, so he wouldn't carry falsehoods to his grave.

"Reidar..." His name burst through her cracked lips like a keening. "You should know... Though you left Éire, you stayed with me always... Even in my tears, even in my dreams, even in my husband's despicable bed... That was how I survived... With you and our Lord, who I begged for you every day of my miserable life." Her voice grew so faint she hardly heard it herself, yet one thing was still left unsaid. "I never loathed you. I love you."

She longed to tell him she was sorry for hiding, even from herself, that she'd known him nearly from the start. And sorrier yet for all her spite and venom. If only she'd been given another chance, she would have spent every breath showing him how much she loved him.

But the world dimmed before she could say more. Then it went dark.

When Brigit was small, she nearly drowned. It had been a warm summer day, and her father was returning from the sea with his catch while her mother tended the fire, unaware Brigit had slipped away to the shore. She had waded there often and thought nothing of it, but that day the waves turned, churning and dragging her under. She remembered little—only the pull of choking water, her father's voice, muddled and distant, and his arms clutching her tight.

It was like that again. She surfaced slowly, as though through a cold, heavy tide, the world flickering back in pieces. A woman's voice, her words running together, devoid of meaning. A rustle, like fabric brushed or turned over. The thud of a drinking cup against wood.

Brigit cracked her eyes open, and light stabbed through—so sharp she shut them at once. The effort sent a jolt of exhaustion through her head. Her limbs were stone. Her mouth tasted of iron and dust. Her lips ached when she tried to part them.

"At last, by all the gods of Asgard!" A warm hand slipped beneath her nape, lifting, while another pressed the rim of a cup to her mouth.

Clean, cool water. She drank too fast, too greedily, coughing and spilling half down her chin.

"Slowly...slowly, child," Gyda—for the voice belonged to her—pulled the cup away. "Or you will be sick."

Brigit blinked. The light had softened. Shapes floated about, morphing into familiar objects. No, not at all familiar. A door—too far from the bed. The slope of a roof beam—too high above. A carved basin—much fancier than before. The bed—twice as grand as Reidar's.

"Wh..." Her heart raced like a wild steed. She parted her lips again, searching the strange chamber for Reidar and not seeing even a sign of him. "Re..."

"Shh." Gyda pressed the cup to her mouth once more. "Reidar is here—in the mead hall, attending to his many new affairs. Listen, and you will hear him!"

Brigit fell silent. A hum of conversation—a throng of voices, some male, some female, some soft, some curt. But one rose above the rest. Deep. Sure. Commanding. It cut through the din, steady as bedrock. The kind people listened to. The kind she had died for. The kind she had given up Heaven for.

She cleared her throat, noticing many new lavish furs pressed around her. She cleared it again. "Where am I?"

"Where, you ask?" With great ceremony, Gyda took the cup away and put it down on the night table beside the bed. "You are in the chamber of Jarl Reidar Haraldsson of Ljosstrond, as befits his wife!"

Brigit blinked, her thoughts a tangle thicker than a briar patch. The fog thinned. The memory returned in a sickening rush. The crushing loneliness in the abandoned hut. The icy breath of death at her brow. Her heart fluttered in a chest too light and empty, and the tears welled, then spilled without notice.

"Ach..." Gyda sat beside her, biting her lip. "Do not weep, child. All is well, hmm? Vargr is dead. Astrid will be punished. Reidar is jarl." She hesitated, then stroked Brigit's hair and told a tale beyond Brigit's imagining.

Upon finishing, Gyda grabbed another cup—this time with the familiar broth—and pressed it to Brigit's lips. "Drink slowly. I will not have the jarl's wife sicken upon awakening!"

Brigit wiped away her anguish and drank the broth through a thick throat, half-wondering if she was dreaming. Half-ready to rise and run to the hall to see Reidar in the jarl's high seat with her own eyes. Half-stunned by the unfathomable wry smile playing on Gyda's lips.

"Have you no fear of my spells now?" Brigit blurted.

Gyda pursed her mouth, suddenly looking anywhere but at Brigit. "I see you more clearly now." She darted a glance. "You are either a very poor sorceress—or no sorceress at all."

Brigit studied the older woman as she busied herself with folding linen cloths. There was nothing special in the movement, but Gyda's unexpected new shyness, mixed with unchecked fondness, made the world shine sure and true.

"I am not?" Brigit said, the word slipping out on a breath of half-moan and half-laughter.

"You find too much trouble." Gyda let the linen fall from her hands and returned to the bed. "Had you any true powers, you would have turned the storm aside and spared yourself the fever. And surely, you would have cursed Vargr and Astrid both and driven them from your path." She reached down to brush a wayward lock from Brigit's brow. "But I think you have no need of spells. The fire within you burns strong enough."

Quickly, Brigit caught Gyda's hand, dry and warm as a river stone in the sun.

"I see you more clearly now, too." She pressed a kiss to the knuckles, ignoring Gyda's lifted brows and tightly pinched lips. "You are kind and...sweet, and not at all the curmudgeon you pretend to be. Besides, we share something that binds us—our love for Reidar."

Gyda blinked, drawing a long, steadying breath, then sank onto the edge of the bed. "Sweet?" she murmured, her voice a bit gruff. "You have no notion of the lengths I have gone to for that boy." She cut her eyes toward the bedside chest. "I prayed to your Christ in secret. Me, a foolish hag, on my old knees before His nailed figure, begging Him to bring you back safe!"

Brigit followed Gyda's gaze. Atop the chest stood a foot-high crucifix, carved from Irish yew and interlaced with dense Celtic knotwork that curled along the arms of the cross. Brigit's breath caught. She knew it—had studied it as a girl at the monastery as the young monk, Padraig, delivered his lovely sermons. Along the cross, Christ still hung bowed and sorrowful, his slender form worn smooth by age but unshaken in this foreign place.

"You?" Brigit whispered, unable to tear her eyes from her girlhood come to life. Her thoughts scattered again. "For me...for Reidar?"

"For both." The old woman pressed her index finger to Brigit's lips. "And do not go repeating it. But what choice had I? It broke my heart to see him so lost. And if he believes your Christ can work wonders, then I believe it, too. For what God is more powerful than One who has the power to give life, pull from darkness to light, and return a birthright to a jarl without starting a war?" She locked her fierce gaze on Brigit. "There is no one I love more in this world than Reidar. I have cared for him since he was a swaddled babe—strong, bright, beautiful, and stubborn as a goat." She shrugged, eyes softening. "And if he loves you, then so do I. Especially now I see you are no spell-weaver but a fragile girl doing her best to live, same as the rest of us."

"Gyda, you... Thank you... I..." Brigit searched for words, aching to say how grateful she was for her and how she loved her, too, for all her selfless care and kindness and loyalty. But she'd never been good at speaking her heart—only at spewing scorn—and the words tangled on her tongue.

The old woman rose, her gaze narrowing as she took in Brigit's bedraggled condition. "Enough of idle chatter." She gave a small, uncomfortable shrug. "Now that you draw breath proper, we will see you bathed and dressed. The jarl cannot lay eyes on you in such a state."

With a cluck of her tongue, she pulled back the furs. "Even if he held you in his arms the whole night, filth and all."

# Chapter Thirty-Nine

## Friend

***Brigit***

**Eighth Night**

*I must learn all my news*
*Before I ride home:*
*How soon will you meet*
*With the powerful son of Njord?*
— Skírnismál, stanza 39

Brigit leaned back against the smooth boards as Gyda knelt beside the tub, ladling in hot water from a bright-copper pot. She'd sipped more broth, along with some mead, and had been promised a crust of bread to dip in stew come suppertime. Her body would need days to mend, and her heart longer still to make sense of all that had unfolded in her absence. But for now, the warm water wrapped her like a cloak; the air carried the scent of ash, wool, and crushed juniper; and thick threads of steam curled up from the brazier in soft, silvery ribbons. So Brigit closed her eyes and let Gyda tend her as she would.

Upon rising, she'd discovered a simple tunic in place of her stained wedding gown, yet she'd neither been washed nor tended. Now, Gyda scrubbed her as if she hadn't bathed in years, passing a rough cloth over her neck, down her arms, and along her flanks.

"Lean forward, child."

Brigit's skin prickled as Gyda worked in silence, washing away sweat, blood, and fear with melted lard-and-lye soap. Reidar had held her through the night—filthy and unkempt. A flush of heat crawled up her neck and burned in her cheeks. After days in the hunter's lodge with neither bathing nor clean clothes, she was keenly aware of her disreputable state. And he bore witness to every bit of it!

"You have more tangles than a net left too long at sea!" Patiently, Gyda loosened her knots, then rinsed Brigit's hair again and again, pouring water from the pot until her strands lay clean and heavy down her back.

Unable to quiet her mind, Brigit watched the flicker of the tallow flame catch and vanish in the whorls of steam. Reidar knew she'd awakened—Gyda had made certain of that, boisterously summoning two men to carry the tub into the jarl's chamber. Yet he did not come. Instead, he remained in the mead hall, his voice carrying strong, sure, and very far away.

Brigit's stomach clenched tight as a hazelnut. Maybe he found her foul now—thinking her ruined and unworthy.

"I will fetch the healer," Gyda said low, steadying Brigit as she rose from the tub. "She will make a poultice—" Her voice trailed off as she swept the drying cloth over Brigit, her hands quick and practiced.

Brigit sought Gyda's gaze, but the woman turned away, reaching for a new linen tunic, finely woven and edged with blue-stitched bands.

"Whatever for?" She raised her arms as Gyda slipped it over her head, fresh and soft. "I have no wounds."

"Your husband saw the dried blood on your wedding gown." Gyda's eyes met Brigit's. "He knows."

Wordless, Brigit let the older woman wrap her in furs and walk her back to the bed. Mouth dry, she sat where Gyda pointed.

"Vargr did not touch me, Gyda, for he would not sully himself with a bleeding woman," she squeezed out. "He merely left me there to die."

The voices in the hall grew louder. The strong, sure one pierced the din, making it fade away.

Gyda studied her for a long moment before grabbing a carved bone comb. Her fingers moved swiftly as she sectioned Brigit's damp hair before weaving tight, intricate braids. She layered them with great care, some thin and others thick, then twisted all into a pattern that framed Brigit's face and cascaded down her back.

"There, now you do not look like something washed ashore." Gyda stared at the top of Brigit's head, jaw rigid as a rock. "He believes you harmed, child. It will be a long time before he lies with you again, no matter what you say."

Brigit blinked as a new furious heatwave rushed from her chest to throat, then flooded her face like a burning ember.

Sighing, Gyda circled her arms around Brigit, pulling her close. "He loves you, do not fret. But he would have you heal—"

"His uncle never laid a hand on me!" Brigit wrenched away, breathless and dizzy. "And neither has Reidar himself!"

Eyes narrowing, Gyda stood. "Now, you have spun one tale too many."

"He has not!"

She lifted her brows. "Not even in Éire, when you were his thrall?"

"No, I tell you!" Brigit blew out a long breath. "I am not a harlot, and he is not a brute!"

"That he is not." Gyda pursed her lips and went to the tub to put away the washing and drying cloths. "Still, I take back what I said about your lack of powers." Her mouth twitched as she glanced at Brigit over her shoulder. "Never in his life has Reidar resisted a woman who caught his fancy—if she was willing. Which they always are."

# Chapter Forty

## Home
***Reidar***

**Ninth Night**

*There is a forest, Barri, that we both know well,*
*A fair and peaceful place;*
*And in nine nights from now, to Njord's son,*
*Gerd will grant pleasure there."*
— Skírnismál, stanza 40

The first day of jarlship broke over Reidar like the ceaseless winter wind. No sooner had he taken the high seat, than men began to press in—farmers with disputes over grazing lines, shipwrights needing timber for longships, traders haggling over coin weights and tolls at the fjord's mouth. All day, he sat in the mead hall beneath the carved crossbeams, the ring-staff heavy in his hand, the hearth snapping and roaring at his feet.

His father's high seat fit him well. Yes, his father's, for he'd outlawed his uncle's name. His new name was *Nithing,* for he had committed the irreversible crime of *Nithingsverk.* Now, he would always be known as an oath-breaker, a dishonorable coward, a vile wretch, and shame incarnate. And as such, he'd received no proper send-off, no funeral feast, and no skaldic songs. Instead, he'd met the very end he'd prepared for Ingrid—his corpse left to the wolves deep in the wilds.

The people of Ljosstrond, though ruled by fear and tyranny for many winters, still remembered the days of Harald Fairblade. And they rejoiced in Reidar's rise, quick to embrace his rule, content with his every command. Indeed, he felt born for his rightful rank in the marrow of his bones. This mantle fit like a second skin—his inheritance, his birthright, his fate. Yet amid the elders seeking counsel, warriors awaiting orders, and traders offering tribute in silver, wool, and amber, his mind kept drifting back to his chamber, where Ingrid lay pale and motionless on his bed.

Yesterday, he watched, cold to the bone, as Gyda stripped away her bloodied wedding gown and slipped a clean tunic over her lolling head. His throat locked when he saw her skin—unbroken, unmarred, and flawless as a goddess'. He'd braced for bruises and cuts akin to those marking Astrid, but *Nithing* had spared her that torment. Instead, he'd left dark rivulets of blood crusting across her loins. Reidar had tightened his fists, gritting his teeth against the roaring in his ears. Even in death, his uncle mocked him. For where he ought to have burned with longing at the sight of Ingrid's lovely body, Reidar had only swayed, sick to his core and trembling with a vengeance no dishonor by wolves could satisfy.

It was then he reminded himself he was now a Christian and not to seek retribution in his heart. But so was Ingrid. And while a woman's guilt in plunder was not the way of his people, Ingrid was not of this place. If a Norse woman was taken by force, the stain of dishonor fell on her offender. But such a turn would bring Ingrid great distress—one she might never outlive. He'd been around enough Christian thralls to know what came after some brute had his sport with them. Shame. Hopelessness. Despair. And despite his new faith, he'd wished to howl, to strike at the walls with his axe, to find his uncle and kill him all over again.

"My lord." Astrid's father, Eldar, stepped before the high seat, face drawn tight as a bowstring. "Whatever sentence you deem fit for my reckless daughter, I beg you to spare her life." He winced. "It was the folly of youth and passion, and lack of sense. Besides, she confessed, shamed herself before all, and paid dearly already." The man set his jaw. "And thanks to the Allfather, her deed did not end your wife's life. I ask only that you temper your judgment."

Reidar gave a slow nod. This was neither the place nor the time to face the bitter failures he'd caused the two women in his life—his beloved and his loyal friend. An oaf. He'd deemed himself wise in the ways of women. But what did he know, when he'd believed Ingrid loathed him while she loved him as fiercely as he loved her? Or when he'd thought Astrid only shared his bed for pleasure, while she'd pined for him since girlhood without end?

"I will spare Astrid's life—you have my word, Eldar." Reidar dug his fingers into the hilt of his ring-staff against the images of her bruises and halting limp. "But she must answer for what she has done," he said low. "You know this."

Before Eldar could respond, the chamber door flung open, and Gyda charged into the hall, eyes wild and face flushed.

Reidar's stomach dropped, heavy as a stone. Ingrid had not survived. What were his misgivings, his vengeance, his burdens, his birthright, his honor—when set against this creeping, consuming emptiness? She was gone. Perished due to his unceasing failure to keep her safe. Reidar flexed his hand; it ached with the urge to deal himself a hard blow. He'd imagined he was bringing her home—instead, he led her inexorably to death. Cheated twice, but not thrice.

"The lady is awake and in need of bathing!" Gyda called, casting a wide-eyed glance his way. "Men, bring the tub outright!"

Reidar's breath trapped in his chest, then rushed back, sharp and bright, like sunlight breaking through storm clouds. She would bathe, for she yet lived. With everything in him, he longed to go to her, to see for himself that she was well, to tell her she was safe. But a jarl could not leave his post amid a gathering. So Reidar steeled himself and turned to his endless affairs.

The rest of the day passed in a pounding, restless haze. Still, he sailed through it with surprising ease, issuing commands without hesitation, weighing disputes with a sharpness that silenced old men mid-grumble. The seal-ring of his father—now his—bit into his hand, and he welcomed the sting, for it tethered his mind to duty.

By the time Reidar returned to his chamber, darkness had fallen, still and heavy. On his bed, Ingrid lay fast asleep, her hair arranged into Norse braids. He blinked. Though she'd never pass for a Norsewoman, it suited her. Still, she must have quite recovered if Gyda thought it wise to dress her hair.

Heart thudding, he stepped closer. This sleep was not the hollow, terrifying oblivion straddling this world and the next, but a clean, sound slumber. Her chest rose and fell with steady breath, her mouth rested soft against the pillow, her color glowed warm and familiar, even in the dim candlelight.

A memory flashed through him, sweet and sour, like the wild strawberry he'd pressed to her lips long ago in her enchanted forest, plundered and desecrated by his people. He didn't know it then, but the fear he saw in her shining eyes would forever haunt his nights and foul his days. He'd never meant to scare her—much less to harm her, yet he'd done both in full measure. And still, she claimed to love him as she was slipping away. Surely, it was a thing of madness, so he refused to let the thrill of it consume him. She hadn't meant it. She was delirious from the fright, thirst, and hunger she'd endured in the hunter's lodge. Reidar lifted his head, blood boiling beneath his skin and rising to his skull—and from his uncle's pillage.

As if in answer, she moaned in her sleep.

Reidar shook himself and knelt quietly before the crucifix. *Thank you, Lord, for this mercy.* As he often did, he struggled with asking without the barter of sacrifice. *By Your kindness, show me how to bring her back from what broke her. Guide me how to make her whole.*

He'd managed to undress without making a sound, but when he lowered himself onto the bed, she opened her eyes.

"Reidar..." She peered at him, frozen, her lips parting and closing without a word.

Unthinking, he reached for her—then stopped, not daring to touch. "I—" His throat burned, heart pounded. Dimly, he recalled offering comfort to a thrall once and promising something that eased her fears. But the words fled him now. "I should have taken better care of you—" he bit out in a voice rough as stone—"instead of running off to chase smoke like a fool." He stared ahead, a bile of self-loathing flooding him, sharp as venom. "I am not fit. I bring you nothing but harm."

A low, choked wail escaped from her. Slowly, she sat up. "I was certain I would never see you again."

He released a shuddering breath. "I believed you had truly perished this time."

"I wish you had not seen me so..." She fell silent, then covered her face with her small hands. "I am so ashamed."

A slow, crushing weight spread through Reidar's limbs. He braced to steady himself, to find the right words. *The blame is not yours. I love you no less. Shame has no place here.*

"I killed him," he bit out instead. "I ran Shadowbane—my blade—through his vile flesh, then I cast his body into the forest to be torn by wolves."

Her hands fell, and she turned to him, pale and wide-eyed. "I am shamed by how you found me," she choked out. "But I carry no dishonor. Your uncle did not touch me."

The night pressed against Reidar, thick and twisting. He swallowed against a bitter taste in his mouth. Would it be kinder to let her keep her lie—or would letting it root between them poison what had only begun to sprout?

He sat up so swiftly, she flinched.

"You need not wear this face with me, Ingrid." He failed to master his voice. "I know what he did. I saw your...blood. But he is dead and gone, and no more harm will come to you. And I think no less of you. I am only in awe of you. I could not love you more if I tried."

She looked away. "I tell you true, he did not harm me."

Reidar kept his face impassive as his mind raced like wind-driven ships. He'd expected sorrow, anguish, despair—but not falsehoods.

"Ingrid." He peered at her. "My uncle was not known to spare his marks. Why would he have shown you mercy?"

She glanced up, color rising in her cheeks. "I..." She bit her lip. "He was deterred by my flow." She heaved a sigh, averting her gaze again. "It came soon after Astrid left me in the lodge."

She sank back and pulled the furs over her head. "I would do anything to blot the sight of me thus from your mind." Her voice drifted low and muffled from beneath the layers.

*Thank You.* Reidar peered heavenward, his heart so full of praise he feared it might burst. No one could lie with such a veil of shame.

He cast aside the furs, taking in her flushed cheeks and pinched lips. "My Ingrid." He gathered her into his arms, ignoring his body's immediate and unflagging response. "If you think I would be put off by your monthly courses when I believed you hurt, struck down, and slain—" He pulled her closer, unable and unwilling to hold back any longer—"then you know nothing of me at all."

Their eyes locked, and he read her plainly—relief, gratitude, love. Longing. Slowly, he released her and drew back. He'd dreamed so long of making her his, and now she was within reach, he dared not touch her—not till she mended in full. A cruel twist of fate: to gain his birthright, to feel its rightness surge in his lifeblood at last, and yet to find the one thing he craved most a prize he couldn't claim.

Her blush grew deeper. She knew it, too.

"Reidar, the things I said to you in the lodge, I meant them." She nudged nearer, her sweet scent making his head spin. "I love you, my Reidar. I have always loved you, and I will never stop." She peered into his eyes. "And I will be whole and a proper wife to you soon, I swear."

Reidar said nothing. All this while, he'd kept most of his misgivings buried beneath the urgency of keeping her alive. But now that she breathed safely beside him, they returned, merciless and unrelenting. With all his heart and soul he longed to belong to her loving, life-giving God. But why would this God want him, with his hands covered in a sea of spilled Christian blood?

Heart sinking, he turned to Ingrid. "I speak of my uncle as if he is the worst of men. But I have done terrible things." He quelled the urge to look away. "I did not kill for sport, like him, but I have taken the lives of so many Christians I lost count." His voice cracked. "Maybe that is why God keeps taking you from me. Maybe He has no wish for you to be wed to the likes of me."

She reached for him, stroking his plaits like he wasn't made of pillage and death. "I had never lifted a blade," she whispered. "But I have envied, scorned, hated, and wished ill and harm in my heart more times than I can count." Her steady green gaze met his. "None of us are worthy, Reidar. If we were, Christ would not have needed to die."

She took his hand—the same hand that had burned homes, torn mothers from sons, and drenched the earth in crimson.

"That is the mercy of it." She laid his fingers over the small cross at her chest. "All is forgiven for those who follow Him, for His grace is stronger than any sin. His sacrifice paid all our debts."

Her words banished his misgivings, replacing them with the steady drumming of her heart beneath his palm. With all his might, he pushed down a powerful rush of aching yearning, searching for something to cool his blood.

"Do you know—" he forced out, his voice low and hoarse—"you are a jarl's wife now?"

Her lovely lips curved as she inched closer and settled her silky head in the crook of his shoulder. "I surely do, my lord."

# Chapter Forty-One

## Valorborn

***Brigit***

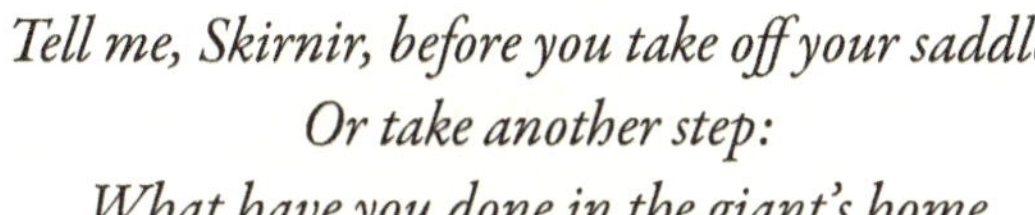

*Tell me, Skirnir, before you take off your saddle,*
*Or take another step:*
*What have you done in the giant's home*
*To make you or me happy?*
— Skírnismál, stanza 41

Brigit lay on her side, stiff and silent, while her new husband tossed and turned, making the bed shift and groan beneath his weight. It had been this way for days—even after she recovered from her ordeal, thanks to Gyda's unfaltering care and endless supply of food and drink. And though Gyda had declared Brigit still unfit to join the jarl at the high seat, her restored health was plain to see. Which made Reidar's hesitation all the more puzzling.

At first, Brigit resolved he was giving her time to heal, wary of putting her out lest she come to some harm. Then she wondered if he was too consumed by his new rank to attend to anything else, gone as he was from dawn to dusk and only returning to sleep. But after she regained her strength—laughing at his jests and devouring each meal with unfeigned hunger—his refusal to see it baffled her.

Worse still, though their marriage had not been blessed by a priest, the lack of bedding did nothing to soothe her unease. Reidar Valorborn was her lawful husband by local custom, with every right to claim her. So why didn't he?

Yet worst of all were the feelings stirring inside her at the nearness of him.

Across the bed, Reidar blew out a slow breath and tucked his arms beneath his head, keeping his eyes shut. He was so warm, so real, so near. Her boy Reidar, her husband—even if unsanctified—her beloved, her champion, her shield. Brigit tried to steady her breath. She failed. This happened every night, and as palpable as the beautiful man beside her, it was happening again. A familiar thought drifted in—something about the lack of proper Christian matrimony and living in sin—but these notions hovered too distant to catch, and they faded like mist on the sea. For they hardly seemed real beside the steady, living heat that pulsed from Reidar, and by some magic, flowed into her, tingling and sparkling in her very depths.

"I am quite healed now," she breathed, shivering, "and I am your wife, my Reidar."

He opened his eyes but remained where he was. "I have a lovely surprise for you tomorrow," he said, a little hoarse. "Then we can lie together as husband and wife."

She shifted closer, certain whatever he'd prepared for her could not rival the aching mystery of his abstinence. "What sort of surprise?" She moved so near they touched.

She waited for him to gather her in, to kiss her, but he only reached out and tucked a strand behind her ear.

"Will you not—" Heart racing, she faltered. "Hold me...for a bit?"

"Hold you?" He withdrew his hand.

His burning, steady gaze on her made her breath catch.

"My Ingrid." His voice emerged so ragged she scarcely recognized it. "Never in all my life have I denied myself a woman's touch. Yet I am learning there is a strange pleasure in such restraint, when it is for one I have desired most of all." He inched away from her. "If I hold you now, my Ingrid, much as I command myself, I fear it would not endure."

*What is this madness?* Brigit closed her eyes. *May it not endure.* But she'd made her meaning clear enough, so she blew out a long, shuddering breath and schooled her mind to anything that wasn't his blazing, thrumming heat.

"Why do you call me Ingrid?" Her voice emerged too eager, grasping for steadier ground. "You know that is not my name."

He blinked, sufficiently distracted. "Ingrid means beautiful goddess. That was how I saw you since the moment I met you." He studied the ceiling, wincing. "I also saw you as my thrall and wished to name you to my liking."

"To your liking?" Brigit rose on one elbow.

"Yes," he muttered. "For that...I am sorry."

"I was christened Brigit after Saint Brigid of Kildare." She searched his eyes. "They say she worked wonders—turned water to ale, fed crowds from scraps, gave sight to the blind. Does Lady Brigit sit ill on Norse tongues? I would keep my name, if I may."

Her words must have stirred something in him, for he suddenly drew her close and held her fast, his heart hammering against her chest.

"I know not what wonders grant me patience to wait, after longing seven winters for you. And yet, though I am raw with it—" his low, deep voice at her neck sent gooseflesh across her skin—"I would wait a thousand winters more, if only to hold you now—alive, unharmed, and so nearly mine."

She dared not move. He was raw with it indeed—blazing and almost undone.

"A thousand winters, is it?" She lifted a brow to mask all that roused within her at his unguarded, if delusory, candor.

"No," he admitted with a strained chuckle, shifting her gently away from him. "But I swear another night of waiting will be worth it, my Brigit."

# Chapter Forty-Two

## Surprise

***Brigit***

*There is a forest, Barri, that we both know well,*
*A fair and peaceful place;*
*And in nine nights from now, to Njord's son,*
*Gerd will grant pleasure there.*
— Skírnismál, stanza 42

Brigit dreamed she was in her forest again, the ground spangled with wild strawberries, their sweet scent filling her with a bittersweet longing. The sky darkened. The scent vanished, replaced by the acrid stench of smoke and fire.

She shielded her eyes, heart thudding. The sky was burning. Her entire world stood aflame.

*Father, help me.*

Gentle arms lifted her; they carried her away from the looming peril.

*Father, help me.*

But she wasn't. Her new home was a cage, and she its captive.

*Father, help me.*

Once more, strong arms swept her up; they pulled her away from danger.

*You are safe.*

Yet she wasn't. She'd only traded one prison for another, awaiting a grim fate at the hands of the beast of Hel.

*Father, help me.*

With an unyielding grip, steady arms seized her, whisking her away from the impending harm.

*You are safe, for I will never let you go—*

"Wake, child. You have slept long enough." Gyda's hushed voice sent Brigit's heart racing. "It is time to rise, for we have much to do!"

Brigit sat up and rubbed the sleep from her eyes, shaking off the dream.

"Here." Lips pursed, Gyda placed a wooden trencher laden with warm bread, smoked herring, and a bowl of thick, creamy porridge in Brigit's lap.

The savory aroma made Brigit's stomach growl.

"What do you know of the surprise Reidar has for me today?" She closed her eyes in bliss at the first bite of the mysterious Irish bread. "Who bakes these loaves, Gyda? And how is it we have grain when all was lost in the fire?"

Gyda lifted her chin, her face impassive as a frozen lake. "Full of questions today, are you? There will always be grain enough for the jarl and his kin. Now eat fast! We yet have your hair to plait, face to paint, and a new gown to squeeze you into—if it still fits, given how you have been stuffing that mouth of yours."

"Gyda!" Brigit put away the trencher and rose, hunger forgotten. "You must tell me what awaits me. I cannot go on in the dark like this!"

"Sit." Gyda reached for her hair and began to unweave the braids she'd so carefully bound but a few days past. "Pester your husband. He is the one driving old Gyda mad with his wild whims and fancies."

She worked fast, threading Brigit's hair with bits of twisted wool, dyed with berries and soot, and weaving it into a crown of elaborate braids atop her head. Finished, she drew forth a square of white linen edged with red embroidery—so thin it was almost sheer—and secured it with bronze pins.

"A veil..." Brigit gasped.

"What is a veil?" Despite her best efforts, Gyda's pursed lips twitched. "I do not know of such a thing."

Eyes creasing at the corners, the older woman headed out. A moment later, she returned with a white gown draped across her forearms.

"Stand." She placed the gown reverently on the bed. "We have no time to spare since you have slept through your own—" She clamped her mouth shut. "Raise your arms and do not question me. I will not break my word to the jarl!"

Brigit fell silent as her mind completed what Gyda left unsaid. But having a wedding was as improbable as it seemed, seeing as they'd already had one.

Despite Gyda's teasing, the gown fit Brigit as if spun for her alone, hugging her waist and falling in graceful folds to her ankles. Made of fine, undyed wool and softened by rinses and sun-bleaching, it shimmered in the morning light. Delicate bands edged the sleeves and hem with intricate red knotwork, and at each shoulder, glimmered a burnished bronze brooch to match her hair.

"Now, your face." Without ceremony, Gyda dipped her little finger into a small jar of coal and smudged the dark powder around Brigit's eyes.

"Hmm, you look near half-Norse now. Boots!" Gyda pulled new boots from a trunk, their soft leather white as snow and trimmed with thick fur.

"Pelts!" She draped cascading white furs over Brigit's shoulders.

With a long, satisfied sigh, Gyda drew back, taking in her work. "Leave it to Gyda to dress a girl so fine no man dares blink!"

Rooted to the spot, Brigit parted her lips.

But Gyda lifted her hand in warning. "No need to ask. You see full well how lovely you are. Now, wait for me to dress, then we will go!"

Speechless, Brigit watched Gyda leave the chamber. If she didn't know better, she'd been adorned like a proper bride on her wedding day. What foolishness! Jaw set, she marched to the door to question Reidar. But the great hall stood nearly empty—a few stragglers sipping from their cups and a knot of *huskarlar* guarding the entrance.

Gyda returned not long after, her steps ringing in the stillness.

Brigit widened her eyes at the sight. The older woman wore a gown dyed a deep shade of crimson; her white braids lay entwined with silver thread; and her eyes were lined with dark coal, lending her an unexpected fierce beauty.

"Something to say?" Gyda set her hands on her waist, no longer able to conceal a grin. "Old Gyda can adorn herself for a special day like today! Let us go now, child. He must be sick with waiting."

Outside, the morning rose cold but sunny. It hovered at once close and distant, as though something wondrous were about to unfold. Dazed, Brigit followed Gyda down a well-trodden path into the woods, her mind spinning with half-formed thoughts, like a child on the eve of receiving a long-desired gift. But they hadn't walked a yard when Brigit's breath caught at the crunch of footsteps behind them.

She glanced over her shoulder. Two armed *huskarlar* followed at a measured distance, their cloaks stirring with each stride.

"Are we in peril?" She stared at Gyda, pulse quickening.

"Do not fret so." The older woman rubbed Brigit's arm, urging her along. "These men are loyal to Reidar and charged by him to guard and protect you everywhere you go."

The drumming in Brigit's chest slowing, she walked beside Gyda until they reached a clearing. At its center loomed a large boulder. Around it gathered all the familiar men—Reidar's most trusted warriors. And in their midst stood Reidar himself, cloaked in a heavy mantle of deep blue wool, fastened at one shoulder with a silver brooch worked in the shape of a wolf's head. Beneath the mantle, he wore a fine woolen tunic, embroidered at the cuffs and neckline with gold thread. A wide leather belt, tooled with runes, cinched the tunic at his waist, and at his side rested the sword he called Shadowbane.

Speechless at the sight of such splendor, Brigit nearly went to him when she noticed a slight, cloaked figure standing apart and facing the wood with a bowed head. She came to an abrupt halt as something in the set of the slim shoulders and a subtle tilt of the head made her heart leap.

The man turned, and the world fell away. It rushed back in an instant like a warm gale, bursting with freshly baked bread, sweet honeycombs, and Saint Padraig's prayer.

*Christ with me,*
*Christ before me,*
*Christ behind me,*
*Christ in me,*
*Christ beneath me,*
*Christ above me...*

"Padraig?" Brigit's voice emerged as if from elsewhere as the monk fixed her with a stunned, glittering gaze.

Before she knew it, she was flying into his arms as she did when she was small, inhaling his familiar scent of warm barley bread and all that was good in the world.

"Wee Brigit..." His sweet Irish voice cracked. "Oh, what have they done with your face?"

She drew back, remembering herself. Padraig had aged—fine lines creased his brow, and a touch of silver threaded through his dark curls, now pulled back in the Norse style. Gone was the tonsure he'd worn, but his large wooden cross still hung from a leather thread around his neck.

Brigit's eyes burned and itched. A priest! And she dressed as a bride. And Reidar as a bridegroom. She clasped her hands together to halt the tears. But they came all the same, warm and copious, and uncaring for all the onlookers, including Reidar, who approached with a small groove between his fair brows.

But before he uttered a word, Gyda swooped in like a brooding hen with a cloth in her hand. "Are you daft, or do you wish to look like something from the midden on your wedding day?" She shrugged with a wry glance at Reidar. "Ach, I said too much, I did. Spoiled the surprise!"

Brigit's heart swelled against her ribs, so full it could burst. "Thank you, my Reidar." The words slipped out in a half-sob, half-whisper.

Through the blur in her eyes, she glimpsed Reidar's unguarded, beaming face. Warm and glowing, his light reached through her every lonely winter. It stripped away years and suffering. And once again, he was the kind boy who found her in the Rathlin wood, tending to her wounds and claiming her forever with his sweet, chaste kiss. And for the thousandth time, she stood on the shores of her ruined island. Behind her—the blaze of the monastery and Padraig's slight form by the longships as she was falling in love with the enemy of her people. And as they spoke their foolish, reckless farewells.

She smiled at her dazzling bridegroom through her tears as Gyda patted around her eyes, clucking her tongue. "Save your weeping for later lest you wish to scare him off! Not that such a thing is possible," she muttered, smoothing the veil over Brigit's crown of braids.

With a wink and a half-smile, Reidar turned to Padraig, and though nearly two heads shorter, the monk peered at him without a hint of fear.

In a sparkling daze, their words mixed and melded with the faint whisper of the pines, the distant caw of a raven, and the crunch of fallen leaves and twigs beneath boots. And like the first light of dawn breaking through the fog, a sense of rightness rushed through Brigit, clear and radiant.

# Chapter Forty-Three

## Steadfast
***Reidar***

*One night is long, two nights are even longer;*
*How can I bear three?*
*Often a month seems shorter to me*
*Than half a night of desire now.*
— Skírnismál, stanza 43

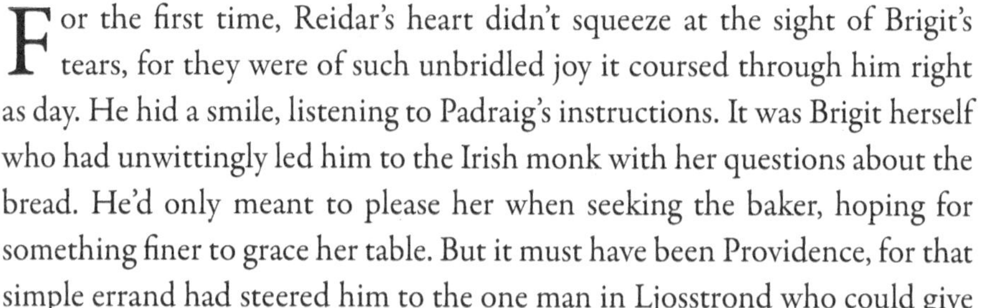

For the first time, Reidar's heart didn't squeeze at the sight of Brigit's tears, for they were of such unbridled joy it coursed through him right as day. He hid a smile, listening to Padraig's instructions. It was Brigit herself who had unwittingly led him to the Irish monk with her questions about the bread. He'd only meant to please her when seeking the baker, hoping for something finer to grace her table. But it must have been Providence, for that simple errand had steered him to the one man in Ljosstrond who could give them the impossible—a Christian wedding.

By some mercy, the monk had not been sent to the slave markets with the others. After the Rathlin raid, he was thrown into the kitchens to scrub the pots, carry wood, and clean the animal pens. Then by chance, he found himself at the hearth, helping with the baking. His bread—crusty, fragrant, and better than any had tasted—won the favor of the cook herself, who claimed him for her own and never let him go.

"Come, my love—" Reidar thrust out his hand. "It is time we wed proper."

Her dainty arm tucked into his, they approached his boyhood boulder. Had someone told him, when he climbed it as a child, that one day he would marry his beloved here in a Christian rite, he would have laughed. Now, its flat surface bore the sign of a cross he'd etched with the point of his dagger. He stood complete at the sight of it. Truly, the Lord's ways were unfathomable.

Brigit's gasp and an awe-filled, "Reidar" flooded him with such warmth it melted away the cooling air. He clasped her hand in his and turned to the small crowd.

His men stood stiff and silent—some glaring at Padraig, others frowning at Reidar.

"Dear friends, I have much to rejoice in today and much to share." His voice carried through the clearing and boomed against the half-dressed tree limbs and his thudding chest. Whether his men turned away or followed, he would remain steadfast, for his faith dwelled in his heart and kindled his soul. How could he deny such light when all power and dominion paled before it?

He squared his shoulders. "It is no longer a great secret, so I will speak plainly before you. All know I sought this woman—whose given name is Brigit—far and wide, for she is my fate. And when I brought her here, half-dead in my arms, I begged our gods to save her." Her hand tensed in his; he gave it a squeeze. "But they stayed mute and deaf to my pleas, and she...died." He swallowed, the memory battering him anew. "I saw with my own eyes her final breath leave her body. With my own hand, I felt her cooling skin. Dear friends, this woman was dead."

The gathering grew so quiet that only Brigit's soft, steady breath and his own thumping heart remained.

"In my despair, I turned to Brigit's God, Jesus Christ." He ignored bulging eyes and raised brows. "Each of you has known me since we were boys. We have fought, conquered, and bled together. You know who I am, my friends, my brothers. And I swear to each of you by all I hold dear, Christ alone brought her back."

The men's faces hardened—lips pressing tight, eyes narrowing.

Reidar bowed his head. *Speak through me, Lord. Show them the way, so they, too, can be free.*

"After that, I wished to offer Him sacrifice, to repay for His mercy—" He fell silent. The unconcealed scorn and bewildered doubt in once familiar faces were enough to freeze the air stiff. How could he make them see the wonder he lived each day?

"But I learned He asks not for the spilling of blood," he said against his racing pulse. "For the Lord sent *Him* as the sacrifice to atone for all our wrongs, even the worst of them. What a God this is—loving and powerful beyond all measure. So, my dear friends, I say before all of you with no shame and great joy: I am a Christian. There is none like Christ in all the world, for how much better is it to worship a God who loves you despite all that you are, than to appease ones who demand and devour and still turn away?"

He released Brigit's hand and approached his men, their eyes on him cold and unflinching.

"Rest easy, friends, the true Christian faith is not one of force, and I will not compel you to believe as I do." Steady and unyielding, he met each gaze. "If you wish to seek the incomparable gifts I have found, Padraig the Monk will guide you. But if your heart clings to the old ways, I will not halt you. I am no tyrant and will never be one. Yet I will pray that each of you receives the dazzling light that now dwells within me."

The men stood silent. Only the rustle of leaves in the breeze and the snap of a twig beneath someone's shifting weight.

Jaw clenched, Reidar returned to Brigit. They would surely declare him unfit to be jarl—or worse.

"You spoke well," she breathed. "It is in the Lord's hands now."

As if in answer, a hush of wind drifted past, soft as a whisper. *The world has hated Me before it hated you.*

A din of low voices rose, rippling through the clearing. His men stirred as one, their breath clouding the air.

"Reidar? A Christian?" Sveinulf the Querulous muttered, shaking his head. "By all the gods!"

"If this Christ brought her back from the dead," said Thorsten, "then I might follow Him, too. No god I know can do such a thing."

"But what of Valhalla?" Ulf gripped the haft of his axe. "What could outrival feasting with our friends and fathers and the gods?"

"A loving God?" another scoffed, his brow drawn tight. "Is there such a thing? All gods demand blood!"

"I will think on it," said one of the youngest men. "Reidar prayed to Christ, and now he is jarl, hmm?"

"I would never betray our true gods!" Another lifted his chin, glaring. "Not for any favor!"

The din grew louder. Some crossed their arms. Others scratched their beards. One spat on the ground and muttered a prayer to Thor.

Reidar turned to Padraig. "Now."

All hushed as the monk stepped forward, taking his place between Reidar and his bride.

"We are gathered here in the sight of God, to join this man and this woman in holy matrimony," Padraig declared in clear, well-formed Norse, unfazed by dismissive shrugs and downturned mouths. "A bond not to be broken, a covenant before our Lord Christ." He rested his gaze on Reidar. "God ordained marriage in the beginning. It is no light thing. It is a covenant and a union of one flesh. Reidar, son of Harald Fairblade, do you come here freely to take Brigit as your lawfully wedded wife, to cherish her, provide for her, and cleave only to her, as long as you both shall live?"

"I do," said Reidar in Irish. Then, in Norse, he repeated, "Yes, I do."

Brigit's small hand trembled in his as it did winters past, when he bound her wrists with his daft rope. He gulped against the familiar thickness in his throat, fighting the tearing memory of her hurt ankle and bleeding knee, her unaffected silky head upon his shoulder, her lilting *Rei-dar* that even then he longed to give up all the world for. The images punched the breath from his lungs—the sight of her lone, helpless shape on her ruined island, the terrible weight of his unforgivable blunder, and the long, dark voyage home, thick with guilt that would gnaw at him for seven bitter winters with neither relief nor resolution.

"And you, Brigit, daughter of Fergal O'Clery, do you come freely, with a willing heart, to take Reidar, as your lawfully wedded husband, to honor him, care for him, and cleave only to him, as long as you both shall live?"

"I do," she said, bright emeralds trained on Reidar.

From the corner of his eye, Gyda reached into her belt for her wiping cloth, her expression at once fierce and vexed—the way it always turned when she was near to tears.

"This man and this woman shall now speak their vows before God and these witnesses." Padraig gave Reidar a nod—their agreed-upon sign.

"I, Reidar, take you, Brigit, as my wife." The words, as he repeated them, shimmered and flared, taking shape, filling the clearing, lifting to the sky. "Before God, I pledge my love, body, and spirit to you. In peace or hardship, in laughter or sorrow, I will not forsake you until our days are ended."

How different Brigit looked now. Not still and pale as she'd been during their rushed, clandestine Norse rites, but pink-cheeked and radiant.

"I, Brigit," she repeated, gazing into his eyes like he was her whole world, "take you, Reidar, as my husband. I give you my trust, my heart, and all that I am. Whether in feast or famine, in light or shadow, I shall walk with you until the Lord calls us home."

Padraig drew a worn psalter from beneath his cloak, opened it, and murmured a blessing in Latin, then repeated in Norse: "May the Lord bless you and keep you. May His countenance shine upon you, and may He be gracious to you and give you both peace."

He pulled a braided cord of wool dyed with berries and wrapped it around their joined hands. "As these hands are bound before all these witnesses, so too are your lives, your hearts, and your purpose—joined not in bondage but in covenant. May this handfasting be a witness before God, and may He bless your union as holy and enduring. May your home be a place of welcome, your bed a place of fidelity, and your hearts a place where His Spirit dwells." He lifted his gaze to the heavens. "What was once two is now one. In the name of the Father, the Son, and the Holy Ghost, I declare you husband and wife. What God has joined, let no man tear asunder."

Like a blessing, the rain fell, soft and cool, the drops clinging to Reidar's beard and shining on Brigit's cheeks.

He turned to his men. Most stood rigid as posts, their faces unmoved, arms crossed, eyes hard.

"Reidar," she whispered, so faint he had to lean closer. "You cannot drag them into the light. They must choose to step into it."

He forced a smile, pulling the pelts tighter around his wife's shoulders. "Friends, I did not make you stand here for nothing! Let us go and feast as befits such a wedding!"

His men's exaggerated exhales, followed by rolling eyes, sardonic jibes, and hungry grumbles wrapped around him like a thick fleece on a cold night. A great weight slipped from his shoulders, and he let out a long breath and lifted his gaze heavenward. *Thank You, Father.*

As they all walked back to the longhouse, he took Brigit's hand and pressed his lips to the place where her sweet pulse drummed. "At last—" he peered down at her, speaking in Irish—"I take you *home*."

# Chapter Forty-Four

## Anew

***Brigit & Reidar***

*Love bears all things,*
*Believes all things,*
*Hopes all things,*
*Endures all things.*
— 1 Corinthians 13:7 (ESV)

Brigit stood in the middle of the chamber, watching the door. The feast had worn on into the night, but after walking her here, Reidar left with a promise of swift return. Now some time had passed, and he still hadn't come back.

Just as the grain store flames surged through her racing mind, the door opened, revealing her husband with a small clay jar in his hands.

"*Heil.*" He smiled.

"*Heill,*" she replied, uncertain why he was greeting her.

"I wish to start anew—" he lifted a brow —"and do it right this time, my love."

She peered at the jar. "Anew?"

"Reidar." He approached, pointing to himself with his free hand.

Brigit swayed against a tingling warmth that filled her limbs and rushed into her face. Memory made flesh. Smoke and ruin made new in light and joy. How good God was.

Silent, he gestured toward her and turned his palm over in question.

"Brigit," she whispered.

"Brih-gid." He nodded. "A lovely name. It suits you."

Eyes twinkling, he placed the jar into her hands, smooth and warm from his touch. "Wild strawberries are past season," he murmured, "but I found these freshly made preserves."

Brigit battled the sting in her nose as a storm of memories drowned her. A tall savage boy pressing a single berry to her lips. His beautiful eyes locking on hers. Her back leaning against the oak behind her, unmoored at her first brush with God's divine purpose.

"Take it," she breathed in Irish, lifting the jar toward her husband with trembling hands. "It is yours."

His gaze trained on hers, he removed the lid, then dipped a finger and brought it to his mouth. "Mmm...all mine?"

The recall blazed through her like a flame. His blinding smile, his warm arms, his chaste kiss. His shape, forever growing smaller, then more distant, then gone as he walked away, leaving her alone. And yet he never had—not with his gentle ways, his kind voice, his firm touch—in her thoughts, in her dreams, in her lifeblood, in her failed counterfeit marriage.

"Brigit?"

Breath hitching, she drew back a pace.

Swift as lightning, he blocked her way.

Once more, she held up the jar. "Take this," she whispered in Irish. "It is time I went *home*."

"*Home?*" With a wry grin, he dipped his finger into the jar and pressed it to her lips.

A burst of sweet tartness rushed across her tongue, sending sparks and tingles throughout. She couldn't unlock her gaze from his. It coaxed and beckoned like a bright ray of sun on a gray winter morning, calling her and pulling her in:

*Home...home...home.*

"*Home*." He bent to her mouth.

His breath smelled of wild strawberries, and his lips were a stark mixture of warmth and iron against hers. His eyes, fixed on hers, were the exact color of the clear summer sky. His kiss was nothing like the one on Rathlin Island, nothing like the time they awaited their grim fate with Vargr. For it was made of stone and fire, and something as tender as flower petals.

Her first kiss. Her new kiss. Her only kiss.

Scented with berries, sea, snow, love, and freedom.

The one she waited for her whole life.

Stolen by a stranger. Returned by her husband.

"The waiting is done, my Brigit." He pulled away with his blinding smile, which made his broad cheeks ride even higher and turned his eyes into bright blue slits. "For now, at last, I mean to take you home."

He stepped behind her as she fought to keep her breath steady. "I—help," he murmured in Irish, removing her brooches.

The gown slid to the floor, leaving her in her linen tunic. Her chest heaved like a breaker as the memory of his turbulent, blood-stained return washed over her, cheerless and desolate. She'd known him almost from the start, yet she pretended and lied, all the while telling herself she was the righteous one.

Doubt, fear, and scorn instead of faith, hope, and love. Which of them had been the heathen? But she, too, would do it right this time, for they would make new memories to bury the painful ones.

"I knew it was you," she breathed, "even if I didn't want to believe it, for you returned as a plunderer and a...captor."

"You'd had me fooled—" his voice at her cheek came forth low and strained—"though I can scarcely fault you. I tried to harden my heart against loving you, my Brigit, but such matters are not ours to decide."

Her pulse raced beneath his touch. She drew a long, shaky breath, floating on a wave of wistful memories and aching longings. This was just how she'd imagined the boy Reidar's hands once he became a man—warm, sure, tender.

His lips found the crook of her neck. Her skin flooded with gooseflesh. A sweet yearning filled every part of her, rushing like an unstoppable surge.

Her husband remained still for a moment, then placed his hands on her shoulders and turned her to face him—steadfast as the oak on a summer day, save for the racing pulse at his throat.

She couldn't say whether she reached for him or he for her, only when their lips met and his arms locked around her, she no longer stood in their chamber. Instead, she floated in a place that tasted of love, safety, wild strawberries, and a sweet ache she wanted to feel forever. Never had she been touched like this. A wonder—in his hands, everything turned shiny and golden.

Her Norseman, her Reidar, her one true love. All the winters she spent in fevered dreams of him, all the days she told herself falsehoods, all the nights she tried to make him into a beast—all of it fell away. There was nothing but him. Only his warm breath and the sure weight of his gentle hands.

The world vanished as he replaced it, claiming his rightful place in it. For in this life, he'd always been her world. Always and forever.

Something soft and small shifted in Reidar's arms. He opened his eyes. She lay asleep, dark lashes caressing her cheek, lips pursed in a pink rosebud, shining hair tousled about his shoulders. They'd been so aflame for each other, never sleeping as he brought her home and made her his, always and forever. As she found her freedom and sealed it with his name and the endless stream of Irish words for beloved that drove him half mad and gave him a home he never knew existed.

Careful not to wake her, he stroked her smooth cheek, brushing away an errant strand of gleaming bronze. All the women he'd known, come morning he was eager to leave. But with Brigit, he only wished the morning would never end. He only wanted to keep her in his arms, to stay wrapped in her warmth, and never let go.

She sighed and opened her eyes—bright green in the radiant light.

"My Brigit." He smiled into them, pulling her close. "How I have longed for this morning."

Oddly thoughtful, she pressed a kiss to his lips and said nothing.

He drew back. "What is it, my love?"

She traced a small blue knot etched into his chest—the one with three interlaced loops. "You could have had countless mornings like this." She bit her lip and fixed her gaze on his. "Why did you leave me behind, my Reidar? You had nearly killed me with it."

He released her, not quite prepared for this long-overdue confession. "I was young and foolish." He glanced away. "I believed I was doing right—honoring my promise to take you home. But I paid dearly for that folly, though surely not as dearly as you."

She rested her head in the crook of his shoulder. "I had been too young to share your bed." Her voice wavered. "What would have become of me had you brought me along?"

"I knew that." He pulled her closer. "I would have waited until you were older."

"You would not have wed me." It was a statement, not a question.

"No." He winced.

"So you would have soon tired of me, and then I would have fallen to Vargr, anyway. Or maybe Astrid would kill me and spare me the trouble. Either way, it would have taken strife and bloodshed to unseat your uncle in the end."

He lifted her chin with his fingertip. "My Brigit, I will never tire of you."

"Nor I of you, but this is the way of the Lord, my Reidar." She peered back at him. "You thought you had made a grave error, and I loathed you for leaving me. But He had a plan for us all along, and it was a better one than either of us could have dreamed up in a hundred winters."

"It is so." He grinned, her words faint against the thrumming in his chest.

"And that plan—" she returned a wry smile, reaching for something under her pillow—"was to bring *you* home, *a chroí*."

She unwrapped the small bundle, lifted her little twig, and placed it upon his head.

# Chapter Forty-Five

## Judgement

***Astrid***

*For I know the plans I have for you...*
*Plans for welfare and not for evil,*
*To give you a future and a hope.*
— Jeremiah 29:11 (ESV)

Astrid stood frozen before the high seat, eyes lowered and heartbeat drumming in her temples, dull as her swirling thoughts. The mead hall pressed in on her, dense with spectators, rank with smoke and sweat, and humming with the low murmur that grated in her ears and tightened around her like a vise.

They had stripped her of weapons, fine raiment, and the freedom to leave her house. Then, as if that weren't humiliation enough, they'd made her wait—first for Reidar's bride to heal, then for the wedding feast to pass, then for the pleasure of his judgment. Now, clad in scratchy, ill-fitting rough-spun wool and with her hair unbound, she stood ready to receive it from the man she once dared to dream of calling husband.

Her father did not believe Reidar would sentence her to death. Through the thick haze made of shame and misery, she remembered him saying he'd pleaded her cause before Reidar and received his word. More the pity. Even without her weapons, she was still a shield-maiden, and she'd seen enough to know death was not always the worst fate.

"Come summer, we will not only raid but also trade, for we have much to offer"—Reidar's voice drifted in and out against the pounding in her head—"fine furs, walrus ivory, chests of amber, timber and iron, honey and fish enough to load a longship. And if our settlement in Dalaradia holds and grows, we shall use it as a foothold and a port..."

She glanced up as he struck his ring-staff against the floor, silencing the din. His new wife sat beside him, fresh and fair as morning dew and glowing with his love. A stark contrast to Astrid's own limp hair and sunken gaze. For all she knew, the blasted woman was already swelling with his child. It mattered not. Soon, Astrid would be branded *Skoggang*—seared on the brow with hot iron, driven to the gate beneath a hail of spit and insults, and cast out into the heart of winter to die alone in the wilds.

She dropped her gaze again. The cruel end she'd plotted for Brigit had come for her instead—the foreigner's God was a powerful and vengeful kind.

"...this day I declare Astrid Eldarsdottir's punishment for her crimes." Reidar's voice came forth too strained, the whole of her name cold and foreign on his lips. "You all know well such a task is not of my choosing. But Astrid aided and abetted a crime against the people of Ljosstrond, which robbed you all of winter grain. And against my wife, Brigit, she committed a grievous act that nearly ended her life."

He fell silent as the crowd waited—so quiet, Astrid heard her own ragged breath.

"Astrid's crimes are deserving of death."

Reidar's flat voice echoed in Astrid's ears like a Christian bell. She clenched her fists, wishing to beg some god for such mercy, yet she believed in none now. So she lifted her chin and locked her gaze upon Reidar's face. He looked pale in his jarl's seat, the weight of his burden pressing down on him like a boulder.

*I loved you too much, Reidar.* She stared into his frozen eyes. *That was my one and only crime.*

He held her gaze, making his face impassive as he always did when steeling himself against a blow. "By all rights, she should be branded *Skoggang* and cast out into the wilds, weighed down by her evil deeds, or slain by any in Ljosstrond without cause for grief."

Astrid's insides churned and roiled, yet she didn't look away. If this was his terrible judgement, she would snatch his dagger from his belt and thrust it into her own heart.

At the edge of her vision, Brigit's face hovered ashen and wide-eyed like a child's. For a beat, she indulged herself and glared at the Irish sorceress. *I do not need your pity, foreigner.*

Reidar swallowed. "Yet Astrid's crimes, grievous as they are, sprang not from malice but from passion. She is not beyond redemption, for she confessed and in so doing saved Brigit's life. I have also struck bargains with two of our neighbors to trade small measures of grain, bartered from the boundless spoils hoarded by my uncle, *Nithing*. And though it will not fill our store, everyone in Ljosstrond will have a portion of bread come winter." He straightened. "Besides, I gave Eldar, Astrid's father, my word to spare his daughter's life. And I keep my word."

The pounding in Astrid's ears broke beneath the swell of angry voices.

"She is guilty!"

"Cast her out!"

"Brand her!"

"Flog her first!"

"*Skoggang!*"

Trembling from head to foot, Astrid squared her shoulders and glowered over her shoulder at the gathering. Her mother's red-rimmed eyes and father's glum face were all that was familiar. The rest—these people she'd known all her life—looked less than human. Twisted with venom, they were rabid beasts hungry for blood. Better that she would never see any of them again.

*Well pleased, are you?* She lifted her eyes skyward. *You, with all Your professed talk of love and mercy, are just as bloodthirsty as any god.*

She flinched as Reidar rose and slammed his ring-staff against the floor so hard the sound stabbed through her chest.

"Astrid's punishment is to be confined to her house through winter, then taken to the slave market in Hedeby come spring." His voice boomed through the hushed hall, then faded as he fixed her with a stare full of shadows. "After that," he said too low for anyone but her to hear, "your fate lies with the Lord alone."

It took Astrid an instant to comprehend—she would not be branded, nor cast out to die of hunger, nor killed. Instead, she'd been spared for a new life, merciless as it was.

Yet in chains or not, she would always remain a shield-maiden, and she would neither bend nor break. For she would face what came with iron in her spine and carve out a future from what remained.

For she would live.

Her knees nearly gave out, but she stayed upright—held fast by Brigit's steady, unblinking gaze. And though its meaning escaped her, it bore neither scorn nor pity. Only a strange light that, had she not known better, she might have mistaken for forgiveness.

---

*Thank you for reading!*

*Visit https://www.verabellauthor.com/of-flaw-and-scorn-deleted-chapter to follow the fifteen-year-old Reidar on his empty-handed journey back to Norway.*

*Vera*

*P.S. If you enjoyed this book, please tell a friend and leave a review. It would mean the world to me.*

---

Stay tuned!

The next installment in the *Gracefire* series follows Astrid Eldarsdottir through pain and suffering, love and duty, despair and sacrifice toward a hard-won redemption.

# Historical Note

Though *Of Flaw and Scorn* is entirely fictional, like all my novels, it was inspired by real historical figures and events. Specifically, Reidar's inner struggle is deeply rooted in the life of Håkon the Good, a tenth-century Norwegian king (c. 920–961 AD) remembered for his wisdom, restraint, and failed—but earnest—attempts to bring Christianity to a pagan land.

The youngest son of King Harald Fairhair, Håkon was fostered as a boy at the court of the Christian King Athelstan in England. There, he was baptized, educated, and steeped in the Christian worldview before returning to claim his father's throne in Norway.

When Håkon came home, it was not to conquer, but to reconcile. He tried to introduce the Christian faith gently, hoping to unite a divided people. But the powerful pagan chieftains, particularly the jarls of Lade, fiercely resisted conversion. To preserve peace, Håkon ultimately relented. Though he built churches and welcomed Christian priests early in his reign, he eventually had to perform sacrifices to the old gods to hold his fragile alliances together. One saga recounts him secretly making the sign of the cross even as he toasted Odin—caught, like Reidar, between two worlds.

Despite this tension—or perhaps because of it—Håkon earned a reputation for fairness, integrity, and courage. Even those who did not share his faith grieved his death and honored his rule. After a reign of nearly twenty-five years, he died from a wound to the shoulder at the Battle of Fitjar, fighting off the sons of his half-brother Erik Bloodaxe. (Håkon's rival king and frequent antagonist in the sagas served as the basis for my character Vargr Bloodgale.)

That detail—the wound to the shoulder—resonates deeply with me. It appears in Reidar's near-fatal injury and, a bit unexpectedly, in two key scenes from my earlier *Always and Forever* trilogy (now unpublished). I first imagined *Of Flaw and Scorn* as a distant prequel to that series, and when I wrote it, I had no idea this same wound held historical significance. Only later, while researching, did I realize how closely the injury mirrored a real event.

Though Reidar is not a direct retelling of Håkon's life, I wrote him as a kind of spiritual predecessor—a man whose story might foreshadow the king to come. Reidar walks the brutal world of early Viking raiders, but his heart is shaped a little different from the start. Like Håkon, he begins to question the old ways. And like Håkon, he learns that real strength lies not only in the sword, but in what the hand chooses to do with it.

# Author's Note

Thank you for spending time with me. I hope you enjoyed *Of Flaw and Scorn,* the first book in the *Gracefire* series! I'm eager to hear your thoughts—what did you love, like, or not fancy much? Reach out at verabellauthor@gmail.com and let me know. I'd love to hear from you.

I also have a small favor to ask. Reviews are the lifeblood of books. They help readers discover our shared worlds. If you could leave a review on Amazon or your favorite retailer site, even a brief one, I'd be over the moon.

For new release announcements, sneak peeks, and other exclusive content, join my mailing list at VeraBellAuthor.com.

Thank you once again for reading my stories. Your support means everything.

Warmly,
*Vera Bell*

# Book Club Discussion Questions

- How do Brigit and Reidar's stories illustrate the idea that God is at work long before we recognize Him?

*Faith Focus: Have you ever looked back on a chaotic season of your life and seen God's hand in it afterward? How did it change your perspective?*

- Reidar is intent on taking Brigit *home*, but the story suggests that our true home is not of this world. How does this theme of earthly vs. eternal home play out in the novel?

*Faith Focus: What does "home" mean to you personally, both in the worldly sense and in the spiritual sense?*

- Brigit hides her brokenness behind scorn, while Reidar buries his love under duty and ambition. How do their struggles reflect common human ways of coping with pain?

*Faith Focus: Can you think of a time when surrendering your brokenness to God brought healing or growth?*

- How does God use Reidar's "flaw"—his love for Brigit—as the very means of bringing about His greater plan?

*Faith Focus: How has God used your own weakness or shame to bring about good in your life, or in someone else's?*

- Brigit knows almost from the beginning that Reidar is the boy who once saved her, yet she denies it. Why was it so hard for her to admit this to herself, and what does that reveal about her inner conflict?

*Faith Focus: In what ways do Brigit's mistrust and Reidar's suppression of love mirror the ways we sometimes resist God's work in our lives?*

- Brigit fears that Christ no longer loves her, yet she clings to Him regardless. How does her faith contrast with Reidar's ultimate disenchantment with Norse gods?

*Faith Focus: What does her perseverance teach us about holding on to faith when circumstances suggest otherwise, especially in seasons of doubt or suffering?*

- Brigit becomes the instrument of Reidar's conversion, even though she sees herself as weak and broken.

*Faith Focus: How does this reflect God's pattern throughout Scripture of using "unlikely" people? Have you ever witnessed or experienced someone's faith drawing another person to Christ in an unexpected way?*

- Reidar's story is loosely inspired by the historical figure, Håkon the Good. How does this historical connection deepen your understanding of the novel's message?

*Faith Focus: Reidar's story echoes how God raises leaders to accomplish His purposes. How does this reminder encourage you to trust that God is guiding history—and your own life's story—toward His greater plan?*

- Brigit's reliance on God might recall a biblical figure, Esther. What similarities do you see between Brigit's faith and Esther's? What differences?

*Faith Focus: Esther trusted God's plan even in danger and uncertainty. How can Brigit's example encourage you to rely on God's strength when you face fear or hardship?*

- Both Reidar and Brigit wrestle with bitterness and vengeance. How does the novel explore the difference between human justice and God's redemption?

*Faith Focus: What does Scripture teach us about leaving vengeance in God's hands, and how might this truth reshape the way you approach forgiveness?*

- Where do you see moments of transformation in Brigit and Reidar, and what turning points made them possible?

*Faith Focus: How has God worked in your life to bring transformation through trials or turning points?*

- Astrid's jealousy and obsession with Reidar lead to actions that will haunt her forever, yet they still play a role in God's greater plan. How does the novel show that God can work all things for good for those who believe?

*Faith Focus: Have you ever struggled with envy, obsession, or selfish desires, only to see God redeem the situation for good? How does that experience encourage you to trust Him with your heart and impulses?*

- Vargr's pursuit of evil leads to his ultimate downfall. How do his choices highlight the contrast between following one's own desires and God's plan for Reidar and Brigit?

*Faith Focus: Are there areas in your life that pull you away from God's will? How can you surrender those and seek His guidance instead?*

- Through her unconditional love for Reidar, Gyda grows to feel compassion for Brigit and sees her as another human being and not a foreign "sorceress." How does her love, shaped by loyalty to Reidar, open her heart to accept and care for Brigit?

*Faith Focus: How can loving others as God calls us—seeing them through His eyes or through the love He has for them—change your heart and open you to His work in your life?*

- In old Norse society, lust, polygamy, and infidelity were woven into daily life and even religious practice. How does the novel demonstrate the emotional and spiritual consequences of these norms?

*Faith Focus: How does God's design for sexual purity and covenantal love provide protection and blessing in relationships today?*

- Viking sagas and mythology often celebrated blood feuds, vengeance, and cruelty. How does the novel show the human cost of living by such a system?

*Faith Focus: How does Christ's call to love, mercy, and forgiveness challenge you to respond differently than the world's instinct for revenge or self-interest?*

- Slavery and societal hierarchies were deeply entrenched in pre-Christian societies. How does Reidar's response to this system reveal its ultimate corruption?

*Faith Focus: How does Scripture teach us to value every human being as made in God's image, and how can this truth shape your daily choices and attitudes toward others?*

- Fatalism—the belief that one's life is controlled by fate—was common in Norse culture. How do Reidar, Brigit, and Astrid wrestle with the tension between fate and free will in the story?

*Faith Focus: How does trusting God's sovereign plan differ from fatalism, and how can faith empower you to make choices that honor Him?*

- Reidar's journey before finding Christ can feel heavy and depressing. How do his struggles make his eventual conversion more powerful and meaningful?

*Faith Focus: How does understanding the depth of our own brokenness help you experience God's grace and redemption more fully in your life?*

- Christianity's radical call to mercy, compassion, and love for others was revolutionary against the backdrop of old Norse society. How does the story illustrate the contrast between man-made customs and the Gospel?

*Faith Focus: In what areas of your life is God calling you to live counterculturally—showing mercy, love, and patience where the world would seek selfish gain or revenge?*

# Acknowledgements

To my editor, Krista Holle, your sharp instincts, thoughtful guidance, and gentle encouragement pushed this story further than I could have ever taken it alone. Thank you for the care and commitment you poured into this book.

To Kathy Hall, Jennifer Reynolds, Molly Sawyer, Susan Pope Sloan, and others who offered their indispensable thoughts along the way, thank you for stepping into the earliest version of this story and sharing your insight so generously. Your perspectives helped shape the book in meaningful ways.

To all the incredible ARC readers, book bloggers, tour hosts, and reviewers, thank you for your enthusiastic support, thoughtful engagement, and for helping introduce this book to readers everywhere. I'm deeply grateful.

To Marius Harridsleff of vikingr.com, my heartfelt thanks for your generous permission to include your lyrical translation of *Skírnismál—The Ballad of Skírnir*—the fifth poem of the *Poetic Edda*.

To Ciara Hall, your expertise in Northern Irish translations and pronunciations has been a gift across my *Always and Forever* trilogy, and I was grateful to rely on your knowledge once again. This story would not carry the same authenticity without your help.

My sincere thanks to the dedicated historians whose work preserves the unfiltered truth of Viking raids and the redemptive paths that followed, including salvation found in Christ. History itself testifies that God uses everything for good.

To Mike, Alexa, and Sean, your constant love and support sustain me more than you know. I would not be here without you.

And finally, to <u>you</u>. Thank you for choosing this story, for trusting me with your time, and for welcoming Brigit and Reidar into your heart. I hope their journey lingers with you long after the final page.

# About the Author

Vera Bell is a Georgia Author of the Year nominee and a recipient of multiple literary awards. Though her faith journey began in childhood, a series of transformative events led her to embrace Christ, reshaping the stories she feels called to tell. After writing a secular historical romance trilogy, she now creates from a place grounded in deeper purpose. ***Of Flaw and Scorn*** is her debut Christian romance. A former graphic artist, Vera lives in Atlanta with her husband, two teenagers, and one fur baby. Her favorite place to write is on her porch, overlooking a pond lined with river birches and magnolias. The topics she never tires of are bygone eras, our universal human condition, and the deeper currents of love, hope, and redemption.

www.ingramcontent.com/pod-product-compliance
Lightning Source LLC
LaVergne TN
LVHW100517110826
845146LV00002B/670

* 9 7 9 8 9 9 4 6 8 0 5 1 3 *